"Are you a rake?"

For a second Brandon's breath caught in his throat. No one ever teased him anymore. No one suspected him of rakish behavior, either. He liked not being the duke and just being Mr. Brandon. It was too bad that this could not last.

"I am certainly not a rake," he answered honestly.

"Well, you have done your duty as a gentleman and have seen me home safely. I greatly enjoyed our walk."

"And I as well," he said. He wanted to tell her it was the happiest hour he could recall, and that he did not want it to end. He wanted to walk to Scotland and back if it meant listening to her and making her laugh.

But he had a fiancée, an inviolable sense of honor, and a life that belonged to the dukedom, not to him. Though he was a master of self-restraint, a man could only take so much temptation.

In the end, he only said, "Goodbye, Miss Harlow."

"Goodbye, Mr. Brandon."

Mr. Brandon, indeed. If only she knew . . .

Romances by **Maya Rodale**

A GROOM OF ONE'S OWN
THE HEIR AND THE SPARE
THE ROGUE AND THE RIVAL

A Groom of One's Own

MAYA RODALE

AVON

An Imprint of HarperCollinsPublishers

This is a work of fiction. Names, characters, places, and incidents are products of the author's imagination or are used fictitiously and are not to be construed as real. Any resemblance to actual events, locales, organizations, or persons, living or dead, is entirely coincidental.

AVON BOOKS
An Imprint of HarperCollins*Publishers*
10 East 53rd Street
New York, New York 10022-5299

Copyright © 2010 by Maya Rodale
ISBN 978-0-06-192298-5
www.avonromance.com

First Avon Books paperback printing: July 2010

Avon Trademark Reg. U.S. Pat. Off. and in Other Countries, Marca Registrada, Hecho en U.S.A.
HarperCollins® is a registered trademark of HarperCollins Publishers.

Printed in the U.S.A.

10 9 8 7 6 5 4 3 2 1

*This book is dedicated exclusively to my Lord Tony,
Baron of Pinner, Viscount of Kentish Town, Earl of
the Eastern Marches, Protector of the Borderlands,
and groom of my own.*

Acknowledgments

This book was made possible thanks to my agent, Linda Loewenthal; my editor, Tessa; and my ideal readers, Ann and Tony. Thank you all!

A Groom of One's Own

Prologue

On her way down the aisle . . .

Chesham, Buckinghamshire, England
June 1822

If she is to marry, a woman must have a dowry and a groom of her own. At an exquisitely inconvenient moment, Miss Sophie Harlow discovered one essential prerequisite was deserting her.

To be jilted at the altar is the sort of thing that happens to someone's cousin's friend's sister; in other words, it is something that only occurs in rumors and gossip. It never actually happened to anyone, and it couldn't possibly be happening to *her*.

Yet here she stood in her new satin wedding gown, hearing the words, "I am deeply sorry, Sophie, but I cannot marry you after all," from the man who ought to be saying, "I do."

She could not quite believe it.

Sophie was vaguely aware of the curious expressions of her guests. The Chesham church—small, quaint, centuries old, and well-to-do like the town itself—was packed with friends from the village, extended family members, and visitors from surrounding counties, as many wished to witness the nuptials uniting two of the most prominent families of the local landed gentry.

Of course they were wondering why the groom had stopped the bride halfway down the aisle. Of course they strained to hear what he said in a voice too low to be audible to anyone else.

She saw her dearest friend, Lady Julianna Somerset, in attendance and as curious and concerned as the rest. Even the church cat, Pumpkin, looked intrigued as she peeked out from underneath a pew.

"I am so sorry to cause you such misery," Matthew repeated quietly, looking pained. His brown eyes were rimmed with red, his skin ashen. His dark hair was brushed forward and tousled in the usual style for a rakish young man. His lips were full and tender, even as he said the bitterest things.

Sophie tried to breathe deeply but her corset would not allow it. She was very glad for the veil obscuring her face.

Misery, indeed.

Her brain was in a fog, and she was pained by every little crack in her heart as it was breaking. Behind the veil her eyes were hot with tears. Her palms were damp underneath her gloves. The cloying aroma of the lilacs in her bridal bouquet was unbearable, so she let them fall onto the stone floor.

It was her wedding day, and he was leaving her. For the occasion, she wore a new cream-colored satin gown with the fashionable high waist and short puffed sleeves, and the delicate lace veil worn by generations of Harlow brides. Flowers decorated the church pews and beeswax candles added to the gentle late-morning light streaming through the stained-glass windows.

All her worldly possessions were packed up in anticipation of the move from her parents' home to her husband's.

And now the dress and flowers were for nothing, and her belongings were packed to go nowhere.

"But why? And when did you . . . and what happened and . . . *why*?" Sophie sputtered.

No one could be expected to form coherent thought in a moment like this.

"Marriage is . . . it's such a commitment . . ."

Obviously.

". . . and I haven't experienced enough. I'm not ready yet. There's so much out there I haven't seen, or done, or . . . I haven't really lived, Sophie," Matthew stuttered while he toyed with the polished brass buttons on his brocade waistcoat. He'd lost enormous sums at cards because of this nervous habit. It had vexed her before, but she loathed it now.

"Hadn't you considered this *before* you proposed? Or in the entire year that we've been betrothed? Or before I started walking down the aisle? Honestly, Matthew, you only realized this *now*?" Sophie tried, and failed, to keep her voice low. Why she bothered, she knew not. This was not destined to remain a secret.

She was not going to spend the rest of her days as Mrs. Matthew Fletcher after all, but as "Poor Sophie Harlow" or "That girl that got jilted."

Sophie turned to go, keenly aware that all eyes were on her. Matthew followed.

"How could you do this to me?" she asked once they were in the vestibule of the church, which provided a modicum of privacy from the dozens of prying eyes. Their curiosity was understandable; she would be nearly falling out of her seat straining to hear, too. Presently, however, she was pacing.

"I know my timing is terrible," he said. "But we have been together for so long already."

Six months of courtship, and a one-year engagement,

to be precise. From the time she made her debut, she had wanted Matthew Fletcher; no one else would do. She had turned down two offers of marriage waiting for him to notice her, and two more as he courted her.

Now she was twenty-one and damaged goods. Sophie the Spinster did, alas, have a ring to it.

"And we were about to spend the rest of our lives together," he continued.

"Yes, I am aware of that," she snapped, never ceasing in her steps back and forth like ringing church bells.

"But there is still more for me to experience before I settle down with one woman for the rest of my days," he said, attempting to explain. It was something in the way he said "one woman" that caught her attention. At that, she paused.

"Who is she, Matthew?" Sophie asked coolly.

He looked in the direction of the heavens.

"Matthew."

"With Lavinia, I feel as I have never felt before! We only became acquainted a fortnight ago, and yet . . . " He could not meet her gaze. His fingers were fiddling with the buttons again.

"Lavinia?" It was a horrible, stupid name.

"We became acquainted at The Swan," he said, referring to the inn five miles over in Amersham. "She lost her husband and is now traveling. She has extended an invitation to me to travel with her."

"Matthew, I'm afraid I don't quite understand. You're leaving *me*—your sweetheart, your fiancée, your bride—for a woman you met at an inn less than a month ago?"

Matthew did not say anything, but his silence was answer enough.

"Oh God," she whispered as the truth began to take hold. All the tiny cracks in her heart added up and now the whole thing crumbled into dust. Sophie clutched her hands over her chest and sank to her knees. Her wedding gown billowed around her on the stone floor.

She had loved him, promised herself to him and entrusted him with her heart and her future. And he was leaving her and the life they had planned.

He murmured her name and attempted to console her by snaking his arm around her waist.

"No."

She shrugged off his hands, for she could not bear to be touched by him now, when he likely had held another woman with those arms and kissed another woman with those lips.

And yet, for more than a year, his arms and his kisses had been the surest comfort she had known. He had stolen that from her, too, at the moment when she needed it most.

Traitorous, heartbreaking bounder.

"Sophie," he whispered, "I'm so sorry."

"Oh! How could you!" She stood suddenly, and he did as well.

"Sophie, I—"

She smacked him on the shoulder. "How could you do this to me?"

"I'm so sorry," he repeated. She didn't want to hear it. He could apologize a thousand times with his sad brown eyes and she doubted she could ever forgive him for this.

She balled her hands into fists and pummeled his chest. "How could you do this to *us*?"

Matthew didn't try to stop her, but he did take a step back. Sophie took one step forward, fists flying all the while. In that manner, they started down the aisle. She might just make it to the altar after all—by beating her unwilling groom every step of the way.

Almost.

Matthew tripped over the bridal bouquet she had dropped in the aisle and he began to tumble backward. With flailing arms he reached out for something to steady himself, and grasped onto Sophie's veil, the very one worn by generations of Harlow brides. He took it with him as he fell, mussing up her elaborately arranged hair and tearing the old, delicate family heirloom.

A hush fell over the church. Not a sound from the entryway to the candles and flowers at the altar, from the hard wooden pews to the high, vaulted ceiling— save for heavy footsteps thudding toward her.

"Sophie, stand back," her brother Edward declared as he marched toward her.

"What are you doing?" she asked as he helped Matthew to his feet.

The thud of her brother's fist against Matthew's face and the hideous crack of his jawbone was her answer.

And with that, all hell broke loose.

Edward pulled Matthew up and planted another facer on him, sending him falling once more. He knocked into the vicar, who stumbled and stepped on Pumpkin's tail. The poor cat yowled and leapt onto the overly decorated bonnet of Mrs. Beaverbrooke, who shrieked once at the initial shock and again when she saw the damage done. The cat jumped from lap to lap, eliciting shouts and cries in her wake.

Mrs. Harlow fainted. Sophie's father was heard arguing with Mr. Fletcher. Matthew's brothers joined the fray, and the guests quit the pews to crowd around. Someone stepped on Sophie's gown and she cringed at the sound of satin tearing. A baby was wailing. The vicar repeated "Let's calm down now" to absolutely no effect.

Sophie was left alone in a torn gown with a damaged veil, forgotten by all.

"You are still standing at least," Julianna said as she arrived at Sophie's side.

They were the very best of friends—born a month apart, raised only a half-mile apart. They learned to walk together and talk together. Sometimes Sophie thought that Julianna knew her better than she knew herself. She was the one person she needed right now, the one who would understand this betrayal, the one who would know what to do.

"I'm never going to live this down, am I?" Sophie remarked dryly as she surveyed the mayhem unfolding.

"I'm afraid they will be talking about it for decades," Julianna answered in her typically forthright manner.

There would be talk, naturally. The story of Matthew throwing her over at the last possible minute and the subsequent mayhem would spread far and wide. She would not be able to go into any town within four counties without stares, whispers, or snide remarks. No man would willingly bind himself to a woman with such a reputation, and a woman was *nothing* without a good, honest, and scandal-free name.

"What do I do now?" Sophie asked. Honestly, she didn't know. From the day she was born, her parents had raised her to one purpose: marry, and marry well.

"There is only one thing, really," Julianna said confidently, linking their arms together and guiding Sophie through the crowd toward the door. "You must come with me to London."

Chapter 1

During a mad dash from a wedding . . .

St. George's Church
Hanover Square, London
One year later, 1823

It was the last place she wanted to be, but no marriage in high life would be complete without Miss Sophie Harlow. This time last year, she had been fleeing from her own disastrous wedding. Now she reported on everyone else's.

Her life had taken a shocking change of direction, and she was occasionally still stunned by it. A combination of heartache, madness, humiliation, and a desire to begin anew had driven her to this grand city where she knew no one, save for her dearest friend.

Within a week of her arrival in London, it was clear that she would need an income, for she hated living on Julianna's limited funds provided by her late husband's estate, and the prospect of starving was equally distasteful. Her options for employment were to be a seamstress, servant, governess, or mistress and none appealed to her.

Out of desperation, Sophie had done the unthinkable

and applied for a man's job—the position of secretary to Mr. Derek Knightly, the publisher of the town's wildly popular newspaper, *The London Weekly*. It had been an outrageous act, and unlikely prospect, but Sophie decided to take the risk.

Even now, a year later, she couldn't quite believe she had done so. Like all girls of a certain social standing, Sophie had been raised to marry advantageously. To work . . . well, it was unthinkable! But so was starving.

Surprisingly, Sophie had left the interview with an offer from Mr. Knightly to write about the one thing she feared most: weddings. Though she had been raised to be a wife, Sophie became a writer.

No man would do it, Mr. Knightly had said. She wouldn't do it either, if it weren't for her other less desirable options of *seamstress or servant, governess or mistress.*

Thus, she became the Miss Harlow of the regular column "Miss Harlow's Marriage in High Life." Inspired by Sophie, Julianna had also turned to writing and had secured a gossip column: "Fashionable Intelligence" by A Lady of Distinction. They, along with Eliza Fielding and Annabelle Swift, were the Writing Girls—and within weeks of their debut in the pages of *The London Weekly*, had become famous.

Mr. Knightly had a hunch that women writers would be scandalous, and that scandals would translate to sales. He was right.

It was all very glamorous except for the small requirement of attending wedding after wedding after wedding . . .

Sophie sat at the end of a pew, toward the wall, away from the center aisle where the bride would pass. It was an escapable position.

Julianna was by her side, surreptitiously taking in

everything that might be gossiped about: who wore what, who conversed with whom, who was in attendance, and who was not.

Everyone looked happy. Pleasant. It was a lovely morning in June and two people in love were going to unite in holy matrimony and presumably live happily ever after.

Sophie felt sick. She never got used to it. Weddings. The nerves. This was her third ceremony of the day—everyone always got married before noon on Saturdays, with a few exceptions—and this was, thankfully, the last one. Still, she was treated with the usual swell and sequence of horrid feelings.

Her stomach tightened into a knot. Her palms became clammy. She was remembering another wedding in June and the slow breaking of her heart as everyone stared on with curiosity and pity. *Breathe*, she commanded herself.

Inhale. She fanned herself with the voucher required to gain admittance—a violation of etiquette, but absolutely essential. *Exhale.*

Seamstress or servant, governess or mistress . . .

She chanted this sequence of her alternative professions, which generally soothed her like a lullaby. As soon as the bride joined the groom at the altar, her feelings would subside. Until that moment . . .

"Still? . . ." Julianna queried. Sophie's breaths were labored and her lips were moving ever so slightly: *seamstress or servant, governess or mistress . . .*

Sophie only nodded, suspecting that she looked ready to be carted off to Bedlam.

"My God, I would like to grievously maim that vile bounder," Julianna said. And though she had made a certain peace with the man who had jilted her, at the moment Sophie's feelings were the same.

"You have spoken my mind," Sophie said.

"Of course, if he hadn't abandoned you like that, then you wouldn't have joined me in London, and we wouldn't be making newspaper history, so we might say that old Matthew Fletcher has done us a favor."

Sophie looked murderously at her friend. As lovely as life in London was—with amazing parties, plays, shops, and company—she'd give it all up in a second for the love of a good, reliable, honest husband.

"Or we might not," Julianna continued.

"What is taking so long?" Sophie asked in a whisper. This is when she became exceptionally nervous—when people were late, and when it seemed like the ceremony might not go smoothly. When someone might, say, *be jilted in front of everyone.*

Honestly, this was not to be endured!

"Probably a torn hem or something insignificant—oh my lord, he is *not*!" Julianna exclaimed.

"What is it?" Sophie asked.

"The groom is leaving the altar," Julianna explained excitedly. The din of hundreds of guests chattering grew louder. This ought to have been welcome news, for it would make splendid additions to their columns. But Sophie's heart—or what was left of it—ached too much.

Sophie forced herself to breathe. "Grievously maimed" would not be sufficient for Fletcher; Sophie was thinking murder now. One year later and she still could not sit through a wedding without suffering the most severe agonies!

"Where is the bride?" she asked her tall friend, who could see much more than she.

"No sign of her," Julianna answered.

"I cannot stay for this," Sophie whispered. She stood up and stepped easily into the far aisle, congratulating herself on having had the foresight to take this seat.

"But your column!" Julianna reminded her, and those seated nearby turned to look at the author of "Miss Harlow's Marriage in High Life," whispering excitedly about seeing her at the wedding.

"Take notes for me. Please," Sophie pleaded, and gave her paper and pencil to her friend.

Sophie kept her gaze low as she rushed out of the church. On a good day she could barely stand it, and today it was all too much. Her only thought was to get away before she began to cry, for this time last year she had fled from a different church, under different circumstances. Perhaps one day she might leave a church with a groom of her own on her arm.

The bright sunlight was blinding as she stepped outside, but Sophie forged ahead through a crowd waiting in expectation to catch a glimpse of the bride and the aristocrats in attendance. She rushed away from Hanover Square toward Piccadilly with eyes to the ground and oblivious to everything until a woman's scream brought her to a halt.

Chapter 2

One month before the wedding . . .

White's Gentleman's Club
St. James's Street, London

"**A**n English gentleman is someone who knows exactly when to stop being one," Lord Roxbury declared. His companions—the usual assortment of peers, second sons, and rakes of all sorts—heartily expressed their agreement.

Henry William Cameron Hamilton kept his disagreement to himself. As tenth Duke of Hamilton and Brandon, he did not have the luxury of even a momentary lapse in gentlemanly behavior. Thus, he never drank overmuch, nor made foolish wagers, nor made an ass of himself over a woman. Vice and excess were strangers to him. Reckless behavior was just not done.

"An English gentleman is someone who knows—" Lord Biddulph did not manage to complete the sentence for falling over drunk. His head thudded onto the tabletop, and his limp arm sent a crystal glass falling and shattering on the floor. His comrades erupted in uproarious laughter.

Brandon, as he was known, noted that it was before noon.

He folded the newspaper he had been reading and set it aside. His friend, Lord Roxbury, caught his eye from across the room and raised his glass of brandy to him, an invitation for Brandon to join them. Regretfully, he declined. Account books were awaiting his review, and doing sums after the consumption of alcohol was not one of his talents.

Though they were his peers in age and in social standing, Brandon felt worlds apart and years older. He had once been as rakish and carefree as the next until he had inherited at eighteen. There had been a time when he certainly would have joined them.

Brandon didn't particularly miss drinking himself into a stupor before dusk, and carousing with opera singers and actresses. He did miss having the liberty to do so without much care for the consequences.

He had forgotten what it felt like to make a decision without considering the effect it would have on his mother, three sisters, the household staff, and the hundreds of tenants who relied upon his judgment and good sense. He wondered what it would be like to feel no obligation to the ancient legacy he had a duty to perpetuate.

To forget he was a duke.

To just be . . . himself.

Brandon did not give voice to such thoughts because no one ever wanted to hear the trials and tribulations of a man of his position. Instead, he took his leave of the others and stepped out of the dark, smoky haven of his club and into the sunshine.

Returning to Hamilton House to balance account books was the last thing any sane person would want to do on a fine summer day like this one. But it had to be done, although a long walk home would be a fine compromise.

As he passed Burlington Arcade, his attention was caught by a woman's scream. She was pointing to another woman in a pale blue dress dashing toward certain disaster. At the sound of the shriek, the girl paused, idiotically frozen with fear, as a carriage pulled by a team of six white horses charged directly toward her.

Brandon bolted forward, knocking over a youth selling newssheets, and sending the gray papers flying high. He lunged forward, grasped her waist with both hands, and yanked her out of the way. She crashed against his chest, knocking the air out of him.

The horses thundered past and the carriage followed.

He held her in his arms. He had saved her.

Brandon held her close for a second longer than was necessary or proper, in part because she made no move to escape and admittedly because she was warm and luscious in his arms. After a moment, he eased her to her feet and let her go. By then a crowd had gathered. He suspected a scene, and he frowned.

But then Brandon caught a glimpse of her plump pink lips and dark curls underneath her bonnet, and the corners of his mouth reluctantly turned up.

"Thank you," she said faintly. She took a deep breath—and his gaze was drawn to the rise and fall of her breasts. He sucked in his own breath. And then she tilted her head back to look up at him with velvety dark brown eyes.

"You saved my life," she said. Her voice wavered. Her pink lips formed a slight smile. She was in shock, but so was he.

For a moment, neither moved.

The longer he looked at her, the more the clatter of the horses' hooves on the cobblestones, the shouts of the merchants, the shoves of the pedestrians all faded, and he was only conscious of an irrational wish to kiss her.

Brandon's heart was pounding and his breath scarce . . . from his recent exertions, of course. It certainly wasn't because of her full, luscious mouth.

He told himself that his inability to breathe had nothing to do with her large brown eyes shadowed by dark lashes, and the way they widened as she looked at him.

Her cheeks were pink, and he wondered if it was because of the sun, or something else?

Brandon yearned to sink his fingers into the mass of dark, glossy ringlets framing her face, to urge her close enough so that he could kiss her.

Here. Now. On one of the busiest streets in London.

That had nothing to do with why his heart was thudding heavily.

He could not lie—it had everything to do with it. He was . . . unfathomably, suddenly, and overwhelmingly entranced by this daydreaming girl who had nearly been trampled by a team of horses.

"Where are we going, miss? I shall escort you," Brandon said. It was clear she was a danger to herself and others, and thus, it was his duty as a gentleman to offer his protection. That, and he did not want to part with her just yet.

"*We* are not going anywhere," she answered, with an uneven smile. She still seemed a bit pale underneath that blush, almost feverish, and certainly still affected by her near-death experience. "Though I thank you for the offer. You've helped me so much already, I couldn't possibly ask any more of you."

In his opinion, it was very clear that she desperately needed him.

"Surely you are not rebuffing my chivalrous offer of assistance." No one ever refused him anything. He was one of the most respected and powerful dukes in the land.

But she didn't know that, did she? No, she most likely did not. His lips curved into a smile. Once, just once, he would indulge and talk to the pretty girl as if he hadn't a dozen reasons not to. What harm could come from an hour's walk and conversation with her? It seemed likely that plenty of harm would come to her if he did not.

"I abhor the thought of you putting yourself out any more on my account," she said.

"What if I phrased my offer anew? I'm looking for an excuse to stay outside as long as possible on this fine day."

"I am a bit distracted," she admitted with a mischievous sparkle dawning in her eyes. "And I am feeling quite out of sorts, as you might imagine."

Of course. But was she also as stunned by him as he was by her?

"It would be my pleasure to see you safely to your destination."

"Do you have a nefarious purpose in doing so?" She eyed him suspiciously, and it might have been the first time that anyone questioned his integrity. It was oddly thrilling. "Or are you really an honest gentleman intent upon helping a lady?"

"I have nothing but noble intentions," he recited. "I am a notoriously upstanding gentleman. However, if you prefer, I will procure a hackney for you. Or I shall leave you to your own devices."

Though he did not wish to, Brandon offered to let

her go even though he was incredibly and inexplicably keen to remain in her company.

"I should like to walk," she said. And then she gave him a long, hard look as if she could determine his moral worth from that alone, and finally she nodded, and her lips formed a pretty little smile. "You may escort me if you wish, but only because you need an excuse to stay outside today and because I owe you a favor."

"Fair enough," he said, exhaling a breath he hadn't realized he was holding. He understood that it was an incredibly delicate situation for a woman to accept the company of a man she did not know, and publicly. But he had just saved her life, and that had to count for something. He suspected she was thinking the same.

And then there was *something* about her that begged for more of his attentions, and for this one hour he was *not* going to be a Perfect and Proper Gentleman.

"Lead the way, my lady."

They started down Piccadilly, toward Regent Street, walking side by side and weaving their way through the masses of pedestrians crowding the streets.

"It's Miss Harlow, actually. Thank you again for saving me. I do believe that makes you my hero," she said with a smile.

"My pleasure. Call me Brandon," he said. "I'm curious to know what has you so distracted."

"It has been one of those years, Mr. Brandon." At that, she issued a heartfelt sigh, and once again, like a cad, his gaze settled upon the rise and fall of her breasts. He was sorry for her distress, but happy for the sigh.

"You must explain, Miss Harlow," he urged, more intrigued by her with each passing moment.

"This time last year I nearly died from mortification, and just today I nearly died from my own stupidity."

Brandon laughed at that, and she smiled, too, but there was still something akin to sadness in her eyes.

"Are you often found to be dashing about London, alone, and distracted—or is today a special occasion?" he asked.

"Rest assured, it is not a habit of mine."

"Glad to hear it. Did you not at least bring a maid with you?"

"I usually do, but circumstances did not permit it today," she said, and she looked away. It was clear to him that she wasn't just an idiotic female not attending to her surroundings. Something had upset her, sending her running.

Brandon wanted to know what had happened, so he could solve the problem for her. He wanted to protect her, from anything and everything. And yet he didn't even know her. He was not surprised when she changed the subject before he could offer to help her.

"I hate to pry, but may I ask what you are avoiding at home?" she asked politely.

"Women never hate to pry," he answered truthfully, and she laughed. It was not the prettiest of laughs, but it was undoubtedly genuine and thus, a pleasure to hear.

"True," she conceded. "We only say so as to sound polite while we seek to unearth all your secrets. So tell me, Mr. Brandon, what are you avoiding at home?"

"Balancing an accounts book," he answered frankly. *And drafting bills for Parliament, managing six estates, carrying the weight of the world.*

And a fiancée. One of the very good reasons why he should not be conversing with Miss Harlow. Lady Clarissa Richmond was a lovely person and would make a perfect duchess, but she did not intrigue him or arouse him the way this dark beauty beside him did. Of course, that is exactly why he proposed to Clarissa—she was not distracting or demanding, which was exactly what he wanted in a wife.

Miss Harlow was merely a pleasant afternoon diversion.

"Say no more, I beg of you. Shall we take the long way, Mr. Brandon?" She tilted her head to look up at him. The expression on her face was one of innocence, but the spark in her eyes was pure mischief. He grinned. He liked her. For one afternoon, he would be an imperfect gentleman and do exactly as he wished.

"Let's take the long way, Miss Harlow."

Chapter 3

Still, after turning onto a quieter street and walking a block or two, Sophie's heart was still beating at an outrageous pace. She ought to have gone back to the church to find Julianna and to take a hack home, but she could not bear to return to St. George's.

She really should not be walking around town with a strange man—and she never would, if it weren't for a certain feeling about Mr. Brandon. The exact feeling could be summed up as: *This one*. She wanted to be with this man.

It was too soon to be seriously entertaining thoughts of that nature, she told herself, so she ignored it as best she could.

What a tumultuous morning!

Her heart raced now, spurring on the sensation of butterflies in her stomach, as happens when one has survived such a dramatic encounter: near death! Romantic rescue! She wanted to laugh with glee, when less than an hour ago she had fought back tears of despair.

Sophie glanced up at Mr. Brandon, and found him stealing a glance at her. He was taller than average, but rather than intimidating her, she felt protected. His hair was dark, and he avoided the fashionable tussled hairstyle in favor of something short. Mr. Brandon's eyes were bright green, and flattered by his hunter green jacket. When he smiled at her—which he did often—there were slight lines at the corners of his eyes. He didn't seem very old, but he did seem wise. Beyond all of that, her rescuer was an undeniably handsome man.

Sophie glanced up at Mr. Brandon—again, and found him stealing a glance at her—again. It was all so very shy, and exquisitely awkward, unbelievably sweet, and like nothing she'd ever experienced before. She had loved Matthew but he hadn't made her heart race. Not like this.

"Miss Harlow, I must warn you of something." She peered at him curiously, for he was suddenly so serious. "We are approaching an intersection. Try not to rush headlong into it," he said, and she laughed. She wanted a man who would make her laugh, instead of cry. Her heart beat strongly: *This one.*

"Newssheets! Only seven pence!" cried a young man standing at the corner with a stack of newspapers.

"Get yer copy of *The London Weekly*!" he hollered, this time to the captive audience of dozens of people waiting to cross the street, including Sophie and Brandon.

"Do you read such rubbish, Miss Harlow? Or are you particular to *The Times*?"

Sophie managed a tight smile while thinking, *Oh, hell and damnation.*

Not only did she read *The Weekly*, but she wrote for it. She could not admit to that, nor could pride allow her to acknowledge *The Times*, archrival to her own paper, as worthy of her attentions. Nor did she wish to lie and say she did not read a paper at all. It would be horrible for Mr. Brandon to think her uninformed, or a fool. She so wanted to impress him.

"I believe most of London reads that rubbish," she said. When the path was clear, he pressed his hand at the small of her back to guide her through the crowds, and she experienced a shiver of pleasure.

"That is the truth. *The Weekly* is the one with those scandalous Writing Girls, writing about yet more scandals?"

"The very one," Sophie answered, thinking that Mr. Knightly would love that description. "And what is your opinion of those scribbling women?" Everyone in town had something to say on the matter. She'd never been so keen to know what anyone thought until now.

"I think it is scandalous, but far preferable to some of the other options available to a woman," Brandon answered and Sophie smiled broadly. He would understand her chant of "seamstress or servant, governess or mistress." She was about to tell him that she was one of those scandalous women writing about scandal, but then—

"Of course," he continued, "I'd probably feel differently if the woman in question was one of my sisters, or my wife."

Sophie was, unfortunately, reacquainted with the sensation of hopes crashing and one's heart sinking.

"Do you have a wife?"

"No," he said, and she waited for him to say "however" or "but" or anything to send her hopes and heart into a tailspin, but he did not, and she dared to dream and entertain thoughts of *This One*.

Brandon was caught off guard by the question, and he had paused in answering. In truth, he did not have a wife. He did, however, have a fiancée. Were he to see Miss Harlow again, he would certainly inform her about his betrothal. But they had only this one afternoon walk—one determinedly chaste walk—so Lady Clarissa didn't really signify.

"It would be very rakish or roguish if you were to be walking around with other young ladies when you had a wife," Miss Harlow pointed out and he hoped she did not notice the furrow in his brow.

"It would be rakish of me," he agreed. "I would need to be reformed."

"Reformed rakes make the best husbands," Miss Harlow recited.

"Is there any truth to that?" Brandon wondered aloud. One couldn't spend ten minutes in town without hearing that hackneyed phrase uttered, yet he was not aware of any evidence supporting it.

"I would not know. Would you? Are you a rake?" Miss Harlow asked. Brandon caught her taking a coy, lingering, sidelong glance at him with those mysterious dark eyes of hers. For a second his breath caught in his throat.

"I don't know," he answered in response to her first question.

"You don't know if you are a rake?" she teased.

No one ever teased him anymore. No one suspected him of rakish behavior, either. He liked not being the duke and just being Mr. Brandon. It was too bad that this could not last.

"I am certainly not a rake," he answered honestly.

"That's what they all say," she retorted.

"I'm sure," Brandon said with a slight bitterness, thinking of his companions back at White's.

"Oh, let's pass through the park," she said as they approached Bloomsbury Square. "I do love the greenery."

Bloomsbury Square was particularly nice with its manicured paths cutting through the lawn shaded by large oak trees. Once in the park, the volume of the city seemed to decrease just a bit, and the air was just a touch sweeter.

"Are you by any chance from the country, Miss Harlow?"

"Yes," she said. "Could you tell that I'm not a native Londoner?"

"I did not suspect a thing until you expressed an interest in trees and grass. How long have you been living in town?"

"Just over a year. I am happy here, but occasionally I miss the countryside. Particularly the sense of space, and the sound of wind in the trees and crickets at night . . ."

"None of those things in London," Brandon admitted.

"Which do you prefer?" she asked.

"I like both," he said.

"That's not a fair answer!"

"But it's the honest one. I enjoy the energy of the city because I can easily escape to the calm of the countryside and vice versa." It was a luxury to be able to go back and forth as he did. It made the management of multiple residences worth the effort.

"Lucky for you to be able to just go whenever you wish, even at a moment's notice," she said wistfully.

"Oh, I never do anything at a moment's notice. Everything is carefully planned far in advance," he answered.

"I used to be that way. But I learned that having a plan is no assurance that it will be carried through," she said.

He was curious about the sadness in her voice. Asking was out of the question. A man of sense avoided a conversation upon sensitive emotional topics that could lead to a lady's tears.

"That is why one must have a secondary plan in place as well," he offered instead and she laughed.

"You must be prepared for everything. I bet you never forget an appointment, or are caught without an umbrella in the rain, or run out of wine at a dinner party."

"How did you know?" Granted, he had staff to assist him with these things, but he was notorious for reminding them.

"You're not bamming, are you?" Sophie asked.

"No," he said. "I am always prepared for any event," he said. *Except for you,* he thought.

She paused before a small gray brick townhouse with white trim. Even though he had no use of the information, he made note of her address: 24 Bloomsbury Place.

"Well, Mr. Brandon, you have done your duty as a gentleman and have seen me home safely. I greatly enjoyed our walk."

"And I as well," he said. He wanted to tell her it was the happiest hour he could recall, and that he did not want it to end. He wanted to walk to Scotland and back if it meant listening to her and making her laugh.

But he had a fiancée, an inviolable sense of honor, and a life that belonged to the dukedom, not to him. Though he was a master of self-restraint, a man could take only so much temptation. Brandon wanted to tell her all of these things, so she would understand why they wouldn't meet again.

In the end, he only said, "Goodbye, Miss Harlow."

"Goodbye, Mr. Brandon," she said with a pretty smile that made him fleetingly consider a second visit. But, no, this was his last glimpse of the lovely Miss Harlow.

Mr. Brandon, indeed. If only she knew . . .

Chapter 4

Twenty-eight days before the wedding . . .

The Offices of The London Weekly
53 Fleet Street, London

"I met someone," Sophie declared to her companions: Lady Julianna Somerset, Miss Eliza Fielding, and Miss Annabelle Swift. Together they were the famed Writing Girls of the popular newspaper *The London Weekly*. At present they were gathered for the weekly staff meeting at the offices on Fleet Street.

Two editors, Damien Owens and Oliver Grenville, looked up from their note-taking, and dismissed Sophie's news as women's stuff, then went back to scribbling notes. Between the two of them, they managed the reporters responsible for news both big and small: acts of Parliament and acts of God, shipwrecks, accidents, and offenses, as well as foreign, domestic, and fashionable intelligence.

The London Weekly offered "Accounts Of Gallantry, Pleasure And Entertainment." Those in search of serious news looked elsewhere.

"Details about this 'someone,' please," Julianna stated. Shortly after Sophie had been hired, her friend wrangled a position as the author of "Fashionable Intelligence," which had quickly become the most adored, feared, and quoted gossip column in London. The column was attributed to A Lady Of Distinction, and its authorship was widely speculated upon but never confirmed or denied. Like Sophie, she had begun her career because of a want of money.

"And how have I not yet heard of this?" Julianna asked.

"It happened while you were at the wedding," Sophie answered, "and I wanted to tell everyone all at once."

There was a pause as writer Andrew Mulligan offered a particularly loud blow-by-blow account of a boxing match to Mitch Radnor, who covered horse racing and cricket.

"Well, don't keep us waiting!" Eliza urged.

"His name is Mr. Brandon. He is breathtakingly handsome, charming, and a perfect gentleman." Sophie sighed once more at the recollection of that completely and utterly magnificent encounter.

He had saved her life. And he had saved her from an intense loneliness that had plagued her ever since Matthew jilted her. Merely knowing that he existed in the world made her hopeful, and was reason enough to consider loving again.

One look into his eyes and she just knew: *This One*. She dismissed the feeling because, really, how could you know something so significant, so quickly?

But then he said something that made her think *yes*, or he laughed at her humor, and he said he was always prepared. It could not be forgotten that he had saved her from certain death.

He was the kind of man a girl could trust her body, soul, and heart with.

And he was handsome, too. Lord, was he ever!

Sophie had relived it all hundreds of times, cementing every moment into her memory.

She knew that his chest was firm, his arms were strong, and that she didn't disentangle herself from his grasp as quickly as she ought to have done.

She adored the faint lines at the corner of his bright green eyes when he smiled at her, and she was sorely tempted to muss up his short dark hair only because it was so neat and perfect.

Even now, at the thought, she felt her cheeks turn pink from desire, just like the other day.

They talked so easily, as if they were soul mates, not strangers.

This one. She wanted this one.

"How did you meet him?" Annabelle asked. Her column, "Dear Annabelle," answered readers' requests for advice. She was possibly the sweetest and kindest person anyone would ever meet. Sophie was incredibly jealous of Annabelle's slightly wavy golden hair, quite the contrast to her own dark, unruly curls.

"Oh, he merely saved me from being trampled by an oncoming carriage," Sophie said, and then she explained their easy banter and lovely walk to her home.

"You let a stranger see where you live?" Annabelle was aghast at the risk. Things were certainly different in London. Had Sophie been in Chesham, walking with a man would be more of a danger to her reputation than to her person.

"I know," Sophie agreed. "But he seemed trustworthy. And he was! He did not take liberties with my person."

They were all distracted by the loud laugh of Alistair Grey, theater reviewer, who was currently previewing one of Randolph Winter's cartoons, mocking the excesses of the new king, George IV, formerly the Prince Regent.

"So he walked you home . . ." Eliza reminded Sophie to continue with the story.

Sophie related the events of the afternoon and concluded with, "But he did not mention calling again. That was two days ago. He knows where I reside, though, so he could have sent a letter . . ."

"Perhaps he doesn't know what to say," Annabelle offered with a slight shrug of her shoulders. Sophie had already thought of that possibility. In fact, she considered every plausible, and impossible, reason for him to simply vanish after what was a magical encounter.

"Such a letter would be easy," Julianna stated. "For example: *Miss Harlow, It was a pleasure to make your acquaintance the other day. I look forward to furthering it. May I call upon you?*"

"Speaking of letters." Sophie nodded in the direction of Fergus, the mail clerk for *The Weekly*, who had just entered with a sack of mail to be delivered.

"For you, Miss Harlow," he said with a grin, and handed her a packet.

"Thank you, Fergus. Who will be marrying this month?"

Not she, that was for certain. A year had passed since Matthew had jilted her and she still grew anxious and suffered damp palms, a struggle to breathe, and a vow that she would quit her position. But as soon as the bride joined the groom at the altar, the symptoms subsided.

She reminded herself of her employment alternatives—*seamstress or servant, governess or mistress*—and decided writing about weddings wasn't such a terrible fate and she would remain a Writing Girl with *The London Weekly.*

"Perhaps there is a letter from your Mr. Brandon included?" Annabelle wondered. She was always so optimistic, occasionally heartbreakingly so.

"No, I did not tell him I was a Writing Girl and he didn't seem to make the connection on his own," Sophie answered, slightly distracted by one letter in particular. "Oh, I have received a personal letter from the Duchess of Richmond! What possible reason could she have to write to me?"

"What does it say?" Julianna asked while Sophie unfolded the sheet.

"It says, 'Dear Miss Harlow,' and that is as far as I read before I was interrupted."

"Just read it aloud," Julianna said impatiently, and Sophie obliged.

> *Dear Miss Harlow,*
>
> *I write to propose a newspaper story to you. I would like to offer you the exclusive opportunity to cover all the details of my daughter's upcoming wedding to His Grace, the Duke of Hamilton and Brandon. You may report upon every step of the wedding preparation, including the selection of the bridal attire, flowers, and wedding breakfast menu. Our social circle is desperately interested in all the details, and I would think your newspaper's other readers are as well.*
>
> *Most sincerely,*
> *Lady Wilhelmina Gordon,*
> *Duchess of Richmond*

"That is quite an offer," Annabelle said, slightly awed.

"It will be a huge story," Julianna stated.

"Hamilton *and* Brandon. As if one dukedom wasn't enough!" Eliza remarked.

"Indeed! Taking two when some people don't have any dukedoms!" Sophie teased, and the girls laughed.

"Do you know him, Julianna?" Sophie asked.

"Not personally. And there is so little gossip about him, I couldn't fill a column on him if my reputation depended upon it."

"Good morning, everyone. Let's begin," Mr. Derek Knightly said as he entered the room. Everyone hushed and turned their full attention to the dark-haired, dashing publisher of the most popular paper in town. They would all take turns pitching their stories, and he would either approve them or request something else.

"Ladies first," Mr. Knightly said with a grin, as he started every meeting. They were all used to it by now, though the inclusion of women had not been tremendously smooth at first. However, once the editors discovered that women were always very interested in hearing they worked with the Writing Girls, and this connection could be capitalized on, relations between the sexes at *The Weekly* had improved considerably.

"I have an exclusive story," Sophie announced, well aware that "exclusive story" were two of Mr. Knightly's favorite words. As expected, his vivid blue eyes brightened even more. "The Duchess of Richmond has invited me to participate in, and report on, the plans for her daughter's wedding to the Duke of Hamilton and Brandon."

It was an unconventional proposal, and yet it made sense. Society hostesses were always angling to have their parties and dinners covered in the newspapers, particularly *The Weekly*—occasionally submitting written accounts that would hopefully be included in the gossip columns. Even if the planning of such a massive social event, as this wedding promised to be, was tremendously dull, people always gobbled up any details about duchesses and other lofty personages.

"Some are calling it the wedding of the year," Julianna added.

"Excellent," Mr. Knightly said, and one could practically see him calculating how many additional readers—and profits—the story might bring in.

"I could focus on wedding-related advice letters in the weeks leading up to the ceremony," Annabelle offered hopefully. It was plain to anyone—other than Mr. Knightly himself—that she was hopelessly infatuated with him.

"Great. Miss Fielding, what is your angle?"

"I could report on the penny weddings of the lower orders, to contrast with the excesses of the aristocracy's weddings," she offered. Eliza's anonymous articles provided a counterpoint to the grandiosity of the ton's behavior. Though not always popular, her anonymous stories were provocative and, as Mr. Knightly often reminded everyone, *scandal equals sales*.

Chapter 5

Twenty-seven days before the wedding . . .

The London ducal residence of the Duke of Hamilton and Brandon was twice as massive as one might expect. To describe it as imposing was an understatement; the surrounding buildings seemed like miniatures beside it. The Palladian mansion was three stories tall, constructed of gray stone, and had so many windows that Sophie suspected the duke paid a fortune in window taxes. It took her a few minutes to walk across the vast cobblestone courtyard to the front door.

Upon her arrival, the butler greeted Sophie, although "greeted" implied a cheer that was not present; "acknowledged" might be a more appropriate description. As per the butler's orders, a maid led Sophie through six drawing rooms (she counted) before they arrived at the intended blue drawing room in the south wing. Thus far, the residence (she hesitated to call it a home) was like nothing she had ever experienced or even imagined.

"Here we are, Miss Harlow," the maid said quietly. Sophie quickly tucked one errant curl behind her ear and smoothed her pink skirts. Then the maid opened the tall paneled door and stepped aside so that Sophie could enter.

The room was a painted pale blue, the color of a robin's egg. Landscapes in ornately carved gold frames hung on the walls. Tall windows overlooked the garden, full of plants in first bloom.

Three elegantly dressed women sat around a small table with a highly polished silver tea service. Two duchesses, one duchess to-be, and she, little Miss Sophie Harlow, daughter of a country squire, was to join them.

This was one of those moments when she was awe-struck by the direction her life had taken. Had Fletcher not been such a monumental cad, she might have been a little wife out in the country, concerned only with housekeeping and child rearing.

"You must be Miss Harlow. I am Lady Hamilton," one of the women said, rising from the moss green velvet settee to greet her. Her dark brown hair was streaked slightly with gray and elegantly arranged. She wore a plum-colored dress that suited her tall figure and highlighted her bright green eyes.

As the duchess of the house performed introductions, Sophie recalled what Julianna had told her about these women.

Everyone adored Lady Hamilton. She was known to be kind, selfless, and pleasant company. She had successfully married two of her daughters, and had one more in the schoolroom. Her son went by the second half of the title, Lord Brandon, to prevent confusion and distinguish him from his late father, who had died suddenly years earlier.

Lady Richmond and her daughter were obviously mother and daughter, for they both possessed the same tall, willowy stature, fair hair, wide-set blue eyes, and milky complexions. The younger had an angelic countenance; the elder seemed a bit more peeved and pinched.

The Duchess of Richmond was considered tolerable. Her rank assured her a prominent presence in society, and invitations to everything, even if her manners and temper happened to be found irksome occasionally. Her primary interest was ensuring her only daughter made an outstanding match.

Lady Clarissa was immediately dubbed a diamond of the first water within the first five minutes of her debut. She had turned down ten offers of marriage her first season.

She scarcely began her second season when she had snared the catch of the season. He was high-ranking, handsome, and supremely wealthy. The Duke of Hamilton and Brandon was known to be a good, honest man, too, but this was generally not considered as important.

"My son sent word that he will be a few moments late and that we should begin without him," Lady Hamilton said while preparing a cup of tea for Sophie. Ten minutes passed during which they discussed the weather— "pleasant, springlike yet with a touch of winter chill still lingering."

And then His Grace arrived.

Sophie's heart skipped a beat, stopped entirely for a second, and then, reluctantly resumed beating.

The double Duke of Hamilton and Brandon was *her* Brandon after all!

There was no mistaking it—though, to see him now, in all his ducal splendor, made her wonder how she ever thought him a mere mister. The Duke of Hamilton and Brandon stood tall and proud, as a duke ought to do. With his broad shoulders, straight spine, and head held high, it was clear that he was a man certain of himself and his place in the world.

Sophie looked him over, trying to reconcile this version of the man she had met.

His hair was dark, cut short, and kept neat—not that faux windblown style that was popular on most young bucks. She recalled wishing to muss it up. The knot on his cravat was perfectly executed with pristine white linen. His waistcoat was a light gray, complimenting the darker gray of his perfectly fitted breeches, which he wore with shiny black Hessians. He wore a forest green coat that exquisitely highlighted his bright green eyes, shadowed by exceptionally dark lashes.

Sophie had not anticipated seeing him like this. Had not dreamed that she had flirted with and fallen for an unavailable, unattainable man. Had never suspected that her funny and seemingly relaxed Mr. Brandon was one of the wealthiest and most powerful men in England. Had never expected that she would have to cover every detail of his wedding to someone else.

"My apologies for arriving late." he said as a footman closed the door behind him. "Mother, Lady Richmond, Lady Clarissa," he said in acknowledgment. When his eyes connected with hers, she saw a flicker of recognition and surprise in his gaze, while his expression remained inscrutable.

She heard his sharp intake of breath.

"You seem a touch out of breath, Brandon. Did you run to be here with us?" Lady Hamilton asked.

"No."

Sophie knew the reason: his breath was stolen by the shock, just as was hers.

"I'd like to introduce Miss Sophie Harlow of *The London Weekly*," Lady Hamilton said.

Miss Harlow of that rubbish news rag, Sophie thought, and declined to say.

"Miss Harlow," he replied with a slight nod of his head. He remembered her, that was clear, but he would not acknowledge it. She understood why; it did not lessen the sting.

"Your Grace," Sophie said, dropping into a curtsy. He was Mr. Brandon no longer. This man before her was a stranger, and she would act accordingly. "It's an honor to make your acquaintance."

At least now she knew why he hadn't called upon her. Because, oh, he was engaged to be married to someone else!

Sophie allowed herself a sigh, resigned to what promised to be a long, awkward, and heartbreaking interview. When it was over, she would return home and cry, but in the meantime, she must focus on the task at hand.

"Shall we begin?" Lady Hamilton suggested.

No, Sophie thought. She did not want to request, record, and report every detail from the first meeting of Lord Brandon and Lady Clarissa to their wedding day. Horrors. Agonies. After this interview, she would tell Knightly she could not complete this story. But first—

"Yes, let's begin," Sophie said as brightly as she could manage, because she had a job to do. She fumbled to remove from her reticule a small tablet and a pencil with which to take notes. She was a touch nervous, since this was one of the first formal interviews she'd conducted and certainly one with the most illustrious personages imaginable. Usually, she based her column on her attendance at the weddings or on written reports submitted by the couples. That it was an interview regarding the wedding of the man of her dreams to another woman did not put her mind or heart at ease.

"First, allow me to say that we at *The London Weekly* are very excited by this opportunity. I'll start today with some questions about the couple," Sophie said.

Lady Clarissa folded her hands in her lap. Lady Richmond pursed her lips. Lady Hamilton smiled patiently. Lord Brandon looked as if he longed to be elsewhere. Though Sophie understood perfectly well, she felt no sympathy for him.

"Lady Clarissa, if I may," Sophie started, "our readers would love to know how the idea for this story came about."

Clarissa opened her mouth to answer, but her mother spoke first.

"As you might imagine, *everyone* has been asking about every little detail about the wedding from the second the betrothal was announced. The material of my dear Clarissa's dress, the flowers, the menu for the wedding breakfast, and so on and so forth. My dear, dear friend Lady Carrington suggested the idea for the newspaper story. I think she might have been jesting, but I took her seriously," Lady Richmond said, concluding with a large intake of breath to replenish herself.

Sophie was afraid to look at her, lest she understand it as an indication to carry on. Instead, she glanced at Lord Brandon and saw that he was gazing attentively at her. She could feel her cheeks turn pink.

"Lady Clarissa," Sophie started, "could you tell our readers about meeting His Grace for the first time?"

She looked at her mother, and at her nod of approval answered, "We met at a ball."

"The ball was hosted by Lady Redleigh, the duchess, and our dear, dear friend Earl Strathmore facilitated the introductions," Lady Richmond added.

Sophie wrote *shameless name-dropper* on her tablet.

Of Lady Clarissa's first impression of His Grace, reported by her mother, Sophie wrote *same as mine*. In other words: handsome, honorable, kind, and respectful, and "not at all like those good-for-nothing rakes overrunning this town."

Oh, she had to see what Lord Brandon thought of that. When she glanced at him, he raised one brow, and inclined his head slightly as if to say, "I told you so."

So he wasn't a rake. He was handsome, honorable, kind, and respectful. Sophie wondered if Lady Clarissa also found him funny and charming, or if his presence made her cheeks turn pink and her heart quicken its pace. Sophie wondered if Lady Clarissa forgot about the rest of the world when he looked into her eyes and smiled.

There was a long silence while Sophie debated asking, and decided it was best if she did not.

"Your Grace, I hate to pry—" Sophie couldn't resist stating. He began to laugh, and covered it quickly with a cough. She bit back a smirk.

"Are you all right today, Brandon?" Lady Hamilton asked with motherly concern.

"I'm fine, Mother," he ground out. "You were saying, Miss Harlow?"

"Perhaps you could share your first impression of your fiancée."

"I noticed her beauty and that she possesses all the qualities of a perfect duchess," he said, providing an answer that made her heart sink. Sophie might have been pretty, but she was no beauty like Clarissa Richmond. And Sophie was so far from being a duchess—due to class and training and education and the fact that she worked—that it was laughable to even give it a fleeting consideration.

She suffered a wave of embarrassment, for she felt

like a fool for daring to dream of love, of Mr. Brandon and herself.

Lady Richmond beamed at his answer, though. Lady Clarissa smiled, gazing down at her hands in her lap, twisting a ring around on her finger.

His answer was complimentary, true, and yet rather bland. She wondered what he had thought of her: feather-brained, a danger to herself and others, and shockingly forward, no doubt. And then she reminded herself that his opinion of her didn't matter.

"And the proposal?" Sophie asked. She did not bother to address her query to anyone in particular, for it was clear Lady Richmond would answer all and any questions.

"His Grace declared his intentions quickly! Within only two weeks we received an offer of marriage," Lady Richmond interjected.

We?

Lady Clarissa sighed. Sophie caught her eye and they shared a smile. Lord Brandon still looked miserable. And Sophie could have sworn she caught Lady Hamilton roll her eyes. But duchesses did not roll their eyes. Everyone knew that.

"After he had secured my father's permission," Lady Clarissa managed to add, "I was called to join them in the library of our home in London. It was there he asked for my hand in marriage."

"Your parents, Lord and Lady Richmond, were present?" Sophie clarified.

"Yes," Clarissa said. She pulled a face, revealing that she knew it was not very romantic at all.

"Lord and Lady Richmond wished to stay," Lord Brandon added, diplomatically blaming his future in-laws for sucking some of the magic from the moment. *Well done,* she conceded.

Utterly unromantic proposal, she wrote on her tablet. But why should she be surprised? Most ton marriages were not love matches, in fact many were seen as merely alliances for the purpose of accumulating and perpetuating wealth.

"Yes," Lady Richmond said, and then continued, "we couldn't very well miss one of the finest moments in Richmond heritage! For more than a century, the Richmonds have married into the best families in England. Keeping this tradition alive and carrying on the family line depends entirely upon my only child, and we are so glad these two illustrious families shall become one, and that, by special order of the king, the Richmond title shall continue through their son."

Sophie began to write all of this down, and then gave up, scrawling only *Richmond's fate so very important, by order of the king*. That was a lot of investment, responsibility, and pressure on a child who had not yet been born or, presumably, conceived.

Sophie glanced at the couple—both of them so reserved and proper and in their bearing—and she doubted they would anticipate the wedding night. Oh, she ought not think of such things!

"Tell us more about the proposal, Lady Clarissa," Sophie urged, pointedly ignoring Lady Richmond and looking at her daughter instead.

"Lord Brandon said he had great admiration for me and asked if I would do him the honor of becoming his duchess. And upon my acceptance he gave me a beautiful betrothal ring."

She and Lord Brandon shared a slight smile; it was the first sign of affection they had displayed in this interview. Sophie's stomach did a little flip-flop.

"The ring is a Hamilton and Brandon family heirloom," Lady Hamilton said. Clarissa held out her left hand so Sophie might see the gold band bearing a large, square-cut emerald, surrounded by dozens of tiny diamonds.

"It is stunning," Sophie said truthfully.

"The proposal was such a very touching scene to witness," Lady Richmond cut in. Again. "In fact, I wept dearly. It's every mother's dream to see her daughter betrothed to a man such as His Grace."

Sophie managed a wan smile and jotted down the words *overbearing and meddlesome*. There was absolutely no way she could tolerate a month of the woman's presence without losing her sanity.

"Indeed," Sophie murmured, looking down at her tablet. All her questions had been answered, except for the grossly inappropriate ones she could not ask, such as:

Why did you not mention you were a duke when we first met? And betrothed?

Why were you so damned charming?

Why did you make me fall halfway in love with you when you knew it would only come to nothing?

"I think I have enough material for the first story," Sophie said. "Thank you so much for sharing your time." She put her tablet and pencil back in her reticule. For once, she would remember her things.

"Miss Harlow, I'll show you to the foyer," Brandon offered.

"Thank you, Your Grace, but it won't be necessary." Eyebrows arched and eyes widened at that. Apparently it was not done to refuse a duke in his own home.

"Are you certain you can find your way?" he asked skeptically.

"Absolutely," she declared confidently.

Not really at all, actually. But she couldn't bear another opportunity to find him charming, handsome, and unattainable. Sophie then took her leave of the duchesses and the duchess-to-be.

Once the doors closed behind her, Sophie marched down the hall, promising herself that the moment she finished here, she would inform Mr. Knightly that she would have nothing to do with the wedding-of-the-year.

But first she had to escape this blasted house! She had been certain this was the way to the foyer, but after a few minutes she did not recognize her surroundings at all and concluded she must have made a mistake. She would simply turn around and try again. Yet after a few more apparently wrong turns, she had to admit she was well and truly lost.

Sophie began to feel the creeping, prickling heat of mortification and panic.

Recalling that she had not passed through a corridor to meet the duchesses, but through a succession of drawing rooms, Sophie began opening doors hoping that one would open to a room that looked vaguely familiar. Or perhaps she would encounter a servant who might point her in the right direction or—even better—personally escort her out.

She might not be allowed back after such an episode, which wouldn't matter because after she quit the story—oh, she prayed Knightly would let her quit the story—Miss Sophie Harlow, Writing Girl of *The London Weekly*, would have no further business with the Duke of Hamilton and Brandon or anyone of his household.

Perhaps this door, Sophie thought, and turned the knob. She pushed the door just a bit, then peeked in.

Drat.

She tried to close the door before she was seen or heard, but it was too late.

Chapter 6

"**E**nter," commanded a firm ducal voice that sounded slightly weary and annoyed. Sophie stepped into the room and saw that she had found her way to the duke's private study.

Hell and damnation!

His Grace sat at his desk, which was a massive, solid, engraved mahogany piece that seemed as though it would require at least six footmen to move.

Bookshelves lined three walls, and held thousands of multicolored leather-bound volumes behind beveled glass doors. A large globe stood in one corner. Matching richly upholstered chairs and settees, and all the usual expensive things abounded.

The duke looked up from his work and gave her a thorough perusal, as if he could not make sense of her presence in his study.

"I'm terribly sorry to intrude. I see that you are busy, so I shall call another time. Good day," she said, and made a move to go. She wondered if she could exit by way of the tall floor-to-ceiling windows overlooking the courtyard, but decided against it.

Staying was out of the question. Miss Sophie Harlow would have no business with a man who could grossly mislead innocent young ladies such as herself. Granted, she hadn't asked if he were betrothed, but still, she had no reason to stay and every reason to quit at once.

"I have a moment now, Miss Harlow," Lord Brandon said, standing from where he sat behind his desk. As if she needed to be reminded of his height and broad shoulders and positively ducal stature. His gaze locked with hers.

Oh, blast, she thought.

"I had thought of an additional question to ask you. That's all. But really, it is not urgent . . ."

"It must be important if you took the trouble to find me here," he said with a faint smile.

"It seemed so at the time, but really, Your Grace, it's not important at all."

"You came all this way, Miss Harlow, to *not* ask a question?" She knew then that he was well aware that she had gotten lost after refusing an escort to the foyer. He was too much of a gentleman to accuse her of such outright, but not so much that he couldn't have a spot of fun with her.

Which meant she could have a spot of fun with him.

"My question, Your Grace, is whether you ever get lost in this house."

His Grace, the Duke of Hamilton and Brandon, gave a shout of laughter. And then that settled into the low rumble of a man's genuine laugh. The sound thrilled her. As if that had broken some sort of spell, he relaxed a little—and she caught a glimpse of the man she'd first met, Brandon the mere mister.

He took a step forward to stand before the desk and casually leaned against it. Glancing left, then right, ensuring no eavesdroppers, he said, "No. At least, it has been some time since I have done so." He paused, then continued: "I grew up here and spent hours exploring. Although, once I was so lost that I could not find my way back in time for dinner, which is when it was noticed that I had gone missing. All the footmen and maids were sent to search for me."

Sophie treaded softly across the plush Aubusson carpets, drawn closer by his story and by the image of him as a young boy bravely exploring such a grand house alone. When, she wondered, did he develop the proud, reserved demeanor she had seen him display during their meeting? It was such a contrast to the mere Mr. Brandon on her walk, and the man talking to her now.

He continued: "But it was my father who found me in the maps room in the east wing."

Maps *room*? How large was this house?

"You must have been very scared. I certainly would be in this house after nightfall," Sophie said. If ghosts existed, they would certainly haunt gigantic ancestral homes such as this one.

"Well, that's because you're a girl," he said matter-of-factly. She was about to protest when she caught a mischievous gleam in his eye.

"I can admit it because I am a girl," Sophie retorted. "Did that misadventure put an end to your explorations?"

"Oh, no. After that, I had Cook pack sustenance for me, because—"

"One must always be prepared," she said, finishing his sentence.

"Exactly."

"I don't suppose that among those papers you have a map of this house," Sophie said, referring to the neat piles on his desk. "I haven't time to get lost again on my way out."

"Let's see," he said, picking up a stack and thumbing

through the lot of them, as if there might actually be a map of Hamilton House. As he did, one sheet escaped from the group and fell gently to floor, resting on the carpet.

Sophie bent down to retrieve it, and so did the duke. Their heads collided.

"Ouch!" Sophie said, laughing a little. It was more shocking than painful.

"Ouch, indeed," he responded, grinning and rubbing his temple.

"You have a hard head," Sophie said, hastily adding, "Your Grace."

"You are not the first to say so, Miss Harlow, but you are the first to speak literally."

"Why does that not surprise me?" Sophie wondered.

"Would it be ungentlemanly of me to say that you, too, have a hard head?" he asked.

"I'm not quite certain of the etiquette on that. I could ask 'Dear Annabelle'," Sophie said, mentioning her fellow Writing Girls' advice column in *The Weekly*. "Should it turn out to be improper, I shall not hold it against you."

"Thank you. I do pride myself upon being the perfect gentleman," he said as he stood and held out his hand to help her up.

She placed her right hand in his. She wore beautiful cream-colored kidskin gloves that were ever so soft to the touch. Brandon's hands were bare, warm, large, and strong—everything a man's hands should be.

With the slightest effort, he helped her to her feet and she stood before him, as close as if they were about to waltz. Sophie tilted her head back so that she might look up at him rather than straight into his chest that she knew to be firm and strong.

Lord Brandon was gazing down at her intently.

They were still holding hands.

She took a deep breath and felt him tense. Brandon released her hand and took a small step away. A sense of shame and guilt tempered her pleasure.

She recalled that troublesome half-sheet of paper, which she held in her other hand the whole time.

"Now, what has caused all this trouble?" she wondered aloud, surprised to find her voice oddly shaky.

"Oh, no, you don't," he said, reaching for the paper.

Years of experience with her older brother made Sophie instinctively turn quickly, presenting her back to Lord Brandon as she held the paper far in front of her, and far from his grasp. Vaguely, she was aware that this was wrong, rude, and in violation of every known rule of etiquette.

But it was too late to surrender. Lord Brandon reached out and closed his hand around her wrist—gentle, but still commanding. Sophie was suddenly hotly aware of him and this strange half-embrace. If she were to lean back, she would certainly find his chest there to stop her fall. Mere inches of air, if that, and a few layers of clothing kept them from touching.

Sophie knew what it felt like to be held by him and that it was worth risking everything for. She ached to close her eyes, surrender, and lean against him to savor the blissful and rare sensation of being held in a man's arms. Sophie gave in to temptation and relaxed into his embrace.

This was inappropriate. She didn't need to ask "Dear Annabelle" about that.

"Miss Harlow," he said softly, and his warm breath swept gently across the back of her neck, making her shiver. If she were to turn her head ever so slightly, her mouth would be in kissing distance of his. It was so very, very tempting.

It was outrageously unacceptable.

Instead she focused her attention on the sheet in her hand, and read aloud: "Desired Qualities in a Wife."

"Miss Harlow . . ." he repeated, and the warning tone was unmistakable.

"Item the first: *'Attractive.'* That is understandable," Sophie commented. "A pretty face across from yours at the breakfast table would be pleasant."

She dared not refer to other reasons why an attractive spouse might be preferred for fear that she could not control the blush.

"I thought so," he said tightly as he loosened his grip and took a step back.

"Item the second: *'Reasonable Intelligence.'* That strikes me as . . . reasonable," she said. The duke now stood away from her, leaning against his desk with his arms crossed over his chest. Obviously he was not pleased with this but would patiently allow her to continue with this ridiculously rude charade of hers. She could not stop.

What did a man like the esteemed and illustrious Duke of Hamilton and Brandon wish for in a wife?

Thus far, Sophie liked to think she qualified—not that she was a candidate for the position.

She thought herself of reasonable intelligence and fairly attractive. No odes and poems had been written to her beauty, as many had done for Lady Clarissa, but she had been called pretty often enough. As for intelligence, well, she was a history-making journalist. If she wasn't smart, then she was absolutely mad. But that was not to be debated at present. There was this list in her hand . . .

"Item the third: *'Agreeable Temperament,'*" she said, and then continued: "Again, I do concur that is a reasonable request in a spouse. One would not wish to deal with hysterical tantrums or violent outbursts or the like."

"I do not care for episodes of disruptive or highly emotional behavior," he remarked. Sophie decided to ignore that and carry on with her disruptive behavior.

"Item the fourth: *'From a respectable and distinguished family,'*" Sophie concluded. That was all. That was all that he required in a wife. An attractive woman, with a modicum of intelligence, placid personality, and distinguished lineage.

"It seems to me," Sophie remarked, "that you have found the perfect woman in Lady Clarissa, for she fulfills all of these qualities."

"I am in agreement with your assessment."

"Anyone would think so. But I notice something, Your Grace. Love is not mentioned on this list," Sophie said, daring to carry on. She had traveled so far out of the bounds of propriety that there was really no going back now. Lord Brandon did not stop her.

"Of course not," he said, responding in the same tone one might have if one were to say, *Naturally, I do not wish to marry someone with a second head.*

"Why would you not wish for love? Or at the very least, companionship, friendship, or affection?" Sophie asked. She had always wondered why one would marry for anything less—if they already had money and status and security. Lord Brandon could certainly afford the luxury of a love match.

"Because, Miss Harlow, the purpose of marriage is to combine assets and protect them for the future generations, which one is to create. Love does not enter into it at all."

"But love will make all of that so much more happy, pleasant, wonderful . . ."

"Or it can lead to crushing and devastating heartache that numbs one to any and all other pleasures in life," Lord Brandon said sharply, and Sophie was taken aback. "I trust that none of this will find its way into your column, Miss Harlow?" Lord Brandon said softly, but firmly.

"Of course not. I should hate to crush the romantic notions of my readers," she retorted.

There was a knock at the door.

"Enter," he said sharply.

Lady Clarissa opened the door and joined them. Again Sophie suffered a rush of guilt for being alone with another woman's fiancé, even though it was an accident, and even though nothing truly untoward had happened. Although, it did feel like *something*. They had laughed, nearly embraced, and almost fought. It was so very wrong.

"I only wished to inform you that my mother and I are departing now," Lady Clarissa said.

"It was a pleasure to share your company today. I look forward to seeing you again at our betrothal ball," he added, taking Clarissa's hand and brushing a kiss across her knuckles.

"I was also about to depart," Sophie said, noticing her opportunity to have someone guide her to the exit of this loveless house. "Goodbye, Your Grace. I shall cease to distract you from important matters of state and other tasks of grave importance."

Sophie set that troublesome list on his desk, curtseyed, received a nod of dismissal from the duke, and crossed the room to leave with the attractive, reasonably intelligent, agreeably tempered, and ancestrally distinguished Lady Clarissa Richmond.

There was a maid with her, who walked ahead, showing the way.

"I still get lost in this house and fear I always will,"

Clarissa confided. And then, horrified at her confession, she begged that Sophie would not include that in her column.

"I would never. And I completely understand. In fact, I got lost myself and stumbled upon His Grace's study."

"I see," Clarissa said. "Please do write to me should you have any further inquiries. I would be delighted to answer them *myself*. " With that slight emphasis, Lady Clarissa made herself clear: she would answer the questions, and not her mother. Clarissa was too polite to say so directly, and Sophie was also too polite to say it herself. But a conspiratorial smile crossed each of their mouths. They understood each other.

"That is very kind of you to offer. Thank you."

Sophie also saw that Clarissa may be quiet, demure, endlessly obliging, but she was nobody's fool.

Chapter 7

In His Grace's Study

That Miss Harlow was *trouble*, and Brandon was glad when she shut the door behind her. No more interruptions, distractions, or head collisions and childhood confessions. He could resume his review of his marriage contract before he signed it.

She had him talking about his childhood and his father! He rarely did so with his three sisters, and merely endured such conversations when his mother brought them up. He never willfully offered information about his ten-year-old self and the hero and idol that was otherwise known as his father. *Was.*

Brandon turned his attention back to the contract he'd been reviewing, then set it down a moment later.

Her luscious figure and wicked sense of humor had managed to pierce all his defenses and shatter his ducal armor.

That was trouble, and it was unacceptable.

It—*she*—would be best avoided in the future.

Brandon took a deep breath and willed his pulse to subside. The worst part—he could barely bring himself to admit this—was that he enjoyed her company. She was quite funny and made him laugh more in their two meetings than he had done in years.

She was quick, smart, impertinent, and adorable. He suspected her notes in that book of hers were devilishly insightful. She was a tempting pleasure to look at.

And in that moment when he held her and kissed her at parting . . . His body was reacting to the memory in a manner his brain and morals disagreed with.

She was trouble. He did not care for trouble.

But, damn it, if trouble didn't feel amazing in his arms.

He definitely must take the greatest care to stay away from her.

Clarissa was like a refreshing and restorative glass of cold water. His good sense returned to him upon seeing her.

Her cool beauty and obliging temperament would not disturb him. She would never interrupt him. He would not be tempted to leave his work and walk halfway across London with her. She would never burst into his study and engage him in chatter about his boyhood self, or tempt him to embrace her, kiss her, or make love to her on the floor. With Clarissa as his wife, Brandon was certain of smooth sailing, free of storms, never to be blown off course.

He would care for her, but he would never fall in love with her.

That was what he wanted.

He found his list—*Desirable Qualities in a Wife*—and reviewed it once more. Brandon was utterly certain that he was correct. These were excellent qualities for a duchess and a wife. He had betrothed himself to the perfect woman. In a few weeks, he would marry her.

Though he hadn't given the contract as thorough a review as he would like, Brandon gave it his signature.

There was really no point to sparing a thought for Miss Harlow at all.

Lady Jane's Salon
Mayfair, London

After her meeting with the duke and duchesses, Sophie met Julianna at the salon of Lady Jane, a witty, eccentric woman who invited writers, artists, scientists, and all manner of interesting people for witty, brilliant conversation. It was the sort of social circle that simply did not exist in Chesham, and was even a rarity in London.

Upon her arrival in Lady Jane's drawing room— decorated in stunning chinoiserie style that had recently become the height of fashion—Sophie found an empty seat next to Julianna on a velvet settee and was served a cup of hot tea, along with a slice of vanilla sponge cake with butter cream frosting. It was just the thing, after the events of earlier in the day.

"Do tell all about the duchesses, darling," Julianna began.

"Lady Clarissa is smarter than given credit for, and Lady Hamilton is guilty of not letting her good nature overpower Lady Richmond's tendency to dominate every conversation."

"Oh, my. And the duke?" Julianna asked, taking a sip of tea.

"Is my Brandon," Sophie said.

Julianna spit out the tea.

"I cannot bring you anywhere," Sophie said with a laugh, and looked around. Everyone else seemed deep in private discussions and did not seem to have noticed, though a maid swiftly appeared with napkins and promptly vanished.

"The Duke of Hamilton and Brandon, engaged to the daughter of the Duke of Richmond, saved your life and escorted you home! I cannot believe it!" Julianna exclaimed. A few people turned in their direction.

"It's true. Of course, he pretended not to know me when we were introduced," Sophie said with a twinge of bitterness in her voice. She took a bite of the cake and found it sweet and comforting.

"Distasteful, slightly rude, but ultimately understandable," her friend replied.

"I know. But it very much made the situation clear to me and markedly diminished my feelings for him," Sophie said, wishing it all ended there. She took another fortifying bite of cake before she carried on. "But then . . ."

"Then what?"

"I am waiting for you to swallow your sip of tea," Sophie said.

"Done."

"Then I accidentally entered his private study. While he was in it . . . Are you aware of how massive the ducal residence is? One could quite easily get lost. In fact, one did get very lost . . ."

"What did you do, Sophie?" Julianna asked, sounding nervous about the answer.

"I might have declined an escort of a maid, or the duke, in a fit of pique," she answered truthfully, with a sheepish smile. Honestly, it had been ridiculous behavior on her part, but it felt so very essential that she not spend any more time with Brandon.

"Oh, Sophie," Julianna said, laughing a little. But then she became serious. "You were alone with the duke?"

"Oh, yes." And then, when Julianna had set down her tea, Sophie related the scene to her wide-eyed friend—particularly the collision of heads, and the dramatic recitation of the list of *Desirable Qualities in a Wife*—to Julianna's great amusement.

Though she wasn't sure why, exactly, Sophie didn't relate the part about their embrace and the dangerous temptation to kiss him. The moment had been too magnificent, and Sophie did not want to be lectured on the impropriety of it. She wanted to keep the memory special. And private.

Her stomach began to ache. She told herself it was the tea, but it was more likely guilt.

"I don't suppose you tried to quit the story on the grounds of extreme emotional distress?" Julianna queried.

"Naturally. Knightly refused, saying it was the equivalent of allowing Mitch Radnor to only cover sporting events in which his team, person, or horse wins."

"Men. Sports," Julianna scoffed, with a roll of her eyes.

"I'm not quite sure that my situation compares to a horse race or boxing match. But his point was taken," Sophie said. She was to suffer for the newspaper and to report the news, regardless of the cost to her emotions and tax upon her nerves.

"Of course, you shall not entertain feelings for him any longer. Really, there should be no distress at all," Julianna said as if it were that simple.

Sophie agreed, even though it was much more complicated. Yes, he was as good as married, which meant that she absolutely would not *act* upon any amorous feelings for him. That was easy to control; her feelings were proving to be much more unruly.

She was just so curious about him now—he was so reserved and imposing one minute, and then laughing easily and flirting the next. And then there was the baser attraction she felt for him, one that she could not discuss in polite company. It was the overwhelming desire to be held by him, to kiss him, to forget the whole world while lost in a long, hot embrace . . .

Julianna noticed her hesitation, and perhaps even her blush inspired by a potent combination of lust and guilt.

"Sophie! You can't. He's married, or as good as married!"

"I know," Sophie said. "I know."

She was only reporting upon every last detail of his amazingly unromantic betrothal and greatly anticipated wedding.

"A match that grand will not be broken," Julianna said firmly. "And, I hate to say it, Sophie, but if it were, it wouldn't be for the likes of us. He is a duke, after all."

"I know." Sophie was the daughter of local gentry, and wouldn't be invited anywhere of significance if it were not for her scandalous and sensational profession as a writer for *The London Weekly*.

Julianna was a widowed baroness, and thus welcomed to *ton* events. Her suspected, but unconfirmed, position as the anonymous author of "Fashionable Intelligence" enhanced her social status.

The finer points of their social status aside, Sophie in no way had the background or position to qualify as a potential duchess. Maybe if he fell in love and forgot about sense and logic, but the duke had made it clear that love was not an option.

"That way lies heartache. Or, at best, a life as his mistress, and Sophie you cannot do that," Julianna pleaded. Her late husband had been an unfaithful cad, and Julianna had never quite recovered from it.

Having been jilted for another woman, Sophie knew

the heartache all too well. It was unfathomable that she act the part of a treacherous, adulterous woman.

Even now, almost one year later, her stomach tightened into a knot at the thought of that awful day. The mortification had faded after a few weeks. For a few more months she had alternated between stunned disbelief and sobs so powerful she could barely breathe. That faded in time, too, thank God. And now she was left with a horror of having it happen again.

Weddings were distasteful. Daring to love enough to walk down the aisle was incomprehensible. That her actions should subject another to that same agony must be avoided at all costs.

"You're right. I shall cease any feelings of an amorous nature at once," Sophie declared. Perhaps it could be that simple. She doubted it, but it was worth a try. She took another bite of cake.

"What are we discussing over here, ladies?" Lady Jane fluttered over and perched on a nearby chair. She was petite, with light brown hair and light blue eyes.

"Do you think, Lady Jane, that it is possible to cease romantic feelings at will for an unsuitable person?" Sophie asked.

"Now, that is a diverting question, Miss Harlow!" Lady Jane said with a smile. "Jocelyn, I suspect you have something to say about that."

"I think that if you could find a way, there'd be a fortune in it—though I personally would be broke!" Jocelyn Kemble, renowned and beloved actress, declared.

All the salon attendees laughed at that.

"All the rakes in London would find themselves suddenly short on admirers," Julianna added.

"Reformed by default!" declared the famous and

beloved actor Julian Gage, to more laughter. Talk of reformed rakes reminded Sophie of Brandon, which was trouble.

"Just imagine a tonic to cure unsuitable affections," Jameson Wright mused. It was only natural that he would think of that, since he was a science enthusiast and frequently conducted his own experiments, and, apparently, invented all sorts of concoctions.

Sophie suspected she would have need of such a tonic, though she also suspected that it wouldn't work.

"It would sell well among concerned parents, cuckolded husbands, and jealous wives," noted Alistair Grey, fellow writer for *The Weekly*, good friend to Writing Girls, and frequent escort to the theater.

"But what would the poets write of?" asked a poet.

"And how would the residents of Gretna find income, if not from elopements?" asked Jack Sinclair, the second son of a baron and renowned rake.

"And would business increase or decrease for brewers and innkeepers?" wondered Jonathan Harris. He was a kind, handsome man and a barrister. He was the sort of man a girl ought to fall in love with, but could never manage to. Sophie offered him a smile, and wished that his smile made her heartbeat race like Brandon's did.

"In short, it would be an economic disaster if unsuitable love was surmountable," Lady Jane summarized.

"Except for the person who sold the remedy. He would find himself possessed of a fortune," Jocelyn said, and she then blatantly made eyes at Jameson to the amusement of all. He merely arched a brow suggestively in response. Julian Gage scowled.

"Thus, it is our patriotic duty to fall in love with all manner of unsuitables: rakes, rogues, married, betrothed . . ." Alistair declared grandly.

"Those above our social station," Sophie said, hoping her voice did not betray too much emotion.

"Or below it," someone added.

"Those prone to drinking, whoring, or wagering," Julianna said, and Sophie knew that she was thinking of her late husband, Lord Somerset. Brandon did not seem like the sort that would indulge is those vices, if any at all.

"Those that spend too much," Jonathan offered.

"Or misers that spend too little," Jocelyn said.

"The excessively vain," Julian Gage proposed.

"Those of whom our parents do not approve," another added.

"Those that do not return our love," said Sophie.

"It is a wonder that any of us do manage to fall in love and live happily ever after," said the salon hostess, and her guests murmured their agreement.

It was indeed a magnificent thing, Sophie agreed, and it was so very unlikely to happen to her. Dukes did not break off betrothals to perfect duchesses a month before a wedding. They certainly did not do so for lower-class girls that worked. Only love would drive a man to do such an illogical, irrational thing, and the Duke of Hamilton and Brandon was not going to fall under the spell of that finer emotion.

She vowed to keep her feelings in check, and to avoid all and any circumstances that would tempt her to do otherwise.

Chapter 8

Twenty-six days before the wedding . . .

Hamilton House

It had been so simple. Logical. Rational.

He, the Duke of Hamilton and Brandon, needed to take a wife. He set about doing so in the same deliberate and methodical manner with which he did every task. He made a list—in this case, of qualities his future wife ought to possess.

His course of action was obvious upon making the acquaintance of Lady Clarissa. He proposed, she accepted, they would marry and that was that—or so he thought.

The decidedly unsuitable Miss Sophie Harlow consumed an embarrassing number of his waking thoughts and all of his dreams. Very wicked ones, too.

Last night his dream began with a vivid recollection of the scene from his study, in which he held her in his arms, flush against him. Her bottom nestled against his arousal, and his hands resting upon his waist. It seemed he could feel the heat from her body, or had he been that hot with desire?

He dreamt that, as he held her, there was a knock at the study door.

She held that damned list in her little hand, and he tore it from her, crumpled it, and threw it aside. Someone persisted at knocking on the door.

In this dream, Brandon then proceeded to kiss her, beginning with the delicate skin at the nape of her neck. Even in his dream, he was aware that it was illicit and indecent. This being his wildest dreams, he did not care about propriety or decency but only about satiating his lust with Miss Harlow. So he caressed her: the ample curve of her hip and moving upward to the full swell of her breasts, cupping them in his bare hands.

She sighed. He groaned in pleasure. The knocking at the door continued.

He was about to kiss her full, pink mouth . . . and then he woke up.

Dressing for the ball celebrating his engagement to the perfect Lady Clarissa was *not* the time to relive that dream, especially if his traitorous body was going to react as it did last night.

Would Miss Harlow be there as part of her story? It was quite likely.

His pulse quickened at the thought of seeing her. Again. Tonight.

To feel excitement at the prospect of seeing this troublesome Writing Girl or to have lusty dreams that he then proceeded to repeat and repent at his leisure was not acceptable. In his head, he began composing a list:

Things he ought to think about other than Miss Harlow:

1. His perfect fiancée.
2. The Parliamentary bill on tax policy reform that he would be introducing.

3. The plight of war widows and orphans.
4. The latest *Waverly* novel (for such books were his secret vice).
5. Dressing for his engagement ball.

Half dressed in his breeches and an unbuttoned shirt—and so heated from his lascivious thoughts that he did not notice the draft that was prevalent in all ancestral homes—Brandon picked up an horrendous scrap of pink satin.

With a curious expression, he turned to his valet.

"Jennings, what is this?" he asked, holding the offensive garment away from his person in one hand.

"It's a waistcoat, my lord."

"Yes, I can see that. Where did it come from? Don't tell me I chose this for myself."

Flowers had been embroidered in scarlet thread. If he selected this, he must have been deep into his cups at the time. Except that he never fell too deeply into his cups, for he had long ago learned exactly how much alcohol he could consume without making an ass of himself or feeling the aftereffects the next morning. He abided by that.

"The elder Lady Richmond sent it over for you to wear this evening, as to compliment the younger Lady Richmond's gown," Jennings explained.

"We need to match?" Brandon asked incredulously.

"It appears that Lady Richmond is of the opinion that you and your fiancée should appear coordinated in your appearances this evening."

"I will not clothe my person in this horrendous item," Brandon declared, still frowning at the thing. Pink? He could not wear pink. He certainly could not wear pink embroidered with flowers. He would be the laughing-stock of London.

"Of course, my lord, you do not need to wear anything you do not wish to. However, it is advisable to placate your future wife and her mother-in-law. If I may be so bold as to speak from personal experience, one does not want to make an enemy of one's wife's relations. They make for unrelenting enemies that a man can never escape."

"I see," Brandon said. He had not been fully prepared for Clarissa's parents. Her mother knew everyone and made sure everyone else knew about it. If her father conversed on a topic other than horse breeding, Brandon had yet to discover it. Still, he supposed it could be worse.

"But Jennings, your honest opinion—is this not the worst garment you have ever set eyes upon?"

"It is an abomination against good taste, my lord," the valet agreed.

"I will give you five pounds if that thing suffers a horrible accident that renders it unwearable," Brandon declared, handing it to his valet, who promptly threw it into the fire.

"Might I suggest the gray waistcoat instead, my lord?" he intoned.

"You certainly may. Thank you, Jennings."

A few hours later
The Ballroom of Hamilton House

It was official: she was the future Lady Hamilton and Brandon. The announcement had been made, the guests had cheered and toasted with glasses of chilled champagne, and now the prospective bride and groom embarked on a waltz as hundreds of their closest friends and acquaintances watched on.

Clarissa desperately wished that she were anywhere else. She'd be an absolute wallflower if her mother would ever allow it.

"Are you enjoying this evening?" her fiancé asked.

"Very much, thank you. Are you?" Clarissa answered, following two of her mother's rules: Always agree with the gentleman, and always ask him about himself. Implied was that she shouldn't discuss herself, lest she bore him.

"I am," he answered, and then he added, "You do look beautiful tonight, Lady Clarissa."

"Thank you, Lord Brandon." She didn't use his first name, Henry. No one seemed to call him that, ever.

She noticed that he wisely wasn't wearing the waistcoat her mother had selected for him. Sometimes her mother embarrassed her by what she said, or how much she said, or the gowns and, now, waistcoats she insisted were "so very much the thing" when they were anything but. Clarissa experienced a pang of jealousy that Lord Brandon could simply refuse to wear the offensive item and not suffer a harangue from her mother. She could never be so courageous.

After a moment of silence, Clarissa dared to hope that they could maintain this comfortable state of non-conversation. She started to relax, just a touch. Lord Brandon was a tall man with a manner of carrying himself that just radiated power, control, and dominance. He was so reserved, too. She never knew quite what to say to him, which didn't quite matter since she often found herself too intimidated to speak anyway.

He did not facilitate conversation or attempt to deepen their relationship. Still, he was a good man. He would be kind to her. She would do her best to be a good wife.

Perhaps she could be silent and smile prettily while he could be impressive and ducal for the remainder of the waltz.

But then he spoke, and he asked the strangest question: "Do you think love is a requisite component of matrimony?"

"I beg your pardon?"

"Do you think love is necessary for marriage?"

"My mother says that love is something that comes to a married couple in time. To fall in love before marriage is to risk all manner of foolish and dangerous behavior. In fact, I daresay my mother thinks love is a fatal disease," she finished.

Her mother often told the story of her dear, departed sister Eleanor, whose passionate premarital love affair had led to her being socially ostracized, heartbroken, ruined, and dead. This ill-fated affair had profoundly influenced her mother and Clarissa even suspected her own life might have been drastically different if things had been a bit less disastrous for Aunt Eleanor.

There was a painting of the two of them hanging above the mantel in her mother's private drawing room. Clarissa, her mother, and her late aunt were practically identical with their honey-hued hair, large blue eyes, and willowy figures. "If only Eleanor had lived," her mother often said with a sigh. If Clarissa was anything less than perfectly obliging, a rare occurrence indeed, she was cautioned to remember her ill-fated Aunt Eleanor.

"I would not go so far as your mother to say that love is a fatal disease, but her point is taken. Love and passion lead to irrational behavior and poor choices," he lectured. "However, an easy and affectionate relationship developing between a husband and wife seems to be a more desirable alternative."

"I'm sure we shall be so blessed," Clarissa said, because it seemed like the thing to say.

If Lord Brandon had asked what Clarissa had thought about love—which he did not—she would have told him that she did not know enough about it to make an informed decision. Her own parents barely tolerated each other. The library of Richmond House was devoid of any fiction other than the most tragic love stories. Poetry was forbidden. Plays were merely an excuse to attend the theater, and one never paid attention to the drama on stage but gossiped with one's acquaintances all the way through. Clarissa had little reason to suspect that love was *not* a tragedy.

Sophie accepted a glass of champagne from a passing footman and turned away from the sight of Lord Brandon and Lady Clarissa dancing. She took a sip, savored the cold bubbles, and wondered what it might be like to waltz with him. She suspected that it would be heavenly, but refused to speculate further. It seemed sensible to avoid any romantic thoughts of him when she was trying to avoid all romantic feelings for him.

"He is incredibly handsome. I hadn't realized," Julianna said thoughtfully.

"It's his eyes, I think. Or perhaps his laugh. His mouth, too . . ." Sophie said, and then silently chided herself for indulging in such thoughts.

"He's everything a man should be—large and strong but not hulking. Truly dignified," Julianna said, continuing the assessment. His black jacket, dove gray waistcoat and breeches were cut well, and perfectly fitted. He put Sophie in mind of statues of Greek Gods on display at the British Museum.

"And his eyes"—Sophie sighed—"they are green, like a forest after a thunderstorm."

"Oh, my, aren't you utterly besotted!"

"Honestly, I'm trying not to be," Sophie said, and it was the truth. The duke was not the same man she had become infatuated with. Brandon the duke was rigid, reserved, and practically married. She wanted the Brandon she first met—quick to laugh, gentlemanly and friendly, and not at all betrothed. But both versions made her heart skip beats and her head a little bit dizzy in a lovely way.

"Is that why you are the only person in this room not watching them waltz?" Julianna asked. A few couples were beginning to join in now, at the duchess's urging. But by and large, most were content to watch the Perfect Couple execute a perfect waltz.

"If only that tonic for unsuitable lovers did indeed exist!" Sophie lamented.

"If it did, it would be a hoax and we both know it. It would contain little more than sugar water, which might actually work if you drank it instead of the champagne you are consuming in copious quantities," Julianna said smartly.

"It is one glass and I had to take it, for not doing so when toasting the happy couple would have been rude. Having said that, I do find myself in need of air."

On her way to the terrace, Sophie successfully dodged encounters with Lord Borwick, a notorious letch, and Lady Rawlings, who could trap a person in conversation for thirty minutes. She and Julianna had renamed her Lady Drawlings for her slow and leisurely manner of speaking.

Once outside, Sophie pulled her shawl tighter around her, for there was still a chill in the spring air. Enough moonlight passed through the fog to faintly illuminate the garden below. Sophie was not alone on the terrace, as other guests had also stepped out, and she freely eavesdropped on their conversations.

"Oh, he is such a bore, I thought I'd never escape!" a woman said to the giggles of her friend.

"Cigar?" one man offered to another.

"We are so very lucky to have this match," a woman said. Sophie could easily identify that voice; it belonged to the elder Lady Richmond.

"Yes, Lord Brandon is a good man," her companion said. She suspected it was the Duke of Richmond. Glancing over, she could see that he had a stocky stature, tufted white hair, and stood as tall as his wife.

Lady Richmond muttered something that sounded like "utterly ruined" but Sophie could not be sure.

"I would have to sell off my stable," the duke said forlornly.

"Hush about your stupid stables, Reginald," she hissed. "They're what got us into this mess in the first place." And then, in a smoother voice: "I was so worried when Miss Selby snatched up Lord Winchester."

"But it all turned out in the end, my dear. You shall have our Clarissa married to a duke, the title will continue, we shall be wealthy again, and I will have the funds to breed my mare Magnolia to my stallion Eclipse. 'Tis my lifelong dream, you know."

"I am well aware," she said bitterly before returning to the ballroom.

Now, that's interesting, Sophie thought. Either Lord Brandon had been duped into believing them wealthy, or he was so rich that he didn't need a bride with a large dowry. If that was the case, then he must have other reasons for marrying her. A list of reasons, in fact.

Sophie reminded herself that none of this was at all her business and she'd best forget it and leave gossiping and speculating to her friend, the professional.

As she heard Lord Richmond returning to the ballroom, she intended to follow, but then she became keenly aware of another male presence.

Chapter 9

Lord Brandon had come to the terrace for a respite, and discovered too late that it was not to be found.

"Miss Harlow, good evening," Brandon said, coming to stand beside her at the banister because she had turned, caught his eye—and it would have been rude to ignore her.

To discover Miss Harlow alone in a dimly lit and fairly secluded place was not what he wished. In fact, it was in direct violation of a rule he had made for himself just the other day: *Avoid her at all costs.*

Rationality dictated that he return immediately to the ballroom. Oddly enough, Lord Brandon did not.

"Your Grace. Good evening."

"I trust I am not interrupting something," he said, and it was not true. If he were interrupting, he would have a polite excuse to make a quick exit.

"I am awaiting an assignation with my lover," she declared. He was shocked first by her boldness to declare her private information. Then he was struck by a wave of jealousy, which was ludicrous, because he did not possess her nor did he want to. And then, finally, he noticed that she was teasing.

"I shall keep you company until he arrives, then," Brandon said, ever the gentleman. It would not do to leave a woman unaccompanied on the terrace where she might be prey to rakes and lechers. She was safe with him, however.

"Then you shall stay a very long time. I am a very respectable girl." To make her point, she tightened her shawl around her.

"As respectable as a scandalous, history-making woman can be," he said lightly. It was happening again: she was teasing him out of his armor, and he couldn't quite bring himself to stop it.

"I'm not scandalous anymore. At first I was gossiped about frequently and I was invited to parties to create a sensation. But I behaved myself and now people have become accustomed to me."

"You are even sought after."

"An interview with two duchesses is surely the stamp of respectability."

"And a duke," he added. He reluctantly noticed how quickly they fell into an easy banter. That had yet to occur between him and Clarissa, and he couldn't imagine that would change. Upon feeling surprisingly disappointed at the realization, Brandon reminded himself that the lack of deep conversation was precisely why he was marrying her.

It all had to do with avoiding distraction and focusing on the things that really matter—but with Miss Harlow before him, it was impossible to pay attention to anything other than her.

"How could I forget?" she teased. "I ought to ask you a few questions," she said.

"For this story of yours?"

"Yes, and because it should look improper for the

two of us to be standing out here chattering away, quite alone . . ."

He liked that she considered the propriety of the situation, even as he was besieged by improper thoughts about her plump pink mouth and all the curves of her figure that begged for exploration.

Miss Harlow reached into her reticule to pull out a tablet. As she sorted through, presumably in search of a pencil, her shawl loosened and slid from her shoulders. One errant sleeve slid down to follow, exposing her shoulder and leaving it quite bare.

It forced him to imagine her in nothing more than a negligee as it slid off her body and onto the floor. His mouth went dry.

Her hair, a dark mass of curls, was swept back, yet a few brushed against this expanse of exposed skin, suggesting the faintest whisper of a caress. He wished to trace the curve with his fingertips, to press his mouth right in the half-moon spot where her neck met her shoulder.

One milky, smooth, beautifully curved *shoulder* and he was utterly entranced.

That he should be so inflamed by a mere shoulder and a wayward sleeve suggested that perhaps he should not have ended things with his mistress just yet.

"My apologies. I can't find my pencil because I'm forever losing things," she said, glancing up at him with a slight smile. "It's a terrible habit of mine."

She had a slight dimple when she smiled. He thought it adorable and erotic all at once.

"It's chilly this evening," she said, pulling up her sleeve and wrapping the shawl tightly around her. The spell was broken—mostly. Moments like those were why he did not like her. She was trouble. She was Dark

Magic and he was Logic. Reason. Rationality. These things were not compatible.

"How are you enjoying your betrothal party?"

"It's a fine event."

She wrote something quickly. He noticed that she had procured a writing implement whilst he was ogling her bare skin like a sailor on shore leave.

"How involved do you intend to be in the planning of your wedding?"

"At the appropriate time and place, I will be present to recite my vows," Brandon replied. What else was a man expected to do? He certainly would not help select the flowers or plan the menu for the wedding breakfast.

"It is a bit silly to ask a man about wedding matters, is it not?" Miss Harlow queried with a grin and a flash of that dimple.

"On that matter, Miss Harlow, we are in agreement," he replied. She laughed at that, a wonderful, genuine sound that he was thrilled to have caused. He caught himself on the verge of leaning against the banister, with the intention of a lengthy conversation.

But dukes did not lean, and decent gentlemen did not ogle or engage with other women at their own betrothal party. Thus he excused himself and returned to the hot, bright, crowded ballroom, even though he desired nothing more than to be alone with Miss Harlow in a dark, secluded place.

Chapter 10

Twenty-five days before the wedding . . .

The Shop of Madame Auteuil, Modiste
Bond Street, London

"**T**he dress ought to be the very height of fashion, yet also timeless," the Duchess of Richmond informed Madame Auteuil, the premier modiste for the aristocracy and the unfathomably wealthy.

Though Sophie had gazed in the windows countless times, this was her first time in the shop. It radiated elegance, glamour, and wealth. The floor was covered in plush carpets the color of crimson. Delicate chairs upholstered in the palest shades of blue with white wooden legs were scattered about. And then the fabrics! Shelf after shelf of silks, satins, cottons, cashmere, velvets, tulle, twill, taffeta, and lace were bolted up and just waiting to be made into a lucky woman's gorgeous gown.

Mirrors reflected everything with Sophie wide-eyed in the midst of it.

While Lady Richmond provided contradictory instructions to Madame Auteuil—who patiently nodded her head in agreement to declarations that it should be kept simple with flounces, lace, and extensive beaded detailing—Clarissa drifted over to Sophie, who was intensely coveting a particular dress on display.

"That is lovely," Clarissa whispered in reverence, daring to brush her fingertips against the fabric.

"Oh, yes," Sophie added. The cut was simple—a high waist with short, capped sleeves and a low, rounded neckline. Clear glass beads and pearls were embroidered close together over white silk. This dress would absolutely shimmer and sparkle as it moved.

It reminded Sophie of moonlight reflecting on freshly fallen snow.

She had never wanted a dress more than she wished for this one.

"Clarissa, my dear," Lady Richmond called out, "we must select the fabric for your gown. Do come."

Ever obedient, she stood still while different swatches of fabric were held to her cheeks to determine which best suited her complexion: an eggshell-colored taffeta, or a milky white satin? A watered silk in pale primrose or a changeable silk in silver and white?

As Sophie looked on, her thoughts drifted from fabric swatches to full bridal dresses, from Clarissa in the modiste's shop to Clarissa at the altar. Each one was more vexing than the last.

Sophie's wedding dress had been beautiful and she'd spent six months making it herself. She had sold it within days of the disastrous almost-wedding. The funds helped pay her way to London.

Thoughts of Clarissa at the altar led, inevitably, to thoughts of Brandon standing there with her and that inspired a full scowl. Against her best intentions and sincere wishes, Sophie found herself daydreaming about him more often than she liked. She thought of the way he had looked at her with bright green, smiling eyes on the day they first met. She imagined witty things to say to make him laugh, because she loved the sound.

"Miss Harlow." The duchess demanded her attention, and focused intently upon her. "What are the other brides wearing this season?"

Oh, yes, all those other brides whose ranks did not include her. Honestly, she was jealous. Her deepest envy was reserved for the love matches, but all it took was a groom who went through the ceremony to make her green.

That aside, it was quite clear that she was not invited to participate in this simply because of a newspaper story, and the glory that brings.

The duchess was determined to have *the* wedding of the year, perhaps even the wedding of the decade. Thus, she needed to know what was popular, what had been overdone, what would be most likely to set tongues wagging, and what would be the newest, freshest trend. Sophie, thanks to her position, knew it all.

"Silver has been growing in popularity," Sophie answered. "Pastels are a classic choice, as always. White is still a novelty."

"Madame, could you tell us about the dress to be worn by Miss Selby?"

"I have been sworn to secrecy, Your Grace, *however*"—Madame Auteuil said, and the duchess's expression went from peevish to beaming—"I can say that it will be silver with white accents."

"Then we shall go with white with silver accents," the duchess declared, and Sophie made a note of it in her tablet.

Once again, Clarissa drifted away to be nearer to Sophie. Her mother, engrossed in the fabrics, did not notice.

"Have you no preference for satin versus silk? Snow white or lily white?" Sophie queried, teasingly.

"No, but even if I did, it would be irrelevant," Clarissa answered. There was no malice in her answer; it was merely a statement of fact. Sophie offered a sympathetic smile.

"Did you enjoy your betrothal ball the other night?" Sophie asked. It had been a pleasant evening. The brief time chatting with Lord Brandon was the only memorable part—and that had been delightful and thrilling, mingled with a slow burn of guilt. Altogether, she felt flummoxed by all the contrary emotions Lord Brandon inspired within her. She shouldn't be intrigued by him, she didn't want to be and yet . . .

"It was a nice party, though I am never quite comfortable being the center of attention like that," Clarissa answered, and she examined a bolt of sea green silk.

"Really?"

"Oh, yes. I dream of being a wallflower," Clarissa said with the slightest of sighs. They both knew that her looks, and her mother, would never allow her to stand unnoticed in a corner and merely watch the people at a ball. As the next Duchess of Hamilton and Brandon, she would never have the chance.

"I would have never guessed. You conduct yourself so well," Sophie said, and it was the truth. Clarissa was so gracious, patient and kind, and everything a duchess ought to be. *No wonder Brandon selected her,* Sophie thought, with a twinge of jealously. She could never compete with such a paragon.

"Thank you. Usually it is tolerable, but to waltz with half the ton watching, and lacking any other distraction, was a real test to my nerves," Clarissa confided.

"You hid it admirably."

"I was reassured by Lord Brandon, for he'd never

allow a lady to miss a step or turn in the wrong direction," Clarissa said.

"He wouldn't," Sophie agreed. "One can rely on him. He's so very assured all the time." It was one of the many reasons she adored him. Some girls fell for the dashing, wild, and dangerous sort. Sophie had learned about those the hard way.

Of course, there was a certain amount of danger surrounding Brandon too but only because of her own feelings, and not his conduct.

"I've never seen him act in any other way than with the utmost composure. I've never heard him raise his voice, or forget his manners, or anything like that," Clarissa continued.

"He sounds almost too perfect," Sophie said, and she realized then why it was so delightful to make him laugh—because it was a glimpse of a part of him that was usually masked behind his reserved demeanor and perfect behavior. She brought that out in him, and doubted that Clarissa did.

"I'm sure he has a flaw. Everyone does," Clarissa said.

"What is yours?" Sophie asked, curiously, because like her fiancé, she seemed so perfect. When Clarissa colored up and looked around to ensure that no one was listening, Sophie grinned with delight.

"Promise not to tell?" Clarissa asked in a whisper.

"You have my word," Sophie answered.

"I cannot sing," Clarissa confessed. That was all?

"Whatever do you mean?"

"I cannot sing on key or carry a tune and live in mortal fear of musicals. I often spontaneously develop sore throats," Clarissa confided with a blush.

Sophie giggled.

"Now you have to tell me yours," Clarissa requested.

"I frequently lose things. I spend a vexing amount of time searching for misplaced items. Earbobs, hair ribbons, reticules, my tablet of notes, my pencils . . ."

"I shall not give you anything of value to hold on to for me," Clarissa said.

"Please don't. I shall certainly lose it and feel terrible," Sophie replied.

"Clarissa!" the duchess called out. "Do come look at these preliminary sketches. Miss Harlow, I wish to know how they compare to the other wedding dresses this season."

Clarissa duly complied, as always.

Harry Angelo's Fencing Academy at The Albany

Brandon lowered his sword and swore under his breath.

"Distracted today?" Harry Angelo asked. This master swordsman was the owner of the school, and he taught there as well. He was the only man in England at Brandon's level. They fenced together regularly, always challenging each other.

What was that?

Yes, distracted.

Brandon was still riveted by the slip of a sleeve and a glance at the bare shoulder of Miss Sophie Harlow from the previous evening.

There were so many things wrong with that preoccupation. First, the object inspiring his desires was a *shoulder*. It was so elementary, the stuff of a green schoolboy.

Alternatively, it suggested to him that he found Miss Harlow *that* alluring.

Warning bells sounded in his head.

Brandon lifted his sword in salute and tilted his head

in an invitation to Angelo for another round. The challenge was accepted.

To lust after Miss Harlow was unacceptable. Because he was an honest man, he could not allow himself to indulge in her pink mouth, or sink his fingers into that mass of dark ringlets, or feel every inch of her with his bare hands. These things were beyond his grasp and thus he was doomed to frustration.

The swords of teacher and student clashed against each other.

He had every intention of being faithful to his wife. But the siren called . . .

Brandon dodged a feint to his lower quarter that almost instantly became an attack to his head. By God, Angelo was damn fast despite his years.

Enough. He would resist the temptation, he vowed, and lunged forward seeking to make his mark on his teacher's near shoulder before dipping beneath the opposing blade and pressing his attack to Angelo's chest.

Brandon would no longer dwell upon ringlets of dark silky hair brushing gently against creamy-skinned shoulders that curved down to the swell of round, luscious breasts that promised to be a good handful. A very good handful.

Steel clanging upon steel, Angelo beat off the duke's attack and advanced so aggressively that Brandon was forced to retreat.

Thoughts of fluttering black eyelashes lowering and rising seductively and dark, expressive eyes would be avoided. He swiftly evaded another attack, but barely so.

To imagine kissing her would be forbidden. To wonder at the softness of her lips, the taste of her, the mere brush of lips against lips that would certainly and inevitably and swiftly become more, so much more . . .

Angelo thrust forward, but instead of the lunge that Brandon had been expecting, he launched his body like an arrow toward the duke, finding his mark and flashing past his student. Caught off guard and off balance, Brandon made the mistake of an amateur. He tripped over his own feet and fell.

"You are not focused today, Brandon. On even an average day you would never let me win with a flèche," Angelo said as he helped Brandon to his feet. "You must recover your concentration. I have heard that one of the greatest swordsmen in Europe, and thus, the world, will soon be coming to London. You will finally have a worthy adversary in His Highness, the Prince of Bavaria."

Chapter 11

Twenty-four days before the wedding . . .

The Offices of The London Weekly
53 Fleet Street

Sophie nodded to Bryson, the clerk in the lobby of the building, and took the stairs to the second floor. She said hello to Mehitable Loud, a gargantuan, knee-quakingly intimidating man of uncertain origins. His sole task was to claim to be the publisher when irate readers invaded the premises. Often, after one look at him, their issue with the paper was resolved.

Mehitable smiled at Sophie, revealing a few missing teeth, and she smiled in return. He was really pleasant when one was on his good side.

As usual, the offices were buzzing with activity. They all used to fall silent when she or another Writing Girl arrived. Now they paused to acknowledge her and went right back to work.

A few of the penny-a-liners were in, offering stories about fires, murders, fights, and the like to Damien Owens. Knightly's door was open, and she considered requesting, again, to quit the story.

Instead she went to the leader-writer's room and sat

at one of the empty rosewood desks. It was supposed to be quiet, but that was a relative term.

Grenville was grumbling as he scribbled furiously upon a sheet.

Andrew Mulligan periodically set down his pen to mime the moves from a boxing match that he was presumably recounting.

Alistair Grey murmured as he wrote: *"Such stupefyingly dull drivel has never before graced the stage of this great nation. The theater does not get much worse than this."*

Grenville glared.

Sophie dipped her pen in the silver inkstand and commenced with the first installment of her four-part story on the creation of "The Wedding of the Year."

First, she wrote the title of her column on the top of her sheet: *"Miss Harlow's Marriage in High Life."* Generally, all stories in the newspapers were anonymous, but Mr. Knightly bucked the trend in order to capitalize on the scandal of a woman writing. Sophie consented because she hadn't had a reputation to lose, but one to create. And that title did have a ring to it.

Julianna, on the other hand, needed a veil of secrecy and thus her column was attributed to A Lady of Distinction.

Sophie thought for a moment and wrote her first line: *There is little dissent that the wedding between the Duke of Hamilton and Brandon and the only daughter of the Duke of Richmond will certainly be the wedding of the year.*

Sophie flipped open her notes. She had written the following: *horribly unromantic proposal, shameless namedropper (Lady Richmond), perfect gentleman (who else?), Lady Sophie, Duchess of Hamilton and*

Brandon, if only, and ~~This One~~ (from the night at the betrothal ball).

In short, a worthless collection of scribbles.

Sophie tapped her pen against the desk. Grenville scowled at her. She stopped, and leaned over to glance at what Alistair was writing.

"I caught up on gossip during the first act, and slept through the second," he said as he wrote.

"What play is that?"

"The Hairy Falsetto."

Grenville shushed them, and they went back to work.

What she really wished to write was not at all publishable, much like how most things she wished to say were just not said.

Just for fun, Sophie proceeded to compose a most unsuitable version of "Miss Harlow's Marriage in High Life" for her personal amusement.

One would hope that the wedding of the year, between the Duke of Hamilton and Brandon and Lady Clarissa Richmond, would be more romantic than the proposal. His Grace, the so very handsome Double Duke, asked the beautiful and sweet Lady Clarissa to become his bride with her parents attending. Lady "Namedropper" Richmond wept; by all accounts no one else was similarly moved.

The Duchess of Hamilton and Brandon has relinquished an exquisite heirloom ring of emeralds and diamonds.

This author has developed amorous feelings for His Grace and is well aware that they are thoroughly unsuitable. Yet she cannot stop dreaming of his eyes, green like ferns, the countryside, or emeralds. She longs to kiss him, and dearly wishes to control these feelings before they lead to heartache.

An advertisement for WRIGHT'S TONIC FOR THE CURE OF UNSUITABLE AFFECTIONS—a new "medicine" that had recently gone on sale—would not be out of place next to this utterly unprintable edition of "Miss Harlow's Marriage in High Life."

On a fresh sheet of paper, she began anew. *A duke,* she wrote, for dukes always sold. *His beautiful soon-to-be duchess,* she wrote, for everyone was always interested in the goings-on of beautiful duchesses. *A Whirlwind courtship* . . . That sounded so much more romantic than the truth.

Chapter 12

Twenty-one days before the wedding . . .

Hamilton House

Like virtually everyone else in the ton, Brandon read *The London Weekly* over breakfast every Saturday morning. Even though he thought it rubbish, one had to read it in order to understand most ton conversations. He had always skipped "Miss Harlow's Marriage in High Life" because he was barely interested in his own marriage, and much less interested in anyone else's. Today, he made an exception.

MISS HARLOW'S MARRIAGE IN HIGH LIFE

A handsome duke. His beautiful soon-to-be duchess. A Whirlwind courtship. There is little dissent that the wedding between the Duke of Hamilton and Brandon and the only daughter of the Duke of Richmond will certainly be the wedding of the year. All the romance of their betrothal and every detail of their upcoming nuptials will be reported in these pages in a *London Weekly* exclusive.

This author had the privilege to take tea with the perfect couple and their mothers (the architects of the greatly anticipated grand celebration) in which they related their romantic story.

After meeting at the ball one evening, His Grace was immediately smitten by the young and lovely Lady Richmond. "She possessed all the qualities of a perfect duchess," he said. After only two weeks, he proposed to the lucky woman at her home in a romantic proposal that "brought tears to my eyes," said the bride's mother, Her Grace, the Duchess of Richmond.

A breathtaking emerald-and-diamond ring was given as a betrothal gift to the young Miss Richmond. Lady Hamilton, the groom's mother, informs that it is a family heirloom.

Wedding preparations are already underway; after all, the big day is just around the corner! There are three more weeks until the wedding . . .

Miss Harlow had a gift, Brandon thought after reading her story about his engagement. The facts were all true, and yet she had managed to make it seem like the stuff of romance and fairy tales. She wrote about a beautiful bride with attentive parents, a doting fiancé, and a kindhearted mother-in-law to be.

He wondered if she was such a truly talented writer, or if she was delusional.

"Miss Harlow's column is perfect," his mother said. She had already read the paper when he joined her at the breakfast table.

"Yes, it is nicely done," he agreed. He was now more interested in the items on his plate—steaming hot scrambled eggs, smoked ham slices, and buttermilk biscuits still warm from the oven and slathered in melted butter.

"You don't seem very interested in the story or Miss Harlow," she said.

Thank God, Brandon thought. No one must know how he obsessed over her against his better judgment and in spite of his best intentions.

"Miss Harlow is an agreeable young woman," he said. "As for the story, I find myself more inclined than Lady Richmond to keep certain matters private. While I agreeably participate, I do find myself less enthused at the prospect."

"You speak as if you were in Parliament and not at the breakfast table."

"My apologies, Mother."

"Oh, it's all very well, dear. I just wish to see you enjoy a more liberated attitude occasionally," she said, taking a sip of her tea.

"I beg your pardon?"

"Not take everything so seriously. Enjoy a spot of fun from time to time."

"I engage in 'fun' activities."

"Other than making your lists and giving orders?" she questioned with a lift of one brow.

"I fence. I particularly enjoy that. And issuing orders is remarkably satisfying."

"Running people through with a sword. So very amusing," his mother replied.

"I read," he continued on, "often of things other than parliamentary bills or estate accounts."

"Clearly, I am in the wrong," his mother said, taking another sip of her tea.

"Why mention all of this now?"

"You had to take on so much responsibility at such a

young age, when your father passed, and now you shall have even more. Life is so precious and I wish for all my children to enjoy it to the fullest."

That did not exactly answer the question, but it somehow made perfect sense to him. Since *then* he had shouldered the burden of everything relating to the Dukedom of Hamilton and Brandon. And now he was taking on more responsibility—a wife. But Brandon never thought of marriage as putting an end to his carefree days the way most bachelors did; the death of his father had seen to that.

"How are your other children?" he asked with a grin.

"That is some way to refer to your dear sisters!" Lady Hamilton said playfully. Her children were very fond and loving to each other.

"How are my dear sisters?"

"They are well. Penelope is redecorating, Amelia's confinement is going well, and Charlotte . . ."

Brandon took a deep breath and exhaled slowly, which is what one did when dealing with Charlotte. One might describe her as exuberant or spirited, but hoyden was an apt description as well. She had a heart of gold, an unquenchable thirst for mischief, and Brandon feared the day she made her debut, for his younger sister did not suffer fools.

"Charlotte has had another fainting spell," his mother said.

"Another? Has she seen a physician?"

"Yes. He could find nothing amiss and the headmistress suspects that Charlotte might be having hysterical symptoms."

"Or is feigning fainting," he added.

"Or feigning. There was an incident when a teacher interrupted a group of girls, including Charlotte, apparently practicing swooning," his mother said.

"She would adopt such a malady," he said, able to imagine his sister developing a habit merely for amusement.

"Nevertheless, it could be serious, and she should have continual visits with the physicians until she is cured. And to think—my daughter, prone to fainting spells!"

At the conclusion of the meal, Brandon left for a long, fast, and dangerous ride around Hyde Park. He skipped Rotten Row in favor of the wilder parts. After a breakfast spent discussing weddings, feelings, and fainting spells, he needed to. A man could only endure so much.

The fog was, predictably, thick. It only slightly slowed his pace. At first his thoughts were like the weather— dense, unclear, hazy. As he rode on, lulled by the steady pounding rhythm of his horse's hooves against the dirt, all his thoughts shifted and fell into place without much effort on his part. And then he understood, after an hour in the saddle, why he was relentlessly bothered by Miss Harlow.

Because she managed to find and bring out the man he was *before* his father died and before everything rested upon him—his sound judgment and his integrity. Before, when he laughed easily, flirted with pretty girls, and, more often than not, engaged in mischievous schemes with Charlotte rather than frowning in disapproval upon learning of them.

He had been happy *before*. He could not return to that time or place or the way things were. To be *Before* Brandon in an *After* world could not lead to anything good, if it was even possible.

Chapter 13

Eighteen days before the wedding . . .

Hamilton House

At the request of the duchesses, Brandon entered the blue drawing room in the south wing with the intention of a short visit in which he would pay as little attention to Miss Harlow as politely possible.

She might invoke *Before* Brandon like a sorceress, but it was very much *After*, and there was no longer a place in the world for his former self.

"We were just finishing up with the guest list," Lady Richmond said.

"Speaking of lists, we have some things for you to take care of," his mother stated, as she handed him a sheet of paper.

Things to do for the wedding:

1. Secure the special license.
2. Find a best man.
3. Prepare a wedding toast.

"I thought the wedding was set for eleven in the morning on a Saturday," he said.

"We've moved the ceremony to half past noon," Lady Richmond declared. Weddings at that time required him to obtain an interview with the Archbishop of Canterbury to plead for a document that he could obtain, with much more ease and much less expense, had they instead moved the ceremony to one hour earlier.

"Is there a particular reason?" he inquired. As soon as he gave voice to the words, he regretted them. It didn't matter the reason, for as a gentleman, he would oblige.

"To marry by special license makes such a statement," Lady Richmond declared. "And we shan't wish to risk anything by having someone protest the wedding when the banns are read."

"Why would anyone do that?" he asked. Never had he heard of anyone protesting the banns, or even coming forth during the ceremony with a reason why a couple should not be wed. He knew just who to ask about this. "Miss Harlow, have you ever witnessed a wedding or heard of an instance of the marriage being protested?"

"Sir Hunt and Miss Bailey, by her former suitor, Mr. Westlake, on the fourteenth of January last."

"How do you remember that?" Clarissa asked. Her entry into the conversation surprised him, but he was glad for he wondered the same.

"I took ill during the ceremony," she said as her cheeks burned pink, and he was intensely curious. "It was very upsetting."

"You see, it does happen. And with all of Clarissa's rejected suitors, I should hate to take the chance. Better safe than sorry, I always say, and to marry by special license . . ."

Lady Richmond did not need to complete her

thought, for they all understood her wish for each and every status symbol.

"I shall obtain one," he acquiesced, because a gentleman honored a lady's wishes, even if they were idiotic or an inconvenience. "And now, if you'll excuse me. I am due at Parliament shortly."

"Are you going right now?" his mother asked.

"Yes, why?"

"Is the fog still terrible?" his mother asked.

"Very much," he answered. It was terrible more often than not.

"Would you mind escorting Miss Harlow home on your way?" his mother asked. "I fear for her safety walking in this weather."

"Oh, Lady Hamilton, it is really gracious of you to offer, but I could never impose like that," Miss Harlow answered. Silently, he thanked her. To be trapped in a secluded, enclosed, and intimate space like a carriage with her would introduce more temptation than he wished to endure.

But there was no arguing with his mother when safety was at stake. And thus, all of his best intentions—namely, to avoid Miss Harlow—were put to the test. In the end he agreed, because it was the gentlemanly thing to do and the fog did endanger pedestrians.

Within seconds of the carriage door closing, and finding himself alone in the secluded, enclosed, and intimate space, Brandon realized that he had made a grave error and there was indeed a time and place for being rude. He should have sent her home in another carriage. He had a dozen, after all. He kept two drivers.

Instead, he braced himself for a self-inflicted torture that could have been avoided.

"Thank you," Miss Harlow said. "I hope this will not inconvenience you terribly."

"It's fine," he replied, eyeing her warily. The green dress she wore was temptingly low cut across the bodice. She carried a pale silver shawl that had fallen off one shoulder carelessly that night at the betrothal ball.

"Are you saying it's fine because it's true or because good manners oblige you to?" she asked, smiling, and revealing that little dimple. Her curls bounced as the carriage clattered across the cobblestones. She was adorable.

"Both."

"After we turn the corner, and are out of your mother's sight, I shall get out and carry on my way," Miss Harlow offered.

"You'll do no such thing. First of all, you are already out of her sight in this blasted fog. Secondly, she'll ask me to assure her that you've returned home with no harm done and I would like to honestly say yes."

"Very well. For the ease of your conscience, I shall stay. For my sake, I hope you are V.S.I.C."

"I beg your pardon?" He must not have heard her correctly; either that, or she was batty.

"Very Safe in Carriages," she explained. "Usually we say V.S.I.C.P.Q. Very Safe in Carriages Probably Queer, but I do not doubt your . . . inclinations," she said, blushing slightly.

"Good." Brandon merely stared at her for a second before arriving at the conclusion that this was the strangest conversation he'd ever had with a woman. If only the novelty didn't make it so intriguing, and slightly thrilling.

"And then there is always N.S.I.C.," she carried on.

"Not Safe in Carriages?"

"Exactly." She beamed at him, and he was annoyed by the rush of pleasure that it brought him.

"What is the purpose of these abbreviations?"

"Quick, discrete communication between women. For example, Lady Somerset—my dearest friend— might be in conversation with a suitor who I've heard is F.U., so instead of pulling her aside and making a scene I can just whisper it to her."

"F.U.?" he queried.

"Financially Unsound," she explained.

"I had no idea," he said. And truly, he didn't.

"Most men don't. Although . . ." Here she paused and he finished her sentence.

"They think they do. I see where this conversation is going and I shall not engage," he said. He fought to keep the corners of his mouth from turning up into a smile.

"If a subject change is in order, then I shall defer to you, Your Grace."

"Call me Brandon."

"Very well, Brandon," she said with a hint of a smile. He liked the way his name sounded upon her lips.

"You seemed very upset at the mention of the Hunt and Bailey wedding today," he said. His curiosity had not faded.

"Oh, it was really nothing."

"You're blushing again. I am now incredibly intrigued."

"Some other time. I've had my fill of discussing weddings for today," she said pertly.

"I did not think that women ever tired of talking about that."

"Some women do not live and breathe weddings, as I do. I suppose for you it might be akin to discussing account books. It is a chore."

He gave a wry smile. He understood her. He was also reminded of their very first meeting, when they had talked briefly of account books, planning excursions, newspapers, and whether or not he was a rake.

The answer was undoubtedly *no*, and yet Brandon thought of what a rake might do upon finding himself in this secluded, enclosed, and intimate space with a woman as alluring as Sophie. Certainly not converse with her about account books or weddings.

An awkward turn of the carriage sent Miss Harlow's reticule flying across the seat and onto the floor. Before he had the chance, she bent over to retrieve it, thus giving Brandon a sublime view of the swell of her breasts. A rake would look.

Brandon made no effort to avert his gaze. His mouth went dry. His hands balled into fists so that he could not touch her. At that moment, he would have traded a house of his for one caress.

"Shall we discuss your account books? Or have you read anything more interesting. The new Wordsworth, perhaps?"

"God, no," he said.

"No—let me guess." She held up one hand to shush him. Then she tapped her fingertip on her lips as she thought, and he was entranced. "Parliamentary reports, agricultural testaments, or improving religious tracts?"

The little minx was teasing, or at least he certainly hoped so. What did it say about him that she thought he was V.S.I.C. and read improving religious tracts in his free time? The answer was mildly horrifying.

It was not how he thought of himself. And he couldn't stand it if she—funny, witty, smart, pretty, daring, and dangerous Miss Harlow—thought him a boring prig.

"Can you keep a secret, Miss Harlow?"

"Oh, yes," she said, slightly breathless in anticipation. Her eyes widened and she leaned forward, providing him with another exquisite and distracting view. So he wasn't hopeless.

"I do not read improving religious tracts. I occasionally read agricultural testaments and parliamentary reports because my position obliges me to. But given the chance and the choice, I read adventure novels," he said.

"That makes perfect sense," she said. "You like to read about long ago, faraway, thrilling, dangerous adventures because you are stuck in England on the same old plots of land."

He stared at her for a second.

"Oh, blast, that was a horribly insensitive thing to say. I do apologize."

"So very astute, Miss Harlow," he said softly. She, of all the people in the world, seemed to understand him, and to know him, after so little time together. It was frightening, of course, and he thought he should *STAY AWAY*. And yet she was so intriguing . . .

"Which ones do you like?" she asked.

"I have just finished *The Pirate*—the latest by the author of the Waverly novels."

"Everyone is reading that one, save for me! I love his, or her, books. Every time I go to the circulating library, it's always checked out."

"Is that a hint, Miss Harlow?" he asked, lifting his brow, and making a mental note to have a copy sent to her.

"It is nothing of the sort and do call me Sophie. It seems we shall be spending a fair amount of time together in the next few weeks."

"It's best that I do not," he said. "I might accidentally use your given name in front of the duchesses and then what will they think?"

"Is there anything for them to think about?" she asked, tilting her head slightly to one side, looking curious and adorable.

"What do you think?" he responded, raising one brow in challenge.

"I think . . . I don't know what to think," she confessed with a laugh.

"Well, I think we are making excessive use of that word." He grinned in spite of himself. He didn't want to enjoy her company, but he—the master of self-restraint—couldn't help himself.

"And I think that was dodging the question," she challenged. And then she smiled at him, and he surrendered.

"It is a constant battle to *not* think of you, Miss Harlow. One that I do not always win. I am betrothed to another, and . . ."

"That is precisely why we should not think of each other, I know. And yet, I cannot stop thinking about you," Sophie confessed.

He had not wondered if she found herself attracted to him, as he did her. But now that he knew the desire was mutual his brain shouted *DANGER* and his heart thudded in an uneven pattern that was not altogether unpleasant.

She thought of him.

If he were not such a perfect gentleman, Brandon would have immediately capitalized upon this moment with a touch, a kiss, or something more. But he was bound by honor, and that was not an easy bind to break.

Still, he considered it. He could easily reach out,

take her hand in his, then proceed to feather kisses along her palm and then to the delicate, sensitive skin of the inner wrist. She would lean in closer to him, of course, impelled by instinct and desire. And then, he would claim her mouth with his for a kiss. What came next was not even worth considering because it would never happen.

"This is dangerous territory," he said finally.

"As if in an adventure novel," she pointed out, perfectly. He felt a twinge in his chest, because, again, he sensed that she seemed to *know* him so well, like no one else, and after such little acquaintance. And they could never be more than that—mere acquaintances.

"I suspect that you would be the adventure of a lifetime," he confessed. His eyes roamed over the curve of her shoulder that he knew fairly well, and he thought of all the other curves he would never get to explore and felt an ache in his chest.

"Just not yours," she said wistfully.

"Not mine," he repeated firmly, for his benefit more than hers.

"Well, this conversation took a rather serious turn. I had not expected that," she stated. A long silence followed in which she looked out the window at the fog, and occasionally glanced at him. Meanwhile, it dawned upon him that she felt the same as he, and hadn't intended him to know of it. She was going to spend countless hours involved in the planning of his wedding—to another woman. She was going to write about it, for all of London to read. And she was going to think of him all the while and tell no one.

It impressed him, that fortitude and sense of integrity. An attraction to Miss Harlow was one thing. An admiration for her complicated that. As if things weren't complicated enough.

Chapter 16

"**A** drink in the afternoon? Are you unwell?" Simon, Lord Roxbury, questioned his long-time friend upon finding him in one of the front rooms at the club, facing St. James Street.

Lord Borwick, Lord Biddulph, and his unfortunately named friend Mitchell Twitchell were attempting to play whist—a four-person game—but otherwise the room was empty.

"I have just spent the morning debating floral arrangements for my wedding," Brandon answered as his friend slid into the leather seat opposite his. It might have been the first time he said *my* wedding, and the words were bitter.

"My God, man! What in the blazes for? Leave that rot to the womenfolk." Roxbury took a sip of his brandy and slouched deeply in his chair.

Why? Because he knew Sophie would be there and could not resist the opportunity to see her. Plus, he thought that a visit with his fiancée would not be out of place. It was his hope that Clarissa would remind him

This stranger sat across the aisle. His observation was not discreet. She'd been the object of a man's attentions before and it bored her. This time, it thrilled her.

She had the distinct impression that he was not just looking at her, but peering into her heart, or her head, or her soul—as batty as that sounded.

Clarissa sat up straighter, and stole another glance at him. *When had it become so warm in here?* she wondered.

The man had shockingly long, dark brown wavy hair that had been tied back in a queue with a black ribbon. His cheekbones were high, sharp slants, his mouth curved into a grin of amusement. His eyes were blue, bright blue, fringed with long black lashes, and they were focused upon her.

Clarissa felt a queer feeling in her stomach—if it was danger or delight, she knew not—but it was certainly caused by the stranger.

"Clarissa, pay attention," her mother hissed.

Dutifully, she focused forward. But then the music began. In two weeks time this would be her, Clarissa thought as she turned in her seat seemingly to watch the bride.

But she only watched the stranger, watching her. A flash of silver obscured their connection for a second. It had been the bride, passing by.

She wanted to ask who he was. Now was not the time.

"Lord Brandon has not returned. Where is he?" her mother whispered, and then frowned.

"I have no idea, Mother," Clarissa said, which was a lie. He was with Sophie, which was not remotely surprising or interesting. Not when that shockingly handsome stranger was right there, with his gaze matching hers.

his nearness and intoxicated by the waves of emotions he inspired in her. "Because when you are flustered and vexed, you are adorable."

Clarissa smiled and asked: "How long shall you stay in London?"

"Eager to be rid of me already?"

"My manners, which I am recovering, forbid me from honestly answering that question," she answered with a sly smile.

It would be shockingly forward to tell him the truth, which was that she hoped he stayed for a long while, because this was the most fun she'd had in ages

"My stay here depends upon the tides, my whims, the weather," he answered. "Why do you ask?"

"Just seeing how long I have to discover one of your flaws, which I may then taunt you mercilessly with," she dared to reply. It was so uncharacteristic of her to tease, but Sophie inspired her, and this man encouraged her.

The prince grinned. Her heart skipped a beat.

"Clarissa—I know you have not given me leave to use your given name, but you should know by now that I do not wait for permission—I like you."

"Your conversation has amused me . . . Your Highness," she said. But her blush and smile gave away her true feelings. She was swiftly on her way to falling madly in love with him.

"Call me Frederick," he told her.

Lord Brandon returned just then. She had quite forgotten about him, and if it had not been for Miss Harlow seated at his other side, she might have felt ashamed for her flirtatious conversation with another man.

The gentlemen eyed each other, suspiciously appraising the other in a manner that put Clarissa in mind of the way her father examined a horse at Tattersall's.

He *knew* he should have sent her home in another carriage.

"Lord Brandon, we have arrived at my house, so this little adventure has come to an end. But you should know that I have tried to quit the story and Mr. Knightly would not accept it. So I shall be underfoot again tomorrow and the day after . . ."

"I've been warned," he said. Like him, she had tried to stay away and he did not know what to make of it. "Good day, Miss Harlow."

And then she flashed him a smile, thanked him for the carriage ride, and disappeared into her little gray townhouse with white trim at 24 Bloomsbury Place.

24 Bloomsbury Place

"Was that the duke?" Julianna asked, stepping back from the window to speak to Sophie as she entered the drawing room.

"Who else do we know with such an impressive vehicle?"

"No one," Julianna said, and she turned to give her friend "a look."

"It was suggested by his mother and one does not refuse Lady Hamilton, and nothing untoward happened, so you can stop looking at me like that," Sophie answered. She set down her reticule on a small table that was littered with circulating library books, ear bobs, hair ribbons, and other assorted female things.

"Nothing? Really? So he is V.S.I.C.?" Julianna asked.

"Not entirely. He said he cannot stop thinking of me!" Sophie told her. She couldn't stop the smile, or the glee in her voice.

"Oh my lord."

"Is it wrong that that makes me so utterly delighted?" Sophie wondered, sinking onto the dark green damask settee and availing herself of the tea tray that Julianna had already set out. Bessy, their maid, had baked Sophie's favorite ginger biscuits, but she was too exhilarated to have an appetite.

"Probably, but anyone would feel so. What did you say back?" Julianna said, sitting down in a blue-and-white-striped chair opposite.

"The same thing, basically," Sophie answered.

"You have captured the attentions of a duke! A double duke!" Julianna declared, and then, in a more sober tone, "It's too bad that nothing shall come of it."

Of course nothing would come of it, but . . . Sophie took a sip of tea, considering this for a moment before arriving at the conclusion that, No, dukes did not jilt fiancées for lower-class girls, and definitely not for scandalous Writing Girls. They did not. Ever.

Perhaps this once?

No.

They did not. Which didn't matter, because she would not indulge in such an illicit affair.

And yet . . . he could not stop thinking of her, and she, him. That meant something—there was a connection and a mutual understanding between them. It was the sort of thing that might one day, under proper conditions, turn into love.

They were not under proper conditions.

And yet, already her heart beat a little faster. He thought of her! The world seemed a little bit brighter and warmer. The man that she had fancied, that she thought about, returned the sentiment. Sophie's smile broadened. It was so rare, so precious, and so sad that nothing could come of it.

But the glow of pleasure remained.

"*The Weekly* sent over a batch of invitations for us. The vouchers for your Wedding of the Year have arrived, too. You mustn't lose yours, Sophie, otherwise you won't be admitted, and then your column—"

"I know, I know. I promise I won't lose it," Sophie said, helping herself to another biscuit. Ton weddings attracted large crowds, and vouchers were often necessary for entrance.

"Also, we have the wedding of the Marquis of Winchester and Miss Victoria Selby—the big rival for the title of wedding of the year," Julianna informed her.

More weddings. "I cannot contain my joy," Sophie deadpanned, and Julianna smirked.

"There are rumors that the groom counts the Prince of Bavaria among his close friends and that the prince shall be in attendance," Julianna confided.

"How on earth does an English earl befriend a Bavarian prince?"

"The earl had an ambassadorship there before he inherited. Apparently, the prince is a very friendly fellow," Julianna said.

"That does explain it. Any other gossip?" Sophie asked, settling into a comfortable position on the settee. This is when she was happiest—with her very best friend in their very own home, sharing delicious gossip before anyone else knew it.

"Well . . ." Julianna started with a sly grin. "You would not believe what I have learned about Lord Roxbury . . ."

Chapter 14

Sixteen days before the wedding . . .

The Duke's Study, Hamilton House

"Your Grace, there is one last order of business," Spencer informed Brandon.

"What is it?" Brandon asked wearily. They'd spent the morning reviewing accounts, correspondence, and documents for Parliament—and Brandon was more than ready to conclude for the day.

"It's a very delicate matter, Your Grace, and I do hesitate to mention it but I have searched my soul, and I am of the firm opinion that you must know about this!" Spencer finished. His cheeks flushed nearly as red as his hair.

The only expression of his curiosity that Brandon allowed was a slight lift of his brow.

"It is about your marriage, Your Grace."

Brandon's heart began to pound.

"I have received a letter . . ." And Spencer related his news about a curious letter from a parish registry in a very hushed tone of voice.

Brandon had known about the Richmonds' debts, and this was something else.

Because he was a man of logic, facts, and common sense, Brandon would not credit such an outrageous tale—unless his secretary could confirm such a shocking, potentially life-altering assertion.

Chapter 15

Fifteen days before the wedding . . .

Hamilton House

That their attraction was forbidden made it so much more alluring. But that was the way of the world, the laws of the universe, and it was even in the Bible. Miss Sophie Harlow was powerless to stop it.

Not that she wanted to.

But she knew she ought to.

"I cannot stop thinking of you, Sophie," he had said, and she relived the memory repeatedly. His gorgeous eyes had darkened from the bright green of new leaves to a dark evergreen. His mouth had been set firm, and she wanted to soften it with the touch of her lips.

But she couldn't.

Even the thought of it now made her feel hot, and her skin tingled in a very lovely way.

But it shouldn't.

Thus, while the duchesses discussed flowers for the wedding, Sophie harbored illicit thoughts and feelings for the groom. She also had done this during previous sessions in which they had determined the guest list and other utterly dull logistics. In short, she hated weddings more with each day, as her romantic feelings for Brandon increased.

Would he join them today? Of course not, she told herself. He had informed her that the extent of his involvement in the wedding would be to attend at the designed time and place.

Perhaps he was here, under this same roof . . .

"I have brought a volume on the language of flowers so that Clarissa's bouquet, and all the other arrangements, shall be both beautiful and meaningful. Lady Effrington gave me the idea to do so at Lady Carrington's soiree."

"It is a lovely idea, Lady Richmond," Lady Hamilton said.

"Indeed, it is sure to become a trend," Sophie added, and Lady Richmond beamed.

Perhaps as Sophie left today, she might get lost again . . . accidentally, of course.

"Clarissa, have you given any thought to what flowers you prefer?" Lady Hamilton asked.

"I'm fond of white irises," she answered. It was the perfect flower for her: tall, delicate, pale, and beautiful. Sophie had always been partial to lilacs, and she had once loved their fragrance. But now it only reminded her of her ill-fated bridal bouquet, trampled on the church floor.

"We shall have roses, of course. Perhaps gardenias as well," Lady Richmond carried on as she paged through the books.

Honestly, Sophie thought, *they really oughtn't take this so seriously. It's merely one hour of one day.*

But then she chided herself because it was a special hour on a special day. If one was lucky enough to find someone to promise oneself to, the event should be honored and celebrated. She may have moments of pessimism, but she was a romantic at heart.

Lady Richmond and Lady Hamilton chattered on about flowers while Clarissa agreed with everything—and Sophie thought that she really ought to pay attention because her work was surely going to suffer due to her romantic daydreaming.

But then the conversation was put on hold, for the drawing room door opened, and Brandon entered in all his ducal glory.

Sophie suddenly became very attentive. The room became warmer, the scent of the bouquet of flowers seemed stronger, her head felt slightly dizzy, and her heartbeat found an excited, uneven rhythm. She was so very glad that she had worn her best day dress for this moment, just in case, because one must always be prepared.

"Good afternoon, ladies," he said with a slight bow. When he caught her eye, there was something in his gaze that made her heart beat faster. "I hope I am not interrupting anything. I heard you were in attendance and I thought I'd say hello."

"We are considering flowers for the wedding," Lady Richmond informed him, setting the book down on the table.

"It is now fashionable to have arrangements that are both beautiful and meaningful, so we are consulting *The Language of Flowers*," Sophie explained.

"Flowers have a language?" Brandon asked, quite naturally perplexed. He sat down on the settee opposite his fiancée and smiled at her. Sophie picked up the book Lady Richmond had set down. It took all of her self-control to keep her hands from shaking due to a potent mixture of exhilaration and desire that must be kept secret.

"Yes, it's quite fascinating," Sophie said, even though she didn't really think so. It was all an excuse to converse with him on what was surely the only acceptable subject, given their company. "For example, were you aware that the spider flowers means 'Elope with me'?"

It was the closest she would ever come to suggesting an elopement to him, though the thought had certainly crossed her mind a time or twelve. It was the one way for her to be with him, without having to suffer through a wedding first. But that was all getting ahead of herself.

He had only admitted to thinking of her, that was all.

"I wasn't even aware of the existence of a spider flower," he answered, and all the ladies laughed.

She saw another one that would amuse him, so she read it aloud: " 'The flower Bachelor's Button means celibacy.' "

Brandon laughed, and Lady Hamilton and Lady Richmond looked like they wanted to share his mirth. Clarissa blushed and twisted her betrothal ring around and around.

"I think you are making this up," Brandon declared.

"Here, have a look at the book for yourself," Sophie offered, leaning over and handing him the book. She thought she detected his eyes straying toward her bosom but did not think he would dare a glance in this company.

As she straightened up, Sophie caught Lady Richmond's narrowed eyes focused upon her. One brow arched up, questioningly. The duchesses pressed her lips into a frown of obvious disapproval.

His glance had been noted. Any pleasure she might have experienced from it was severely diminished.

"Ah, here we go: hyacinths, rhododendrons, and oak leaves," Brandon said. Sophie glanced questioningly at Clarissa, who shrugged, indicating she didn't know.

"Translation?" Sophie asked.

"If I'm doing this correctly, I believe that, taken together, it should mean 'Beware, I am dangerous and brave at games and sports,'" Brandon said. All the ladies laughed uproariously at that. Sophie even needed her handkerchief to dab at her tears.

"Wonderful for one of your fencing matches, Brandon, but perhaps not for the wedding," Lady Hamilton suggested, but she was smiling at her son.

"I concede your point. Let's do another," Brandon said, and then he flipped through the book again before offering another bouquet: "A gardenia, red camellia, and Heart's Ease."

"I have no idea," Lady Hamilton said.

"Clarissa, do look it up," her mother said. Brandon handed his fiancée the book and they exchanged bland but polite smiles—or so it seemed to Sophie.

"'You're lovely, you're the flame in my heart, and you occupy my thoughts,'" Clarissa read aloud. With her gaze on the page, Clarissa did not see "the look."

This was no fleeting glance. Brandon's gaze found Sophie's and settled there. Without words, with only the look in his eyes, she knew that she was lovely, the flame in his heart, and that she occupied his thoughts.

"The color combinations would not work with the rest of the ceremony," Lady Richmond said dismissively.

But this had nothing to do with his wedding. It had everything to do with Sophie, and she knew it. Forcing herself to break the gaze, she looked around at the others and it was all too clear by their expressions that they suspected something untoward.

Lady Richmond's cool fury was disconcerting. But it was Lady Hamilton's thoughtful expression, and Clarissa's impassive face, that bothered Sophie most. In fact, she felt a wave of shame, for her feelings rebelled against her best intentions.

The conversation returned to the matter of flowers. Blossoms were required for the bride's bonnet, for her bouquet, for arrangements at the altar, and for the table at the wedding breakfast.

Clarissa was not the slightest bit interested.

Her attention was riveted by the rare and unusual presence of her fiancé. Previously, he had not volunteered to attend to the slightest detail relating to their wedding. Which was perfectly fine, because that was what one expected of a man with regard to weddings.

It was now plain to Clarissa that her fiancé was not at all interested in flowers, weddings, or her—but that he only had eyes for Miss Sophie Harlow.

It should bother me more than it did, Clarissa thought. She ought to be mad. She merely felt lonely.

Clarissa watched the way Sophie easily made witty remarks, or cast warm sidelong glances toward Brandon. With Sophie, he was less of a duke, and more of a man. So much so, that her heart ached a little—because, Clarissa thought, *If I could only be a bit like Sophie, her own fiancé might care for her more.*

But it did rankle that she could not bring that out in him. But she did not know how! He was so reserved, and she so shy, and her mother was constantly hovering. Clarissa hadn't a prayer of flirting with her own fiancé. She wished for someone that would draw her out, because she didn't know how to do it.

It was silly to dwell upon all of this because she was

going to marry him no matter what. It must be all that talk of love going to her brain, just like her mother had warned. People fell in love after marriages, and so it was perfectly fine if she did not love him now. It did not matter that she was so quiet and withdrawn around him, for eventually they would grow close. Or so she hoped.

Clarissa could not simply declare that she thought those two would suit admirably, and she didn't want to stand in the way of true love, and would they please marry each other and leave her free to . . . to what?

Very few would wish to marry her after being jilted, and Clarissa suspected that her family was in desperate need of a fortune they had no way to procure other than by her marriage to a wealthy man.

Everyone burst into laughter, and Clarissa rushed to join in, lest they notice that she had been woolgathering. She'd been doing that frequently of late. Ever since Lord Brandon asked her about love the other night, Clarissa had dared to consider it.

Could love happen to her? Could love end happily, unlike the tragic fate of dear, departed Aunt Eleanor? Or was it too late for her?

"What do you think, Clarissa?" Lady Hamilton asked, and she was mortified to discover she had no clue what they were talking about.

"Roses, orange blossoms, and tulips?" Sophie said, sensing her distress, and reminding Clarissa why she liked her.

"I would like that," Clarissa answered.

"I was hoping you'd pick the other option," her mother sniffed.

"That would be nice as well," Clarissa agreed, because that's what she always did.

As they were gathering their things to go, Clarissa

noticed heated glances between Lord Brandon and Sophie. Clarissa knew that Lady Hamilton saw because of the sweet smile and the gentle squeeze of her hand. Her mother noticed, too, judging by her pursed lips and narrowed eyes—both a very bad sign.

of what he wanted—a cool, collected woman like her.

But then he was drawn into an amusing conversation with Sophie, which he greatly enjoyed against his better judgment. She distracted him.

He *did* want to marry Clarissa. He did not want to be perpetually distracted. And yet . . .

"I have involuntarily developed an inconvenient, undeniable, and intense attraction to Miss Harlow," Brandon explained.

"Who is Miss Harlow?"

"She reports on weddings for *The London Weekly*," Brandon said. He did not expect Roxbury to own a familiarity with the wedding section of the newspaper. It's likely that his butler clipped out that section before leaving the rest of the issue next to his breakfast plate.

"So you are besotted with one of the *Weekly* wenches. Splendid," Roxbury said with a smirk.

"She is not a wench."

"That's neither here nor there. You are simply panicking at the looming doom and gloom of matrimony. The thought of for better or for worse till death do you part is giving you a fright—which it ought to do if you are the slightest bit sane, or male."

"But why her? Why now?" Brandon wondered, sipping his brandy. He'd made it so long without any inappropriate or inconvenient passionate attachments.

"Because you don't pursue women, they have to come to you. And then this one just happens to turn up right when you are in a moment of panic about fidelity and matrimony and all those other dirty words," Roxbury explained.

"So you are saying that any woman would inspire such . . ." Brandon hesitated to use the word *feelings*. "Such interest, were she to appear in my life at this time?"

"Precisely. I'm sure Miss Harlow is delightful and delectable," Roxbury said, then paused.

Oh, Roxbury had no idea of the numerous charms of his Writing Girl and, God willing, would remain ignorant.

Roxbury continued: "But it's all a matter of timing. Had you been unengaged, I wager you wouldn't have looked twice at her."

Brandon thought of his list, *Desirable Qualities in a Wife*, and suspected that he never would have taken much notice of Miss Harlow. She was not what he wanted, and yet the attraction was present in an almost palpable way. Funny, that.

"You know, your bachelor days are dwindling," Roxbury pointed out. "Don't squander the last, precious few."

"Are you suggesting that I embark on an affair with her?" Brandon took a large swallow of his brandy.

Roxbury lifted his brow.

"Point taken," Brandon agreed, and took another sip.

His friend knew less than nothing about matrimony, other than what he gleaned from the married women with whom he frequently wooed and bedded. But Roxbury did know a thing or two (or ten or twenty) about being a rake, having affairs, and all the highs and lows of living bachelor life to the fullest.

And so, if Roxbury said that Brandon was merely panicking at the prospect of matrimony—even though he never panicked—he was slightly inclined to believe him.

If Roxbury said that there was nothing especially attractive about Miss Harlow, other than her showing up at this particular moment—even though Brandon could list more than a few of the traits that made her very well suited to him—then he was inclined to believe him.

Roxbury looked left, then right. When he had ascertained that Borwick, Biddulph, and Twitchell were immersed in their card game and not at all interested in their conversation, he leaned over the table and spoke quietly.

"So have you . . . ?"

"I am a faithful man, Roxbury."

"I suppose that I have committed enough indiscretions for us both," he said, settling back in his seat.

"I shall decline to comment," Brandon said, adding a grin.

"But in all honesty, Brandon, you have three options. Here's a list for you, I know you like them: first, you can tup her, second you can abstain, third you can jilt your fiancée and see what happens with you and the Writing Girl."

"It is that simple, isn't it?"

"Yes. You're spending too much time with women if you think there are thirty-nine different ways of examining a situation and twice as many courses of action," Roxbury stated.

Brandon laughed at this. He had sisters and he had endured many such conversations.

"Now, I have need of your advice," Roxbury said. "Lady Derby is under the impression that I am to attend your wedding with her."

"And the problem?"

"Lady Belmont assumes that I shall attend your wedding with her," Roxbury said, looking slightly sheepish to be caught bedding not one widow, but two.

"And you need help to decide which one?" Brandon asked.

"Or you could tell me how I could get out of attending with either of them. Attending such an event with a lady implies a level of commitment I couldn't possibly follow through with."

"Yes, and I suppose it would ruin their friendship if you were to publicly attend with one of them and not the other," Brandon said.

"Actually, they are already mortal enemies. It's perfect for my plans. I know they won't talk to each other and discover that I am visiting each of their beds on alternating evenings," Roxbury said with a giant grin.

"I am appalled," Brandon stated. "On second thought, knowing you, I'm not shocked in the slightest. In fact, it shows a streak of intelligence."

"Someone must compensate for your excessively perfect behavior," Roxbury said. "So how do I get out of it?"

"I couldn't say. But I might ask you to be my best man only so that you cannot plead illness and skip the ceremony."

"Devious bastard," Roxbury said, but he was smiling.

Brandon walked home from the club. It was a beautiful, warm day not unlike the one in which he had met Sophie. Perhaps, if he could just retrace his steps, he could find the moment when the path turned from the perfectly straight and narrow one he had been traveling on to this increasingly winding, tangled road of conflicting thoughts and—*damn it*—feelings.

Clarissa was everything he wanted in a wife. With her, he would enjoy a quiet, calm, unperturbed existence. He would care for her, but he would never love her, and thus he would be safe from devastation should he lose her.

Adventure was for novels, not for every day.

But Sophie called to him. She managed, with a witty retort or a flash of her eyes, to make him laugh. She was like a spark of light, revealing the darkness he usually existed in—and bringing Brandon *Before* back again. And then, of course, there was the undeniable fact that he wished to seduce her and to possess her in the most exquisite, earthly way.

He did not own such feelings for anyone else.

Brandon suspected that Roxbury might be wrong—it wasn't just any woman at this deuced inconvenient time, it was Sophie. Either way, an affair was out of the question. As was jilting Clarissa. He was a man of honor and a man of his word. The contracts had been signed and the betrothal publicly celebrated. There was no backing out now.

Chapter 17

Fourteen days before the wedding . . .

St. George's, Hanover Square

The wedding of the Marquis of Winchester and Lady Victoria, daughter of Lord Selby, rivaled Brandon and Clarissa's for the title of Wedding of the Year. The groom was a well-respected marquis; the bride was the daughter of an earl. It was also a love match.

As was her custom, Sophie sat at the end of a pew, toward the wall, not the center aisle where the bride would pass by, so that she could easily flee if necessary.

Julianna accompanied her, as she often did, partially to gather material for her own column, and partially to comfort Sophie.

"No need to get upset just yet," Julianna told her. But Sophie was already nervous. *Seamstress or servant, governess or mistress . . .*

This wedding was different than all the others. Brandon was in attendance. She watched as he arrived and took his seat—he sat at the other end of the same pew. If she were to lean forward just a bit, and casually glance in that direction . . .

She caught his eye and smiled as much as she was able to, given that weddings upset her and anything reminding her of his looming wedding—such as seeing him here—upset her all the more.

Focus, she commanded herself. *Breathe.*

"Seamstress or servant . . . Oh, hell and damnation," she muttered. It was no use.

Sophie had her pencil and tablet at the ready to mark down all the details of the ceremony: the names of those in the bridal party, what they wore, if anything unusual happened, and, most interesting to her, how the bride and groom acted toward each other.

She had taken the following notes this morning: *love match, pink roses and orange blossoms, crowded church, a fortnight until . . .*

A fortnight left until what? In that time, would she convince Lord Brandon to jilt his perfect fiancée for a girl reporter? Or did she have fourteen days to steel herself against the oncoming heartache?

Both seemed impossible.

She glanced in his direction again.

He caught her eye. That was the thing, she thought: it wasn't just her. He thought of her, too. He glanced at her, too. It was so very magnetic; there was a pull to him that was impossible to resist. She simply could not look away.

"What do you keep looking at?" Julianna asked. And then she saw Brandon and said, "Oh."

"I know," Sophie admitted, thinking that the sensation of butterflies in one's stomach was overrated and quite unpleasant.

"I thought you did not care for him because he is going to be married to someone else in two weeks time," Julianna stated so matter-of-factly. It was not that simple, and her friend did not seem to grasp that.

Sophie didn't care to try to convince her otherwise, at least not presently. It would require confessing to deeper feelings than she wished to own.

"Thank you for reminding me," Sophie said instead.

"You don't sound glad of it," Julianna remarked.

"I'm not," Sophie replied. She knew she had to confront the facts that she was falling for a man who would marry another in just a fortnight. Perhaps some other time; getting through a wedding was difficult enough.

"What is going on?"

"I'm falling for him, Julianna," Sophie whispered. She began to fan herself with the voucher for her admittance. Why did it always get so blasted hot in St. George's?

"Oh, my," her friend murmured.

"Where is the bride? The ceremony is supposed to start now," Sophie said, changing the subject. The symptoms were beginning in earnest now: her stomach was queasy and her palms were damp. Oh, how she hated this!

Seamstress or servant, governess or mistress.

Perhaps she *did* want to be a mistress—Lord Brandon's mistress. She glanced in his direction again; he did not see her. He was standing to greet the Richmond ladies.

"And for that matter, where is the groom?" Julianna wondered.

"Is he not here?" Sophie asked, worried. This was another reason to have Julianna—she was taller and had a better view of the altar.

"Not that I can see."

"Oh, bloody hell," Sophie whispered fiercely.

"Sophie!"

"I'm afraid I cannot stay," Sophie said, as she stood

to go. Julianna knew better than to stop her. Instead of running out into the streets, Sophie took refuge in the vestibule and proceeded to pace. Brandon was here, and her desire to be near him won out over her desire to quit the church.

As she paced back and forth on the stone floor, she cursed Matthew Fletcher and grumbled about how she suffered for her work. All of those brides, and she wasn't one of them—and it didn't seem likely she ever would be.

She thought of Brandon—he was never far from her thoughts—paused and sighed. She wanted him, yet he could never be hers.

She wiped away a tear, because what ought to be a pure, magical love was a dangerous, hurtful, complicated emotion she couldn't control.

This time last year, she had been blindsided by heartache. Now she was positioned to experience it again. First, she had fallen for the man that left her and now she was falling for a man that would never leave another woman *for* her.

"Sophie. Are you all right?"

She spun around and saw to her surprise that it was Lord Brandon, with concern fixed upon his face. She did not want him to see her vulnerable and emotional. And yet, with an equal fervor, she wished to throw herself into his arms and rest her cheek on his chest. But she kept herself in check.

"What are you doing here?" Sophie asked, looking around for Clarissa, or his mother, or a reason for his presence.

"I noticed you leave, and that you seemed unwell," he answered, as if that explained anything. So she waited for a moment, to see if he would explain himself further, and it dawned on her: He cared. For her.

"I hate weddings," Sophie blurted out. Only the Writing Girls knew that *The Weekly*'s celebrated wedding columnist despised, loathed, and reviled those lovely ceremonies that were the subject of pages that paid her wages.

It was clear in his expression that he had not expected that.

Brandon stepped aside, pulling Sophie into an alcove that would provide some privacy.

"Every Saturday morning I subject myself to ceremony after ceremony, when each one makes me . . . makes me . . ."

The words would not come; it felt as if they were stuck in her throat and she would choke on them. She wanted to tell him that each wedding broke her heart anew, and that she never dreaded a wedding the way she did his.

For every man that stayed at the altar, she wondered why she hadn't fallen in love with that one. For every bride that progressed more than halfway down the aisle, Sophie wondered if she would ever take those steps. And the whole damned ceremony and celebration made her feel inadequate and panicked all over again.

Brandon clasped his hands gently around her upper arms and looked intently into her eyes.

"Sophie, take a deep breath," he commanded, and she complied. His voice was so sure and steady. It calmed her significantly. "Tell me why you hate weddings."

Would the truth make him find her less desirable? It made her feel that way, like secondhand goods, or a purchase that had been returned to the shop because it wasn't quite the thing. It might be for the best if he thought less of her.

For each passing moment that he stood here with

her, hidden away from prying eyes—exactly when she needed him—she could feel herself falling more and more in love with him.

"I was jilted." It came out in a whisper.

"He's a fool," Brandon said.

"I made it halfway down the aisle . . ."

Brandon took her hands in his and gave a gentle, supportive squeeze—and she fell for him a little more. "And now I feel sick until the bride meets the groom at the altar. And just now, the groom walked off and the bride is late . . ."

"Shhh . . ." Brandon placed his finger over her lips, because her voice was rising in panic. "Look."

He pulled her deeper into the shadows as the bride entered the vestibule from a side chamber. Sophie thought she was so beautiful in her silver satin gown dotted with pearls, like moonlight.

The bride took no notice of them as she smiled happily at her father, stood up straighter, and looked determinedly down the aisle. Sophie guessed that she saw her groom at the altar, for her smile positively dazzled.

Sophie remembered this moment when it had happened to her, and it had been quite different. She had been late, and she hadn't paused to look down the aisle to smile at her groom to see if he smiled in return. Instead, she rushed straight into disaster.

She had learned later that Matthew had been trying to speak to her before, but had been shooed away from her chambers; and then she had been late, and he had been ushered up to the altar when he hadn't been ready. To meet her halfway had been his only opportunity.

The music started. The bride took one step, and then another, toward her future. And all the while Brandon stood at her side and held her hand.

Her eyes became hot with tears. *This* was what she wanted: the man who would stand beside her and hold her hand just when she needed it most.

"Was yours a love match?" he asked.

"It had been for me. But love wasn't enough for him."

"What happened?" Brandon asked.

"He wished for adventure. And for one Mrs. Lavinia Tibbits, a traveling widow whom he had met at the local pub a fortnight earlier." It still hurt to mention it.

"You were jilted on your wedding day—" Brandon repeated carefully.

"Halfway down the aisle, to be precise," Sophie said.

"For another woman?" he finished.

"And now I write about everyone else's perfect weddings," Sophie said bluntly. She could tell by his expression that he was stunned. She watched as he processed the information, calmly and thoughtfully.

Presumably he could understand now that this—whatever it was between them—was no light flirtation for her, but dangerously similar territory.

Brandon did the one thing to do in this situation: he wrapped his arms around her, and urged her closer. Sophie thought of her ill-fated wedding day, when Matthew had tried to hold her, to comfort her. She had wanted the refuge of a man's arms.

Finally she had found her haven.

Sophie leaned her cheek against his chest. It was warm, strong, and she could hear his heart pounding in a certain and steady rhythm. This was a man that could be trusted with a girl's heart and love for a lifetime.

Brandon held her with one hand resting on her lower back, one at the base of her neck, and she felt utterly under his spell, and his command.

She burned with desire and she burned with jealousy of Clarissa.

His slightest caress sent delightful shivers down her spine. Her wits were fleeing as primal, wanton sensations were beginning to take over. With her last shred of intelligence, Sophie pulled back and gazed up at him.

His eyes had darkened considerably, to a shade not unlike grass in the moonlight— dark, but with a hint of color. Sophie loved his eyes, but that paled in significance to the fact that they were engaged in a heated embrace in a church vestibule during a wedding.

In two weeks time, he would be here for his own wedding to Clarissa.

The intensely splendid heat she'd been feeling was starting to fade, leaving her cold.

"What are we doing here?" Sophie asked.

"Getting into trouble," Brandon answered with a smile.

"You do like trouble," Sophie responded.

Brandon said, "I do."

To hear Brandon say those particular words to her, in a church, made her wonder: How far would either of them go for this magical, magnetic thing between them? Would this man of honor break his word and marry her?

Lady Clarissa wondered why Miss Harlow had dashed off. She did *not* wonder why her fiancé went after her; Clarissa's fiancé, that is—not Miss Harlow's, though at times it seems one would never know. That idle thought faded in light of a much more interesting matter.

Namely, who on earth was that gentleman brazenly staring at her?

Who is he?

She felt, for the first time, a shiver of anticipation of pleasure—and the first fluttering of butterflies in her belly.

Clarissa glanced at him again, completely unable to look away. He winked at her. Winked! She blushed, and her lips formed into a genuine smile for the first time since her betrothal.

Chapter 18

Twelve days before the wedding . . .

The Offices of The London Weekly
53 Fleet Street

T hanks to Julianna's notes, Sophie had ample
material with which to write her column. There
were the mentions of all the weddings she had attended
that week, and review of the Winchester and Selby
wedding, as well as the progress report on the "Wedding
of the Year."

She also had a disturbing letter from the Duchess
of Richmond, detailing the selection of the cake and
relating plans made during meetings that Sophie had
not been invited to. Which was fine, really, as Sophie
did not particularly enjoy hours spent planning the
wedding of a man she adored to someone else.

She thought of the duchess's narrowed eyes and
pursed lips upon seeing particularly heated glances
between Sophie and Brandon.

It was immediately obvious to Sophie that the
duchess was trying to separate them, and she could
not find fault with that. But if she lost this story,
Mr. Knightly would not be pleased and writers who

earned his displeasure did not write for *The London Weekly*.

A staff meeting was due to begin in an hour, so she had no time to sigh or lament any of it. As she read over her column, she couldn't resist adding a dash of snark.

MISS HARLOW'S MARRIAGE IN HIGH LIFE

Weddings, weddings, everywhere! (*So sick of weddings am I.*) This author particularly enjoyed the beautiful ceremony of Lord Winchester and his bride, Lady Victoria Hodges, daughter of Earl Selby (*after being nearly sickened by it*). The affection the couple had for each other was noticeable and the joy in the room was palpable as all were swept up in the romantic spirit (*including Lord Brandon and myself*). Who doesn't love a love match? (*Really, what's not to love?*)

The bride's gown was a stunning silver and white satin creation by the talented Madame Auteuil. (*Very wished for.*) This modiste is also creating Lady Clarissa Richmond's dress, for her much-anticipated ceremony to the Duke of Hamilton and Brandon (*not anticipated by this author, though*). The plans for that ceremony continue at a fevered pace—the cake and flowers have been selected—only two short weeks until the Big Day (*two weeks in which anything might happen. Dare a girl wish for an upset for a love match?*)

She finished a fresh copy (without parenthetical asides) for Mr. Knightly to edit with just enough time to join the rush to the staff meeting.

"Miss Sophie Harlow, we want an explanation," Eliza declared, once they were all seated.

"You've made the gossip columns," Annabelle explained, and held up a copy of *The London Times*, which was *The London Weekly*'s principal rival. Sophie's heart sank; this could not be good.

"Let me see," Julianna said, taking the paper. She turned to *The Times* gossip column, "Man About Town," which was her arch nemesis, and read aloud:

> At the wedding of The Marquis of Winchester and the daughter of Earl Selby, Writing Girl Miss Harlow made a quick exit just before the ceremony, only to be followed by the Duke of H— and B—. We, along with everyone else in London, wonder why and suspect the perfect duke might, for once, be up to no good.

"I can explain," Sophie said, forcing herself to speak with a calmness she did not feel. "I did not feel well, so I stepped out for a moment. The duke had business of his own to attend to. It was merely a coincidence of timing."

If I lost my column . . . The thought was too horrible to contemplate. She may not love it, but she took pride in her work and cared little for her other options.

Alistair Grey smiled, and affectionately placed his hand upon hers. "Darling, it is nothing to be ashamed of if you've captured the attentions of a handsome duke."

"Unless he is betrothed to another," Julianna said.

Sophie suffered an intense pang of guilt because of Clarissa, and a surge of indignation because it was indeed a marvelous thing to have captured the attentions of a handsome man like Brandon. But she couldn't completely revel in it because of his betrothal.

"Are we really discussing this?" Grenville cut in.

"Yesterday in parliament one of the royal dukes requested an eighteen-thousand-pound increase in his allowance! When people are starving in the streets! Isn't that more worthy of our *attentions*?"

"Undoubtedly," Alistair answered. "Oddly enough, it is not nearly as fascinating as what our own Miss Harlow may or may not have done with a duke, in a church vestibule."

She had done nothing but fall further in love.

It had begun so innocently and she keenly missed the exhilaration of those few days between when they first met and when she discovered they could never be together. And though she had tried to put a stop to any sort of romantic feelings for him, it was too late. He stood by her and held her hand when she was at her most vulnerable. How could she not give her heart to him?

The conversation ceased when Mr. Knightly entered the room.

"Good morning," he said to the staff. His gaze settled on Sophie, and her stomach began to ache. "Miss Harlow, I saw you made the dailies."

She nodded, suddenly terrified. What if she did lose her job over this? Was she ready to starve for Brandon? Or become a seamstress for him? No, she was not that far gone. Yet.

"I have a hunch that a scandal involving one of our own will lead to an increase in sales," Knightly said, and she exhaled a little.

"Scandal equals sales," the entire staff recited in unison.

"However, should it jeopardize the content of your own column, Miss Harlow, I shall feel differently," Knightly said. "If Lady Richmond were to take her story to another paper, I would not be pleased."

"Yes, sir," Sophie answered. She understood him: an adulterous spinster reporting on weddings wasn't quite the thing.

"Now, ladies first, of course," Knightly said, flashing a grin. Sophie exhaled with relief. She was safe for today, though with Lady Richmond very aware of the flirtation between Sophie and Brandon, she had to watch her every step.

"I will refute the rumors about her supposed liaison with His Grace in my column," Julianna said.

And then they went through the rest. Sophie would continue with her wedding reports, Annabelle was answering letters that asked wedding-related questions, and Eliza would report on the efficacy of Wright's Tonic for the Cure of Unsuitable Affections. It had been started as a jest, but the sales of this potion were tremendous.

The rest of the pages of the next issue would be full with the usual assortment of foreign and "Fashionable Intelligence," Parliamentary accounts, and passionately biased political articles, scathing and raving theater reviews, reports of accidents and offenses, and stock numbers.

Sophie left the weekly meeting feeling out of sorts. *Infatuation. Scandal. Dukes and Writing Girls.* When and how had this become her life?

Chapter 19

Eleven days before the wedding . . .

*The Residence of Lord and Lady Westbrooke,
Mayfair*

The crowd was thick at Lady Westbrooke's musicale,
but Sophie quickly spied Clarissa standing off to
the side, by herself.

"Good evening, Lady Richmond," Sophie said.

"Call me Clarissa, please," she implored. "Otherwise I shall look over my shoulder for my mother, who
is at home with a megrim this evening."

The two women exchanged a look that spoke volumes about the significance of the elder Lady Richmond's absence.

"I'm sorry to hear that she is unwell," Sophie said.
Clarissa must have arrived with her fiancé. Sophie sti-
fled the urge to look around for him.

"It's nothing fatal, and it is rather interesting to be
out without her," Clarissa said, looking around at the
other guests before pausing to gaze at one in particular.
She looked away before Sophie could determine who
had captured her interest.

"Clarissa, I wanted to apologize for the other day, at

the Marquis of Winchester's wedding. I had been feeling out of sorts and Lord Brandon came to ascertain that I was well. And then the ceremony began and . . ."

"It's fine, Sophie. I've noticed that you two seem to get on well together," Clarissa said, and Sophie was not sure how to reply to that. Her tone did not reveal much. Nevertheless, Sophie wondered if, perhaps, Clarissa did harbor feelings for her fiancé that she dared not show.

"It must be nice," Clarissa said, filling in the silence.

"Indeed," Sophie replied, not knowing what else to say.

"May I ask you something, in the strictest confidence?" Clarissa asked, leaning in closer.

"Of course," Sophie said, intrigued.

"Who is that man?" Clarissa asked, ever so slightly inclining her head toward a small gathering of guests. Sophie paused a moment, and quickly peeked over her shoulder.

First she saw the lecherous Lord Borwick with a brandy in hand and his face already red from drink. She quickly dismissed him as a candidate for Clarissa's interest, and then noted a striking stranger.

He was a tall man, with brown hair that was shockingly long, reaching almost to his shoulders. It was an oddly attractive style, especially combined with the perfectly refined evening attire he wore. So wild, yet so civilized. He leaned easily against the mantel, with a crowd of men and women surrounding him while he looked past them, with a slightly amused, slightly bored expression.

"I have no idea, but he is deuced handsome," she answered.

"He *is*," Clarissa said, with a faraway look in her eyes.

"Let's ask Julianna. She'll know who he is, and everything pertinent about him, along with a few irrelevant details," Sophie suggested.

They wove their way through the crowd of guests who had yet to take their seats before the musicale.

"His name is Frederick von Vennigan and he is the Prince of Bavaria," Julianna informed them when they found her.

"Oh," Clarissa said, breathlessly. "A *prince* . . ."

"I remember now! You spoke of him the other day," Sophie said.

"He's been mentioned in the papers," Clarissa said, her face lighting up.

"He is friends with the Marquis of Winchester, and they met when the Marquis held the ambassadorship to the Bavarian court. The Prince is in town for the wedding, and, I understand that he is in no rush to return for he left in the throes of a scandal."

"A scandal over what?" Clarissa asked, obviously curious.

"Oh, the usual. Women and wagers or something of the sort," Julianna said flippantly.

"Good evening, ladies. I hope that I am not interrupting," Lord Brandon said with a smile that seemed to be just for Sophie. To see him, to hear his voice, to be near him—all made the whole world seem brighter, and she couldn't help but smile at him.

He handed Clarissa a glass of lemonade that had presumably been requested earlier. She thanked him, took a sip, and her gaze darted in the direction of the prince.

"My friend Lady Julianna Somerset was just telling us about the Prince of Bavaria," Sophie explained.

"Apparently, he is scandalous," Brandon said dryly. Everyone, it seemed, was discussing him. One did not encounter young, handsome, scandalous princes every day.

"And you are now as well, Your Grace. I noticed your debut appearance in the gossip columns," Julianna said to the shock of her two friends. And the duke.

"Something every man should do once in his life," Brandon remarked. Clarissa took a sip of her lemonade and Sophie saw her glance in the direction of the prince. Again.

"Ah, but I am not certain that most men can restrain themselves to only once," Julianna replied.

"This is when you ought to declare that you are not most men," Sophie told him.

"That is the expected retort, is it not?" he replied with a grin.

"Indeed, I had set you up admirably for it," Julianna said, smiling.

"You have my deep and eternal gratitude," Brandon replied, ever the gentleman.

"You had better take care, Lord Brandon, or you might find yourself making your second appearance in the gossip columns," Sophie warned. Everything and anything was fodder for her friend—not that anyone knew that she authored *"Fashionable Intelligence,"* though it was widely suspected.

"It seems that we are encouraged to take our seats for the musicale portion of the evening," Julianna said. They made their way into the large, airy ballroom, which had been filled with an assortment of chairs and settees.

Two enormous chandeliers, lit with hundreds of candles, hung from the ceiling, which had been painted to look like heaven with clouds, plump cherubs, fair-haired angels, and golden rays of sunshine.

One settee was sufficient for the four of them. When

it became clear that some delay was in effect, Brandon left to procure lemonades for Sophie and Julianna, who fell into conversation when they saw that Clarissa was otherwise occupied by none other than the Prince of Bavaria.

Within a second of Lord Brandon's departure someone took the seat on Clarissa's other side. She turned to politely acknowledge whomever it was, and was stunned to discover the mysterious, staring stranger from the Winchester wedding and, as she had been lately informed, the Prince of Bavaria.

She was overwhelmed by excited, nervous energy because this was a situation she'd never expected to find herself in: she was with a man who aroused her interest—and her mother was on the other side of town.

Clarissa smiled, truly smiled.

"Are you going to sing for us this evening?" he asked without any sort of polite introduction, and her smile vanished because he caught her off guard.

She was also distracted. Up close she noticed that he had one fine-lined scar on each of his chiseled cheekbones. She wondered about them, and him, and why it was suddenly so very warm, yet she shivered.

"Are you?" he asked, again. How embarrassing. What strange manners!

"Oh, no," she replied, and her pleasure was fading, to be replaced with panic. Of all the subjects in the world, of all the things they could possibly discuss, their first conversation had to be about her greatest flaw!

She twisted her betrothal ring around her finger.

"Why not?"

"Lady Westbrooke has already selected the musical performers for this evening," she answered.

"Exceptions are made all the time. I shall offer to

play a tune, and you shall sing," he said. He smiled and she was too nervous to respond in kind.

"I have a sore throat this evening," she told him.

"You sound fine to me," he rejoined, and she despised him for calling her a liar in so many words.

"I'm certain that is not necessary, or even desired by the guests," she answered, growing more mortified by the minute. This was *not* how this was supposed to go!

"I wish for it," he said plainly. *Typical of a prince,* she thought, *to wish for something and expect it promptly.*

"Sir, we are not even acquainted! I am in no position to grant your wishes, nor do I intend to ever do so," she replied confidently. Really, he was rude, intrusive, and strange-looking with his long hair, scars, and unnervingly blue eyes.

She had no idea what had come over her previously that she should be so attracted to him.

"My name is Frederick von Vennigan. I am the Prince of Bavaria."

"Lady Clarissa Richmond." Good manners were so instilled in her that she answered automatically.

"Is it because you are nervous performing in front of an audience?"

"No," she answered, and then thought better of it, saying, "Yes."

"Or are you not confident in your singing abilities? I'm sure that you sound like the angel you appear to be."

"I am, in a fact, a wretched singer. Were I to regale the audience with my talents," Clarissa said, "I should be shunned from society." She might as well admit it, since she no longer cared about impressing him.

"That bad?"

"Yes."

"We can't all be perfect, I suppose," the prince said. "I am, of course. Perfect, that is."

"What you are is excessively provoking," she muttered. Too late, she clamped her gloved palm over her mouth. She had just told a member of royalty that he was excessively provoking.

But he was! His presence and his conversation were making her out of sorts. He teased her, and she was not used to it. Something about him made her shiver, and now her heartbeat had quickened and it was so loud she was afraid he might hear it and tease her about that, too.

"Has anyone ever told you that you are delightful?" he asked, to her shock. She had just been horribly rude and he liked it, and liked her for it. How peculiar.

"Yes," she answered. This was the first time it was for something other than her pretty face or sweet disposition.

"You have received many compliments, I suspect. Raves about your beauty, to start. I can't imagine you receive many on your manners," he persisted.

Clarissa paused at the sound of Sophie's laughter. That reminded her of the other afternoon: how she was so witty and at ease, how she made Brandon seem human, and how Clarissa wanted to be like her.

This was her chance to try something different. Her mother wasn't here and, she suspected, the prince would be amused by it.

"My manners are usually exquisite. You bring out the worst in me," she dared to say.

"So it is my fault that you have been impertinent to visiting royalty?"

"I couldn't say," she murmured.

"I'm not going to apologize and I shall tell you why," he said, leaning in closer to her, and she was thrilled by

He studied the creature for strength, character, intelligence, and dominance. No doubt that Brandon was noting the slim scars on the prince's cheeks. Clarissa was outrageously curious about them. Rather than ask, she performed introductions.

"Your Highness, may I introduce His Grace, the Duke of Hamilton and Brandon. My fiancé. Lord Brandon, this is Frederick von Vennigan, the Prince of Bavaria."

Before further conversation could occur, Lady Westbrooke informed a hushed crowd that it was her great pleasure to present the lovely singer Miss Octavia Catalani. After a round of polite applause, she began to sing.

Clarissa snuck a glance at the prince and caught his eye. She blushed, he smiled, and she was smitten, and, though Lord Brandon was seated next to her, she forgot entirely about the man she had promised to marry.

Chapter 20

Lord Brandon's fiancée was openly flirting with one of the few men that outranked him. It was a strange and novel sensation to see his fiancée act thusly.

Brandon had never thought of Clarissa as the flirtatious type, and didn't know anyone who did, other than this prince—von Venison, or whatever his name was. This, naturally, led him to the conclusion that the prince was the one to unlock that part of her that he had not.

To his surprise, Brandon experienced something like jealousy, or annoyance. Perhaps it was shock; she was not the woman he thought. He couldn't make sense of the situation, which rankled all the more.

Spencer's alleged secret only complicated matters more. Though he wouldn't credit it without actual proof (which he had yet to receive), Brandon occasionally had trouble dismissing the thought from his mind.

To his left was his fiancée—a bright-eyed, blushing, suddenly intriguing stranger.

On his right was Sophie—a tempting woman for whom he had a temporary infatuation. Or so he hoped.

At night, he was plagued by erotic dreams in which

he explored every inch of Sophie, with his bare hands or even his mouth. He dreamt of her below him as they made love—and then above him, inside her and passionate with frantic kisses.

During the day, everything made him think of her.

A man could only continue for so long in this state.

Brandon tried to ignore such thoughts, but it was presently impossible. The settee they sat on was not large, and thus he and Sophie were quite close. If they were alone, he'd need only to turn his head to kiss her.

He'd slide down one sleeve of her bodice, and then the other, and then the whole damn thing. He'd cup her breasts, caress them lightly and then . . .

Brandon took a few seconds to banish the image from his mind. During a musicale in the drawing room of Lord and Lady Westbrooke was neither the time nor the place to have vivid daydreams of an erotic nature about the young woman seated next to him.

Sophie tapped his arm, which was crossed with the other over his chest, mainly to keep his hands occupied with not touching her. When she had his attention she gestured, with the slightest inclination of her head, in the direction of Lord Borwick. The old fellow was asleep, his bald head lolling back with his mouth wide open.

In spite of himself, Brandon grinned. Sophie did, too. And they both turned to focus again on the music.

Brandon was then distracted by a loud snore from Lord Borwick. It was audible enough to only disturb those in his immediate vicinity.

Sophie had her hand pressed over her mouth. Her cheeks were turning pink and she tried to hold in her laughter. Her friend was similarly occupied. Clarissa was not laughing; she was making eyes at her prince.

He pressed his own mouth into a firm line and willed himself to scowl disapprovingly. He could not manage it.

"You are a terrible influence on me," Brandon whispered to Sophie.

"I have no idea what you are talking about," she said, smirking.

"Cheeky wench."

She gasped. "Your Grace!" But she was smiling, too, and trying so hard to look affronted. He was shocked that he had actually called a proper young woman a wench.

"Bad. Influence. I am now calling proper young ladies 'wenches' to their faces," he said, wondering what the hell was happening to him. His brain warned, again: *DANGER! BEWARE!* Every other part of him vibrated, hummed, and pleaded for more of anything Sophie.

At that moment Lord Borwick's snoring ceased for a second, recapturing their attention. His eyes fluttered open only to close again and then his head abruptly fell forward, in a manner suggesting that the muscles in his neck had taken a moment's respite. The ensuring jerk of his head woke him.

Sophie turned pink and shook with pent-up laughter.

"Do I need to escort you out to ensure that you are well?" he asked, managing to appear utterly calm even though he was desperate to shout with laughter.

"I'm fine," she gasped.

"Because you know what happened the last time that happened—I caused a scandal and I'm not sure I've sufficiently recovered from the thrill."

"I'm reminded of a saying," Sophie stated. " 'What happens once never happens again and what happens twice shall happen thrice.' "

"Interesting logic, Miss Harlow. Are you suggesting that if I were to escort you out this very moment, I shall eventually do it again, a third time?"

"It's merely a saying," she said.

"What happens after the third time?"

"I'm not quite certain. At any rate, I'm fine. So long as Lord Borwick stays awake."

"Are you sure? Because women always say they are fine when they are not," Brandon said, provoking her further.

"Men do that as well. And, yes, I am sure."

"*Shhhhhh*," Lady Endicott urged then, and gave "a look," which quite nearly sent them both over the edge. They were being unpardonably rude, but it couldn't be helped. He'd never enjoyed himself more at a *ton* event.

"I haven't been shushed since I was a mere lad. You are trouble, Miss Harlow."

"But you like trouble, do you not, Lord Brandon?" she said coyly.

"I find a little trouble amusing," he said. More than amusing, actually.

He liked her and desired her from the start, but it was her confession at the Winchester wedding that fascinated him. She was not another spoiled, isolated debutante. He had never known another woman like her. A woman jilted, writing about everyone else's perfect ceremony.

If she became so upset at every wedding . . . He wondered how she would fare at his, then immediately shut down and refused to consider it. At that thought, he shifted uncomfortably in his seat.

On his left, Clarissa brazenly flirted with a prince.

On his right, Sophie's fingers brushed against his, hidden in the folds of her skirts.

He remembered that the marriage contract had been signed.

Sophie spent the better part of the musicale wondering how Brandon could have such a splendid time with her when Clarissa was right there, and not consider, maybe, perhaps, changing his bride or, at least, the date of the wedding.

He couldn't possibly go through with it!

He gave every sign that he intended to go through with it.

The ceremony was scheduled for eleven days, and there was so little time to make a life-altering decision.

Unless he had no intention of changing his mind, or his bride.

Why, then, did he laugh with her, and secretly entwine his fingers with hers?

If things weren't so exquisite when they were together, she would walk away. But she and he were so perfect. When her heart wasn't beating with the pleasure of his company, it was aching at the prospect of losing him forever.

It was a delicate situation.

One that may or may not have been complicated by the arrival of the prince. Sophie had noticed the attention he paid to Clarissa, and how she responded to him. And she wondered . . .

"Goodbye, Sophie," Clarissa said. Her eyes were so bright that if Sophie didn't know better, she'd think the girl was feverish.

"Good evening, Miss Harlow," Brandon murmured, and she barely managed a smile because she knew he was about to spend unchaperoned time with Clarissa in a dark carriage and she'd give just about anything to trade places with her.

Sophie sighed and a few moments later was jolted from her maudlin reverie by the arrival of His Highness, the Prince of Bavaria.

Sophie looked over her shoulder to see whom he might wish to speak to, but there was no one else.

"Your Highness." She sank into a curtsey, wondering why on earth he deigned to give her his attentions.

"Let's not bother with formalities, Miss . . ." he said, prompting her for her name.

"Miss Harlow."

"If you would please give this to Lady Clarissa Richmond," he said, handing out a letter.

"A letter?" she queried, stupidly. Of course it was a letter.

He nodded.

"I thought you only just met," Sophie asked, and then chided herself that she really ought to refrain from asking inane and invasive questions of royalty.

"It was a small matter to slip into our host's study and use his writing supplies. I'm sure that he would not mind terribly that a prince would write a love letter upon his stationery," His Highness replied, even though he didn't need to explain himself to the likes of her.

"You have a point. She is betrothed, you know." Sophie felt it her duty to warn him away from suffering the same as she.

"I am as aware of the fact as you, Miss Harlow."

It dawned on her that the letter in her hand could change *everything*.

Chapter 21

<u>*Things Brandon MUST do before the wedding:*</u>
1. Secure special license.
2. Enlist a best man.
3. Prepare a toast for the wedding breakfast.
4. Cease all and any attraction, infatuation, and manner of interest in Miss Sophie Harlow, otherwise known as *Trouble*.

It was unlikely that he would accomplish any of those items this evening. He was already wondering if Sophie would also be attending the ball, and remembering that Clarissa would be there, too. *Of course.*

But first, there was a carriage ride to be endured. Not a ride fraught with restrained passion and lust, as with Sophie. No, he would be enclosed with his mother, and then Clarissa and her mother. *Joy.*

"How are you faring lately, Brandon?" his mother asked once they were in the carriage, driving through Mayfair.

"Fine, thank you. And you, Mother?"

"I'm a bit troubled, actually," she responded, frowning.

"Is Charlotte still fainting?"

"Yes. But the headmistress and the doctor are of the opinion that it is all a hoax. However, it is you that I am concerned with."

"Whatever for?" he asked, hoping it wasn't anything to do with women or weddings.

"You appear to have a great interest in Miss Harlow," she said.

"She's an agreeable woman," he replied. Definitely something to do with women and weddings.

"Allow me to rephrase. You obviously harbor a preference for Miss Harlow over that of your fiancée."

Oh God. Was he really going to have this conversation with his mother, at this age, now? *Things he would rather discuss with his mother: anything else.*

"Appearances can be misleading," he said with the hope that this was in some way relevant enough and an acceptable answer.

"I only mention it because your wedding, to Clarissa, is in less than a fortnight. If you do not wish to go through with it for any reason . . ." his mother's voice trailed off.

"I gave my word. The contracts are signed," he said in a tone that declared the conversation finished.

Precisely because he had given his word and signed the contracts, there was nothing to say on the matter. Unless Spencer's report confirmed . . . No, he would not pin his hopes and future on small-town rumors.

Brandon could no longer deny a passionate infatuation for Sophie. But it was, as Roxbury told him, merely symptomatic of pre-wedding jitters. Not that he was the jittery or panic-stricken sort. He frowned at the dissonance of those two facts. Whatever it was, it wasn't a reason to cancel "The Wedding of the Year."

They paused in front of the Richmond residence.

"Good evening, everyone!" Lady Richmond declared after settling into the carriage. She began chattering on and on about the weather. They all agreed that it was warmer than the previous day.

"You look especially beautiful tonight, Clarissa," Brandon said. And it was true. There was something about his fiancée that was different than usual. It could have been a new way of arranging her hair, but he suspected it was the first blush of romance that was the cause.

His future wife's first romance was with another man. Brandon frowned. If it was his heart or only his pride that rebelled against this, he knew not.

"Thank you," she replied sweetly, folding her hands in her lap, smiling, and reminding him that she would be a perfect duchess.

"She's been corresponding with Miss Harlow all day," her mother said.

"Will she be in attendance this evening?" Brandon asked. Even in the darkened interior of the carriage, he could see his mother arch a brow.

"She didn't say," Clarissa answered.

"All those letters and not one word about the ball tonight! How strange," Lady Richmond said. Brandon agreed.

He was not aware that the two women had become such close friends in such a short time as to necessitate the exchange of numerous letters in one day. But that was women for you. A man of sense, such as himself, did not trouble himself to understand their odd workings.

"How was the musicale last night?" Lady Hamilton asked. "I'm sorry I wasn't able to attend."

"I was home, too, with a megrim," Lady Richmond

answered. And then she paused to accept sympathies. "Everyone is raving about it."

"I heard the Prince of Bavaria was there! Were either of you introduced?" Lady Hamilton asked.

"Yes. In fact, Clarissa sat next to him all evening," Brandon answered.

"My daughter seated next to a prince! Even if he is a German one, and you know about the Germans," Lady Richmond said.

No one did, but no one cared to discover it, either.

"What was he like?" Lady Hamilton asked Clarissa.

"He's not what I had expected. But he is . . . diverting," she answered. In the darkness, Brandon thought he saw her blush.

By diverting, Clarissa really meant that he was dashing, thrilling, vexing, endlessly fascinating, and a million other wonderful things because he made her feel a million new, exquisite feelings. To think, they had only just met.

It had been only a day since their first encounter. Yet, in that time they had exchanged dozens of letters so that Clarissa knew more about him than anyone else. The curious scars on his cheeks—fine slash lines just under his marvelously high cheekbones—were from a duel he'd fought at sixteen with an older fencing master over a slight to the von Vennigan family. He had recently celebrated his twenty-eighth birthday. He favored Wordsworth and the romantic poets. He spoke six languages and swore in twelve. He had three sisters and was the middle of two brothers and thought she must have been terribly lonely as an only child.

She told him of things she had never told anyone.

It had been terribly lonely as an only child and she had often wished for siblings, or more friends, but her mother hadn't thought anyone was good enough. Clarissa found that unfair and wrong. She had just turned twenty, spoke French, and did not know any swear words and wished he would teach her some.

Perhaps it wasn't a million feelings but one particularly magical feeling: being understood, and wanted because of who she was and who she could be, not because of her complexion, or eyes, her pleasant countenance, or distinguished family name.

For the first time, she had lied to her mother. The letters she had been feverishly composing all day were not to Sophie because she could not confess to a correspondence to another man, particularly a German one. A German prince would not be welcomed in the Richmond household—not after her mother's father had met his end due to one. But that was neither here nor there for Clarissa because her prince had finally come.

And now she finally felt those proverbial butterflies in her stomach; they'd been there all day, with a diminishing effect on her appetite. If she sparkled, or glowed, looked especially beautiful, walked on air or burst out in song, it all was because of Frederick von Vennigan, the Prince of Bavaria and of Clarissa's heart.

Shortly after his arrival in the hot, crowded ballroom, Brandon spied Sophie precariously near the dowager and spinster corner of the ballroom, engaged in conversations with Lady Rawlings.

Correction: There was no such thing as conversation between Lady Rawlings and other persons. One served as an audience for her monologues.

One thing was certain: Brandon must save Sophie from certain boredom. Or, more precisely, that was the excuse he gave for proceeding directly to her. In truth, this temporary infatuation he had admitted to impelled him to seek her out and spend every possible moment with her.

After all, they didn't have many moments left. Every day brought him closer to the wedding. *And after the wedding . . . ?* He did not entertain such thoughts.

Not when Sophie looked so pretty in a violet-colored dress, and he wished to dance with her.

"Good evening, Lady Rawlings, Miss Harlow," he said.

Seven excruciating minutes later, after a lengthy ramble about Lady Rawlings's gout, Brandon whisked Sophie away under the pretense of introducing her to a dear, dear friend of his.

After they had walked a sufficient distance, Sophie spoke: "We call her Drawling Rawlings."

He gave a shout of laughter that turned a few heads. "That is brilliant."

"So who wishes to meet me?" she asked, looking around at the other guests as they passed through. *By God, she is adorable.*

"I'm afraid that was merely an excuse to save you from her talkative clutches. Perhaps we might dance instead?"

"I'd love to," Sophie said. And then her eyes lit up, as they do, and he was proud to be the reason. He wouldn't have many more chances to do that, before the wed—No, he would not think of that now.

They lined up for the next dance—it was not a waltz, as he wanted, but a slow dance with complicated steps and constant switching of partners.

His fiancée stepped up with the prince.

They all nodded politely, as if there was nothing untoward about this arrangement.

Partners were exchanged and Brandon went through the same motions with Clarissa.

He pressed his palm to hers, and she looked away.

They spun, and he thought that she was such a stranger to him. He wouldn't love her because he didn't *know* her. That would change after the marriage, would it not?

After the wedding. It was unfathomable. And yet, in only a few days' time . . .

Brandon caught sight of Sophie with von Vennigan, and to see her touched by another man made him feel as if he were punched in the gut.

He despised the inventor of this dance. The ton had thought the waltz scandalous, because of the temptations of the constant proximity. But this damned dance gave and took away, and only made him want more of what he could not have.

There was a tightening in his chest every time Sophie's deep brown eyes met his own.

What was she thinking? He wished to know.

Partners were exchanged again, and Sophie was back with him, hand to hand.

What was happening between them? It was something—of that he had no doubt. In his waking hours he sought her out. As he slept, he dreamt of her.

With that gorgeous mouth of hers that he ached to kiss, she would say something to make him laugh. Slowly, but surely, his pulse would rapidly increase and his nerves would hum with energy, and he would feel more alive than ever—all as he battled certain disaster.

When he was with her, logic and reason became irrelevant, everything became slightly and delightfully off kilter, his senses were heightened to a nearly intolerable level.

He imagined what it would be like to embrace her, to taste her, to possess her. When they were apart, he thought of when he would see her again, and he wondered what would happen next.

Sophie Harlow was his adventure story.

But the course of action was not clear to Brandon. He could not withdraw from his marriage for a multitude of reasons he did not care to dwell on presently. He could always indulge in Wright's Tonic for the Cure of Unsuitable Affections, but enough logic remained for him to know that it was sheer quackery and it would take far more than that to diminish her allure, or to cure his symptoms of joy, agony, exhilaration, and ecstasy he experienced when he was with her.

For this moment, he savored the brief touch of Sophie's hand against his. And he looked into her beautiful brown eyes and allowed himself to get lost in those depths.

One step closer. He could not get close enough.

Hand to hand. He ached for her touch.

Step, step, slow spin around. He could not look away.

Hand in hand, they turned to the left and took four steps. They stopped, turned, and took four more steps, only to end up where they began: hand to hand, like heart to heart. Step, step, slow spin. Always, always looking into each other's eyes.

And then the dance concluded, and the din of the ballroom overpowered the sweet music. The controlled and organized formation of the dancers gave way to a chaos of bodies as some left for air and lemonade, and others crushed in for their turn. Brandon placed his hand on the small of Sophie's back to draw her close to him so that he might protect her from the jostling crowds.

She looked at him questioningly. He nodded that, yes, something had just happened in those few minutes. Sophie's smile quickly faded.

"Clarissa, darling! Lord Brandon!" It was the Dragon Duchess herself, with some dear, dear friends eager to be introduced to the couple of the season.

"Lord Brandon, may I introduce you to my dear, dear friends Lady Endicott and Lady Chesterfield?"

He considered saying, "No," but suspected it wouldn't make a difference. He nodded his assent. She began her introductions, including His Highness, and neglected to mention Sophie. In fact, Lady Richmond positioned herself so that Sophie was entirely cut from the circle.

That was not acceptable.

"And I would like to introduce Miss Harlow of *The London Weekly*," Brandon said, drawing her in.

"Oh! You are one of the Writing Girls! I read your column every week, and I utterly adore it," Lady Endicott exclaimed, fanning herself in excitement. Most journalists were reviled; the Writing Girls were an exception.

"We've been eagerly awaiting each installment of the story on Your Grace's wedding. I do love hearing all the details," Lady Chesterfield added with an equal measure of enthusiasm.

They embarked on a female conversation with a flurry of wedding details—something about satin, seating arrangements, and hyacinths—which he, as a man, was fundamentally incapable of comprehending. They chattered away about Sophie's writing, too—what it was like to work for a newspaper, how she started, gossip about the publisher— and Brandon paid attention to how Sophie responded.

She was so gracious. Every question was patiently

and modestly answered, joyfully even. She laughed with Ladies Endicott and Chesterfield and asked them questions, such as what they liked best about the paper. Within moments, they were all acting as if they were dear, *dear* friends.

Lady Richmond was seething. Her face had taken on a hue that was beginning to blend remarkably with her crimson gown.

Clarissa looked genuinely interested in the conversation. Her wide blue eyes focused upon whoever was speaking, and she laughed with the others.

Von Vennigan seemed bemused, when he wasn't mooning over Clarissa. Brandon assumed that it was not often that princes were not the center of attention, and exceedingly rare that they be upstaged by girl reporters.

"Clarissa, did you not promise this waltz to your fiancé?" Lady Richmond cut in with a fantastic lack of subtlety.

"I did. Thank you for reminding me, Mother." Clarissa had done no such thing, of course. She did not contradict her mother, and Brandon, as a gentleman, never contradicted a woman. However, he wondered what else Clarissa would do for her mother without voicing complaint.

The prince took that opportunity to take his leave and Lady Richmond ushered her friends along. Sophie was left there, suddenly alone.

Brandon smiled at her—a sad sort of smile—as he walked away. It was the correct, honorable thing to do and yet he was disgusted with himself.

His waltz with Clarissa reminded him of two things:

1. She would be a lovely wife and duchess: end-lessly obliging, deferential, and beautiful.
2. He would care for her, but he would never love her.

Brandon wondered why, if this was what he wanted, did his thoughts stray to a woman who was not at all what he wanted in a wife or a duchess?

As he waltzed with his fiancée, Brandon saw Sophie walking out onto the terrace—alone. As soon as the damned dance ended, he followed after her.

Chapter 22

Sophie went to the terrace and lingered there. It was easier to avoid conversation, and she was not in the mood to make polite chatter. Even though she was not surprised by it, receiving a cut direct from Lady Richmond frightened her. That woman, along with her dear, dear friends, could destroy Sophie socially.

If she were not invited to weddings, she couldn't write her column. If she couldn't write her column—Sophie sighed. There was no need to mull over the details of such a downward spiral, not when there was an awful cut from Brandon to contemplate. Sophie understood that he had to go waltz with his fiancée, especially given the circumstances.

The fact remained that if he wouldn't cry off for a waltz, then he would never cry off his engagement.

The truth of it was harder and harder to accept, or ignore. Only ten days until the wedding . . . for there certainly would be a wedding.

Oh, she would *not* weep. Not here. Not now.

"There you are," Brandon said as he joined her. "I've been searching for you."

"Hello," Sophie said softly. There was nowhere she'd

rather be than with him, but she loathed that she had to wait to take her turn for his attentions.

"You should not be out here alone. It isn't proper," he said firmly.

"Really, there is no need to worry. I am chaperoned by half the party," she said with a sweep of her hand. Many people had also elected to take a stroll on the terrace.

"You do have a point," he said, taking her hand and leading her around the corner of the terrace to a significantly more secluded alcove formed by the wall of the house and two large stone pillars. A sconce high on the wall above their heads created flickering shadows and sparks of light.

Oh . . .

They were alone—except for the hundreds of people just around the corner, any one of whom could stumble upon them at any moment.

It was very dark—except for the moonlight and fire-light providing faint light and gray shadows.

The setting was ripe for the particular kind of trouble known as seduction. Given the things they risked— her livelihood, his honor, and their reputations—they should not be here.

There was no way she was leaving.

"I must apologize about that situation earlier," Brandon said.

"With Lady Richmond? It is perfectly understandable, and I cannot blame her," Sophie said. It had been hurtful, it frightened her, and she did not want to talk about it when she had a moment alone with the man of her dreams.

"She was snubbing you. That is not acceptable," he said. She loved how he championed her—until she realized that he only did so up to a point.

"I am obviously a rival to her daughter for your affections. What you witnessed was simple feminine warfare, and a very gentle form of it," Sophie explained. A cut direct from a duchess was mortifying—until one had been jilted at the altar, and then it felt like little more than a bee sting.

It could have much more disastrous repercussions, though.

"I confess that I do not understand why women cannot solve their problems as gentlemen do—with fisticuffs and a brawl."

Sophie laughed, and her fear and dismay started to fade. "I'm not certain I would wish to engage in hand-to-hand combat with Lady Richmond."

"I don't think I would, either," Brandon answered.

"We shall hide here on the terrace, then," Sophie suggested, even though that was a terrible idea. Honestly, she'd be delighted to stay hidden here with him for hours. "Though it is cowardly of us."

And far too dangerous . . . and far too pleasurable.

"I prefer to think of it as wise to avoid a battle one does not wish to fight," Brandon replied.

"It's not always possible is it?" she asked, and he shook his head no. "At any rate, it is much more pleasant out here than in there," she said. It was easier to pretend that he was hers, and only hers.

"Yes," he agreed, leaning against the wall, and gazing down at her. Oh, how she loved the way he looked at her! As if she were his very own secret treasure.

"Though it is surprisingly warm," she added. It was a hot summer night. Sophie allowed her shawl to slide further from her shoulders, and she heard his sharp intake of breath.

She entertained a fleeting thought of disrobing for

him entirely—*lud,* if that did not make her blush and inspire some very exquisite sensations!

"I suspect that one familiar with such matters would say this was all very romantic," Brandon said, adding that dashing grin that weakened her knees and her resolve to be good.

"Yes, the stars, and moonlight, and . . ." Sophie added, allowing her voice to trail off.

"You," Brandon murmured.

"And you," Sophie whispered.

Would he kiss her?

God only knew how she wanted him to, wanted him so much that she'd been waking up from heated, wanton dreams. Wanted him so much that, in weaker moments, she considered being his mistress even though her head and heart rebelled against such immoral behavior, for she was desperate to be with him. Her heart longed for him, her brain said that he was a very suitable candidate (other than that damned betrothal), and her body tormented her with its cravings for him.

And yet, she did *not* want him to kiss her. Whether Lord Brandon or Mere Mr. Brandon, he was a man of honor and that was not a small part of his appeal. She adored him for his honor and goodness, and did not want her illusions dashed. She also did not want a kiss that was rightfully owed to someone else.

She ached to kiss him and loved him because he wouldn't.

"I have a question for you, Sophie," Brandon said, and her heart started fluttering. "Did you love him?"

That was not the question she was hoping for. In fact, the last thing she wanted to think about was a massive heartache just as she was facing an even bigger one.

She couldn't be anything but honest with Brandon, and she could not refuse him anything.

"Oh, I loved him as if there was no such thing as heartache and as if happily-ever-after was for certain," Sophie answered truthfully. "But I don't think that's nearly as brave as knowing about the hard parts, and loving anyway."

He paused thoughtfully. She was dying to know his thoughts, because what she had said was massive—even though she knew deeply and intimately how horribly wrong love could go, she was still taking the leap and falling in love.

"Or perhaps it's just foolish," she added.

"But how do you recover from something like that?" Brandon persisted.

"I'm not entirely certain that I have completely recovered. I loved and I lost, and that is horrible. I had plans, Brandon, and they changed on me. I know that you understand the horror," Sophie said with a teasing smile. It was necessary to lighten up a little in such a serious conversation. "There is still a part of me that wonders what might have been."

"Yet you still laugh and smile and write and . . ." Brandon added.

"My heart still beats, yes. I can wring some enjoyment from life. Quite a bit, actually," Sophie said, and here she longed to touch him, but knew that one caress could lead to their downfall.

With her luck, that would be the moment they were interrupted by one of the hundreds of party guests milling about, just around the corner.

In the life she had planned with Matthew, there had been no allowance for soulful conversations in the moonlight on the terrace at a London ball with a man like Brandon. And now, in this moment, she wouldn't trade places for anything.

"Impressive," he murmured.

"Have you suffered the same?" Sophie asked him softly.

He leaned against the wall of the house, angled toward her, and much less than an arm's length away. Sophie felt it was not close enough.

"Something similar, yes," he answered quietly. She could hear the snap of the flames burning in the sconce above, and the low hum of chatter from a far part of the terrace.

"A woman?"

"No, my father."

"Your tone suggests that we do not speak of this," Sophie observed.

"We do not."

"Shall we converse upon another subject?" she asked, more brightly.

"Yes. Let's talk about how adorable you are," Brandon said, smiling.

"Oh, Your Grace," Sophie teased, with batting eyelashes for the full effect. It was flirtatious, and it also kept back the tears. How could they have heartfelt conversations and flirt outrageously and not talk about The Big Wedding that was only ten days away.

"What did I say about calling me that?" he said sternly, but mockingly.

"Very well, Brandon. Tell me how adorable I am," Sophie said with an exaggerated sigh, as if it were a massive trial to undergo the reception of compliments from the man of one's dreams. In her situation, it was indeed bittersweet.

"To me, you are so damned adorable. You are so

beautiful, and I never want to stop looking at you. And . . ."

"There is more?" Sophie asked breathlessly.

He belongs with me, she thought, and she could barely tolerate the fact that he did not.

"Here," Brandon said, daring to trace his finger along the curve of her neck to her shoulder. "I have dreamt of kissing you here ever since the night your sleeve slipped down, like this," he murmured, and then he slid the scrap of fabric acting as a sleeve down just a touch. The slide of the silk against her skin, along with the warmth of his hand, was an irresistible sensual combination. She swiftly surrendered and closed her eyes to savor it all the more.

"My brave, and beautiful, damned adorable Writing Girl," Brandon murmured with a small laugh. "I'm not much of a poet."

"It's a perfect compliment. From a perfect gentleman," Sophie said, and she meant it. To be told she's beautiful is every girl's dream, but to be declared brave by a man like him . . .

Brandon knew her, really understood her, and found her adorable.

For the love of anything holy, how could he possibly marry another?

Sophie bit her tongue to silence the words. She would not have this conversation yet, and certainly not in this moment. A kiss—that is what she wanted. Wasn't it?

"I'm not a perfect gentleman right now. My thoughts are decidedly impure," Brandon murmured, and in the moonlight she saw that although there was a note of jesting in his tone, he definitely was Very Serious.

Would he kiss her *now*?

Would this be the moment that desire and an intoxicating connection overwhelmed their better judgment so much that he would lower his mouth to hers? She could see the intensity in his gaze, darkened so much that his bright green eyes appeared to be black. She could see the tension in the line of his jaw. She placed her poem on his chest. Underneath the evening coat, waistcoat, shirt, and hot skin, his heart was beating in a strong and steady rhythm.

Sophie was aware of her back arching slightly, tilting her forward and closer. She was drawn to him by a force that she did not understand and could not control. Every part of her—every nerve, inhalation, heartbeat, exhalation, thought, or sensation all whispered the same thing: *This One.*

He wanted her. But something was holding him back: Clarissa, his honor, and a reluctance or even refusal to surrender, to love.

"Sophie . . ." Brandon murmured her name and she loved the sound of it from his lips.

"Yes?" Her face tilted up to his, not expectantly but hopefully. *Will he kiss me now?*

"I can't." His voice was a harsh whisper.

Then he left.

money—or even a house or two—on the turn of the cards.

He was considering it when that damned Bavarian prince arrived. Brandon watched him, with narrowed eyes, as he graciously accepted the attentions of the other club members. He had also spent the better portion of the evening graciously accepting the attentions of Brandon's fiancée, which he could not complain about without sounding like the worst sort of hypocrite. Still, it rankled. Clarissa might not be the woman he thought she was.

A quarter of an hour after his arrival, von Vennigan intruded with an offer for a game of billiards. Brandon agreed. Hitting something would be just the thing.

Von Vennigan started at Brandon's urging, striking the break.

"The ball was enjoyable," the prince said in an attempt to initiate conversation.

"Yes," Brandon replied as he lined up his shot. He did very much enjoy dancing with Sophie, probably as much as von *Venison* enjoyed waltzing with his fiancée. There was something wrong about that.

"Was it an example of a typical English ball?" the prince asked.

It had been hot, crowded, and loaded with romantic intrigues.

"Yes," Brandon said.

Von Vennigan sunk two balls into the pocket.

"Cigar?"

"No, thank you."

His father had frequently smoked cigars, and stank accordingly. It was the one thing that Brandon had not liked about the man he so idolized.

As he lined up his next shot, Brandon idly wondered how things might be different had his father lived.

Brandon would have had more years free of the responsibilities that came with a seat in Parliament and the management of six estates. He would not know the fear of losing someone close to him, and thus he might have married for love.

Brandon took his shot, and sent the balls careening across the table. Was he really going to entertain thoughts of love, marriage, and what might have been? No good could come of that, only misery. These thoughts turned his mood blacker.

"It seems that you are not very interested in social niceties and pleasantries," von Vennigan mused.

"Yes," Brandon said. He took another shot, and sunk another three billiard balls. He missed a few, too. Instead of focusing on the game, he recalled Sophie gazing up to him adoringly, and the glow of the moonlight on her skin. As a duke, there was very little that he could not have—Sophie Harlow might have been the only thing, and because of a trap of his own making.

"So I shall not, what is the saying? . . . Beat around the bushes. None of that," von Vennigan said.

Brandon paused expectantly. The prince's eyes were far too blue.

"We are rivals," von Vennigan said. Bluntly.

Rivals. There it was again.

"Yes," Brandon said, now tempted to crack a smile. It was good fun to be less than perfectly obliging.

"I wonder, Your Grace, at the attentions you allow me to pay to your fiancée," von Vennigan mused, leaning against the billiards table. Apparently they were taking a break from the game.

"Did you hurt her?" Brandon asked. This prince did not seem interested or capable of hurting a woman. He might bore her to tears by reciting poetry perhaps—the

prince was a known devotee of the Romantic poets—
but was no actual physical danger.

"Never," von Vennigan vowed, looking straight into
Brandon's eyes.

"Did you take advantage of her?" Brandon asked.
He, too, leaned against the billiards table, holding his
cue stick with both hands. It kept his hands occupied
and from something other than pummeling his so-
called rival.

"No," von Vennigan answered.

"I will not tolerate the slightest mistreatment of her,"
Brandon said firmly as he looked von Vennigan in the
eye. It was the truth. She was under his protection. A
man did not take that lightly.

Clarissa seemed to take great pleasure in this prince's
attentions, and the distraction afforded him more time
with Sophie. It would all end soon enough, when he
and Clarissa married. Because they would marry.

He'd invested too much, and there was too much at
stake to back out because he was temporarily infatuated with another woman—or because a longhaired
sapling of a prince fancied himself in love.

Sooner or later he'd return to his senses and recall
that Clarissa was what he wanted, and the most suitable
wife for a man of his position and disposition.

Dukes did not marry scandalous girl reporters, and
Brandon never did anything that was just not done.

"Good," von Vennigan said, nodding approvingly, as
if Brandon needed his approval. "I also wonder, Your
Grace, how you might react differently if I were to pay
the same attentions to Miss Harlow. For example, if I
were to waltz with her, and have long conversations with
her in a dark, secluded alcove . . . no liberties taken, of
course, but it would be dimly lit, intimate . . ."

The cue stick Brandon had been holding cracked under his grip and snapped into two halves.

"I suspected as much," von Vennigan said smartly. "We are rivals, of a sort. You would fight for Clarissa out of duty, but I would fight for her out of passion."

"Are we fighting?" Brandon asked. Clarissa was not a prize to be won, for she had already been claimed.

"Do you wish to?" von Vennigan queried.

"Not particularly," Brandon lied.

"I have heard that you are a master swordsman," von Vennigan said, slightly changing the subject.

"I've heard the same of you," Brandon replied.

"So we shall fight and see if we can discover if duty is a stronger motivation than passion," von Vennigan proposed.

"Or merely who is the superior swordsman," Brandon stated.

He would certainly fight von Vennigan, and would take great pleasure in it. But he was not prepared for a full-scaled battle for a lady's favor. It was much more complicated than that—not that this young pup could be expected to understand that. There were contracts, debts, and reputations at stake—all things far greater than one's *feelings*.

Chapter 24

Nine days before the wedding . . .

Hamilton House

Brandon dreamt of that moment last night when he almost kissed her. He had seen the conflicting desire in her eyes, and it mirrored his own feelings. In this dream of his, however, he kissed her, deeply, hotly, and fervently.

He dreamt that he pressed her up against the wall, and that she liked it. He grabbed fistfuls of her satin skirts, hiking them up so that there was nearly nothing between them. Slowly but surely, he did away with those last remaining scraps of fabric.

She did not protest, but she did blush.

First he tugged down her bodice, and cupped her naked breasts in his bare hands. He dreamt of taking the pink centers in his mouth, and he heard her gasp with shock and moan in pleasure.

In his dreams his bare hands roamed over her, exploring all those curves: her breasts, her hips, her derriere. In his dream, he kissed her passionately, held her close, and was on the verge of owning her when he woke up to crushing disappointment and unsatisfied desire.

A short while later, when his brain resumed functioning, he recalled other parts of his evening—namely, the game of billiards with that strangely longhaired prince of Bavaria. He thought they were rivals. It was a quaint interpretation of the situation.

Brandon was not going to step aside because someone else took a liking to his fiancée, or even just because he had taken a liking to someone else. It wasn't that simple.

He may have vividly erotic dreams about another woman, but that didn't mean he was prepared to change his mind about values that had governed his existence. He wanted a wife he would not be preoccupied with, a wife befitting his station, a woman he could never love.

Passion ought to be tempered with restraint. Brandon's feelings were always held in check by duty. He wondered what this young prince knew of anything other than indulging his desires.

He did not doubt the young puppy's feelings for Clarissa, but Brandon wondered if that romantic, starry nonsense might fade when he learned about the debts, and other obligations, never mind Spencer's startling assertions. Then again, the prince was young, in love, and rich. It might not matter at all.

For better or for worse, Clarissa was under Brandon's protection, and he would not take that responsibility lightly.

Brandon rang for Jennings, his valet, and Spencer, his secretary. Upon their arrival, they got quickly to work. While Brandon shaved himself—an unusual habit for a man of his position, but a preference of his— Jennings readied his clothes and Spencer recited a list of the day's events.

"First, you are due at Parliament," Spencer began.

"Are we voting or just listening to inane and mind-numbing speeches?"

"The latter, Your Grace. The topic will be the Marriage Act."

Brandon set down the razor and took a bracing sip of hot black coffee.

"Following that," his secretary continued, "you have allotted time to review your accounts book and other business."

"Fine."

"Lady Richmond has written, requesting to know your progress regarding the special license. I have looked into the matter. The peer who wishes to marry must make the application to the Archbishop of Canterbury himself, but from there I may make all the other arrangements."

"Remind me to do that later."

"I have also noted your other obligations for the wedding. I have taken the liberty of making a list of potential best men, and have drafted some possible toasts for the wedding breakfast."

"Spencer, you are a godsend."

"Thank you, Your Grace," he said. "This evening, you have planned to escort the Richmond ladies to the theater with His Grace, the Duke of Richmond."

Brandon finished his shaving, took another sip of his coffee, and thought of what an impossibly dull day he had ahead of him.

"Spencer, would you say this is a typical day for me?"

"Yes, Your Grace. Parliament, estate management, social engagements. Every day."

Horror was dawning upon Brandon. His life was

dull. By God, he hoped that *he* wasn't dull. Now he understood why his mother was forever nagging him to "enjoy a spot of fun."

"Thank you, Spencer," Brandon said, and his secretary quit the room. "Jennings."

"Ready, Your Grace. That is quite a day you have ahead of you, Your Grace, if I may be so bold as to say so," the valet said as he assisted with the boots.

"You may be so bold, Jennings."

Brandon knew it was not very ducal of him to encourage such liberties with his servant, but he was often amused by Jennings's outspoken opinions on anything and everything.

"By quite a day," the man went on, "I mean it sounds bloody boring."

"We *are* being so very bold today," Brandon said. But he agreed. He put his waistcoat on. It was gray. Plain gray.

"Don't misunderstand me, Your Grace. I am glad to have a sober, intelligent man like yourself looking after government matters."

"Thank you," Brandon said. His valet continued talking as he helped him into his coat.

"And then the theater with your future in-laws. Don't worry, Your Grace, I won't go on being so very, very, very bold today."

Brandon was well aware of what his valet thought of the Richmonds. His opinion was based upon one pink-and-red-satin waistcoat, and that was reason enough to despise.

"Your point, Jennings?"

"You're a young, wealthy, healthy man. Do something for yourself for once. Oh, blast. I've got to get another length of linen to get this cravat just right. Be right back, Your Grace . . ."

"Don't worry about it. This will do."

"My God, Your Grace, you can't possibly go out with your cravat like that!"

"Thank you, Jennings. Have a good day."

Out in the hall, Spencer was pacing nervously.

"Your Grace! There is one other matter of business I need to discuss with you," Spencer said. "Privately."

Brandon indicated that they should speak quietly as they walked. Spencer related his news about further correspondence from informed persons who had promised to offer proof of the scandalous assertions. All of this was related from secretary to duke in a very hushed tone as they traveled from the master bedroom to the grand foyer. Boots thudding on marble floors covered the sound of their voices.

If there was proof—well, that would change everything.

Madame Auteuil's
Bond Street

Finally, the wedding dress was ready for Clarissa to try on, and she modeled it for them now. The gown was fashioned from white satin in the current style of a high-empire waist, capped sleeves, a modest square neckline, and three lace flounces at the hem. What made it truly stunning was the overlay of the palest silver lace in an intricate pattern of plump roses. A small pink sapphire adorned the center of each ornamental bloom, providing the faintest glow of sparkle and color.

This was a gown for a duchess, the bride of the year, or even a princess.

Sophie took notes on the dress—not that she would forget any detail of it, but just in case. Out of the corner of her eye, *her* dress, as Sophie thought of it, was still there. She put away her paper and set down her pencil in order to trace her fingertips over the beadwork, and the silk, and imagined that she could afford it.

"I agree with you," Lady Hamilton said, surprising Sophie as she came over to stand beside her. "That is a gorgeous gown."

"It's like nothing I've ever seen," Sophie said. She had browsed many shop windows and perused hundreds of ladies' fashion periodicals. The quality of this dress was unparalleled and it was just ornate enough without being overwhelming.

"Have you tried it on?" Lady Hamilton asked.

"Oh, no. I couldn't," Sophie said with a shake of her head. "It would be torture to wear it for just a few moments in the shop, and then to change into my regular day gowns."

"You wouldn't purchase it if it fit you perfectly? I know you have many occasions to wear it," Lady Hamilton said. Sophie bit her tongue to resist pointing out that they were not all duchesses with accordingly sized purses.

"There are other things to consider," Sophie said delicately.

"So you shall admire it from a distance, but never make an effort to own it?" the duchess asked quizzically.

"Yes," Sophie said with a sigh. "Rather tragic, isn't it?"

"Not if we are just talking about a dress," Lady Hamilton said cryptically, before giving Sophie a smile, a pat on the hand, and leaving to attend to the matter of her own dress for the wedding.

Clarissa, finally free from her fitting, took a seat at the small table that had been set with a tea tray. Sophie joined her.

"Is something wrong?" Sophie asked. Clarissa seemed rather downcast for a girl trying on her wedding dress.

"I was having a bittersweet moment. The dress is lovely, of course. And Lord Brandon is so nice . . ."

Nice! *Nice*? The weather was nice. New hair ribbons were nice. Lord Brandon could not possibly be considered in the same breath as such banal, nice, items. He was a man, *the* man, who made her heart pulse with longing, who occupied all her dreams and nearly every waking thought, who aroused in her sensations that could not be discussed in polite society. *Nice* was not the word for him.

". . . And as I stood there in the dress, it made me realize that soon I would be saying goodbye to Frederick and donning that gown, and facing the rest of my life. Without Fredcrick," Clarissa finished.

Sophie bit her tongue, and refrained from asking if Clarissa considered crying off.

She must have done, surely. But it would be lunacy to back out of a match like hers without another one secured. The prince, she presumed, had not proposed.

One might use, say, a dress as a metaphor for the situation. Sophie couldn't just ask Clarissa to give up her dress simply because Sophie liked it and wished to have it—because the dress fit her perfectly, complemented her strengths, and disguised her weaknesses, because it made her happy and exhilarated—and she ached to feel its touch on her skin, and to kiss it . . .

Very well, she was not talking about a dress. Lady Hamilton hadn't been talking about the dress, either. The fact remained that one could not ask for another woman's dress, or fiancé.

"What are you going to do?" Sophie asked.

Please say you'll jilt him. Please say you'll jilt him . . .

"What can I do?" Clarissa asked with a shrug, eyeing her mother who was on the far side of the shop examining different fabrics.

"I couldn't say," Sophie responded, even though she thought of a dozen things. For starters, Clarissa might cry off, or she might simply elope, or she might refuse to marry a man she did not love. She could not voice any of those options. Sophie was acutely aware of her place, and the limited liberties attending it.

"The contracts have been signed, and even if I were daring enough to speak to Lord Brandon, my parents would . . . make things very difficult for me."

"I see," Sophie said. It was as plain as day: Sophie ought to steel her nerves and harden her heart, for in nine days' time, Clarissa was going to marry Lord Brandon, even though she loved another.

How she could do that boggled Sophie's mind. But she remembered a conversation between the Duke and Duchess of Richmond that she had overheard. They needed funds. Brandon had plenty. Their daughter was all they had to trade.

Still . . . there was a glimmer of hope! If Brandon was the one to end things—if the most honorable, trustworthy, notoriously upstanding gentleman would just break off a *very* public engagement . . .

It was an unlikely prospect, Sophie grudgingly admitted.

"And if he were to break things off with me, I'm certain my parents would sue for breach of contract," Clarissa said, continuing to hammer nails into the coffin bearing Sophie's hopes and dreams for a loving marriage with Lord Brandon.

"Scandalous," Sophie managed. A broken engagement, and a subsequent lawsuit would mean that the Wedding of the Year had become the Scandal of the

Decade. Reputations did not recover from incidents of that magnitude.

Sophie could not expect the most obedient girl in the world to suddenly disobey when the stakes were that high, nor would a Perfect Gentleman like Brandon risk the blow to his finances and reputation.

Her situation was hopeless, and she wanted to cry.

"Very scandalous," Clarissa echoed. After ascertaining that her mother had gone into a dressing room and was thus out of earshot, she abruptly changed the subject: "Did you know that Frederick speaks six languages? Isn't that the most amazing thing you've ever heard?"

"Yes," Sophie said, because it was the thing to say to a girl in the first blush of romance.

Clarissa selected some pastries for herself, and when she removed her gloves, Sophie noticed her very ink-stained fingers.

"Letters to Frederick. My mother thinks I am corresponding with my cousin in Bath," Clarissa explained. The she proceeded to speak of all the things she was learning about him that she adored, only concluding when her mother emerged, intent on departure.

As Lady Richmond's gloves were buttoned up by two of Madame Auteuil's girls, she issued instructions: the carriage was to be brought round, and Clarissa was to don her bonnet.

Then the duchess turned to Sophie.

"Oh, and Miss Harlow, we will be meeting to discuss the menu for the wedding breakfast. I will have a copy sent to you for your column. You need not attend."

The shop door slammed shut behind her.

That was not good.

Obviously, she and Brandon had not been discreet enough during their interactions: laughing together

It was a thought-provoking sight to see Clarissa and Sophie standing next to each other.

Clarissa was tall . . . Sophie barely reached his shoulder.

Clarissa had blue eyes . . . Sophie's eyes were velvety brown and always alight with some sort of mischief or humor.

Clarissa was blond . . . Sophie's dark curls were up-swept, revealing the graceful curve of her neck, and that spot at her shoulder that he longed to kiss. A few tendrils hung loose around her face, framing her lovely features.

He ached to kiss Sophie's full, pink mouth.

He refused to acknowledge that he never would, or what that kiss would cost him if he did.

The orchestra began to sound the first notes, and the gentlemen bowed to their partners, who curtseyed in return. Brandon took a small step toward Sophie, while she took one small step to meet him. He raised his palm to press it against hers—hand to hand, like heart to heart. With their hands pressed together, they embarked on a slow spin, reversing positions before reluctantly parting and beginning again.

He could not look away from her.

Clarissa may be a renowned beauty, but Sophie possessed the luscious looks of a true temptress. She, and only she, aroused him and tormented him.

After little more than a moment of this, Brandon discovered a new kind of torture. He could only anticipate a fleeting touch of hands; he wished to hold her close.

Hand to hand was insufficient. He wanted the length of her pressed against him.

He could only watch as she spun around him, always moving, and moving away.

Chapter 23

White's Gentlemen's Club
Later that evening

Brandon suspected that his slumber would consist of tossing, turning, lusting, wishing, and cursing it all. In short, a mockery of sleep. Instead of returning home, he went to his club. A drink was in order.

He had been dangerously close to throwing away his pride, his honor, and the value of his word for a kiss. It would have been one hell of a kiss, and probably even worth it. But old habits died hard, and to act recklessly rather than hold back was unfathomable to him.

There was a time and a place for rules to be—if not broken—at least bent. Though he could not go so far as to indulge his desires of a hot, deep kiss with Sophie, he could go for a drink at White's, even though he almost never went out after a ball.

With rule-bending in mind, His Grace, the Duke of Hamilton and Brandon also deigned to loosen his cravat—something he never did in public. He took a sip of his brandy and considered joining the game of whist being played in the far corner. If he were so inclined, he could wager an outrageous sum of during the meeting about flowers, flirting openly at the musicale, shamelessly making eyes at each other as they danced, and then nearly kissing in an alcove at a ball.

This was not good at all.

In fact, it was very troubling and Sophie anxiously mulled it over as she began the walk home.

White's Gentlemen's Club

Brandon's intentions were to proceed directly from Parliament to the archbishop, but he took a detour by way of White's. He found a seat in the front room, near the famous bow window. And then, instead of coffee, he had brandy. Rather than silence, he accepted Roxbury's company.

Thus, he drank in the afternoon, kept company with persons of dubious morals, and lusted after unsuitable women—all to prove to himself that he could be a bit rakish, a bit dangerous, and not at all dull.

"How fares the grand plans for the wedding of the year?" Roxbury asked.

"I am happy to say that I know not," Brandon said, taking a sip.

"The lengths a man will go to for a woman! I thought duels might be the worst of it, but to endure a discussion on flowers . . ." said Roxbury with a grin.

"That is behind us now, thank God."

"And what of your infatuation with the Writing Girl? Actually, I see that you are drinking brandy in the afternoon, so I know *exactly* how things stand."

"I'm eager to hear it."

"Your attraction to her is becoming so strong that you are beginning to crack under the strain of suppressing it," Roxbury stated.

"For someone who has never indulged in a deeper emotion or thought in your life, that was remarkably perceptive and astute," Brandon conceded.

"Because I live my life to avoid the pressures of restraint, I've learned to identify the symptoms in others to ensure I never suffer the same," Roxbury declared.

"Congratulations," Brandon said. "And how is your dilemma? Any closer to resolution?"

"No. I have thus far managed to avoid a definitive answer whenever Lady Belmont or Lady Derby asks me about escorting them to your wedding. But either way I'm doomed. I suppose I shall have to break it off with both of them, but just before the ceremony . . ."

"Oh, the troubles you have."

"Identical to yours. Deciding between two females," Roxbury mused. "It could be worse."

"My decision has already been made," Brandon declared. "The contracts have been signed."

With that fact already burning in his gut, he downed the rest of his drink. "And now, I have account books to manage."

"Duty calls. At the very least, you are drunk for it. You'll be as debauched as the rest of us in no time at all," Roxbury called after him as he walked out of the club and headed toward Hamilton House.

Chapter 25

Had it only been three weeks ago that Sophie was walking this same route with Brandon? Already so much had changed. The weather was significantly warmer, for one thing. Then there were her feelings for Brandon, growing hotter and more intense by the day.

They were also more obvious about their affection for each other—dangerously so. Lady Richmond clearly noticed. Naturally, she did not approve and definitely was not going to sit idly by and hope that things proceeded accordingly to plan.

Sophie suffered a tremor of fear. If she lost this story, she could lose her column.

If she lost her column, she would lose her livelihood.

She could sum up her declining fortunes thusly: from jilted girl, to Writing Girl, to servant girl.

Her stomach ached at the prospect. When she came upon an apothecary, Sophie paused. Wright's Tonic for the Cure of Unsuitable Affections was on display in the window and she wondered if solving all her problems was as simple as taking a sip of the strange blue potion.

"Miss Harlow!"

She looked around to see who might have called her name. Then she saw Brandon, standing taller than everyone else and striding purposely in her direction. Her heart gave a little lurch of excitement, mingled with panic.

What if Lady Richmond saw them? She could still be in the vicinity.

No, she'd be gone by now. At any rate, Sophie could not ignore him, and could not pass by what might be one of her last chances to be with him.

"Hello. Fancy meeting you here. Again," she said, holding her gloved hand up to her eyes to block the sun. She could see only his face with the bright sun shining behind him, as if he were an angel with a halo. It was only slightly misleading.

Then she noticed something was amiss with him.

"Is everything all right?"

"Everything is fine, why do you ask?" he asked, looking perplexed.

"Your cravat is *not* stunningly perfect," she pointed out. In fact it was barely tied, and hung limply around his neck. Still, he managed to appear ducal. He grinned and his green eyes were bright in the sunlight.

"Call the Bow Street runners," Brandon deadpanned. "I lacked the time, energy, and motivation to be perfect this morning,"

"How I wish I had been there to witness that. A first."

"Jennings was horrified. I hope he's sufficiently recovered," Brandon said, and then he added: "Enough of this standing about. I shall walk you home."

"Oh, really?" she asked pertly.

"Really," Brandon said firmly.

"It led to a bit of trouble last time you did," she

reminded him, thinking that "a bit of trouble" was a tremendously inadequate phrasing.

"What's a little more?" he asked, lifting one brow.

If only you knew, Sophie thought.

"Account books again?" Sophie guessed. She started walking and Brandon fell in step beside her. As they walked toward Bloomsbury, Sophie relaxed in the safety the swarms of pedestrian traffic offered.

"Yes, after a long day in Parliament," he answered, and she was pleased to know him so well, though that made their looming separation harder to fathom.

"What great matters of state were debated today?" she asked. She didn't want to discuss their situation now, not on a pleasant walk on a lovely summer day.

"The Marriage Act," he said with a grimace.

"There is no escaping it, is there? Weddings and marriages everywhere," Sophie said. And to herself, she sang a little tune: *Weddings, weddings everywhere and not a groom for me*.

"Bloody hell," Brandon swore, and stopped short. A pedestrian grumbled and he dodged him. She turned around to look back at him, perplexed.

"Oh? And now you are swearing before a lady!" Sophie chided him. "I am shocked. Why were you swearing just now anyway?"

"I intended to apply to the archbishop about the special license today," answered Brandon.

Her heart flip-flopped. He meant to go, which meant that he still intended to marry Clarissa. And yet, he was not at the archbishop's office but walking with her.

How in the world was a girl to make sense of his intentions? She opened her mouth to demand that he declare his intentions but then he spoke:

"Instead, I had a drink at the club," he confessed.

"How debauched of you," Sophie teased. A serious conversation loomed and she wasn't ready for the resulting heartache.

"It's a whole new me," Brandon stated.

"I like the new you. I liked the old you, too," Sophie said as they paused at an intersection to allow carriages to pass.

Brandon lightly grasped her arm to hold her back and keep her safe. She was reminded of their first encounter, and wondered if she could count on him to save her a second time, should she lose her column because of what was happening between them.

When the road was clear, Brandon gave his arm to an elderly woman and assisted her across the street. Clearly, he had not been completely corrupted. He was still a Good Man.

"What brought you to this part of town?" Brandon asked after the elderly woman thanked him profusely before entering a shop.

"Wedding dress fittings," she said plainly, watching him closely for his reaction, as if that might reveal anything about his intentions.

"Fascinating," Brandon said dryly. She understood that he did not wish to talk about it. She didn't, either—if only she could stop thinking about it, too!

"Not particularly," Sophie remarked. "Although, I do like looking at all the gorgeous gowns at Madame Auteuil's, and do wish Knightly would allow me to write about fashions instead of weddings."

"Have you asked him?"

"Not yet. My columns have proven to be too popular to discontinue, but my patience with other people's weddings is coming to an end." And it was his that was pushing her over the edge, and might just be the end of her—the column *and* her writing career.

Sophie bit her lip nervously. She didn't love attending weddings, but she did love everything else about her position at the paper. She loved the sense of purpose and satisfaction that came from her job. She loved the Writing Girls and she respected Mr. Knightly. She loved being a part of something bigger than herself. She even enjoyed the writing—except for when she had to write about certain weddings.

"And what of a wedding of your own, Sophie?" Brandon asked, turning to look at her. Sophie smiled faintly and resisted the urge to say, "I don't know, you tell me."

"My catastrophic failure of a wedding? Or a future one?"

"How bad was it?" he asked with a faint grimace.

"My former fiancé's face was unrecognizable, thanks to my brother's fist. My mother was more upset about the torn Harlow veil, which my intended used to stop his fall by grabbing a handful of the lace. Mrs. Beaverbrooke's hat was ruined because the cat jumped onto her head when Matthew stepped on her paw as he stumbled, then fell. A baby was crying, too, I think. All for a widow named Lavinia that Matthew met at the pub."

"I'm so sorry," Brandon said. But he sounded oddish. Sophie peered at him curiously. His mouth was pressed into a firm line and he was staring straight ahead.

"Are you laughing?" she asked, aghast.

"I'm trying not to," he choked out.

"Guests were standing on the pews to gain a better view of the brawl," Sophie said deliberately to taunt him.

Brandon burst out laughing. He paused, bent over with his hands on his knees, and laughed even harder. Again, pedestrians speeding on their way grumbled and cursed at his sudden stop and his blocking of their path.

"I fail to see the humor in this. I would so love an explanation when you have recovered yourself," Sophie declared.

"It's just that . . ."

"Take your time. Really there is no rush at all," she said as people jostled around her.

"Very well. Sophie, what you have described to me is so utterly horrific."

"I know. I was there."

"It's so horrific, horrible, and the stuff of farce and tragedy. It's so bloody awful, and you survived it, and now the only thing to do is laugh at it. Laugh, because you have emerged strong, brave, beautiful, lovely, wonderful, and spectacular from an experience that would have destroyed a lesser person."

For a stunned moment, she just stood there, further blocking pedestrian traffic while she enjoyed a revelation.

"I have, haven't I?" Sophie said with awe. Truly, that interpretation of the situation had never occurred to her. All this time she had pitied herself for what had happened, how she had suffered, and what she now had to endure as a wedding columnist.

In truth, she was blessed not only for narrowly dodging a man who would not have been faithful to her, but also because she had an amazing life now. She had been brave to start anew in London rather than hide in Chesham, brave to take on a scandalous profession, and, she thought with a deep glance at Brandon—brave to love again.

But could she rebuild her life again, if she lost him, and her position at the paper? Where did a girl go after making history and stealing the heart of a duke?

"Look at you—a beautiful woman taking London by storm," he continued. "You write for the most popular newspaper in town. A girl from a small town is now a society darling. You're making history. Seducing dukes . . ."

"Yes, the Duke of Radley did succumb to my charms," she retorted.

The Duke of Radley was rumored to prefer his own sex.

Brandon laughed. She always made him laugh. It was her favorite sound in the world. And besides, it was necessary to make a joke because if he kept going on about how wonderful she was, Sophie feared she might start bawling, and perhaps even propose to him herself.

How could he say such things and still intend to marry Clarissa?

Honestly, it confounded the mind and tormented the heart.

"So are we going see more debauched, rakish, and scandalous behavior from you?" Sophie asked, changing the subject. Now was not the time to ask him whom he intended to marry. *There probably isn't any point in asking,* she thought, *in light of the conversation with Clarissa.*

"I did do one other thing today that was not in keeping with the typical behavior of a perfect duke, such as myself," Brandon confessed.

"And modest," she added.

"Yes, I am the most modest, perfect duke in England," he said. "Except that I didn't quite pay attention in Parliament today."

Sophie burst out laughing. Of all the debauched and nefarious activities one could do—seduce virgins; wager and lose fortunes; commit robbery, murder, or arson; excessive drunkenness—his sinful behavior was a lack of attentiveness.

"What distracted you?" she asked. Her heart began to pound.

"I was thinking about you," Brandon confided.

Her pleasure at this news was tempered by the fact that it might be her downfall.

"Thank goodness they were only discussing the Marriage Act and not something truly important, like labor laws or feeding the poor," Sophie remarked lightly.

"That would be taking this too far," he conceded. And then he grinned and she couldn't help but smile in return.

The moment was bittersweet. She wanted nothing more than to laugh and chatter with him, and yet she knew a Serious Discussion was in order. But the words that would ask him to declare his intentions stuck in her throat so she could only smile, laugh, and try to forget that the wedding was little more than a week away.

Brandon saw her home safely to Bloomsbury Place. Sophie began to wonder if it would be up to *her* to stop the wedding—for it was clear that neither Brandon nor Clarissa would—or if she would allow this love to slip away.

Chapter 26

Eight days before the wedding . . .

<u>*Things Brandon would prefer to do rather than*</u>
<u>*attend the theater with the Richmonds:*</u>
1. Be with Sophie.
2. Balance his account books on a perfect summer day.
3. Be with Sophie.
4. Swim across the Channel in December.
5. Be with Sophie.

And yet, despite his wishes, he found himself in the carriage with the Richmonds en route to Drury Lane for a play—which one, he neither knew nor cared not.

Clarissa's father dominated the conversation in the carriage. The Duke of Richmond was horse-mad, however his passion was not for the exciting sport of racing but the more scientific aspect of breeding. That very few people cared to discuss, at length, the mating habits of horseflesh did not concern him.

"My favorite mare, Magnolia, has been demonstrating all the signals that she is ready to mate,"

Richmond said. "Do you know what those signals are, son?"

The duke called him *son,* which rankled. First, because he wasn't Richmond's progeny; and secondly, because he feared that this aged duke viewed him as the son he never had.

It was that lack of an heir that was part of the problem. Clarissa was the last of the Richmond line. By special arrangements with the king, the title would be allowed to pass through her to her firstborn son, who would be the Duke of Hamilton and Brandon *and* Richmond. A triple duke.

It had seemed like a powerful maneuver at the time. Now Brandon wondered if one title might be sufficient.

"Really, Reginald, this is not the time," his wife said.

"Nonsense! Of course Brandon is interested in breeding. All young men are!" Here the duke chuckled heartily. "Now, do you know the signals?"

"I confess that I do not."

"Magnolia has been raising her tail to reveal her lady parts, if you understand me," Richmond said with a grin, and another chuckle.

"Oh, for Lord's sake," Lady Richmond sighed with exasperation. Though he couldn't be sure in the dim light, Brandon suspected that Clarissa was blushing furiously.

"My stallion, Samson, has been showing interest in her by nipping, nudging, that sort of thing. Now, I had planned to breed her with Lord Carrington's stallion, but considering Samson's interest, I might just have to revise my plans! After all, his stamina with her coloring would make for a splendid mount. On the other hand . . ." The Duke of Richmond went on.

Brandon now understood why the Duchess of Richmond spent so much of her time at public functions without her husband. For the first time, his feelings toward her were not of horror or annoyance, but understanding verging on sympathy. Her husband all but ignored her, leaving her with nothing to attend to but her social calendar and daughter.

The duke's monologue, at least, allowed them a respite from idle chatter. Clarissa still had that glow, making him wonder if she had planned an assignation with her dear, dear von Venerable tonight at the theater. Lady Richmond stared out the window of the carriage—out of *his* carriage, actually. Unable to afford repairs, theirs was not in any condition to be taken out unless life or limb depended upon it, and then one ought to say their prayers.

But they had a splendid team of matching carriage horses.

If it wasn't horses, the Duke of Richmond wasn't interested. Carriage maintenance, ancestral estates, and personal relationships were not given his notice.

"Ah, we have arrived," the Duchess said with unconcealed relief, and fifteen minutes later they were seated in Brandon's box at the theater and scanning all the other attendees.

"There is Lady Endicott with Lady Carrington—they told me they were going to be here. I must go say hello at intermission. And Lord and Lady Brookmore, too. Oh that Prince of Bavaria is here, too, with the Marquis and Marchioness of Winchester. They must be back from their honeymoon already!"

"Miss Harlow is here, too," Clarissa mentioned. Brandon snapped to attention and began searching for her.

"Indeed," Lady Richmond remarked with notable disdain. Brandon eyed her curiously.

Clarissa, seemingly oblivious, said, "I should like to visit her at intermission."

"She's beneath us, Clarissa," Lady Richmond said, and that was that apparently.

It was interesting that the duchess's favor should have diminished so markedly. It was, after all, her idea to involve Sophie. Brandon suspected he knew precisely why her sentiments had changed.

He did not hide his interest in someone else as well as he ought. Neither, he noted, did his fiancée. Clarissa was currently beaming in the direction of von Vennigan.

One could snub a reporter, but not a prince.

In spite of this recent realization, Brandon continued his search for Sophie.

He saw that she was not alone.

In fact, she was with a dandy wearing an embarrassing fuchsia waistcoat and numerous rings that sparkled when he gestured as he spoke. His hair was messy, but Brandon supposed it was deliberately shaggy and tousled, and wondered if he hadn't better things to do with his time.

But such thoughts paled when he saw that Sophie was laughing at something the sissy fop had said.

Brandon was halfway out of his seat before he realized it.

"Are you going somewhere? The play is just about to start!" Lady Richmond said, lowering her binoculars.

"I'm just getting comfortable," he said, settling into his seat. He had been on the verge of storming over there and brawling with that sorry excuse for a man, to rescue Sophie from him, as if she needed it.

As if he had claim to do so.

As if he wasn't sitting next to his betrothed, with her family. As if that wasn't the behavior of a lunatic, or a man in the throes of passion.

He was neither. He was a Duke and a Civilized Gentleman.

Sophie placed her hand on the man's arm—a gesture of affection. She wore elbow-length white satin gloves. Brandon yearned to strip them off, one by one. That midnight blue dress she wore would look so much better on the floor.

She said something that made her companion laugh.

Brandon nearly growled and his hands balled into fists. He was on the verge of conducting himself like an irrationally, besotted, uncontrolled fool. Ridiculous.

"Oh, and I see Lord and Lady Bickford, too!" Lady Richmond cried out, delighted.

"Indeed? I've been meaning to talk to him about breeding one of my Highland ponies with his," Richmond said.

This was intolerable. This—the name-dropping, the horse breeding, the fiancée infatuated with one of the few men in the world that outranked him—this could not possibly be his reality. But it was, and his future, too.

However, he was not a man who pined, or lamented, or bemoaned unfortunate situations. Something had to be done.

Sophie peered over the edge of the box at the rabble in the pit below. She counted three scuffles, one bout of fisticuffs, and four women of seemingly negotiable affection plying their trade. English audiences were notorious at the theater for having no manners to speak of. Well, the aristocrats in their boxes were well mannered, perhaps, but not those down below.

Alistair Grey, theater reviewer for *The Weekly*, and her host for the evening, focused his attentions on the higher classes. Julianna, who had also joined them this evening, was trolling for gossip in the lobby.

They were there for a performance of *The Rivals,* by Sheridan, featuring their friends Jocelyn Kemble and Julian Gage.

"By the way, darling, your duke is here," Alistair remarked.

"Where?" she asked excitedly, and quickly scanned the crowds looking for him. She hadn't known he would be here tonight. He hadn't mentioned it when they walked together yesterday. In fact, there was much he hadn't told her, such as whom he might marry.

"Front and center. Where else do dukes sit at the theater?" he replied.

"Oh, I see him!" She couldn't help but smile as she suddenly felt warmer from his heated gaze. Just knowing he was here made the evening more magical.

"And he sees you," Alistair said, for the duke was clearly gazing intently in her direction. "I expect you shall make eyes at each other all evening. You won't attend to a second of the play."

"I'll read the review," Sophie responded without looking away from Brandon. Even from a distance, across a crowded room, he had a mesmerizing effect on her.

"Are you suggesting that my columns are so amazing that they can replace the actual experience of seeing the play?" Alistair asked.

"Yes, precisely," she agreed. The mention of his column made her think of her own, and how it might not exist for much longer. She was staring at the potential demise of Miss Harlow's High Life. She did not want to think of it right now.

"You are ridiculously and outrageously infatuated," he declared.

"He's so handsome," Sophie said with a sigh. Alistair trained his binoculars upon the duke and after a second replied with a brief, "Yes."

The duke of Hamilton and Brandon was, by all accounts, undeniably handsome.

"I get butterflies around him," Sophie confessed, turning and touching her palm to Alistair's arm for emphasis.

"The hallmark of true love," Alistair remarked dryly. She laughed, but it didn't last long.

"He's with the Richmonds," Sophie said forlornly.

"I see that."

"He's always going to sit with the Richmonds at the theater. Never with me." She hated to acknowledge that. It was difficult not to, given that it was right before her eyes, for the whole world to see.

"Men take their mistresses to the theater all the time," Alistair remarked flippantly.

"Alistair—I'm not! I wouldn't! I won't!" That jolted Sophie away from her mooning over Brandon, and she gave Alistair her full attention.

"I'm sorry, Sophie. I was not minding what I said. I didn't mean it. I know you, and that you would never enter into such a situation. And as for Lord Brandon—"

"He would never, which is one of the things that I adore about him," Sophie said firmly. It was. He was the reliable, honest man she had sought.

"He is a notoriously upstanding gentleman," Alistair agreed.

Perhaps even too upstanding, she thought.

"Did you know that we had the perfect moment for a kiss and he wouldn't do it? He wanted to. I wanted him to. But he is an honorable man, so nothing occurred."

"Of course. Honestly, Sophie, I don't think that. But I just saw Wainthrope with his mistress—look they're over there, on the left, and so it was on my mind and . . ." Alistair looked truly pained to have offended her.

"I know. It's just that as the wedding looms, I become more and more nervous. What we have is electric, Alistair. I feel so much for him! I think that he can't possibly marry Clarissa, yet I don't see any other outcome. Can you?"

"Oh, all sorts of things could happen, darling," Alistair said with a reassuring pat on her hand.

"Such as?" Sophie asked, tucking a stray curl behind her ear.

"Lady Clarissa could be abducted, or run off with a footman. It could be discovered that she had a secret baby. He would be obligated to cry off at that point. You might discover that he is a terrible kisser, which would significantly dampen your affections for him. There could be another great fire causing the destruction of half of London and her population. Anything could happen, Sophie."

"You are ridiculous. If she'll run off with anyone it will be von Vennigan, not a footman," Sophie retorted.

"I have consoled you. Excellent. Now shush and let me attend to the drama on stage."

Julianna, wearing a stunning bronze silk, returned just then, slipping into her seat on the other side of Alistair at the last possible moment. The curtains parted and the play began. Sophie did not attend to a second of it. How could she when there was a drama unfolding right before her eyes, and of which she was a principal player? The man of her dreams was just over there, and he was looking at her with longing, pent-up passion, and self-restraint on the verge of breaking.

She responded in kind, and marveled how he could be so close—just there, on the other side of the theater, that was all—and yet so very far away from her.

The box she sat in was owned by her employer—one who might fire her. Brandon owned his. She attended with her fellow newspaper reporters. Brandon sat with a duke, a duchess, and his fiancée. Sometimes, when she thought of what separated them—his obligations, his fiancée, his honor, and social status—it all seemed hopeless.

Instead of walking home with Brandon yesterday, she really ought to have gone into the apothecary, purchased Wright's potion, and consumed it all at once.

But she didn't, and so she thought the magical connection and sweet understanding between them was palpable. She confided in him, he in her, and she felt that she knew him and he knew her like no one else. The mere touch of their hands sustained her as she dreamed of kisses and giving herself to him completely.

Whatever was between them was too good, too rare, too sublime to relinquish. Yet it seemed like there was no alternative, for though he flirted with her, he still spoke of his intentions to marry Clarissa.

She watched as he stood and exited his box. Her heart began to beat faster in anticipation. Would he come to her?

Chapter 27

"Sophie." Brandon murmured her name from the dark recesses of the box. The sound of his voice sent her heart racing and she savored a small measure of triumph. He had come for her, and he was calling for her.

"Ah, young love," Alistair remarked. Julianna scowled.

She reminded herself to distance herself from him—for the sake of her column, and for her own good. It was easier said than done. At the moment, her career and her survival was the last thing on her mind. Brandon was here, for her.

Sophie slid into the shadows to meet him without a second thought. It was so dark, but slowly her eyes adjusted enough so that she might discern his outline. It was utter madness to be here with him. Lady Richmond could note their absences and then she might . . .

"Sophie," he whispered her name again, and all thoughts vanished save for *This One*.

Brandon was so tall, so strong, and, in this confined space, overwhelming with his masculinity. Her imagination took over, offering all sorts of wicked activities they might engage in. It was dark, so he could not see her blush, and she was glad.

She wanted this—the intimacy, the touch, the triumph of him coming to her. But it was dangerous, and she acknowledged that. Her heart was long gone, but they had been so good so far, and to be alone with him in the dark tempted all sorts of wickedness.

"Sophie," he murmured again, sliding his arm around her waist. She raised her palms defensively against his chest, and felt the steady pounding of his heart. Her own heart was beating at a feverish pace.

"What do you want?" she whispered to him, because it would not do to be overheard.

"Who is that man you are with?" he asked in a low, commanding voice.

In the dark, she smiled, as the truth dawned on her.

"Jealous?" she asked coyly.

"Yes," he admitted with a rush of breath across her neck that was unbelievably erotic.

Though she hadn't any intention of using Alistair thusly, she could not deny the delight she felt to know that Brandon was feeling something akin to what she regularly suffered every time she saw him with Clarissa: a soul-consuming, heartbreaking envy.

He needn't be jealous, but she did not tell him that. Alistair was V.S.I.C.P.Q.: *Very Safe in Carriages, Probably Queer.* But that was none of Brandon's business and, frankly, not something she wished to discuss presently.

She decided not to allay his fears—let him be jealous!

"What are you doing here? You belong elsewhere," she said softly. Brandon's warm hand splayed across her lower back, and pressed her against him, as if to say no, he belonged here, with her. If the way her nerves vibrated with pleasure at his touch was any indication, her body thought so, too.

"You belong to someone else," she whispered fiercely, to remind him as much as herself.

"I cannot stay away," he confessed, and she melted against him a little more. She would give herself to him in a heartbeat—if he would do the same, in an honorable way.

"You have to," she managed. "Unless . . ."

She felt him stiffen against her.

Lady Richmond undoubtedly had her binoculars trained on Sophie's empty seat. It would not escape her notice that Brandon was gone, too.

It was one thing to lose her heart and quite another to lose her means of support. She did not want to be a seamstress or servant, governess or mistress—even to Brandon. She had entertained the thought, and dismissed it. When all was said and done, though she loathed weddings, she loved being a Writing Girl.

She also loved this man, and had from the start.

Brandon's hand caressed her lower back, and slid lower and pressed her closer. She could feel his arousal pressing against her skirts between her legs. Her lips parted, but no sound came forth.

She felt his touch in a hot, wonderful way she had never before experienced. This was desire.

Fighting her instincts, she took a step back. He followed. Her back was up against the wall, and he was trapping her against it.

It was not at all unpleasant.

"Unless . . ." she offered, grasping his shirt in her fists and aching to raise her lips to his. His hands grasped her hips and with an exquisite lack of speed, slowly skimmed up to her waist, and higher still, spurring a trail of deliciously wicked sensations.

"There is nothing I can do, Sophie." The pain of his words clashed with the pleasure of his hands upon her.

"I don't think that's true," she challenged. He was a man, a double duke. Surely there was something he could do—if he wanted her enough. Unless he did not, but if so, what was he doing here, holding her and having this conversation with her?

Such thoughts, and his touch made her dizzy.

He wanted her. She was sure of it. But what of it, if he would marry Clarissa anyway? Her breath caught in her throat.

He pressed one light delicate kiss upon her temple.

There was nothing *she* could do, and she despised it.

"The contracts have been signed."

His words ignited a war within her. She loved his honor. If he cast Clarissa aside quickly, on a whim, she would always live in fear that he might do the same to her. His struggle was a good thing.

She understood. But she didn't like it.

"Then what are you doing here?" she cried, struggling to escape from his embrace. Brandon would not let her go, and she wouldn't have expected this possessiveness from him. She was reminded that he was not always only a gentleman, but a powerful and hot-blooded man.

"I don't know," he said. She could hear, and she could feel his frustration.

He moved against her, and she bit back a sob, or a sigh. His lips brushed over the shockingly sensitive skin of her neck, pausing just around the earlobe and moving lower still. Brandon pressed a hot kiss against the place where her shoulder curved into her neck. And then she did sigh and arch against him.

He might have groaned. It was an exquisite agony for them both.

He moved so that his lips brushed fleeting across hers. Just as the kiss was to become real, and deep, and truly magnificent, the audience outside broke into sudden thunderous applause.

Chapter 28

Sophie was right: he was not powerless.

What he could not confess was that, for the first time in his life, he was unsure of how to employ that power. It was not merely a matter of his desire. Even if it were, he could not say what he would do.

He desired Sophie in such a base, primal way—with an urgency that shocked him.

Yet he also wished to lead a quiet life. One in which he was not tormented by passion, or love. One where he would not be possessed by jealousy, and driven across a crowded theater for a heated, yet hushed, whispered discussion combined with a decidedly erotic encounter.

He vowed to consider his options, and made a note to request the marriage contract so he could review it, just in case there was a clause that he might invoke so as to dissolve the engagement without disastrous repercussions.

When Brandon returned to his seat, von Vennigan had taken it, and Clarissa was laughing. It might have been the first time he'd seen her do so. Her parents, he was told, were visiting the box of some dear, dear friends.

"Frederick was just saying the funniest thing," she said, giggling slightly. So it was Frederick now, was it?

"In my country . . ." Frederick started. But Clarissa began to laugh again. It was obviously a private amusement between the two of them, and one he had no interest in sharing.

When, he wondered, had they become so intimate?

"Oh, never mind. It is clear that he is in no mood for humor, Clarissa," von Vennigan said. And then he remembered his manners and acknowledged him, "Your Grace."

"Your Highness," Brandon responded in kind. Privately, he thought the prince was ridiculous, though he was the only one in London to hold that opinion. It was probably due to his long hair, but also the lack of gravity in the man's demeanor as he hopped from one party to another.

"When are we going to fence?" von Vennigan asked. Reluctantly, Brandon was interested in this offer. He remembered, vaguely, that Harry Angelo had declared him one of the best fencers in Europe. Brandon looked forward to thoroughly trouncing him.

"At your earliest convenience," Brandon said, "provided I have room in my schedule."

"I am due to spend the afternoon at Court tomorrow, but I think I shall excuse myself," the prince declared, and Brandon thought that this was why he could not respect the man, and certainly could not entrust Clarissa and—he hated to recall this—all the obligations that attended her.

Responsibility cast aside when more pleasant activities were offered. This attitude made Brandon wonder how the prince's feelings might change should he learn that Clarissa's hand in marriage came with monstrous debts, or if he learned of some other details of her past that Spencer had told him.

"You'll both be careful, won't you?" Clarissa said, worried. She anxiously twisted her betrothal ring around on her finger.

Brandon eyed the token, remembering that his father had given that emerald and diamond ring to his mother upon their own engagement. She had loved it, but not nearly as much as she had loved his father. Once upon a time, it had symbolized a love match.

Brandon ignored the tightening in his throat and returned his attention to the conversation at hand.

"Of course, Clarissa, I would never slay your fiancé and claim you for myself," von Vennigan said with a sly smile. Clarissa offered a little laugh and Brandon maintained his stony expression.

"That would be an unsporting way to win her."

"Positively archaic. Medieval. And we are enlightened men," von Vennigan stated grandly. Brandon did not return his smile.

"I will enjoy our fencing session. Tomorrow," Brandon said pointedly.

"In my country," von Vennigan said, sending Clarissa into giggles again, "we can take a hint. Good evening, Your Grace. Clarissa, till next time."

"Clarissa, a conversation is in order," Lord Brandon began.

Clarissa's heart began to beat faster at his words, and not in a pleasant way. She could think of nothing for them to discuss, other than her shameful behavior with Frederick and his shameful behavior with Sophie. Both were conversations she'd rather not have.

"What is on your mind, Lord Brandon?" she asked politely, thinking it prudent not to presume anything.

"You," he said, and she immediately thought, *That's a first,* and she felt ashamed. He was a good man, and it would be an honor to be his wife. But he did not love her, and she did not love him.

"You and I, our marriage," he finished. "You did not choose me, did you?" he asked bluntly, and she was taken aback.

"I didn't *not* choose you," Clarissa answered.

"You'll have to explain. And please, Clarissa, speak honestly to me," Lord Brandon urged, and it was a good thing he had, for it reassured her. Slightly. Her fiancé had always intimidated her, with his size, and how he seemed so remote. And so ducal.

Her father was a duke, but he bumbled about in the muck with horses most of the time and there was nothing fearsome about that (other than for one's shoes and hem).

Frederick seemed to her to be more like Prince Charming than intimidating, highly ranked royalty.

Brandon was different. And now he was sitting next to her, initiating a serious and heartfelt discussion. She found it strange.

"My mother," Clarissa explained, "strongly championed you and I had—*have*—no aversion to you. You are a very good man."

He managed a slight smile. She feared she might have offended him, but he had asked for the truth and thus he had been given it. She was nothing if not dutiful.

"Thank you," he said. "But why me? There are other rich peers. Wealthy princes, even."

"I suspect it all has to do with my aunt Eleanor," Clarissa said with a sigh.

"Your aunt Eleanor?"

"It's unlikely you've heard of her. Are you prepared for a long tale of love, loss, and unimaginable woe?" she asked with a halfhearted smile.

"We are at the theater. Of course," he responded, and they managed smiles at each other.

Clarissa took a deep breath, and gathered her courage to tell a story she had only told once before, to Frederick, in one of their many letters. It was a lot to confess to a man she found difficult to talk to. An abbreviated version would do, Clarissa decided, because he had to know the essential details so he could understand her, and her mother, the way things are and had to be.

"Aunt Eleanor was my mother's younger sister and she fell madly and passionately in love with a dashing rogue. When she found herself with child, he vanished. Thus she was shunned from society and utterly penniless before she and the child expired during the birthing."

"Oh my God," Brandon said under his breath.

"Yes. It's a horrible, wretched story. I suspect it might even be exaggerated. But this is the story of love and marriage—or lack of—that has defined my mother's life, and mine."

"Not very inspiring," he remarked dryly.

"Not at all. She had already married my father when this happened, but it certainly solidified her disdain of the rakish in favor of more upstanding gentlemen. She is obsessed with the social whirl because her sister was cut out from it. She is overprotective of me because her sister lost her child . . . You see how this all goes on."

"Yes," Brandon said softly. "It does explain everything."

"She sees you as the savior of our family. Because you are wealthy, composed, and can be counted on, and are unlikely to cause any sort of scandal. As a duke, you will always be welcomed in society. And you are a man who will always stand by your wife."

It all made sense to her. It was why she must marry Brandon and why to marry anyone else, particularly a dashing, rakish foreign prince, would kill her mother.

While everything she'd said was the absolute truth as she understood it, she did glide over the part about Lord Brandon's wealth, and how necessary it was for her family. Clarissa was so thankful for this hot weather, since they wouldn't have been able to afford wood for fires otherwise. The money they now had left was spent on keeping up appearances.

"I don't know what to say, Clarissa, other than you have given me much to think about."

"I recognize that this puts a lot of responsibility upon your shoulders," Clarissa said.

"I know nothing else," he said.

"No one doubts that. Please don't mention to anyone that I've told you this. My mother doesn't like to hear about it," Clarissa said.

"Understandably. We shall change the subject, as I suspect she will return any minute," he offered, and she thought that he was very considerate and perhaps not as intimidating.

"One last thing, though, Lord Brandon. I know she's"—and here Clarissa faltered, not sure exactly how to describe her—"I know she's a challenge, but she's my mother. I'll do anything to see that she's happy."

"Even if it's something you don't wish to do?" Brandon asked.

In other words, why would she deny her love for Frederick to marry a man she had no deep affection for?

Of course, he had noticed the devotion between her and Frederick; he was not blind and they were not discreet. She had merely assumed that he had been so involved with his own affair that he hadn't noticed hers or cared. But it was clear that he was watching out for her after all. This was comforting, yet also made her feel slightly ashamed. He knew that she had no particularly strong desire to marry him.

"If it makes her happier than it makes me miserable. Does that make sense?" Clarissa hoped it did, because she couldn't bear to explain how she would marry him even if her heart wasn't in it.

For the money. For her mother's approval. Because those things mattered more than her own happiness.

Because being disobedient was such a strange notion that she couldn't imagine herself capable of it.

"It does," he answered. Brandon placed his hand on hers in a comforting manner, and too late did Clarissa remember the ink stains on her fingers that he really shouldn't see.

She had taken her gloves off to show Frederick, and likewise, he had removed his. Her prince had then delicately traced his fingertips along her palm, making her skin tingle with pleasure.

Oh, she shouldn't have allowed that liberty, and she certainly should not think about it while holding the hand of her fiancé! Discreetly, she tried to pull her hand away.

Lord Brandon saw the ink stains.

"What have you been writing?" He seemed benignly curious. His lack of suspicion made her feel all the more guilty.

"Oh, nothing," she said, quickly pulling on her gloves. If her mother saw, she would have a fit, and likely remove her dwindling supplies of ink, pen, and paper.

"Clearly you have been writing something," he pointed out kindly.

"Merely correspondence. Nothing of interest," Clarissa lied with a blush.

It was so interesting and fascinating to exchange soul-bearing letters with Frederick! To learn so much about another person, and to share the deepest parts of one's own self was to forge a bond, the likes of which she had never experienced. The letters were splendid, and wonderful, but still she ached to be near Frederick.

This, of course, she kept to herself for she had shared enough. In fact, this was certainly their lengthiest and deepest conversation to date. Part of that was due to Frederick encouraging her to speak her mind, and Aunt Eleanor had been on her mind of late.

Secretly, in the dead of the night, Clarissa dared to consider a scandalous elopement with her own dashing rogue, à la Eleanor.

She would never do it, of course. That was utter madness.

And so, she had to explain to Lord Brandon why she would still marry him when their hearts belonged to other people.

Because it would make her mother happier than it would make her miserable.

Because passionate love, the sort flaring up between her and Frederick and Brandon and Sophie, never lasted. It would fade, or it would spectacularly implode and they'd all be devastated and ruined in the end.

But she and Brandon could, in time, develop a strong affection for each other.

And then there was the matter of her outrageously expensive dress that had taken half a dozen seamstresses forty hours to sew, the two hundred handwritten invitations, hundreds of hothouse flowers and beeswax candles, a massive vanilla cake with lemon-flavored icing, a special license from the Archbishop of

Canterbury, and a reoccurring story in the newspaper about all of it.

Furthermore, the contracts were signed, and the creditors were looming, and the fates of many were resting on her delicate shoulders. All she needed to do was proceed according to plan.

The lights dimmed and Clarissa was thankful to have the second act to distract her from her own drama. And yet, she kept stealing glances at Frederick and wondered *if only* . . .

Chapter 29

Six days before the wedding . . .

24 Bloomsbury Place

Things had been so heated, so charged, and so un-settled there at the theater, and Sophie had not heard from him since.

As promised, Lady Richmond sent over a copy of the wedding breakfast menu. Sophie was not sad to miss an afternoon in her company, but she did lament the loss of the opportunity to see Brandon. It was better she did not.

Though the wedding menu detailed dozens of unde-niably delicious dishes, they were not at all appetizing to her. Still, she included it with her other notes, such as: *Fancy dress. Silver lace. Lady Sophie Brandon.* And, *How could he!*

She had not yet figured out how to compile it into a column that would not result in her dismissal. The threat loomed like a storm cloud over her life.

Sophie had no appetite, so she merely sipped tea whilst her fellow Writing Girls enjoyed freshly baked ginger biscuits and chattered on about the latest install-ment of the ongoing Darcy Darlington mystery story, the new fabrics that had arrived at Madame Journelle's, and who Lord Roxbury was supposedly bedding this week.

"Speaking of scandalous Lords—" Julianna started with a sly grin.

"You and Lord Brandon made the dailies again!" Annabelle said gleefully. Sophie's heart sank. Lady Richmond would see it. Clarissa would see it, too. Sophie shifted in her chair, feeling awfully guilty. When she was with Brandon, it felt so very right. When she imagined how Clarissa might feel, she despised herself.

But then again, Clarissa was admittedly in love with another.

"It was noted that you both disappeared during the first act of *The Rivals* the other night," Eliza informed her.

"Curses," Sophie swore.

"It's scandalous and shameless. Am I the only one that remembers the man is betrothed?" Julianna remarked with a strident tone of voice.

They all mumbled that they did indeed recall that pertinent detail.

"His fiancée is madly in love with another man and would not think twice about enjoying a romantic interlude with him," Sophie replied defensively. "Provided her mother allowed it."

"So that excuses everything, does it?" Julianna retorted.

"It certainly means the situation isn't so black and white, right and wrong," Sophie countered. It felt like a dozen shades of gray. Clarissa loved Frederick, but did not seem to consider escaping her match with Brandon, who was definitely infatuated with her. And then there was the matter of von Vennigan, to complicate, or solve, everything, she knew not. Gray, gray, gray . . .

Yet the contracts were signed, and that thought elicited a sigh.

"I just do not understand how you can persist in doing this when you know what has happened to me. This is just like Somerset," Julianna challenged. Out of the corner of her eye, Sophie noted Annabelle and Eliza's heads swiveling back and forth.

"It is not the same. It has nothing to do with you, and everything to do with the fact that it's something bigger than me, bigger than him," Sophie replied. Somerset had been indiscriminate in his affections. Brandon and she had something unique.

"You can't help who you love," Annabelle sighed. "If you could, I would love someone who paid attention to me." She was referring to Mr. Knightly, the unceasing object of her desire, who only had eyes for society ladies and women of dubious morals. In other words, absolutely not Annabelle.

Julianna appeared to consider this for a second, and then rejected it. "It's exactly the same. There is the woman who is legally entitled to her husband's affections—me, Clarissa. And then there are all those other women who steal it—all of Somerset's paramours, Lavinia, *you*."

Lavinia. Sophie had not thought of her in a while. She did not care to.

"Can you really legislate affection like that?" Eliza mused. "Particularly when people do not marry for love, as is the case with Lord Brandon and Lady Richmond?"

"And would you really want kisses that were contractually obligated?" Annabelle said, picking up the more philosophical and less personal thread of the conversation in hopes of distracting Julianna and Sophie.

"I wouldn't," Eliza said, and Annabelle agreed.

"Why can you not be supportive of me, and my feelings, in this?" Sophie asked. For the first time in her life, she felt as if there were things she couldn't tell her best friend.

"I don't want to see you get hurt," Julianna answered.

Sophie shoved a biscuit into her mouth so that she would not be able to say the thing that had just popped into her head: Did her friend not want to see her get hurt, or did her friend not want her to be happy? It was a horrible accusation (thus, the mouthful of food preventing her from saying it).

Julianna's protests were valid, and Sophie understood their origin—infidelity had wreaked havoc on her friend's life—her father first, and then her own late husband. Sophie wished for some compassion, though, rather than being told that it was hopeless and that she was no better than Lavinia.

Fortunately, she had Clarissa's friendship, for she, oddly enough, understood how Sophie felt. Still, she missed the compassion and empathy of her longest and best friend. When had they become so distant?

"Do you know what this is the perfect occasion for?" Eliza asked. "A test of Wright's Tonic for the Cure of Unsuitable Affections."

"Oh, yes!" Annabelle agreed, clapping her palms together with a glee that Sophie could not match. She may have considered taking it, but she had rejected it.

"I'm sure it's nothing more than sugar water, or laudanum," Julianna added.

"And I'm not sure I want to give up my unsuitable affections," Sophie said to Julianna's darkened expression.

"It probably won't work," Eliza replied. "So you could try it and . . ."

"Are you trying to experiment on me for an article?" Sophie asked suspiciously.

"Perhaps," Eliza admitted, and eyebrows arched skeptically all around the table. "Oh, very well, yes."

After some cajoling, Sophie was persuaded to take a sip of the strangely blue liquid that promised to cool the blood, soothe the heart, and otherwise end one's unsuitable affections.

Chapter 30

Hamilton House

When he arrived in his study the next day, Brandon saw the document he'd requested on his desk. It was the marriage contract, detailing the merging and transfer of wealth that would occur with the union of himself, "Lord Henry William Cameron Hamilton, Tenth Duke of Hamilton and Brandon" (and here follows a list of the fifteen other lesser peerages he held) with "Lady Clarissa Elizabeth Gordon, the sole of issue of Lord Reginald Jonathan Francis Gordon, the Sixteenth Duke of Richmond" (this, too, was followed by a list of his numerous other holdings).

If it were not for his heated encounter with Sophie at the theater last night—and, in fact, every encounter with her—he would not be reexamining his marriage contract.

He would be blissfully betrothed to the perfect wife and duchess instead of infatuated with a magical temptress.

Oh, and temptress she was! He'd had a taste and, by God, he wanted more. Having finally taken the liberty of pressing his mouth to that place where the curve of her shoulder met her neck—a spot he had long craved to taste—he was dismayed to discover that it had the odd effect of increasing his desire when it was supposed to be satisfied. It was like crumbs when one wanted a loaf of bread.

He was thinking in such mundane metaphors. But, as he had said, he was out of sorts. Brandon did not dare to even reconsider the more emotional aspects— the jealousy, the longing, the searing pain of seeing her with another man and understanding how she must feel to see him with Clarissa, or how it must feel *to write romantic stories about him and Clarissa for all of London to read.*

Brandon swore under his breath and, for the first time in his life, strongly considered drinking before noon.

Brandon knew he must review the contract and consider *all* of his options.

And yet, after his surprisingly revealing conversation with Clarissa last night, he wasn't sure it would matter if he did find a loophole as wide as the Pacific. He would not break her heart if things did not go as planned, but she had been clear—she had no intention of breaking their engagement.

All because of the long-dead Aunt Eleanor.

Brandon now understood the Richmonds in a way he had not before. While it did not make them more enjoyable company, he did feel some sympathy—and plenty of responsibility.

That the tragic tale of dear departed Aunt Eleanor was exerting its influence upon his present situation struck him, in his more heartless moments, as a bit ridiculous. How could love go so wrong, so horrifically, and still have such potentially devastating consequences decades later? And upon people she had never met?

In a way, it was not unlike the loss of his father—twelve years and ten months ago. He was still reeling from it. But that was an agonizing soul search for another day.

With low expectations, but desperately hoping, Brandon picked up the contract. An hour later, he set it down.

There was one possibility. If Clarissa were undeniably, absolutely and shamelessly compromised, he could withdraw with no financial consequences.

But there were other points to consider:

Reasons why he could not jilt Clarissa:

1. The damage to her reputation. She would likely never marry.
2. The damage to his reputation. Even double dukes had to be wary.
3. Lord and Lady Richmond were up to their necks in debt—as was all their tenants and the tradesmen that depended upon them. There would be no hope for any of them without Brandon's infusion of funds into the Richmond estates.
4. Von Vennigan might marry her. But would he do so if he knew of the debts? Was his love the abiding, eternal kind, or a fleeting infatuation? He was so young, so flippant, and Brandon did not trust him with a matter of this magnitude. He would not even trust him with a book from the circulating library.
5. And then there was the matter of Charlotte, his fainting-prone sister. The condition may or may not have been medical, or it could be symptomatic of a mischievous temper.

Neither bode well for her chances after making her debut next year. She did not deserve to come out under a cloud of suspicion and scandal.

6. There was also the matter of that Awful Secret that may or may not be true.

There was a knock at the door and Spencer entered.

"Your Grace, if I might remind you that you are scheduled for an appointment at Angelo's with His Highness, the Prince of Bavaria, shortly."

"Yes, thank you."

"And if I might also have a word with you," Spencer asked.

Brandon looked at the clock. Half past three. Good God, he would be late. He was *never* late.

"Some other time, Spencer."

"But Your Grace! It is of the utmost importance—" Spencer cried out.

At the moment, Brandon did not care to know. He quit his study, and Hamilton House.

Drinking in the afternoon, barely knotted cravats, searching for ways to break contracts, postponing business in favor of fencing, and being late. He really was well on his way to becoming a complete reprobate.

"You do not seem like the type to be late," von Vennigan said when Brandon rushed into Angelo's.

"I make it a habit to keep royalty waiting."

"It does keep us in line," von Vennigan said with a smirk.

Harry Angelo was utterly beside himself to have not only a prince and a duke in his school but two of the very best swordsmen in Europe. He hovered. He offered to assist. He sent servants running for beverages and food in case the two worked up an appetite. Angelo sent inferior students home; he did not wish to be embarrassed by them.

"I believe we both have the requisite skill to dispense with masks," von Vennigan said, and Brandon agreed.

As they suited up, and prepared for their match, they discussed the weather. With swords drawn, the genuine conversation began.

"I am curious to know, Your Grace, what made you late," von Vennigan began, advancing and bringing his point to bear on Brandon's chest.

"Very important business to attend to," Brandon replied with more than a touch of ducal haughtiness in his voice. He suspected his opponent did not have very important business, other than being a foppish princeling and flirting with other men's fiancées. Cutting his hair certainly wasn't on his list.

He enveloped von Vennigan's blade with a circular parry, removing the imminent threat to his waistcoat. Just because he had dozens did not mean he had to ruin one. He took care of, and protected, his possessions.

"You must tell me more," von Vennigan urged.

"I was reviewing contracts."

"Ah. Of what business? Not that it is any of my business," von Vennigan said with a grin. Brandon resisted the urge to say, *It isn't—* because, in a way, it was.

"If you must know, I was reviewing my marriage contract," Brandon said casually.

His Highness stumbled. Brandon restrained a grin and beat the prince's blade away, forcing him further down the floor.

"I also like to review contracts before I sign them," von Vennigan replied.

"I've already signed," Brandon said, and he noticed his opponent pause for a second as he processed the information, leaving his guard a little more open than usual. It was the faintest of opportunities.

"And Clarissa?" he queried.

"She has also signed in exquisite, ladylike penmanship," Brandon took pleasure in telling his opponent.

Von Vennigan leaned too heavily on his back foot and Brandon saw his chance: a beat to the blade, a parry evaded as von Vennigan struggled to move backward, and Brandon's point hit true.

Touché!

Von Vennigan swore under his breath at being caught in such a manner but composed himself.

"And your conclusion upon reviewing the marriage contract?" von Vennigan asked casually, though Brandon knew it was put on.

"Ironclad."

It was difficult to say whose shoulders sagged more at his words. Both men paused to catch their breath.

"A philosophical question for you, Your Grace," von Vennigan started as he engaged Brandon's blade again. "Action or honor?"

"Honor. Always." Brandon did not need to think twice about that. For the very beginning, his father taught him that honor was everything. A man that couldn't be trusted was less than useless. To hold another person's trust was the most precious gift and one bore a sacred duty to protect it.

Honor. Always.

He parried the prince's steel and pressed his attack.

"Why does that not surprise me?" von Vennigan asked, stepping back under the onslaught.

"My honor is legendary. I have a reputation as a 'Perfect Gentleman,'" Brandon recited.

One that, in his own eyes, was slipping away with

every glance in Sophie's direction, every traitorous erotic dream of her, every time he spoke to her, and every time he wished to kiss her.

In other words, he was becoming less of a Perfect Gentleman with every passing second.

"Your reputation precedes you," von Vennigan said. "Rather confining, isn't it?"

"Honor? Yes," Brandon agreed. Occasionally it felt like a straightjacket or a ball and chain. One still bore it with dignity, however.

"I meant one's reputation, whatever it may be. I, for example, am known to be charming, flirtatious, and utterly rakish. Being a prince, I am forever expected to rescue fair maidens," von Vennigan said, pressing forward with his sword, circling the duke's in search of any advantage.

Brandon would have rolled his eyes had it not been dangerous to do so.

"If you are tired of being charming and flirtatious, I hadn't noticed."

"Are you not going to ask me about rescuing fair maidens?"

"No," Brandon said. He did not care to discuss fair maidens, princes, or any of that romantic nonsense. "It's your turn to answer. Action or honor?"

"Action. I think it is more honorable," von Vennigan answered.

"That you must explain," Brandon said, for he was intrigued.

"Often, it is more difficult to act than to remain passive. Action requires thought. One must determine the best course, then one must overcome inertia and find the strength to put thought to action," von Vennigan said casually.

With a speed that gave lie to the laziness in his voice,

he lunged forward, catching Brandon with a ringing blow to his hand guard that the duke was barely able to turn in time.

"It is simply more complex," von Vennigan said succinctly, knowing that if his point had not found its mark, his words had.

"Indeed."

"I think the weak and ignorant are passive. Honor is often passive," von Vennigan continued.

"And when it's not?"

"It's action."

"I suspect that your argument is flawed and illogical," Brandon said.

"The point remains, however, that my honor compels me to act. Yours compels you to be still. I probably should have asked which was more noble, action or restraint, and our conversation might have been much the same," von Vennigan answered.

The parrying continued with the sound of steel clashing against steel echoing around the Spartan room.

Brandon did not like von Vennigan's insinuations that he was a coward. Had they not already been fighting, Brandon might have challenged him just to prove a point.

"Nothing to say to that?" von Vennigan reiterated.

"If my honor didn't compel me to inaction, as you are suggesting, I'd tell you to go to hell."

Von Vennigan's laughter was short lived. Brandon renewed his attack with a vigor that clearly surprised his opponent.

Brandon was covered in sweat from the exertions, deeply irritated by this Bavarian's conversation and presence in his life, angry at the confining contract he had drawn up and signed, and fueled by masses of pent-up lust for a woman he might never touch.

Even here, now, she was in his thoughts.

Brandon lunged clumsily and von Vennigan forced his blade to the floor with such force that it splintered, leaving Brandon with a shorter but far more deadly blade in his grasp. He slammed his foot onto the flat of the prince's weapon, forcing him to the floor.

Brandon stood above him with the razor-sharp shard of steel pointed at the young prince's chest. His life was there for the taking, should Brandon care for it.

"It is my honor that restrains me from finishing you off."

Chapter 31

The Duke's Study
Hamilton House

His honor, his honor, his damned, damned honor. It all came back to that, did it not? Brandon had found no satisfaction from his match with von Vennigan. He paced his study like an exotic animal in a cage, full of unleashed fury and frustration.

Sophie—he wanted Sophie. He craved her, against all of his best intentions and better judgment. He couldn't and shouldn't see her because of his honor, his honor, his damned honor.

Damn his honor.

He needed to see her. There was a new opera debuting at Vauxhall tomorrow night, providing the perfect occasion for him to see her discreetly. In the end, he sent her a note that read:

> *Meet me at the grove in Vauxhall tomorrow night, eight o'clock.*
>
> *—Brandon*

Clarissa's Bedroom
Richmond House, London

She clasped the latest note from him to her heart for merely a second before she just had to read it again:

My darling Clarissa,
   I must see you. Meet me by the supper boxes in Vauxhall tomorrow night, 8:00.
                              Passionately yours,
                                    Frederick

Chapter 32

Five days before the wedding . . .

Vauxhall Gardens

Sophie had answered Brandon's note with a re-sounding *yes*. She dared to hope he would confess his love, or ask her to run away with him. She tried on every dress she owned before settling on a forest green gown. She counted the hours, and the minutes, and even the seconds until they were to meet.

She also wondered how long it would take for Wright's Tonic for the Cure of Unsuitable Affections to work; thus far, it seemed to be completely ineffective for she could think of nothing but Brandon, her love for him, and her desperate wish that he might love her enough to leave Clarissa.

If he loved her, he might make the sacrifices necessary to be with her.

Time was slowly laboring on until she was to meet him at the grove at eight o'clock. But from there, it would be easy to slip away unnoticed from the massive crowds attending the debut of a new opera. They would leave the public areas in favor of the more private garden walkways.

* * *

Arm and arm, Lord Brandon and Sophie strolled through the dimly lit, dangerous, and seductive paths of Vauxhall. They spoke of love, but it was not exactly romantic.

"I have reviewed the contract," Brandon began, and she did not need to ask which one. Her heartbeat and her breath were suspended, awaiting his next words.

"And?" she queried. It was all she could manage to say. She peered up at him, but Brandon faced straight ahead, not meeting her glance—and she knew, just knew . . .

Her stomach twisted into a knot. *Damn useless potion.*

"It's complicated, Sophie," Brandon said.

"I see," she said, waiting and hoping for him to say, *"However, there is a way . . ."*

Instead, Brandon rambled on about how so much depended on the value of his word, and his reputation as a man of honor. He pointed out that many people depended upon his sound, sober judgment.

"No wild bouts of passion for you, then?" She had to tease him; the alternative was to weep and her eyes were already hot with tears. He would not be with her!

"No," he answered, sounding surprisingly forlorn.

"No staying up late, drinking copious amounts of brandy, and writing fevered poetry?" she went on. *Must not cry,* she cautioned herself.

"You know how I feel about poetry," he said dryly. She laughed, a little, because she did know that and Clarissa probably didn't, and for some idiotic reason he wasn't going to marry the woman who *knew* him, who belonged with him.

They continued to walk, passing by other couples

or small groups, and Sophie carried on with her list of Things He Would Never Do: "No waltzing through a public square, or brawling in the streets, or shouting your love from the rooftops?"

"It would be utterly unseemly," Brandon stated.

"But wonderful all the same," she replied, sighing. "Except, perhaps, for the brawling."

"And except for being in love. From what I have witnessed, I have no desire to succumb to such a state," Brandon said. "You know that."

Oh, she did. He was explicitly clear about what he had wanted in a wife, and that he had no inclination for love. She was the fool for persisting in following her heart, for it had led her here: in love with a man who wouldn't love her, yet they strolled down a secluded, moonlit path in the pleasure gardens of Vauxhall.

If only the tonic might take effect!

"You do not want to love because it leads one to shout from rooftops or waltz through town and write poetry?" Sophie reiterated.

"I'm mortified to even be discussing it." The gravel crunched under their feet and they could hear voices from the other side of the hedge reminding them that they were not alone.

"But not everyone in love does those things. That cannot be your only reason," Sophie persisted. It was rude to pry, but she felt an explanation, at least, was owed to her.

"I fear this conversation might verge into deeply personal territory," Brandon said evasively.

"I do hope so. For I would like to know, Brandon, why you will not be with me when we have this something between us . . . something like love."

He was silent for a moment, and she waited while

they walked on, down the gravel path bordered by tall hedges. They could be discovered together at any minute. Her heart beat hard in her chest.

"My parents' marriage was a love match. After my father died, my mother was never quite the same."

"It's like you lost both parents," she said softly, reading between the lines and understanding the pain within. Her heart ached for him. "I trust you haven't been the same, either."

"No."

"How old were you?"

"Eighteen."

"That's a terrible time to have lost him," Sophie mused.

"I should think any time would have been terrible," he responded.

"Yes, but that is the age when you are finally about to experience freedom! You were just old enough to throw yourself into idiotic, youthful pursuits of drinking, women, and such. And you could not. You went directly from childhood to all the responsibilities of adulthood."

"It's not important," Brandon said, but she knew it was.

"And now you are about to be married . . ." she continued, for it was all coming together for her now. He did not want to love her, in case he lost her. He clung to his honor and responsibility as a defense. He did not know anything other than duty to his estates. She tempted him to throw away his closely held beliefs. She tempted him . . .

. . . Oh, how she tempted him! Every second brought Brandon closer to throwing it all away for a kiss or even a caress.

"If I cry off, I'll be no better than that demented bounder that left you," Brandon said, explaining to Sophie yet another reason why he couldn't leave Clarissa. "I don't understand how he could have done that to you."

"You don't understand how he could leave his bride at the altar, or leave *me* at the altar?" she asked, turning to look at him.

God, she is so pretty. He so easily remembered his first glimpse of her— plum mouth, bright eyes, and those dark curls and milky skin—and how his heart raced and he could hardly breathe, all for wanting to kiss her.

Nothing had changed.

He hated that he had to hurt such a pretty thing.

"First, there is the matter of honor," he said, answering her question.

"Are you suggesting that he should have married me because of the plans we had made, even though he did not wish to?" Sophie asked. She sounded aghast, and he did not understand why. It made perfect sense to him.

"He gave you his word," Brandon said plainly. A group of drunken young bucks swaggered by, hollering and stumbling, and he tightened his grasp upon her.

"While I was utterly and absolutely devastated that he broke his promise to me, I am glad to have suffered the short-term heartache over the long-term agony," Sophie explained.

"Really?" Now it was his turn to be taken aback. He understood that honor did not come in only black or white, but shades of gray, too.

A dangerous thought occurred to him: *Could it be honorable to break his engagement to Clarissa?*

A woman's laugh, sounding vaguely familiar, from somewhere in the gardens, intruded on his thought before he could wrestle down that shocking thought and make sense of it.

"Do you wish to spend your life with someone who does not love you?" she asked, and he knew she was driving at something about him, Clarissa, and von Vennigan, but he stubbornly refused to acknowledge it.

"I told you my thoughts about love," he replied.

"But what about someone loving you?" she persisted.

He had never given much thought to that, actually; he only took care that he should never fall in love with someone else. Did he wish to spend his life with someone who did not love him? Maybe even someone who resented or despised him?

He did not care to ponder that at the moment, so he turned his attention away from this new, shocking thought and back to Sophie.

"I would not wish to be the wife of a man who does not love me," she stated.

"I don't see how he could have left *you*," Brandon said.

And then Sophie fell silent for a few moments. He glanced at her, and saw her deep in thought, with a slight frown and a furrowed brow.

"I am a different person than I was then."

"Were you less beautiful, intelligent, kind, and funny?" he asked.

"I was a young woman from a good family in a small village. I had a very narrow view of the world and my place in it. I may have possessed all of those qualities, but they were certainly sharpened and refined by London," she answered.

And then he understood her: like him, there was Sophie *Before* and Sophie *After*.

He was so very sorry for the heartache she had suffered, but that intense pressure had turned her into a diamond. The process may not have been easy, but the end result was exquisite.

He wanted to possess her, but would he? He wanted to belong to her, but could he?

On a different dimly lit path
in the gardens of Vauxhall

Frederick Maximilian Wilhelm von Vennigan, Prince of Bavaria, had fallen in love. He and the object of his desire walked arm and arm through the paths of Vauxhall in a companionable silence. Simply to be near Clarissa was a pleasure, because he was deeply and truly in love.

He had first noticed the symptoms at the wedding of his friend Winchester. He was shockingly unable to turn his head in any other direction from that which enabled him to look at *her*.

When he first set eyes upon Clarissa, he noticed her beauty—but he was more intrigued and entranced by the air of sadness that hung around her. From the curve of her shoulders, and how she ducked her head, he could see that she wished to be overlooked. He could do no such thing.

Frederick pulled Clarissa closer as they strolled along the path, and she smiled up at him. He did not know how he could let her go . . .

Letters followed. Dozens upon dozens of pages, full of her lovely ladylike script confiding in him. He sent just as many letters in which he revealed his true self to her: not Frederick the prince, but Frederick the man.

She was beautiful, but that had nothing to do with it.

It did add nicely to the fairy-tale-like quality of their situation, though: He, the dashing prince on a white charger (he ought to acquire a white charger). She, the gloriously beautiful damsel in distress, held captive by a wicked (step) mother and a grim fiancé with his blasted ironclad contracts.

Frederick's heart thudded in his chest whenever he caught a glimpse of her. He was reminded of a shooting star making a rare, sudden, and all too brief appearance. He held her now, but could he hold her forever?

Frederick's breath caught, his stomach knotted, and his heart thudded faster. He could not fathom how he could manage to sail away without her small hand enclosed in his. Leaving her did not seem in the realm of humanly possible, yet he saw no alternative.

Well, other than abduction, but that really wasn't done anymore. But who knows? Perhaps he might bring it back in fashion.

Lord Hamilton and Brandon had made himself clear: he would not relinquish Clarissa, even though he was obviously deeply in love with another woman. It defied logic, good sense, human decency, and grossly offended Frederick's romantic sensibilities.

A good man protected what he loved. Brandon was a good man. But he obviously did not love Clarissa. It did not add up, no matter how often Frederick thought it through. *There must be a reason,* he concluded. What it was, or how he would discover it, or what he would do when he knew . . . these things were irrelevant at the moment.

"This is all so romantic," Clarissa said with a pleasant sigh. It was—the moonlight, a beautiful garden, her prince.

"Romance is what princes do," he said.

"What else do princes do?"

"We fight battles, rule over the court, and lead the country. We waltz with the belle of the ball, rescue fair maidens, and provide fantasy material for legions of women."

Clarissa laughed. Frederick loved the sound.

"We travel to foreign lands and find treasure untold. And we write volumes of love letters to fair maidens we fancy."

Clarissa smiled at that, but there was sadness in her eyes. "Will you write to me once you've gone?" she asked, and her words hit him like a punch to his gut. She did not mean to go with him.

But then again, he had not asked her to.

Frederick paused, and stepped off the path, pulling her with him into a secluded alcove formed by the tall hedges. It was a space purposely designed for intimate moments between lovers.

"Perhaps," he answered, taking her hand in his and drawing circles on her palm with his thumb.

"Perhaps? You might not?" she asked, aghast. He pulled her close against him.

"I might not need to write to you if you come with me," Frederick said, lowering his gaze to hers. Clarissa's big, blue-sky eyes were dark now, and wide with surprise.

"I . . . but . . . I . . . you do know that . . . I couldn't poss—"

"I will write you love letters if you come with me," Frederick whispered to her. He was leaning in very close now, scandalously so, but he could not stop and could not withdraw from this heavenly nearness. "Little notes by your place at the breakfast table. I shall have footmen send you messages throughout the day, just to tell you that I am thinking of you as I rule over the court, the government, the battlefield . . ."

"And rescue fair maidens," she added.

Frederick cupped her cheeks in his palms.

"You are the one fair maiden for this prince, Clarissa." He spoke softly, whispering the words into her ear. From there, it was so easy, natural, destined that he should grace her lips with his.

They shared lots and lots of little kisses with their lips caressing each other's. Gently, slowly, he urged her to part her lips. He hadn't known it could be like *this:* so sweet, yet setting him afire; slow and gentle, yet full with indescribable passion.

It was clear to him that this was her first kiss, and he felt a surge of pride, and gratitude that it should be with him. No matter what else happened, he had claimed her first.

He prayed that he would be the only one, and the last one.

Chapter 33

Sophie saw him right away, and she stopped suddenly, halting Brandon as well. She offered a little prayer of thanks that he was with her for *this* unfathomable and unexpected encounter.

For even after all this time, there was no mistaking the man she'd almost married. If she had any doubts and needed confirmation, there was the way the ground seemed to tilt, her palms felt clammy, and breathing was well-nigh impossible.

It was Matthew Fletcher, after all this time.

I'm so sorry, Sophie. I'm so sorry, Sophie, but I cannot marry you after all.

That moment was perfectly frozen in her memory. His words, his voice, and the way he played with the buttons on his waistcoat—and how he seemed sorry but she couldn't accept it.

"Sophie?" Brandon asked her, but she only barely registered it. She had been frozen in place upon seeing Matthew. With another woman.

Matthew saw her just then. Sophie watched the play of emotions upon his face: disbelief, confusion, shock.

"My God. Sophie!" Matthew exclaimed. He stepped toward her and clasped her around the upper arms, looking at her, and, it seemed, debating if he should embrace her. He looked past her, at Brandon, presumably, and then promptly let go of her and took a step back, with a nod to the gentleman behind her.

"This is unexpected," Matthew said. He seemed glad to see her, but a touch nervous as well, and she could understand that. She felt paralyzed by a rush of emotions: shock, of course, a wish to flee, a wish to harm him, a burning desire to ask *why*, and a dozen other questions, and the urge to give him the cut direct.

And then there was the matter of the woman beside him—she could only presume it was Lavinia. They eyed each other appraisingly.

"But a pleasure nonetheless," Matthew added. He smiled.

The nerve! Their last interaction had been when he jilted her at their wedding and now he smiled at her!

"Lord Hamilton and Brandon," the duke said smoothly, introducing himself, because Sophie had apparently lost the ability to speak. "And you are?"

"Matthew Fletcher. Sophie and I . . ." His demeanor changed when he registered that Sophie was in the presence of a gentleman, a lord, perhaps even one to whom she had not informed of her past.

"Matthew is the man that jilted me," she said, recovering her voice. Matthew flinched at that introduction, and she took a small amount of pleasure at that.

"Ah, I see." Brandon lifted his arms, only to cross them across his chest and stare down at her former fiancé. Matthew took another step back, probably recalling her brother's repeated blows on *That Day*. With Brandon standing intimidatingly behind her, Sophie felt her confidence increase.

Maybe, just maybe, this needn't be an encounter that would make her feel completely wretched.

"Are you going to introduce us?" Sophie asked. The woman beside him was pretty, with petite features and light brown hair. Sophie had her suspicions, and they were promptly confirmed.

"Sophie, this is Lavinia. My wife."

Wife. So it wasn't that he didn't wish to marry, but that he did not wish to marry her.

She felt Brandon's palm on the small of her back. She lifted her head high.

Sophie managed a tight smile. What on earth was she supposed to say to that? What exactly was the etiquette for this situation? To say "it's a pleasure to make your acquaintance" would ring false. She had to say something, though, rather than stand there like an addlebrained ninny.

"Congratulations," she managed.

"Thank you," Mr. and Mrs. Fletcher responded in unison.

An awkward silence reigned. Matthew cleared his throat. Lavinia smoothed her skirts. Brandon stroked her lower back. Sophie had a dozen questions to ask, all of them rude, and thus she bit her tongue.

"Well, it was nice to encounter you like this. Quite surprising and nice," Matthew said, and Lavinia smiled, nodding. They were about to walk away and Sophie would likely never see them again, nor get the chance to ask even one of those dozen inappropriate questions.

"Before you go," she blurted out, "I have a shockingly forward question for both of you, and I sincerely wish for an honest answer."

"Sophie . . ." Matthew said, visibly uncomfortable. "Now might not be the best occasion for this."

"Matthew, you jilted me on our wedding day, subjecting me to extreme mortification, and a life-altering inconvenience. I'm sure you have a moment to answer a question of mine."

"Of course," Matthew acquiesced. Lavinia nodded. Sophie resisted the urge to say, *"I thought so."* Out of the corner of her eye, she saw Brandon subdue a grin.

"Did you regret leaving me, Matthew? Lavinia, have you felt any regret for stealing him?"

They were silent at first. It was a long silence, more awkward than the first.

Matthew toyed with the buttons on his waistcoat. Still, he had not broken his nervous habit. Lavinia noticed, and took his hand in hers. Sophie wondered why she had never thought to do that for him.

"I know it's so very unpleasant of me to ask, but I shall be vexed with myself for the rest of my life if I do not take this opportunity."

"I understand perfectly," Lavinia said. "I had no prior knowledge of Matthew's actions. He came to me afterward and explained what he had done. My heart did ache for you and I absolutely took him to task for the manner in which he, ah, conducted the conversation. I am so very sorry that we hurt you. It was not our finest hour."

To reiterate her point, she turned and smacked him on the shoulder. Matthew flinched, but did not complain. Sophie smiled wryly.

"And yet," Lavinia continued, her tone gentle. "I felt, and still feel, that he is the man for me. I could not let him go."

Sophie nodded. She understood. "Matthew?"

"Sometimes, Sophie, I wonder how things might have been if I had gone through with the ceremony," Matthew began. "We'd be married, obviously. We'd probably have a baby by now. We'd still be in Chesham—I would have never traveled and you would have never gone to London."

"You don't regret it at all," Sophie said plainly.

"I hate how I hurt you, and I'm sorry for that. Deeply, deeply sorry. But I don't think I would have been happy with the life we had planned and I am very happy now. In short, I regret the hurt I have caused you but I do not regret my choice." Matthew punctuated this by clasping Lavinia's hand. *His wife.*

"Thank you for your honesty," Sophie said, and though she felt quite numb at the moment—surprisingly—she recognized a gift.

All of them were eager to move on, so goodbyes were quickly said. With that, Matthew Fletcher vanished from her life once more.

Brandon handed her a handkerchief, but, oddly enough, her eyes were dry. It was the shock, most likely. Or her store of tears for Matthew Fletcher had been exhausted long ago. It had been some time since she missed him.

"He's not sorry," she repeated, once they had walked a suitable distance. She had to say it again. She hoped that Matthew burned with remorse, and expected a small measure of regret. She was shocked he did not, and confused as to what Brandon might think of it all.

"He's not sorry that he left me. He's not sorry that he left one woman for another," she echoed again.

Good sense had deserted Brandon when he had invited her to walk with him. He was compelled by a mad and wild desire to take the woman he desired far into the gardens of Vauxhall, to a secluded space that declared *ROMANCE* and *SEDUCTION*.

He's not sorry.

Brandon stepped off the path and brought Sophie with him, only pausing when he'd found a suitably private area. It was shaded by trees and hidden with tall hedges. He turned to face her. There was just enough moonlight for him to see the deep pink of her lips, her smooth, pale skin. She looked into his eyes in a way no one ever had and, he suspected, ever would.

He did not regret it . . .

He wanted her so much that staying away from her was the great and only failure of his renowned and usually reliable self-control.

Brandon reminded himself that he was a gentleman.

In that moment, for the first time, Brandon absolutely understood the saying, *An English gentleman is someone who knows exactly when to stop being one.*

This was that moment.

Brandon pressed his mouth to hers.

And then he knew what it felt like to be swept away, to lose oneself, to surrender, to fully ignore logic and reason in favor of tasting, touching, and kissing a woman he couldn't have, but could not let go of. It felt like a rush of heat, it felt unreal and unbelievable, and it felt like he was suspended between two worlds.

They could be discovered at any second. Hundreds of people were strolling along these same pathways.

But he wasn't thinking. For once, he allowed those strange things called feelings full supremacy. And thus he was only aware of darkness; the sweet, intoxicating scent of Sophie, like roses and woman. Faintly, he heard strangers talking and walking nearby, but mostly he heard the roaring of blood coursing through his veins and his heart thundering.

Her lips were soft and tender under his. As gently as he could manage, he urged her to open to him. Her lips parted, his heart thudded hard.

The last remaining shreds of his self-control were devoted to preventing him from completely plundering and ravishing her, for now that he had allowed himself to let go this far . . .

No, this could be all they would ever have.

She tasted sweet and wild and like something he could never possess. He explored the contours of her mouth, and his tongue tangled with hers, save for when he urgently needed to nibble upon her plump bottom lip. And then he urgently needed to taste her again, so he did. Brandon sunk his fingers into her mass of soft curls to cradle her head and hold her close, and he wondered how he would ever let go. He banished the thought and focused upon Sophie, upon her delicious mouth, and her wicked and wonderful kiss tempting him to abandon everything for her.

"Sophie," he murmured.

"Yes," she answered.

When his lips had pressed against hers, Sophie's heart had slammed in her chest: *This One!*

She swiftly bowed to the perfect pressure of his mouth upon hers, and parted her lips. She was surprised, she was hot with desire, and she wanted to give him everything, or, the one thing the double duke in possession of numerous estates and unimaginable wealth did not have: Her. Her love.

The kiss deepened. Sophie arched her back, pressing closer to him, because it was impossible to be too close.

She vaguely recalled that they were in public and might be found at any second. The thought, and its attending fear, passed when he cradled her head with his strong hand, but then let go to trace his hand along her breasts, the dip of her waist, her hip, and back again, leaving a trail of heated skin that tingled, desiring more.

She moaned softly, and he captured the sound with his kiss. She reached up to run her fingers through his hair, mussing it up as she had longed to do the first day they met.

She pulled him to her. He did not resist.

"Oh, Sophie," he murmured.

"I know," she whispered. Some things were too perfect.

With this kiss, she gave herself up to him, and he pleasured her with his mouth, and the way his hands roamed over her, and she thought she'd explode from all the deliciously wicked sensations.

She grasped a handful of the fabric of his shirt because she needed to hold on to something before she was completely lost. His kiss was hot, strong, and sure. She'd never experienced anything like it and she'd give anything to be able to kiss him forever.

The kiss came to an end, as all good things must.

"What are we doing here?" Sophie asked.

"My desires are not honorable," he said, and she turned her head to look at him. He looked her in the eye. "Though my intentions are."

"You desire me, though you will not—" Sophie started. *Take me, have me, kiss me, love me . . .* She couldn't bring herself to finish the sentence. She didn't have to.

"I want you, but I cannot," Brandon said. He opened his eyes—gray green like a field on a cloudy day—and he gazed upon her. "I have reasons, Sophie. It's not just about me."

She knew this feeling—the little cracks in one's heart, multiplying so quickly that a small cut suddenly turns into a big wound and hurts accordingly.

"It's almost quite funny," Sophie remarked. "On my ill-fated wedding day, I vowed—to myself, mind you—

that I would find an honorable man, a reliable man, a man who would not jilt a girl."

"And you did."

"Funny how the universe works," Sophie said, finding it not at all funny in this moment.

"Uproariously hilarious," he said dryly. They understood each other, then. She smiled at him, but it didn't reach her eyes. The smile he returned to her was the same.

It was clear—he would marry Clarissa, and he would *not* marry Sophie. That was not a thought that she could dwell on presently—perhaps later, in a dark room with a thousand handkerchiefs.

How could he possibly marry anyone else after that kiss?

Honestly, it was unimaginable.

She could ask him why, but she knew he could offer her no answer that she would like. Besides, he had, in so many words, explained it to her.

He didn't love her, couldn't love her, or was afraid to love her. He had the dukedom to consider, and his reputation as a man of honor. Knowing him, he likely had a list of Reasons Why He Must Not Marry Sophie.

She did not care to hear them. In the end, she said, "It's getting late. We ought to return."

They stood and walked in the direction they had come from.

This situation was a mess and had all the makings of a spectacular disaster, and she would have to report it all. She had managed the first week. The second installment had been hard, but this one would surely make her heart hurt and her stomach ache. She could not even fathom having to write the fourth, and final, installment.

Provided, of course, that she did not lose her position.

Sophie sighed at the thought. Brandon took her hand in his. Just before they came to the end of the path, he ducked into another alcove and pulled her with him.

Lord Brandon dared to kiss her once more.

This kiss was fierce, and urgent, and quite possibly the last one. His mouth was hot and passionate upon hers. She sucked on his bottom lip, he groaned. He cupped her cheeks in his hands and she sighed.

She placed her hands upon his chest, as if to steady herself, and she felt his heart pounding. Hers was beating in triple time. She felt faint, and she wanted to cry because this was too magical, too exquisite, and too damned perfect. Sophie didn't have much experience, but she knew that kisses like these did not come along every day. Because they did not, she kept her tears in check and kissed him thoroughly, with all of her wild, fiery desire.

Brandon enfolded her in his arms, and kissed her back with a passion to match.

And then this kiss, too, came to an end. They could not spend all night together. She bid him goodnight, but not goodbye.

Sophie emerged from the garden paths, alone. Brandon would wait there until a suitable time elapsed. She cursed every minute they had to stay apart for the sake of propriety, for decency, and because he was a stubborn fool who refused to fall in love with her.

She wove her way through the crowds and unintentionally stumbled upon a horrible sight: Mr. Knightly in conversation with Lady Richmond, while Clarissa stood by her.

Sophie's heart leapt into her throat and stuck there. While she was debating whether or not to join them, the duchess spied her.

"There she is! Ask her where she has been, and who she was with," she huffed.

"With all due respect, Your Grace, you seem to have me confused with someone who cares. I am her employer, not her parent or guardian," Mr. Knightly informed an increasingly enraged duchess.

Sophie's panic subsided. Slightly.

"I could have you banned from the best society," Lady Richmond hissed.

"I have yet to be welcomed anyway," Mr. Knightly remarked.

"I demand she be taken off the story," Lady Richmond demanded. Clarissa's eyes widened.

Sophie held her breath and resumed her internal panicking. Clammy palms—yes. Aching stomach— affirmative. Labored breathing—indeed. Urge to cry— absolutely. *Making lists like the man she loved?—Oh, dear.*

"I'm afraid that is not possible," Mr. Knightly said evenly. Sophie exhaled. He caught her eye and nodded, but she didn't understand it.

"Then I shall take my story to *The Times*," the dragon duchess threatened. Sophie thought she might be sick.

"By all means do so, Lady Richmond," Knightly said, much to Sophie's surprise.

But then he grinned and said, "Nothing like a high-class wedding covered by a second-class newspaper."

Lady Richmond pursed her lips, and turned her back to him. His aspirations to be welcomed by the aristocracy had just suffered a tremendous setback.

Then the dragon duchess focused her narrowed eyes upon Sophie.

Obviously, she was trying to decide what she wanted more: Sophie off the story, or the story in the best paper.

Sophie held her breath.

Chapter 34

Later that evening

Clarissa finally understood the sonnets and the dramas, and all the other love stories—for love had happened to her at last. It came in the form of a letter, and a kiss, and a Bavarian prince.

That kiss! Oh! In the carriage ride home, she relived it again, instead of listening to her mother.

He had held her cheeks, and she had liked that. His lips were soft, and feeling them against her own set off strange and delightful sensations within her. And then when his tongue slid past her lips to make it more intimate she felt, for the first time, a little bit wicked. It was surprisingly delightful.

It was also another reminder that something had to be done about her fiancé—and their wedding day.

With Frederick's kiss still burning on her lips, Clarissa vowed to confront her mother and father before they retired.

"I had the loveliest time talking to Lady Bickford about flowers for your wedding. We must, I think, reconsider the lilacs. And did you see Lady Millicent Merritt wore a dress that was quite the wrong shade of red for her," her mother said, handing her rabbit-fur wrap to a maid and proceeding into the drawing room.

Her father sat by the fire, smoking his pipe and resting his muddy boots on a small footrest. He must have been out in the stables until late. It was his usual position; something seemed different about the room, though Clarissa could not discern what had changed.

"Mother, Father. I need to ask you something," she started.

"And then Lord Radley . . ." she continued, apparently not having heard Clarissa. As Lady Richmond nattered on, she strolled around the room, readjusting the frame on a picture, brushing lint off the upholstery, and picking up the few remaining knickknacks, examining them and setting them back down.

"Mother," she said firmly, in a higher volume than before.

"Yes, dear. What is it?" she said absentmindedly.

"Must I marry Lord Brandon?" The words tumbled out, and upon saying them, Clarissa realized she had waited a long time to release them.

"I beg your pardon?"

Her father removed his pipe and looked at her curiously.

"Is it imperative that I marry Lord Brandon?" Clarissa repeated.

"Is it imperative that you marry Lord Brandon?" her mother echoed. And then she exploded: "Of course it's bloody imperative that you marry him! You are betrothed. The contracts are signed and the invitations have been sent."

"But, Mother . . ."

"You will marry him and do you know why? Because the fortunes of this family depend upon it. We are broke, Clarissa, utterly broke. Have you not noticed that half the paintings in this room have been sold?"

Now she saw what was different about the room: half the paintings had been removed and the remaining ones had been rearranged to cover the losses.

"And all because of your father's stupid horses," her mother said meanly, with a glare in the direction of the duke, who continued to calmly smoke his pipe.

"Your dresses cost a pretty penny, too, madam."

"Those are investment pieces and what would you know of any of it, spending all your time in the barn?" she snapped, and then turned back to her daughter. "I have selected a good husband for you. I can't believe you would be so ungrateful as to refuse him. And at this late date!"

"But I don't love him!" Clarissa cried.

"That is irrelevant," Lady Richmond declared.

"I don't think it is," Clarissa said, stomping her slippered foot on the carpet (at least that had remained) to no effect.

"Your opinion is of no consequence," Lady Richmond shrilled, and Clarissa had to agree with her, though she wished it weren't so. "It's done, Clarissa, done!"

And then, from somewhere deep within her, a courage that she hadn't known herself to persist, emerged in one defiant syllable: "No."

" 'No'?" her mother repeated, though with a touch more hysteria in her tone.

"I don't want to marry a man that doesn't love me, that I do not love," Clarissa stated calmly.

"You want to ruin us all! Just like Eleanor! You want our creditors carting out the furniture, and our good name dragged through the muck so you can be *in love*. I cannot fathom where you got such ridiculous, corkbrained notions."

Clarissa bit her tongue. Certainly not from her mother, that much was clear.

"We are finished with the conversation," Lady Richmond said, every inch the duchess. "You are going to be the Duchess of Hamilton and Brandon and your marriage will restore this family's fortunes. You will not embarrass me by refusing a perfectly good match."

"So I am to give up true love for your dresses and Papa's horses?" Clarissa retorted, emboldened now.

The crack of her mother's palm connecting with her cheek was answer enough to that. The sting . . . oh God, the sting!

Clarissa held her cheek with her hand, as Frederick had done so sweetly, and gently mere hours earlier. She hated her mother in that moment, for striking her, but mostly for defiling the place of her lover's tender touch.

"You may retire now, Clarissa. Please do recover your sense with all possible haste."

She turned to go, still too stunned to speak to declare the truth, which was that she had finally come to her senses, and acknowledged her love for one man and the impossibility of a successful marriage to anyone else.

"Clarissa," her father called to her. She paused. "Your mother was wrong to strike you."

"How dare—"

"Quiet, wife," he said sharply, and Clarissa turned to face him. He looked so old, so sad, so wretched in the firelight with smoke from his pipe lazing around his head, and almost blending with the white of his hair. "However, dear daughter, she tells the truth about our fortunes. Or lack of. I beg of you to marry Lord Brandon so that we may not resort to begging from our creditors and friends. Please, my daughter, *please*."

Chapter 35

Three days before the wedding . . .

Hamilton House

Brandon was dreaming again. Nothing this amazing could possibly happen in his real, waking life.

He was back, to that luscious and perfect moment with Sophie in the gardens of Vauxhall. Once again, he was kissing her. Layers of clothing vanished. Just vanished. No fumbling with buttons, corsets, cravats, or stays. In this dream, he could feel the radiant heat of Sophie's nude body beneath him.

This dream was evilly vivid, for he could swear that he could feel her soft curves under his palms, and that he could taste her skin when he pressed his lips to her neck, as he dreamt he did. Oh, and there was more, too: the way her small hands caressed his chest and then splayed upon his lower back, pressing him into her.

And then he imagined kissing her everywhere: her breasts, the curve of her hips, her inner thighs, her belly, and everywhere in between. And in his dream, this cruelly tempting and tormenting dream, she did the same with her plump, plum mouth.

There was only so much of this torture a man could take.

Brandon was keenly aware of the pounding of his heart. Was that real? Or the dream? There was a whisper between each beat—*forever*. She wrapped her arms tighter around him, pulling him closer into her and he . . .

Woke up.

Brandon woke to a cacophony of horrendous noise. Men shouting. Something big fell. The sound of dozens of boots stomping on the gleaming marble floors. Jennings appeared shortly after Brandon rang the bell.

"The decorators for your wedding breakfast," the valet said by way of an explanation.

"The wedding is not for . . ." Brandon paused, needing to count.

"Another three days," his valet informed him.

"What the bloody hell are they doing to my house?"

"I tend to avoid coming between women and their decorating, so I haven't the slightest notion. But I shall discover it for you."

"Thank you."

It would be another unseasonably hot day, he could feel it. Already, he missed the coolness of the previous evening, the silver light of the moon instead of the raging gold of the sun. He wished for Sophie's dark eyes, her laugh, her kiss. His resentment for everything that kept him from her had been growing for some time and now he felt the pressure of it pressing hard from within.

But he was a duke, he knew his duty, and he was not a coward. And so, Brandon dressed with the assistance of his valet. In this atrocious heat, he still donned the proper attire of a gentleman: white fitted breeches, black leather Hessians, a snowy white shirt with a matching cravat, a hunter green waistcoat, and a dove gray jacket.

"Good morning, Brandon," his mother said when he entered the dining room.

"Good morning, Mother." It was then that he recalled his conversation with Sophie. About love, loss, and asking someone who knew better than he. It was too early in the morning for that.

"I trust you noticed the decorators have arrived for your wedding," she remarked dryly before taking a sip of her tea.

"One would have to be a blind, deaf mute to miss it," he said. "Although they seem to have quieted down somewhat."

"They were rather loud and I have spoken to them," she said.

"Ah," he said with a smile. His mother was a diminutive woman, who listened more than she spoke. He'd never heard her raise her voice and had learned, from her, that a quiet, calmly worded command achieved more than blustering and hollering.

"Your wedding day is fast approaching," she pointed out. "You must be so eager for it."

"What makes you think that?" he asked, helping himself to a plate of fried eggs, rashers of bacon, freshly baked biscuits loaded with melting butter, and hot coffee.

"You have taken such an interest in the planning of the big event," she said.

He just nodded. Gentlemen did not speak with their mouths full. This elementary rule of civilized behavior was often broken, but never by him. Especially when it was convenient for him to remain silent.

"Lady Richmond is of the opinion that you harbor illicit desires for Miss Harlow. She is terribly concerned."

"Is she?" He responded carefully and evasively, hopefully eliciting further information without expressing excessive interest.

"We are both aware that the fortunes of the Richmond family are utterly dependent upon this marriage," his mother said. "She'll go to great lengths, I'm sure, that everything occurs according to plan."

That sounded like a warning.

"And you? Are you concerned?" he asked.

"I only wish the best for my son. Whatever makes you happiest, Henry."

It was not the answer that he was looking for, but he thanked her all the same. He knew that he was long past the age of receiving instruction. But for a second he wished that she would interfere or tell him plainly her thoughts. He wanted her to give him advice, or anything other than leaving it up to him and looking at him with a trace of sadness in her eyes.

"I have an appointment to attend to. If you'll excuse me, Mother. Do have a nice day."

In the hall, his secretary found him.

"Your Grace, I have news for you. Private, urgent news."

They retired at once to his study. His secretary related his news that the reports had been confirmed by numerous sources. Old servants, in abject poverty due to their master being unable to pay their pensions, were willing to talk for coin. They would also never speak a word of it again, for more coin, should His Grace wish for it.

Brandon frowned, before quickly masking his feelings with an appropriately inscrutable ducal expression.

"She is not who she says she is, Your Grace," Spencer said in a hushed whisper, because such massive secrets called for such tones, even when dozens of servants were making obscene amounts of noise. "Do you realize the implications of this?"

He did. It complicated everything.

Harry Angelo's Fencing Academy

Once again, Brandon met von Vennigan for a fencing match. Other than making long, loud love to Sophie, the thing he wanted to do most was engage in violent activity. He was tense, irritable, and—he realized upon arriving at Angelo's—unshaven. He wondered why Jennings hadn't said anything.

"You look ready to fight," von Vennigan observed.

"I am. Consider yourself warned."

"Done. You should know that I, too, am in somewhat of a temper today."

Usually, Angelo's was busy, with a dozen or so men engaged in swordplay at any time. Today, Brandon and his adversary were alone. It was likely due to the heat. It weighed on a man, made him feel like he was suffocating.

It wasn't just the temperature. Between the glorious kiss with Sophie last night and his secretary's outrageous news this morning, Brandon was divided and at war with himself. His desires, his obligations, his wishes, his values—everything was in opposition and he wanted to explode from the tension.

He knew he should have taken better care to avoid her.

Yet, he loved every minute with her.

If he lost her . . .

But if he married Clarissa, he would be safe from an excess of sentiment. If he lost Sophie before things went too far, he might have a chance. As far as he was concerned, they hadn't. They had not made love, or confessed to a love. To do that would be a new *Before* and *After* and he feared that *After* like a child feared the dark—stubbornly, irrationally, and utterly intensely.

Yes, Brandon was in the mood to fight today. He wanted to concentrate on the slashing of swords, of dodging blades and attacking his opponent. He did not want to think of anything else at all.

"Ready?" von Vennigan asked, settling into en garde.

Brandon took his position opposite. With his notoriously remarkable self-control, he willed himself to avoid thinking of Sophie, and from sparing even a fleeting thought to the news Spencer had delivered. Then he curtly nodded yes, he was ready.

At first no one moved, each keeping a perfect defensive position and daring the other to find the gap in his guard.

"Have you heard from Clarissa?" von Vennigan asked, taking a quick step forward to test Brandon's parry.

"Clarissa?" Brandon repeated pointedly as he brought his blade across his body to cut off von Vennigan's line.

"Your fiancée," he remarked dryly.

"You mean Lady Richmond," Brandon corrected, engaging his opponent's blade and using brute strength to force his way through the young prince's suddenly urgent defenses, almost scoring had von Vennigan not been so quick on his feet. The words were bitter in his mouth for reasons he would not dwell upon.

"That may be the formal way to address her, but it puts me in mind of her mother, and I would rather not have her on my mind."

"That we can agree on," Brandon said.

"And she has given me leave to use her given name," von Vennigan added, moving back and forth just outside Brandon's range, almost daring the duke to lunge.

"Is there anything that your honor as a gentleman compels you to tell me?" Brandon asked. *Best do it now, whilst swords were already drawn.*

"No. My feelings are my own. And hers."

"I care not for your feelings," Brandon told him, and pressed forward, forcing von Vennigan toward the far wall and causing the first bead of sweat to form on the young prince's brow.

"But you do care for the purity of your intended," von Vennigan said in a tone that made Brandon curious.

"Very much," he answered, though for a very particular and unsentimental reason.

And then he paused, considering whether or not he wished to share a certain piece of information with his opponent.

Because he was reckless and stormy inside and because things were already so complicated, one more additional revelation could not possibly hurt. Brandon added, "In fact, the marriage contract would be rendered null and void were it discovered that she was compromised."

Von Vennigan's head whipped up and he parried Brandon's attack forcefully, halting his retreat down to the floor and giving Brandon pause.

"I thought this contract was, in your words, *iron-clad*," von Vennigan reminded him with a devilish gleam in his eye.

"That point is the one way out." Brandon banished thoughts of another way . . .

"Unfortunately," von Vennigan remarked dryly, "it is grossly insulting to the woman in question." As he pressed forward, he almost seemed to collapse, and too late did Brandon realize his intentions. The point of his blade found Brandon's foot, a reckless move that among one less skilled would have left von Vennigan open to a vicious counterattack.

"I find it more pleasing to have my sword on your foot than I did your foot on my sword, Your Grace," von Vennigan gleefully remarked. Brandon winced at both the reminder of their previous bout and the throbbing pain in his foot as both men moved to take up the en garde position.

"Would compromising her—grossly insulting her—be an honorable action, if the end result was marriage. To you?" Brandon asked, testing the prince's defenses of his head.

"That is an interesting question," von Vennigan asked. "One I have not yet had sufficient time to analyze." His voice was labored as he attempted to stop Brandon's blade from coming too close to his face, and Brandon wondered if von Vennigan regretted his previous remark about dispensing with masks.

Perhaps not—with those scars he already possessed, what was one or two more?

"There is not much time for you to decide," Brandon said.

"A fact of which I am achingly aware."

"So you might, then, stand by your previous principle of action being honorable?" Brandon asked. He knew exactly why he persisted in this line of conversation and questioning. Because of Sophie, and kisses in the moonlight. Because he was not yet certain if he could jilt Clarissa. He was also not certain that he could leave his fate in the hands of a Bavarian prince, either.

"There are many possible courses of action," von Vennigan mused. "Some less humbling than others."

"You would not humble yourself for love?" Brandon asked mockingly. His blade danced around von Vennigan's, first threatening the shoulder, then the chest, then the head.

"I think there might not be anything I would not do for love. And you?"

"Love is an irrational emotion that leads to excruciating heartache. As with drinking to excess, I prefer to abstain for I care not for the aftereffects." These were words he had no trouble saying even in the midst of an intense swordfight, amid an intense heat.

He had said them before. He had lived them. He would say them again.

He still meant them. It was just that he feared he might be heading for said heartache. Like a drunk, he might prefer to abstain but he could not help himself.

Von Vennigan took the initiative and with a balletic step that Brandon had never seen before, closed the distance between them so fast that his only defense was to force both blades heavenward.

At that moment, von Vennigan was mere inches from him and he felt the young prince's hot breath on his face.

It was hard, fighting so many battles at once: against von Vennigan with swords, against his feelings for Sophie with rationality, and then wrestling with his honor.

"You are either an outrageous liar or a delusional fool," von Vennigan stated as they disengaged.

"Unfounded," he said, and then he lunged, a move that was swiftly deflected.

"Miss Harlow," von Vennigan challenged. Brandon thrashed forward with emotion rather than calculation. Instead of retreating von Vennigan took advantage of his opponent's wayward blade and counterattacked with a quick lunge that caught Brandon on the sternum and drove the breath from his lungs.

"Is a temporary aberration," Brandon said, through labored breaths. He needed it to be true. He did not know what to do if it wasn't. "A temporary bout of madness. I'm certain it shall pass after the wedding."

It was the right thing to do. Or was it? He did not know anymore. He did know that mentions of it taunted his opponent, and so he wielded it like a second sword.

"To Clarissa," von Vennigan said bitterly.

"To my intended."

Von Vennigan renewed his attack, though his approaches had lost something of their previous precision.

"But you have not heard from her?" von Vennigan asked with concern blatantly etched on his features.

"No. Is something amiss?" Brandon asked, parrying and forcing von Vennigan back.

"I suspect something might be. Out of respect for her reputation, I dare not call upon her."

"She has not canceled our plans to attend the annual dinner hosted by Lord and Lady Byrnham," Brandon said with a casualness that belied his vigor. It was to be a small, exclusive, and intimate gathering of the most socially prominent.

"I will see you both there," von Vennigan said.

"Are you sure you were invited? It commemorates Marlborough's campaign in Germany," Brandon asked.

Von Vennigan paused. "I shall secure an invitation. After all, princes are never refused," he said pointedly. Dukes generally weren't either, but that was neither here nor there.

Their swordplay continued. Brandon was soaked with sweat, and increasingly exhausted, though not enough to put an end to thoughts of his Epic Dilemma of a Lifetime. He stamped his foot loudly, a feint that von Vennigan took for an attack and mistakenly parried, leaving his right side open. Brandon scored a palpable hit.

Did von Vennigan truly love Clarissa, beyond her beauty? Brandon wasn't sure, and how could he be when the man was a known jester, so often spouting poetry and philosophic rot about honor. Looking at him as he rubbed his shoulder, the prince did not seem in the mood for jokes now.

Would this prince still love her if he knew what Brandon knew?

He might love her, but would that be an honorable married love, or an illicit one? Or would von Vennigan set sail for his native land, alone, by sundown?

In short, Brandon doubted von Vennigan's love for Clarissa. And he knew that she *needed* him in a way that Sophie did not.

But Sophie called to him. If Clarissa appealed to his brain, then Sophie tempted the rest of him. When she was near, it felt like his blood coursed faster, driven by a swiftly beating heart. Sophie was heartbeat and lust, the air in his lungs, and a feeling in his gut. How could he possibly live without her?

It was the final point. Both men labored up and down the floor, their swords weighing heavily in their hands, the sweat stinging their eyes. Brandon decided, against all rationality, to follow his teacher's example. With what little energy remained, he feinted to von Vennigan's inside left and then threw his body into a desperate flèche, arrowing his sword toward the prince's chest. His sword jarred as it hit true and Brandon continued past the prince only to stop, panting a few paces beyond.

"It seems you can be a man of action when the circumstances demand," von Vennigan said ruefully as he rubbed what would surely be a welt by morning.

Chapter 36

Sophie had never been so overjoyed to attend a staff meeting. Knightly had no intention of firing her. In fact, he said he owed her. The paper had been doing well, but it hadn't been the stellar success it was until she came in and gave him the idea to hire a woman and cause a scandal.

Irate duchesses were a dime a dozen, Mr. Knightly had said, but there were only four Writing Girls.

She had confided in Julianna about the events of the other night. Mostly. She had not mentioned the kisses because merely mentioning the long, private, moonlit walk had set her off on a lecture about propriety, decency, and yet another reminder that the man she loved was practically married to another woman.

The story of Matthew and Lavinia had been of great interest to her, however.

"Sophie had a chance encounter with Matthew and Lavinia," Julianna informed the group, and repeated the story. Naturally, the Writing Girls asked what she was doing in the gardens at Vauxhall, and it wasn't long before the entire story of Sophie's magical evening had been told (minus the kisses; those she kept for herself).

"What is so sad to me is that we are so perfect together, and yet it seems that he is going to marry her," Sophie explained. "I can't understand how he can go through with it."

"I thought we knew that he was going to marry Clarissa," Eliza said.

"He can't possibly cry off, and neither can she," Julianna said.

"Julianna . . ." Annabelle murmured, wanting her to be supportive.

"He does not love her, and she loves another and neither of them believe in marriage for love. *And* Matthew told Brandon and me that he did not regret jilting me. So I hope that perhaps he would consider it," Sophie said. And then he had kissed her passionately! Just when her hopes had been dashed utterly after that long conversation about his refusal to love, Brandon had kissed and restored her hope.

"It would be such a scandal," Eliza remarked.

"The likes of which we've never seen," Julianna repeated, smiling eagerly at the thought of it, and the exclusive she would land. Sophie turned away; this was about true love and the rest of her life, not about a gossip column.

"What, oh what, do I do, dear Annabelle?" Sophie asked. That was the problem—she did not know what to do now, and Brandon's intentions were still unclear. She did not know when she would see him next, or speak to him.

"Have you spoken to the gentleman about the situation?" Annabelle asked.

"A little."

Julianna's brows shot up. Apparently, she thought it less serious than it was.

"Did you?" Eliza said, leaning in excitedly. "What did he say?"

"He said it's complicated. I did not want to force the matter," Sophie said, explaining why she did not have a more concrete answer. She wished Brandon would just come to his senses and say he loved her, and ask her to marry him—all without her initiating a truly intimate conversation.

"But Sophie, that awkward conversation might become the splendid moment he decides to marry you," Annabelle pointed out. Sophie had not considered that.

"I should talk to him," Sophie concluded.

"Yes," Annabelle and Eliza answered in unison.

"That sounds rather sensible," Sophie agreed. *It sounded like a disaster.*

"It is. Remember, I am expert advice-giver," Annabelle said, smiling sweetly.

"I thought maybe I could have a near-death experience so that he might truly realize his love for me and that he cannot live without me. I shall recover and we'll live happily ever after." Sophie sighed.

"Talk to him," Annabelle said firmly. Eliza, and even Julianna, nodded in agreement.

"Ladies first," Knightly declared, as he always did at the beginning of a staff meeting. "Miss Harlow?"

"The third installment of the 'Wedding of the Year' has been completed." She finished it early this morning with the notes previously provided by the Dragon Duchess herself. She'd had to rewrite it once, because her teardrops caused the ink to run on the first draft.

"See that you attend the wedding itself, by any means necessary," Mr. Knightly told her with a firm stare.

"Yes, sir," Sophie said with a sinking heart.

"What Fashionable Intelligence do we have this week?" he asked.

"Everyone is talking about The Duke of Hamilton and Brandon's attentions to a certain Writing Girl. When they are not discussing that, the other favored topic is his fiancée's affections toward the visiting Prince of Bavaria."

"Love triangles, dukes, princes, *The London Weekly*'s Writing Girls. Well done, Miss Harlow. I love it. Miss Swift, your next column should offer advice, solicited or not, to the couples."

"Of course, Mr. Knightly," Annabelle said, fluttering her eyelashes.

"Miss Fielding, what is your angle?"

"I'm reporting on the efficacy of Wright's Tonic for the Cure of Unsuitable Affections."

"Is Miss Harlow one of your subjects?" Mr. Knightly jested.

"Yes. It doesn't work," Sophie declared.

The meeting went on, and Sophie had not paid attention to a minute of it. Three days until the wedding! It was not much time to change a man's mind, or even to find the time to have a conversation to tell him her true feelings, which may or may not factor into his decision to marry Clarissa.

Perhaps these three days were best spent becoming accustomed to the idea of no more Brandon and addressing Clarissa as Lady Brandon. Her breath caught, and she struggled to breathe.

He couldn't!

What about love?

He didn't believe in love.

"Annabelle, what if I talk to him and he is still going to marry Clarissa?" Sophie whispered.

"Then you have to let him go," Annabelle answered with an affectionate squeeze of Sophie's palm. That was not what she wanted to hear, though she knew in her heart that it was the right thing to do.

Chapter 37

Later that evening
Clarissa's Bedroom

It had been so long since Clarissa had last corresponded with Frederick. Her mother was refusing the letters; she knew, because she had taken to spying, and eavesdropping, and soliciting information from her maid, Nancy, who was not terribly forthcoming. She had also been unable to send letters. Her attempts had been thwarted and her writing supplies confiscated, except for one small, secret and dwindling stash.

Furthermore, her mother had insisted that she stay home and rest for The Big Day, which was only three days away.

It had been a miserable existence to live without word from Frederick. Was he worried for her? Did he miss her? Would he rescue her after all? Oh, how she wished he would simply steal into her room and carry her off in the night!

Nancy was currently styling her hair for this evening's dinner honoring Marlborough's military campaign in Germany. It was highly unlikely that a Bavarian prince would attend, and thus, Clarissa had little interest in it.

Clarissa's gaze traveled away from her reflection in the mirror (the very image of a distressed, melancholic maiden), to the bottle of Wright's Tonic for the Cure of Unsuitable Affections that had arrived with her breakfast tray. She had yet to sample it, but she had certainly considered it.

The Royal Society Dinner Commemorating Marlborough's Campaign in Germany

Like everyone else in attendance, the elder Lady Richmond was clearly surprised to see a Bavarian prince at the dinner. He wouldn't have gone, except that he desperately needed to see Clarissa. When he wasn't watching her, which was most of the time, it did not escape his notice that her mother was hawkeyed in her attentions to Clarissa. Whenever Frederick dared to get close, she swooped in and made it impossible for him to come closer.

Brandon, the lucky, ungrateful bounder, did not leave Clarissa's side. He had tried to but Lady Richmond always dove in with a dear, dear friend to be introduced to the couple.

Frederick slipped away from the drawing room and took a liberty with the hostess's seating arrangements so that he was next to Clarissa and Lady Richmond was below the salt.

Alas, the hostess caught the violation of her sacred seating arrangement and fixed it before all the guests arrived in the dining room. Frederick found himself seated next to persons of no interest.

Instead of making conversation, he gazed intently at Clarissa. What had caused their sudden silence? What was happening in her heart?

She lifted her eyes away from her plate—she was

not eating, darling little bird—and focused her gaze upon his. He thought he detected tears, but that might have been a trick of the candlelight. That he could not go to her, could not reach out to her, could not console her was utter anguish.

He despised this situation.

Clarissa touched her mouth—her sweet, gorgeous lips he had tasted in that soul-stunning kiss—with her fingertips, and he saw that the ink stains were gone. She had not been writing at all.

She had refused his letters. She had not written her own. And yet, he could read her face as if someone held a mirror up to his own.

"Clarissa, Lady Byrnham was asking about your wedding dress. Do describe it for her," Lady Richmond cut in.

How, how, how, how was he supposed to stand idly by while she married another?

Frederick understood that Clarissa was, in a way, confined to a tower, stowed away from his grasp and his kiss.

With Clarissa's attentions occupied elsewhere, if only for the moment, Lady Richmond darted a glance at Frederick. Upon catching his eye, she smirked, as if she had outsmarted him. As if she had won the battle. As if she was certain Frederick would never possess Clarissa because she was locked up.

Frederick excused himself. He proceeded directly to the host's study, and availed himself of the writing supplies. A maid was liberally supplied with coins and clear instructions for the fate of the letter.

Chapter 38

Two days before the wedding . . .

Hamilton House

"**N**o, no, no, *no*, NO! The orchestra should be on the *other* side of the room," Lady Richmond said impatiently to one of the footmen. She fanned herself furiously because of the heat, and because of the sheer pressure of pulling off the perfect wedding for a couple that had little interest in each other, and even less in their big day.

Sophie hung back, trying to be as little noticed as possible. That she was still invited to participate in these proceedings was only because Lady Richmond's quest for social fame and her name in the papers exceeded her loathing for a girl she perceived to be her daughter's rival. Little did she know that she had selected the perfect husband for her daughter and for this scenario. The one who wouldn't leave a woman.

Even if . . . Sophie sucked in a gulp of hot air, which did nothing to ease her feelings of suffocation. It was the heat, of course, and the fact that everyone and everything was proceeding as if the wedding were going to happen as planned. Clarissa would walk down the aisle, to where Brandon waited. They would promise to love, honor, cherish, etc, etc.

But . . . but . . . and yet . . . they couldn't possibly . . . No, no, no, *no*, NO!

Sophie's heart rebelled. Her stomach ached. And *breathing*—that was proving to be a challenge. How could they carry on? Clarissa didn't love him, and Lady Richmond had to know about her daughter's affections. Brandon did not love Clarissa, and . . .

That didn't mean that he loved her. He hadn't said it and he had told her frankly his thoughts about that tender emotion. If he wasn't going to call off the wedding for love, why would he?

It wasn't as if she possessed all four of his Desired Qualities in a Wife. She was a lowly, slightly scandalous, passably socially acceptable newspaper writer. Dukes didn't marry women like that; if anything they set them up in little apartments with spending allowances and discreet late night visits.

Perhaps . . . oh, it ached to acknowledge this . . . perhaps he wasn't going to leave Clarissa for her. Sophie could tell that he enjoyed her—in spite of himself. She could tell that he desired her—and that he didn't want to.

But did he want her more than he wanted that calm, quiet, well-ordered life of his?

Sophie closed her eyes and willed such thoughts to cease.

Lady Hamilton was quietly and calmly meeting with the housekeeper. Clarissa had been put to work recounting replies to the invitations. Sophie wanted to talk to her, but every time she approached her, Lady Richmond asked a question about how this person had arranged the tables at their wedding breakfast or how many servants per guest so and so had, and all other sorts of distracting nonsense.

"This weather is horrible," Lady Richmond complained, beating her fan at a fast clip. "The heat is unbearable."

Everyone, duchesses and servants alike, nodded and muttered that, indeed, it was far too hot for comfort.

"Some more lemonade perhaps?" Sophie offered.

"It shall be my third glass, but I think I must," Lady Richmond answered. Any minute now she would need to use the necessary and Sophie could have a frank conversation with Clarissa.

"No, no, no," Lady Richmond corrected. "The potted palms should be centered between the windows."

"Yes, Your Grace," a footman mumbled as he and the others moved the heavy pots of palms a few inches in the other direction.

"I'd be so very appreciative if you could manage to do something right while I step out for a moment," Lady Richmond said bitterly. She fanned herself furiously as she left the ballroom. Lady Hamilton pursed her lips disapprovingly.

Sophie set down her notebook and pencil on the sideboard and approached Clarissa, seated at the large, long dining table.

"We finally get a moment to chat," Sophie whispered conspiratorially. "How are you today, Clarissa?"

"Oh, I'm fine. And you?" Clarissa said, and her voice wavered. She decidedly was not fine.

"As well as you are," Sophie said.

"So you are wretched, too?" Clarissa asked.

"Utterly," Sophie sighed. And then Clarissa handed her a sheet of paper that had clearly been read and reread (and read and reread).

"You must advise me, Sophie."

Sophie read the letter:

My darling,
  I love you, and cannot live without you. Come
away with me, as my bride. Your prince wishes to
live happily ever after with his princess. Marry
me, Clarissa.

                    Yours, with everlasting love,
                                  Frederick

"Oh, Clarissa," Sophie said with a heartfelt lilt in her voice. "He has proposed, and yet you look sad!"

"I must say no!" Clarissa said, and then there was a strange sound, as if she was choking back a sob. "I must refuse."

"Because of Brandon?" Lady Hamilton glanced in their direction.

"That is not the only reason. There are delicate family matters that I mustn't speak of, but they are . . . it makes it so that . . ."

"He's a prince, Clarissa, and princes fix everything, no matter the problem," Sophie said, because she knew about the decline of the Richmond fortunes but did not want to share her knowledge. "And he loves you. Everlastingly."

"But what if it's like Aunt Eleanor, what if it fades, and I've ruined everything and what if . . ." Clarissa whispered with panic.

Sophie, to her shame, wished to shake her and yell, "It's true love! It can last forever!" She wanted to remind Clarissa that *this* was the escape plan that they both desperately needed if they wished to even attempt a happily ever after.

But one did not have an easy time being rebellious after a lifetime of blind obedience, and Sophie knew this was a large part of what was holding Clarissa back. Unfortunately, now was not the time to talk sense into her (the clock was ticking away), for out of the corner of her eye, Sophie saw Lady Hamilton walking toward them. Sophie turned back to Clarissa, who swiftly snatched the letter and stuffed it into her bodice.

"What was that?" Lady Richmond demanded, and Sophie nearly shrieked from the shock of the other duchess's unexpected approach. She hadn't heard her at all. Suddenly, Sophie and Clarissa were surrounded. With one illicit proposal letter from a prince stashed away.

"Hand it to me, please, Clarissa. Pray, do not make me ask twice," her mother ordered. The footmen and maidservants greatly slowed the pace of their work and ceased their chatter to divert their attentions from the unfolding scene.

"It's nothing, Mother." Clarissa was, as one might expect, a terrible liar. She stared at the floor, and colored up tremendously.

"Then you'll have no qualms about giving it to me," Lady Richmond declared. Her voice echoed off the gleaming parquet floors and the high ceiling. *The acoustics in this room are remarkable,* Sophie thought.

"Really, it's insignificant, Mother. No need to concern yourself," Clarissa mumbled. Sophie bit her lip.

"Lady Richmond, I'm sure it's nothing to fuss about," Lady Hamilton said in a very duchesslike voice: commanding but absolutely gracious.

"I'll thank you to tend to your children and leave me to mine," Lady Richmond snapped, apparently impervious to commands from her peers. And then she turned her attention back to her daughter. With only *a Look*—a very strong, terrifying look that made even

Sophie wilt a little, she obtained the obedience she sought.

Clarissa, with tears in her eyes—from sadness, defeat, and mortification—handed over the letter.

" *'My darling, la, la, la. Marry me, la, la. Yours with everlasting love, Frederick.'* A marriage proposal?" Lady Richmond questioned, looking accusingly at her daughter.

"It's mine. It's to me," Sophie blurted out.

"Miss Harlow, do you mistake me for an idiot?"

Sophie declined to provide an answer.

"Ah, smart enough not to answer that. I know very well that Frederick is that blasted Bavarian that keeps waltzing with my daughter, who I only tolerate because he is the toast of society and it would look bad to make a fuss about it—even though a Bavarian murdered my father. I do not hold them in high esteem."

"Mother—" Clarissa said.

"Lady Hamilton, I am mortified that you had to witness this episode. Clarissa will pen her refusal this very moment."

"What if she wishes to accept?" Lady Hamilton asked, casually fanning herself. This perplexed Sophie.

"I assure you she does not."

"She might," Sophie said, daring to enter the conversation.

"You have ulterior motives in this, and thus, cannot be trusted," Lady Richmond said dismissively.

"I'm most interested in Clarissa's feelings," Lady Hamilton said, and then she turned to her. "Dear, do you wish to marry Frederick?"

Clarissa nodded yes while refusing to look up from the floor.

"How dare you," her mother hissed.

"Why, Lady Richmond, can she not marry a prince? He outranks my son. He is wealthier than my son. She obviously cares for him more than my son."

"The Richmonds are an English family and have been for generations. They live here, marry here, procreate here, and die here . . . with other English," Lady Richmond said, and Sophie was taken aback by her lack of tolerance for anything non-English (other than, one had to presume, French fashions).

The duchess continued: "The Richmonds keep their word and honor their commitments. They do not embarrass themselves with scandalous affairs with long-haired foreigners. They do not refuse sound matches for a little thing like love, which shall fade and lead to the ruin of us all. They put their family first, above themselves."

Lady Richmond took a heaving breath after venting her spleen. It was surprising to witness such an outburst.

"Hmmm," Lady Hamilton murmured. Sophie suspected that she did not quite agree, and probably did not wish to provoke her further.

"Clarissa, you are writing a refusal," Lady Richmond reminded.

"Mother, please don't make me do this," Clarissa gasped as she choked on her tears. "Please, Mamma."

The duchess stood still, unyielding and impervious to her daughter's pleas. Clarissa was sobbing now, creating quite the scene.

The servants looked away and Lady Hamilton stroked Clarissa's back. Sophie took her hand and stared at Lady Richmond wondering how on earth she could be so unmoved by her daughter's heartfelt and heart-wrenching sobs. It struck her as downright unnatural.

"You may do it now or you may do it at home. But you will refuse him."

Sophie watched, tense and on edge, because her own heart was on the line, too. She was hopeful when Clarissa lifted her chin and swiped the tears away with the back of her hands.

"Fine," Clarissa said, and picked up the pen. She spoke aloud, and her voice echoed for all to hear, as she wrote,

"My darling Frederick, My horrible mother insists that I refuse you. You have my love, my heart, and my desperate pleas that you shall rescue me. Yours, Clarissa."

She handed it to a very shocked Sophie.

"You are the only one I trust to deliver this," Clarissa said.

"Absolutely. Even if I must deliver the message to him verbally," Sophie said. She hoped that von Vennigan was as dashing, romantic, and heroic as he seemed. Perhaps he would whisk Clarissa away, so they might live happily ever after in Bavaria and then Brandon would be free to be her hero.

"You, Miss Harlow, are an ungrateful, low-class, impertinent hussy and I rue the day I invited you to participate in my daughter's wedding," Lady Richmond informed her. It was a very understandable sentiment, and one Sophie elected not to respond to. "My ungrateful, wretched daughter and I will depart. Terribly sorry for the scene, Lady Hamilton. We'll return on the morrow to complete the preparations for the wedding, which will go on as planned."

Sophie immediately sent the letter to von Vennigan. She then related the entire tale to Julianna who offered to pepper her column with unflattering rumors about

Lady Richmond, and declared that this pretty much cleared up the matter of who would marry whom. In other words, Sophie should plan on writing an excruciating, gut-wrenching version of "Miss Harlow's Marriage in High Life" which did not, actually, detail Miss Harlow's own marriage in either high or low life.

Even with the dramatic turn of events this afternoon, Annabelle's advice to Sophie to speak to Brandon had not been forgotten. She did have questions about his intentions, especially in light of Frederick's proposal, and she deserved answers. After pacing and debating, she wrote him a note. "I must speak to you. Urgently. Yours, Sophie."

Chapter 39

Within the hour, Brandon's carriage was outside of her door and it was too late to second-guess herself. Sophie had questions, and now she would obtain answers. With a fleeting prayer that she would receive answers she liked, Sophie climbed into his carriage.

"Where are we going?" she asked, hoping he would say Gretna Green.

"I thought we'd drive around town. This was the only private, discreet place I could think for us to meet," Brandon explained.

"Perfect," she said. She was nervous to be alone with him, even after all this time.

It was dusk outside, and rather dark inside the carriage, though a little periwinkle light shone through the windows providing sufficient illumination for her to see Brandon.

Oh, he took her breath away with his green eyes, noble nose, the strong line of his jaw, and his mouth. Oh God, his mouth and his kiss. Knowing it made her crave it all the more. His posture was perfect and she wished to crawl onto his lap and be clasped in his arms.

"What did you need to speak to me about?" he asked.

"So many things," Sophie said. "Have you heard from your mother?"

"I have not. She's engrossed in some book and took a tray in her room for supper."

"You missed a very dramatic scene this afternoon, in which Clarissa was caught with a letter from von Vennigan by her mother and yours."

"What did the letter say?" Brandon asked.

"He asked her to marry him."

Brandon merely nodded, and Sophie did not know how to make sense of it. If he cared so little that another man had made such a blatant claim on his fiancée, then he really shouldn't be marrying her at all. But then again, Sophie was biased. It was still remarkable, though.

Unless, of course, Brandon had already heard and already run von Vennigan through with his sword. Always an option.

"Her mother insisted she refuse. Your mother almost sounded as if she supported the match."

"How so?" he asked, finally expressing some curiosity and interest in the matter. It was a very interesting matter, one in which their fates depended upon.

"She was the only one to ask Clarissa what she wanted, or what was so wrong with her marrying a man who outranked you, and was wealthier."

"And much more handsome, talented, and charming," Brandon deadpanned.

"I find you much more handsome than von Vennigan." *Or any other man.* No one else made her feel so many things, and so intensely. Brandon made her feel like the brave, beautiful woman she'd always wanted to be. But then when he smiled at her, she felt shivers of delight. To laugh with him was divine. To touch him was heavenly, except for it being so very wicked. *He had to feel all these things, too,* she thought.

She wondered, again, *How could he marry someone else?*

"Thank you," he said, and he offered a shy grin. Sophie forged on with the conversation.

"In the end, Clarissa was forced to write her refusal then and there. I was entrusted with the letter."

"The affection they hold for each other is no secret," Brandon said, stating the obvious. But what did he think of the situation or how did he feel about it all, and, for lord's sake, *was he going to do something or not?*

Honestly, men—even one a woman was madly in love with—could be tremendously vexing. Though she was scared to initiate a conversation about them, she knew that she had to if it was going to be discussed at all.

"I'm more interested in the affection we have for each other," Sophie said, and then rushed on nervously: "We do, do we not? Or am I the only one that feels this way?"

Her words drifted in the air, unanswered, for what seemed like an eternity before he finally said, "No, Sophie, I do as well."

"I hate to pry," she said, and he grinned faintly at the recollection of their first meeting. "Brandon, but I must know what your intentions are. Are you going to marry Clarissa? What is going to happen with us?"

A long silence ensued. Sophie looked out the window at all the people the carriage was passing and marveled at how they were blissfully unaware of the agonies she was enduring. She had asked him to state his intentions and hadn't thought to fear that he might not have any to declare.

Within her gloves, her palms were becoming
clammy. Her throat was tightening, breathing was a la-
borious activity, and she feared she would faint or cast
up her accounts. In short, as she waited for Brandon
to speak, she felt as she did at her own wedding and at
every other one she attended.

She felt rejected. Unwanted. Unloved. So very
alone.

Those weren't feelings that could be soothed by her
chant of "seamstress or servant, governess or mistress"
because this had nothing to do with weddings, or being
a Writing Girl, and everything to do with a lonely
woman offering her heart and no one taking it.

"Brandon, I am beginning to panic," Sophie managed to say, willing him to speak.

"I don't know, Sophie," he burst out. "I have feelings
for you—feelings so intense that I am kept awake at
night, and I question everything I've ever believed or
held to be true. But I don't *want* to have these feelings
for you."

"Why?" It was a whisper.

"Because love is the one thing that I cannot afford.
Because it complicates things, and it makes what I fear
I must do so damned hard. I am also a man of honor.
You know that. I am not the kind of man that would jilt
a woman. That is one of the things you like about me. I
know that, too. I cannot win."

"But she'll marry von Vennigan . . ."

"Will she? Now that she's refused him, will he still
wish to have her?"

"He loves her," Sophie said, as if that was enough. It
was, was it not?

"But would he still wish to marry her if he knew
of the masses of debt that she comes along with, or if
he discovers certain secrets from her past that I hate,

which I am privy to? Will he still want her then? And what of my sister making her debut next year? And what of my conscience? What of the life I had planned and wished for? A quiet life, uncomplicated by—"

"By love, or honor, or jealousy, or anything in the realm of feelings. Yes, I know," she retorted. She made a note to ask later about the certain secrets from Clarissa's past.

"You saw the list of qualities that I looked for in a wife," Brandon said. "You knew all of this."

Clarissa was cool, calm perfection. Sophie was a mess, a walking disaster, and a constant intrusion. She was the sort of woman a man dallied with, but did not marry.

It was clear that he was torn by trying to accommodate so many conflicting interests. As he said, here were more than feelings at stake. But it was also true that he wanted her, too. She knew he could provide no answers, and little consolation. She could push now, but she sensed she would not like the answer.

"I would like to go home now," Sophie said. Brandon, ever the obliging gentleman, informed the driver even though she keenly wished that he would refuse and instead order the carriage to drive all the way to Gretna.

"We'll find a solution, Sophie," he said calmly.

"When? Your wedding is in two days' time!" she cried.

"It's not simple and I have a lot to consider," he persisted. Oh, she knew that! She didn't expect it to be easy, but was it too much to ask that he arrive at some course of action sooner rather than later?

All he had to do was follow his heart, she thought, but then she conceded that wasn't such an easy thing when one had been ruled by his head for so long—and a very hard head, at that.

She also understood that in his position, as a man—as a head of a family, as a duke, as a powerful double duke—meant that he was delicately trying to balance competing interests, and often neglected to consider his own.

She also knew that as a powerful duke, no one spoke to him plainly and told him when he was being vexing, bullish, or simply wrong.

"You are hiding behind honor. I think it is cowardly, not heroic. I think that is just an excuse because you are afraid to trust von Vennigan, afraid to love me, and terrified to upset the order of things to do something for yourself for once."

"I am a duke. Many people depend upon me. I do not have the liberty of doing something for myself."

"Brandon, I have defied all expectations of what a woman has the freedom to do. I will not accept that excuse from a man, least of all a duke. If anyone can do whatever he pleases, it is you. But I shall not argue or debate this with you. If you can't see this . . . then I cannot make you."

The carriage stopped promptly at the perfect moment for her to make a grand exit. She reached for the latch to open the door. Brandon's hand closed over hers.

If he kissed her now . . .

Involuntarily, her lips parted at the thought. If he kissed her now, she knew that it would not merely be a kiss, but that she would be thoroughly, utterly, wonderfully ravished in a carriage. Her skin tingled at the mere suggestion.

She would finally be able to run her fingers through his hair, to slide her hands beneath the fabric of his shirt, and feel his heartbeat under her bare palm. They would be skin to skin, heart to heart. They would kiss, oh yes, for hours. Hot, frantic, delicious, and illicit kisses. Yet pleasure would tangle with uncertainty within her. Would it be the end? Or would duty compel him to make it their beginning?

Sophie felt herself leaning toward him slightly, involuntarily, and he was, too. His hand still covered hers, holding her captive.

A kiss seemed to be suspended in the air between them. One need only to lean forward a little more to find soft, yielding lips. Such a kiss would swiftly lead to an act that would not be lovemaking, but only another complication.

They had been so *good.*

If that was going to happen, she wanted it to be a consummation of their love, not a hurried, frantic affair in a carriage because they were overcome with passion and could not think clearly. They could do that later.

But his hand still covered hers, covering the latch, thus keeping her in.

"Brandon, I'm trying to make a grand exit here," Sophie said frankly. That elicited a faint smile.

"This is not goodbye," he said, and then he let her go, when she wished he would ask her to stay forever.

Chapter 40

Brandon ordered his driver to take him to White's. A drink was absolutely in order. Upon his arrival, he took a seat in the back room, which was, thankfully, mostly empty save for a few second sons of minor lords playing a game of billiards. Lord Biddulph and Mitchell Twitchell were drinking and watching the billiards game, and occasionally absentmindedly rearranging the balls, to the great frustration of the players.

As he proceeded to consume an excessive amount of brandy, Brandon composed a list in his head:

> *<u>Truths that must be acknowledged, though he desperately wished to avoid them:</u>*
> 1. He had been an ass during that carriage ride with Sophie. But he had felt as if he was on the rack, and the screws were tightening, and he must not confess at all costs.
> 2. He might, in fact, be acting like a coward. This he preferred not to dwell on, but might return to it after, say, six or seven more brandies. The one he'd had thus far was not enough.
> 3. Sophie had a way of saying just the right thing.

4. It wasn't that he was a coward, just that he was finding it difficult to reverse course. All his life he had been raised to put The Estate first and now he was tempted to consider making a duchess out of a lower-class girl because he was in l— No, he was not yet ready to acknowledge that truth. Not after only two drinks.

5. Where was he? Ah, yes, changing plans, revising lifelong values, etc, etc. Did he really want to marry Clarissa? Yes, she would be calm and composed, would never intrude upon his study or his thoughts, and honestly, he did not imagine loving her and thus he did not imagine heartache upon losing her. Why, then, was he so reluctant to give her up? Note to self: do order more brandy before contemplating that.

6. Responsibility (see previous point four— in charge of the world and it's contents), and von Vennigan not being trustworthy (as Sophie had pointed out in the carriage, see previous point three). If Brandon told von Vennigan about The Awful Secret that Spencer, that too-damned-good secretary of his had discovered, and von Vennigan refused Clarissa because of it, then Brandon, out of duty, would have to go through with the wedding. If he could accept the Awful Truth about her then perhaps an elopement would be in order, but that still left the matter of what he wanted to do about Sophie.

7. Sophie always said just the right thing. Which meant that . . .

8. He was a coward, von Vennigan was trust-worthy, and he, Brandon, was terrified to love her because he was even more terrified to lose her.

9. Another drink was certainly in order.

10. He had the most blinding insights into things with some alcohol coursing through his veins, and brain. Must drink to excess more often.

"Dear God, it's the apocalypse," Roxbury declared when he arrived to discover Brandon in the advanced stages of intoxication. He was sprawled on the chair, with a half-empty glass dangling dangerously from his fingertips. It appeared that some of the contents was soaking into his shirt (unbuttoned) and waistcoat (also unbuttoned). Cravat: whereabouts unknown. Hair: disheveled as much as it could be.

Roxbury continued, vastly amused by this unexpected scenario of the Perfect Duke outrageously foxed: "It *must* be the end of the world if you are drinking so much. Although . . . No, you would organize everything, ensuring that judgment day ran smoothly and efficiently, and that all the plagues arrived as scheduled . . ."

"Are you finished?" Brandon slurred.

"I'm shocked. I haven't seen you like this since your father died. Oh *God*—has someone died?"

"No."

"This must be a case of women troubles. Typical. What has happened?" Roxbury availed himself to a seat and took a sip of his drink, already in hand. That was the great thing about Roxbury. He was always ready for lamenting, particularly about love affairs, whether his own or, less frequently, someone else's.

"Another man has proposed to my fiancée. Sophie does not understand why I cannot just jilt my betrothed for her."

"Why doesn't your fiancée jilt you?" Roxbury asked. "I would if I were her."

"Her mother will not allow it."

"And why will you not jilt your fiancée?"

"Yes, why, Lord Brandon?" another voice demanded. It was von Vennigan, and he had just arrived. For some reason, he was dressed in military attire, or so Brandon assumed due to the medals decorating his jacket. A cape was thrown over one shoulder, revealing his sword, ready to be unsheathed at the slightest provocation. "Why will you not release her from the bonds you hold her in?"

"You're being overdramatic again, von Vennigan," Brandon said, bored. Then he noted that *again* and *von Vennigan* rhymed and this occupied his thoughts for a few more seconds than it ought to, due to the drink, of course.

"I am a man in love. It cannot be helped," von Vennigan stated grandly. "And you are the obstacle standing between me and my love."

"He's sitting, actually," Roxbury pointed out, though no one paid him any mind.

Von Vennigan drew his sword. The room fell silent.

Lord Biddulph, deeply in his cups and intrigued by the sword, leaned forward to get a closer look and fell out of his chair. As this was typical behavior for him, no one paid any attention to him, not even Mitchell Twitchell.

"Put your damned sword away, von Vennigan," Roxbury cut in. "He's too drunk to stand, let alone fight. It would be embarrassing for you both to challenge him now."

Turning to his friend, Roxbury continued: "I beg your pardon, but I still don't understand, Brandon, why you can't let this bloke have your fiancée so that you can run off with that *Weekly* wench you are utterly besotted with."

"I'm not besotted," Brandon mumbled.

Roxbury and von Vennigan laughed uproariously. Biddulph and Twitchell joined their laughter, though they could have no idea what they were splitting their sides over. This vastly increased Roxbury's amusement with the situation, and diminished Brandon's.

"You damn well are!" von Vennigan declared when he had recovered sufficient breath to speak.

"Just admit it, man, you are in love," Roxbury said, between gasps of laughter.

"Love is an irrational emotion that leads to nothing but heartache, trouble. It distracts one from important things, like managing the world," Brandon lectured. Perhaps, if he repeated it enough, it would be true.

"Do go on," Roxbury said with a smirk.

"Love makes one lose all sense, rationality, and self-control. It makes a mess of a man. This will *not* happen to me," Brandon declared firmly. That is why he had to hold on so tightly to Clarissa. Because if he let go of her, then he could let his heart go to Sophie and then he would always be distracted thus, somehow that meant the estates would be mismanaged and parliament wouldn't be able to function, and thus England would lose her supremacy over other nations and the world would end.

It didn't quite make sense, but it felt like it did. Everything depended upon him.

Von Vennigan looked a bit red in the face, Brandon noted.

"For the love of God and anything holy, it's already happened to you!" von Vennigan exploded.

"He has a point," Roxbury said. "The famously restrained duke has lost it. Drunk. Cravat lost. Waistcoat unbuttoned. You are outrageously drunk, all over a woman. It's too late. You are in love."

"I beg to differ—"

"The sooner you realize it, the sooner we can plan a way out of your wedding, which is scheduled to take place a mere six and thirty hours from now."

"There are other things to consider, von Vennigan. Perhaps when you are older you'll understand," Brandon explained. Horrible secrets and lies, for starters. Ones that made the marriage contract null and void, should he deign to bring it to anyone's attention.

"I'm old enough now to know my own mind, and my own heart."

"But do you know about anything else? Responsibility, duty, contractions, debts, *deception*? Your own heart and mind are the least of it."

"I will learn," von Vennigan retorted. "You did. After all, you could not possibly have been born with the weight of the world on your shoulders."

Brandon wasn't born with it. It was dumped upon him one night when he was eighteen, when his father failed to survive the overturning of his carriage one stormy December night. He'd lost a lot that evening—his father, his innocence, his freedom, and his desire for love.

Chapter 41

Richmond House
Earlier that evening

Clarissa pushed open the door to her mother's private chamber without invitation, and without knocking. She sat at her dressing table, brushing out her hair. It was long and golden, like Clarissa's, like dear, departed Aunt Eleanor and every other woman on their side of the family.

"Why?" Clarissa asked, her voice raw from hours of sobbing.

"I'm glad to see you have progressed to leaving your bedchamber. Perhaps tomorrow you'll dress and join us for breakfast."

"Why can't I marry Frederick?" Clarissa asked again.

"I don't wish to speak of this."

All her life she had been the most docile and obliging daughter. This was the moment when she needed to find her voice and her courage. She thought of Frederick's kiss, and how delighted he'd been when she told him he was excessively provoking. She could *do* this.

"Why? He's rich, and he loves me. We can both

be happy," Clarissa cried. "Why can I not marry for love?"

"You're being overdramatic, Clarissa. Spare me—"

"Oh, now you're going to mention dear, departed Aunt Eleanor again, are you not? Just because she had rotten luck doesn't mean that—"

"That's a fine way to speak of your mother!"

From the look upon her face, Clarissa swore she hadn't meant to say it. At least, not like that.

"What did you say?"

"Sit down, Clarissa. I'm tired of keeping this secret and you shall learn why you must marry Lord Brandon."

Clarissa sat down on the settee before the fireplace—there was no flame burning. The heat wave in the city still raged on. And yet, Clarissa was chilled.

"You are not my child, Clarissa. You are Eleanor's bastard child. Your father was a charmer—like your prince—who had his spot of fun with my sister. She died giving birth to you."

Clarissa's gaze immediately went to the portrait of the two sisters. It was one of the few that had not been sold. Clarissa could easily be either of their daughters, for they all shared the same straight golden hair, wide-set blue eyes, and porcelain skin. The picture was proof of nothing, other than this revelation being a possibility.

"I had been married for a few years by then, and it was clear that I was not able to have a child. An heir. It was agreed that I would raise you as my own, as far as the world knows."

"How did you manage that?" she asked skeptically.

"Oh, it's easy enough to take an extended tour of the country with my sister as a companion and come back with a baby," her mother said breezily.

"So Father—I know not what to call him now—he doesn't know?"

"It would break his heart should he learn that the Richmond line will die with him, or that the title is going to an illegitimate girl child not of his blood."

It would kill him. He was obsessed with breeding, and he had failed to do so himself. He was so interested in tracing the bloodlines of broodmares and stallions and the truth of his own family's line was unknown to him. Her heart started to ache for him, and for her dead parents, and for herself.

"Why did you do all this?"

"Like all women of our station, there were two things expected of me in life, Clarissa," she said coldly. "I was to marry well and to deliver an heir. I've always been determined to succeed at the only thing the world gave me a chance to accomplish. It is rare that a woman can find success outside of the home, like Miss Harlow. I hadn't that option. Because of you, Clarissa, I was able to fulfill my duties. I have taken us far, but only you can complete this."

"I still don't see why . . ."

"It's too risky! We have arranged by special order of the king—*the king!*—for the title to pass through you. Do you know what a rare honor that is?"

"I don't care!"

"Should Frederick discover this secret of yours, he could never marry you. No one would marry you, and we would be penniless. Lord Brandon—"

"Does he know?"

"I don't think so. God forbid he learn of it. Either way, the marriage contract is ironclad. In a few days' time, the estates, the fortune, our futures will be secured. I've kept this secret for twenty years, and it needs to remain a secret for two more days."

"He loves me, so perhaps . . ."

"Princes have to care about bloodlines and lineages. More so than dukes."

"Were my parents in love?" she asked. It was vitally important that she know. It would, she was certain, determine her fate.

"Very much. It led to utter stupidity. To a mad dash to Gretna Green in winter. There was an accident and your father did not survive. Eleanor was already pregnant."

"Can you tell me more about them?" she whispered. She could hardly believe it, but details might make it real.

"There are hundreds of love letters and Eleanor kept a diary. I shall give them to you when you are married to Lord Brandon."

Up until that moment, Clarissa had been ready to flee to Frederick no matter what. But the chance to know the whole truth of her real parents and her own existence was a tempting offer. All she had to do was marry a man she did not love and keep him from the woman he ought to be with. How badly did she wish for those love letters, knowing the wealth of secrets and details contained within her own loving correspondence with Frederick?

Chapter 42

The day before the wedding . . .

Hamilton House

Brandon opened his eyes, saw that he woke in his bedchamber, could not recall arriving there, and closed his eyes upon the excruciating pain that occurred when he tried to think.

He did wonder why someone was pounding on his head. A moment later, he concluded that his head ached independently from the hammering, which was likely due to the servants preparing for his wedding. Tomorrow. A wave of nausea coursed through him.

Slowly, fragments of the evening returned to him.

He'd been at White's and he'd been drinking. Roxbury had been there, and von Vennigan, too. Mostly, though, he had indulged in a good drinking and thinking session. He remembered being amazed by the insights and stunning revelations about himself and his situation. Unfortunately, that was all that he recalled.

One thing was clear: he had been driven to living rakishly and it did not suit him. Brandon resolved to return to his sober, gentlemanly habits as soon as he was able to.

He was a gentleman who dressed appropriately and

completely (no more of this gadding about without a cravat), who kept a clear head, and did not indulge in drunken, emotional outbursts, who did not make an ass of himself over a woman.

Last night, he had failed on all counts.

He held on to one consolation: he had not gone and fallen in love, and given his heart away. One could recover from the aftereffects of alcohol in a day; heartache took longer. But he would not suffer from heartache because he had not fallen in love. In fact, he very clearly remembered lecturing Roxbury and von Vennigan about this very thing.

Something about how love would never happen to him, and if it did the world would come to a crashing halt. Brandon actually groaned as he recalled their response: hysterical laughter.

The door to his bedchamber opened.

"Good morning, Your Grace," Jennings said brightly.

"Good morning, Your Grace," Spencer echoed.

"What is it?" Brandon asked irritably.

"Your Grace, we are attending to you at eight o'clock as we always do," Spencer said.

"I'll assist with your dress, whilst Spencer goes on and on about all the tedious tasks and Very Important Appointments in your day," Jennings explained.

"Are you unwell, Your Grace?" Spencer inquired.

"He's fine, just overdrank himself last night. I've been waiting years to witness this," Jennings said. He clapped his hands together and grinned broadly.

"Do not clap, or make any loud noise, or I shall fire you," Brandon mumbled.

"Of course, Your Grace. Shall we carry on, then?" Spencer said.

"Tell me what awaits me today, Spencer," Brandon muttered.

"Your sisters and their families are due to arrive this afternoon. Your family will dine with the Richmonds. According to my notes, you have not obtained the special license, or secured a best man, or composed a toast for the wedding breakfast. Knowing you, that must be an inaccuracy on my part . . ."

At that, Brandon was suddenly wide-awake.

He had not obtained a special license.

In fact, he had not obtained any license whatsoever.

He thought he might be sick—due to either alcohol poisoning, or a lack of preparation for the biggest day of his life, or because his mother just burst into his chamber, uninvited, and without notice. He pulled the sheets up to cover his bare chest.

"I should like an interview with my son. Privately."

Spencer and Jennings fled.

"You have been drinking. You never drink," his mother said, stating the obvious.

"I'm a grown man, I'm allowed to overindulge from time to time," he said sullenly, sounding much more like a schoolboy than an adult.

"Of course you are. I'm only concerned about the timing," she said.

"Living like a bachelor at least once before I settle down," he said grandly.

"Bollocks."

"Mother!"

"Honestly, how on earth have I raised such a stick-in-the-mud? You didn't always used to be like this. In fact, you used to be quite the little devil," she told him. "Don't you remember the fun we used to have as a family? We are a lively bunch, though it's been so long since we've all really been together . . ."

"Since Father died."

"It is time for us to have a Serious Discussion."

"I think I am going to be sick," he said, and closed his eyes.

"I think you are going to listen," she stated firmly. "Your father would be so proud of the way you manage the responsibility of the estate and as head of this family. I am so proud of you. Brandon, you are a strong, reliable man. But your father would be so disappointed in you if you let go of true love."

Brandon opened his eyes and looked at his mother. Her cheeks were flushed, her eyes were bright, and she was utterly serious.

He had always hated to disappoint. To hear his father say "I'm very disappointed with you, son" was a worse punishment than a week locked in the attic with naught but stale bread and water. Or so he'd imagined, for he had never suffered such because 1) he was good, and 2) his parents had not been horrid and cruel. They'd been lovely and loving, in fact.

But about true love, and letting it escape . . . it was a Noble Sacrifice.

"I don't know what you are talking about," Brandon said.

"Don't play the dunce with me," she retorted. "You need not answer me now, but you will listen. Your father and I were madly in love from the day we met until the day he died. Yes, it destroyed me to lose him, as you saw. When he was alive, it wasn't sunshine and roses all the time. But I wouldn't trade a second of the heartache so long as I got to spend all those years with him, and raise such a lovely family with him."

Brandon nodded. There was a knot in his stomach and an ache in his chest. Things had been so damned glorious—a house full of laughter, the shouts of children, and a duke who read bedtime stories and a duchess who took tea with her daughters and their dolls.

And kissing. He remembered now, they were always kissing.

They had been happy, truly happy.

"I want you to consider that as you are deciding whom you shall marry tomorrow," she told him.

"Mother, it's already been decided . . ." He had signed the contract. He had given his word. He had learned too much about Clarissa to cast her out into a cruel and unmerciful world, and von Vennigan could not be taken seriously or trusted.

But Sophie . . . A fresh wave of pain washed over him. If she knew him so well, why could she not understand why he had to keep his word?

If he left Clarissa, he wouldn't be the man she loved. If he didn't leave Clarissa, he'd be the man she loved that broke her heart. *He could not win.*

Had he more strength and less of an aching head, he'd howl at the unfairness of it all. No, actually, he would not. That was an uncivilized thing to do. As a gentleman, he would stifle the desire.

"No, Brandon, it is not too late," she said with an exasperated sigh. "Now, if you'll excuse me, I have to return Miss Harlow's notebook to her."

"You have her notebook?" Brandon asked. She was constantly scribbling notes in it. He had suffered pangs of curiosity over what she had written.

"Yes. She left it here the other day."

"She's always forgetting things accidentally," he said with a bittersweet smile.

"Is she? What else?"

"She always says just the thing to make me laugh when I am being too serious."

"You need her," his mother said.

"I'll take the notebook to her," he offered.

"We'll see," she said, pursing her lips.

Richmond House
Exterior

To the surprise of no one, the Richmonds were not "at home" when von Vennigan called upon them. The errand was not entirely a failure, however, because he was able to glimpse into the grand foyer and glean a faint idea of the layout, as he waited to learn if he would be allowed a visit. It was information that might prove useful should one, say, be sneaking through the house in the dark with a fair-haired angel in tow.

It was very clear to him: Lord Brandon was not going to make things easy by breaking the engagement. It was necessary, then, for von Vennigan to resort to extreme measures to secure his future happiness. She had, after all, asked him to rescue her.

He strolled around the house, and wondered which window opened to Clarissa's bedroom, and if she saw him strolling around the garden in search of a way into the house and, most importantly, a way out.

After a quarter of an hour, von Vennigan had seen enough. He returned to his hotel and ordered his staff to pack the things. He would leave tomorrow, as originally planned. If God, Fate, Fortune, etc., etc., smiled upon him, his ship would sail away from England with him and Clarissa hand in hand and looking toward the horizon, and their future together.

Richmond House
Interior

It was a strange thing to have breakfast with one's parents who were not, actually, one's parents. Clarissa had never suspected a thing . . . in fact, she even wondered if this was just a convenient lie told to coerce her into marriage with Brandon. *When you marry Lord Brandon, I'll give you their love letters and your mother's diary,* she had said.

She wished, desperately, to know about her real mother. And her father.

Her mother—or should she call her Aunt?—was adamant that she should marry the duke, and reject the prince. Clarissa's writing things had been confiscated. Though she hadn't been locked in her room, she hadn't been encouraged to leave it, save for breakfast with the people who had raised her, the Duke and Duchess of Richmond. Oh, and she'd go out for the final dress fitting later today. Escorted by half a dozen maids and footmen, no doubt.

It went without saying that none of Frederick's letters had reached her. He rang the bell this morning, but Lady Richmond did not permit him in. Her heart had soared, and then crashed.

The question remained: The prince or the duke?

She loved the one; she did not love the other. She could marry von Vennigan and leave behind her family, her country, everything she's ever known. She could marry Lord Brandon and learn about her real mother and her real father. She could also live in a loveless marriage in which he pined for Sophie, or perhaps would even make her his mistress.

The choice was very clear. She must marry Frederick.

And yet, she was not sure that she possessed the requisite gumption required for the dramatic, scandalous, incredible act of ditching the duke at the last minute in order to run off with a prince.

Merely considering it now induced a wave of nausea. Her skin felt tingly, though not in an altogether unpleasant way.

Her father—or uncle?—was speaking about his usual subject. Clarissa tuned him out and wondered how to refer to her parents in her head, and decided to maintain the charade that had defined all of their lives.

"Lord Burbroke and I were debating—quite a lively debate, I should say—over which parent had more of an effect on the foal: the sire or the dam," Lord Richmond informed his wife and Clarissa. The ladies wore feigned expressions of polite interest; their thoughts were clearly elsewhere. Clarissa, however, was making an effort to listen.

"And I had to point out," he continued, "that the offspring almost always inherits the status in the herd that its mother had, as they are usually of the same temperament, you see."

That sounds like mothers and daughters in the ton, she thought. Would she take after her real mother, or the duchess? Would she elope with the man she loved, as her real mother had? Or would she, like the mother she had known, marry for the grand opinion of England's beau monde?

"Perhaps we needn't discuss this over breakfast," Lady Richmond said in a tense and bored tone, but to no effect. It was so sad, Clarissa thought, how no one ever wished to talk to her father about his favorite subject. It was almost tragic that he should be so obsessed with breeding, and have not even sired his own child, who would, provided she marry Lord Brandon, pass on the title to a child not even of the Richmond blood.

He had been a good father to her. She vowed that he should not discover the secret.

The duke ignored the duchess. They were not fond of each other; that was no secret. She did not want to live like that. If she married Frederick . . .

She did not believe that a love like theirs could fade. She would not allow it. Now, if only she could steady her nerves and find the recourse to commit her one act of disobedience.

"In fact, if you think about it, which I have done at considerable length, I assure you, the foal spends more time with its mother—in utero, being the prime example. And I cannot help but offer my experience with my favorite mare, Magnolia. No matter the sire, her foals always took after her," Lord Richmond said. "Calm and obedient, but quite spirited when the situation called for it. Excellent qualities in any female."

Clarissa snapped to attention at that.

True love was certainly one of those occasions that called for spirited behavior—if her real mother had done it, then perhaps Clarissa could, too.

24 Bloomsbury Place

This time tomorrow Brandon would be saying his vows. The thought intensified the horrendous pressure in Sophie's chest. Honestly, she feared her heart would burst from a potent combination of love, passion, anxiety, uncertainty, anger, and desire.

The copious amounts of tea she had consumed earlier—in an effort to settle her nerves—had made her jittery. She tried to lie down. She could not stay still. And so, she paced.

It was the previous evening's conversation in the carriage that she replayed in her mind. Brandon had too many things to consider and it was paralyzing his decision-making abilities. In trying to please everyone, no one was happy.

But it was her own words to him that her thoughts kept returning to: I have defied expectations . . .

She was, as Brandon had helped her to see, a brave woman. She blossomed when others might have wilted. After all, when Matthew left her, she hadn't stayed in Chesham to fade away, but had done the unthinkable and moved to London. And then, she had dared to apply for a man's job, and look how that turned out!

Rather well, she thought.

But it was something that Lavinia, of all the people in the world, had said that confirmed her course of action: He is the man for me, she had said, implying that there was little one should not do for the man she loved.

It was clear: Sophie would have to do something.

With that decided, she only needed to figure out what exactly to do to ensure that she and Brandon married, and that Clarissa and Frederick were able to marry, and that no one was left stranded at the altar.

"Hell and damnation," Sophie swore.

Sophie's pacing was interrupted by Bessy informing her that there was a caller waiting in the drawing room.

"And you'd better get dressed up all fancylike for this one," the maid added.

"Is it Brandon?"

"No. Methinks it's his mother," Bessy said. The fact that a duchess was calling at their little house did nothing to jolt the maid out of her typically sullen demeanor.

"Help me into the green dress and then prepare a tea tray."

Bessy nodded. Within record time, Sophie was dressed to receive the duchess. One did not dawdle upon such occasions, if only because one could not stand the curiosity.

"Your Grace." The duchess had availed herself of a seat upon the settee. Sophie sat opposite her on the brown étoile chair.

"Miss Harlow," the duchess said. "I found your notebook and I have come to return it."

"Oh, thank you so very much, Your Grace! I'm always forgetting my things; it's a terrible habit of mine," Sophie said. And then she wondered why the duchess was personally returning it when it would be more convenient and appropriate to send a servant to deliver it.

And then Sophie suddenly understood: "You read my notebook."

"Against all my best intentions. But your notes from our first interview caught my eye, particularly your comment about Lady Richmond being a shameless name-dropper."

"I'm sorry . . ."

"It's spot on," the duchess continued. "And then I couldn't resist the rest. So I have come not only to return it to you, but apologize for reading your personal material."

"Thank you. I completely understand," Sophie said. She probably would have done exactly the same thing.

"I have also come to inquire on your plans to win my son for yourself and prevent his marriage to Clarissa."

It was such an unexpected question from the duchess that even though Sophie had been scheming all morning, she could say nothing. The duchess's matter-of-fact tone struck her speechless.

"Your Grace! I couldn't possibly . . ." Sophie demurred. It seemed like the polite thing to do.

"Miss Harlow, I have read your book and know your feelings for my son, and that you are a smart and resourceful girl. I wish to speak to that girl and not a doormat."

"Yes, Your Grace."

"Now, what are you going to do about his well-intended but idiotic idea of honor and marrying the wrong woman?" Lady Hamilton asked.

"Any plan would have to ensure that Clarissa and von Vennigan can be together," Sophie said quickly.

"Of course."

"And *no one* can be left alone at the altar. It's a personal horror of mine, and I wouldn't wish it upon anyone."

"Right. We'll need special licenses, too. I shall take care of that," Lady Hamilton declared, and Sophie sighed with relief. That was one part that kept tripping up her plan. There was one other thing, too, that she'd had trouble accommodating.

"And one problem—"

"Yes?"

"He doesn't want to marry me!" Sophie confessed.

"He does, Miss Harlow. He'll figure it out any minute now," Lady Hamilton answered breezily.

"We haven't many minutes before it's too late! This time tomorrow . . ." Sophie persisted. This was the other part that gave her pause—that Brandon might not wish to marry her and she might find herself alone at the altar, again.

She shuddered. Actually shuddered.

"Which is why we must plan," the duchess said calmly, and Sophie understood where Brandon had inherited quite a few of his more notable character traits.

"Yes. Planning," Sophie said, hoping that Hamilton and Brandon family composure would rub off on her.

Bessy brought the tea tray in just then. The two ladies paused to pour, add sugar, milk, etc., and then, finally, they each took a fortifying sip.

"The easiest thing would be if Clarissa and I could somehow switch places," Sophie said.

A rush of planning ensued. They kept their voices low, even though there was no one to overhear. Occasionally, they whispered. They considered the movements of the bride, the habits of the bride's mother, the volume of skirts on the bride's dress. They rejected this idea in favor of that idea. They factored in the massive crowds expected to gather outside of St. George's. Sophie paced. Lady Hamilton sipped her tea and smoothed her skirts. When a brilliant idea occurred to one of them, they smiled grandly at their own genius and mischief.

Approximately one hour and one pot of tea later, the Duchess of Hamilton and Brandon and her future successor had developed a plan to ensure that Clarissa married Frederick and that Sophie married Brandon. Tomorrow.

Nothing was required of the men, other than that they stay in the proper places—

Brandon at the altar and von Vennigan at the docks, where he would be boarding his ship.

The real daring and disruptive actions were left to the two brides. They were the ones with the wits, courage, and sense to be trusted with a mission of this magnitude—disrupting the wedding of the year and turning it into the wedding of a lifetime.

"Now all we must do is ensure Clarissa's participation," Sophie said. That was one of the few weak points of their plan: it required a grand act of disobedience from the most dutiful and obliging creature in the world.

"She and her mother will be at Madame Auteuil's

for a final fitting. I am supposed to meet them," Lady Hamilton said.

"Oh, that's right. I was supposed to join, but I doubt that I am welcome after yesterday's scene."

"Likely not, but you shall come anyway. I will engage Lady Richmond's attention while you have a moment with Clarissa and explain everything."

"Perfect."

Sophie, the Duchess, and Bessy gathered their things, donned their bonnets and gloves, went out, and climbed into the duchess's carriage. Twice now she had been in this carriage, which reminded Sophie of a saying: What happens once shall never happen again. What happens twice shall happen thrice.

She took it as a good omen, one she very much needed.

Their plan was good. But she hadn't forgotten that, as of the previous evening, Brandon had not wanted to marry her. And that if he did not come around, *then she would be jilted at the altar again.*

Such was their plan. Sophie tried to change that part of it, but they could find no other way. It was a risk that she would have to take. Already her stomach was working its way into knots.

"Why are you doing this, Lady Hamilton?"

"Because this will make more people happier than otherwise. Because if we leave it up to men, it will be some slapdash last-minute scheme riddled with flaws. Because he's my son and I want what is best for him. Because a mother knows best. And because it is so very exciting, and because it's *true love* and one cannot sit still and idly watch it pass by."

"All excellent reasons," Sophie replied.

"I should confess that I do not fancy the Richmonds as my in-laws."

"You have not met my family," Sophie pointed out. It occurred to her that, should everything happen as it ought to, they would miss her wedding. She would also have to do without the Harlow veil (which had been repaired, her mother informed her, in one of the numerous letters they shared). Considering how that had gone for her before, Sophie did not miss it.

"I'm sure they are lovely and, if not, they at least live in the country," Lady Hamilton said. The carriage came to a stop in front of the shop.

"They are good people and they are not name-droppers."

"Splendid. Wait here for a moment, until I will have taken Lady Richmond aside."

Sophie remained in the carriage and tried to sort out the welter of thoughts and feelings storming around within her. One horrid thought kept bobbing to the surface: what if she was jilted at the altar again?

It would be so much worse this time because she loved Brandon so much more.

It would be so much worse because it wouldn't happen in the tiny little church in the sleepy town of Chesham but in St. George's of Hanover Square in front of two hundred members of the ton, with another large crowd outside.

The last time she'd just been Sophie Harlow, small-town girl. Now she was Miss Harlow of "Miss Harlow's Marriage in High Life" of *The London Weekly,* the largest newspaper in London and thus the largest in the world. All the rival papers would relish the story of the wedding columnist that got jilted. Twice.

Sophie suspected that she wouldn't be able to feel the slightest shred of embarrassment because the heartache of being rejected by Brandon would nullify her capacity to feel anything, ever again.

His hesitancy scared her, but it would not scare her off. She was sure they belonged together and she was hopeful that he would figure that out before it was too late.

But to be jilted *again* . . .

Oh, she would *NOT* be sick in the carriage.

And then she remembered that she was brave and that he admired her for that.

Brave, beautiful, Writing Girl Sophie emerged, scaring away the small-town, panic-prone version of herself.

The woman who had once before dared to go after a grand fate emerged from the carriage. She would dare to do it again.

She entered Madame Auteuil's shop and quickly found Clarissa—standing in her wedding dress.

"If I have a plan for you to marry Frederick and for me to marry Brandon, would you do it?"

Clarissa continued to stand perfectly still while her hem was slightly altered and she considered Sophie's question.

"I have always been so very *good*," she said finally, and Sophie's heart seemed to stop beating. "But if ever there was an occasion for disobedience, it is now."

Sophie exhaled with relief and felt her heartbeat quicken.

"It will require me stealing your wedding, to an extent," Sophie said, keeping her voice low.

"It's my mother's wedding, as she selected everything, and I couldn't care less about it. Now, tell me what must be done."

Sophie wasn't sure what had occurred with Clarissa to make her readily agree when Sophie had been braced to convince her of the merits of this plan. She did not take time to question it. Instead, she whispered the details—the devilishly simple, unfathomably scandalous, potentially life-altering details—to Clarissa.

"But what if something goes wrong? And what about the carriage driver?"

Sophie whispered more instructions.

"I think I can do this," Clarissa said finally. "Although I am already terrified."

"I as well," Sophie said. And then she reached out for Clarissa's hand and gave it an affectionate squeeze.

"I'll miss you, Sophie."

"I'll miss you, too," she answered truthfully. They were from different circumstances, they lived in different worlds, and they had little in common except for a few very important things: Lord Brandon; illicit, secret love affairs; and, now, high-stakes gambling for a love match.

"And you must select a dress now," Clarissa said, and urged her out of the dressing room. Sophie knew just the one.

But first, Lady Richmond took notice of her. "Miss Harlow, what are you doing here?"

"Good day, Lady Richmond. I have come to purchase a dress for the wedding tomorrow."

"You are still attending?" she asked in disbelief, with a scowl upon her features.

"Unless you do not wish for it to be written about in the newspaper," Sophie answered lightly, knowing full well that she very much did.

"Is there not someone else that could write about it?"

"No, there is not," Sophie said proudly. The column was "Miss Harlow's Marriage in High Life." She wrote it, and it belonged to her and no one else. And yet, on the spot, Sophie decided that tomorrow's wedding would be the last one she reported on, whether she married Brandon or not.

Perhaps she could convince Mr. Knightly to allow her to write about ladies' fashion. Or perhaps she would be a seamstress, servant, mistress, or governess after all.

Maybe, she might even be a duchess.

Sophie hadn't considered it that way before. A tremor of fear at the magnitude of the events of the next twenty-four hours coursed through her.

"If you must, Miss Harlow," Lady Richmond conceded. Her passion for social glory far surpassed her disdain for Sophie. "Do sit in the back, though, to save the prime seats for our more esteemed guests."

Sophie merely nodded and turned away. She said hello to Lady Hamilton, as if they had not arrived together.

"Hello, Miss Harlow. I'm sorry that I cannot stay longer, but I have an urgent errand to take care of," Lady Hamilton said with a wink. She was off to procure the special licenses.

Finally, Sophie had the attention of Madame Auteuil herself.

"You are here for a dress?" the modiste asked.

"Yes. How much is this one?" Sophie asked, gesturing to the gorgeous one she thought of as Her Dress. It was made of snow-white satin, which contrasted stunningly with her dark hair and eyes. On the bodice, hundreds of glass beads were sewn in, nearly covering the satin. They splayed out on the skirt, and intermingled with pearls. As before, it made her think of moonlight reflecting upon freshly fallen snow.

"For you? It is gratis," Madame said with a smile.

"I'm sorry, I do not speak French," Sophie answered, hoping that "gratis" was not a very large number.

"Free, my dear, for you."

"No, you couldn't possibly mean that!" Sophie exclaimed. Her mouth dropped open. Even in her wildest dreams, she had never considered free dresses.

"Absolutement! Since you have begun mentioning my shop in your columns, my business has increased tenfold. It is the least that I can do. Besides, I have watched you admire it for a month now."

"I adore it," Sophie said softly.

"Come on, try it on. We haven't much time for alterations," the modiste urged. An hour later, Sophie and Bessy and The Dress hailed a hackney to return them to 24 Bloomsbury Place.

Hamilton House
Later that afternoon

When Brandon returned from his errand to procure a special license from the Archbishop of Canterbury, his butler informed him that his sisters and their families were due to arrive shortly. Thus would commence the wedding celebrations. They would dine with the Richmonds this evening.

Brandon thanked the butler and retired to his study.

He had not actually seen the archbishop, because he was engaged with someone else, but he quickly provided the necessary document after being alerted to the urgency of the situation. After treating the clerk to his most haughty, lofty, ducal stare, Brandon had left with a license lacking any names.

Brandon set the incomplete special license on the desk, adding it to the growing pile of papers scattered all over the surface in no conceivable order. Not so long ago, the top of his desk was polished to a high gloss and devoid of clutter. His habit was to neatly sort his papers, which Spencer filed promptly. Lately, he had been too occupied with other things.

Sophie. Something seized up in his chest at the thought of her.

Because of Sophie, he had woken up hungover, his desk was a mess, his mind uncertain, and his heart actually ached. His life was a disaster and he was a stranger to himself. All this disarray and confusion was her fault.

Brandon tried to recall how things were before Sophie, before that moment he looked into her smiling face and felt his breath knocked out of him.

He had been at his club, not drinking, thinking he knew better than everyone what it meant to be a gentleman, and wishing that he wasn't so damned constrained by the dictates of everyone else all the damned time.

He had indulged in selfish behavior, just a little. And, as if he had allowed himself one sip and then finished the bottle, there had been no turning back. This was inevitable. She happened to be present at his weak moment, that was all. It was not Sophie's fault.

Brandon did not care for the results of his overindulgence—his mind was muddled, his desk was a mess, and his life was a fiasco. Longing for calm, for order, for logic, for reason, for his damned head to stop throbbing overtook him.

Because he had brought this upon himself, it logically followed that he would be the one to sort it all out. Beginning with his desk was a capital idea.

Methodically, he began to sort through his papers. Parliamentary papers formed their own pile. Matters pertaining to his estate were another pile, and then those were ordered by estate (alphabetically, of course). There were stacks of personal correspondence, invitations, and legal documents. There were also personal notes and lists, namely, that troublesome list of *Desirable Qualities in a Wife*.

A review seemed prudent.

Attractive:

It would, as Sophie pointed out, be nice to look at a pleasant face across the breakfast table. He had been thinking more along the lines of bedding. Clarissa was beautiful, but he had no desire to touch her. But Sophie . . . he hardened at the thought of their naked limbs tangled as they made passionate love to each other.

Reasonable Intelligence:

Sophie was smart, well-educated, well-read and could certainly write, but she was far more than reasonably intelligent. She knew truly important things, like how to make him laugh, say just the right thing. She knew *him*. That was far more important than being able to maintain household accounts and find England on a map, which had been his original and inadequate definition.

Easy Temperament:

He had meant that she would not bother him. But he found his gaze settling on the door, and recollecting the memory of Sophie getting lost, entering, finding this list, and giving him her unsolicited opinions upon it. During that same interview, he had been sorely tested to wrestle her to the ground for this damned sheet of paper and have his way with her. Oh, she bothered him in *every* possible way. Oddly enough, he didn't mind.

From a Distinguished Family:

This one had been included so that he didn't think to consider any attractive, biddable servant in possession of a modicum of intelligence who would qualify. Brandon knew little of Sophie's family, other than they were gentry in some small country town. Translation: they were respectable enough and not near enough to meddle. And as for Clarissa . . . She was not who she said she was, and he sincerely doubted that she even knew it. It was a secret that he would keep.

It was logical and reasonable to conclude, based upon this review of his list, that Sophie was, in fact, the perfect bride for him. She was a scandalous choice for a duchess for many reasons, but she would be a good one. More importantly, she would be a good wife and he would be happy with her. Because he l—.

No, not yet.

Brandon placed the list in a drawer and turned to the last remaining document requiring his attention: the special license. He filled in his own name on the place marked for the bridegroom.

As for the bride . . . he hesitated.

Sophie was the one for him, that he was certain of now. But could he, notoriously perfect, upstanding gentleman, cause what would surely be the scandal of the decade?

If von Vennigan did not marry Clarissa, she would certainly be a spinster. The Richmonds' fates depended upon his wealth. They would attempt to sue him for breach of contract and he would either have to pay or blackmail them with that awful secret.

His reputation and the good name of his family would be blackened.

Charlotte, his younger unmarried sister, wouldn't have a prayer of finding a suitable husband when the ton would have legitimate cause to suspect that she, like her elder brother, might cry off at the last possible minute.

Could he do it? Could he risk everyone's fates so that he might marry Sophie?

There was a knock at the door.

"Your sisters, Amelia, Penelope, and Charlotte have arrived, as have their husbands and children," a servant informed him. Brandon quit his study to greet them.

By the time he had arrived in the hall, his mother had returned. The front foyer, typically the quiet and stately domain of the butler—the one man more organized, orderly, and neat than Brandon—had become unrecognizable. There were massive piles of luggage, which footmen attended to. Shouts and exclamations echoed on the marble floors and off the epically high ceiling. There were embraces, tears of joy, small children running and shrieking. It was an explosion of activity.

It was rare that the family all gathered under one roof. Amelia and Penelope lived some distance far away, and for the past few years one or the other was in her confinement. It made it easy to forget what it was like. One by one his sisters launched themselves into his arms. He shook hands with his brothers-in-law. He made the acquaintance of his newest nephew, who promptly spit up on Brandon's jacket.

The baby's mother, Amelia, laughed and said she finally had her revenge for the time he pushed her in the mud, ruining her best dress. They had been seven and five, respectively.

At long last they were all together for their only brother's wedding. They would celebrate with singing, dancing, feasting. It would begin tonight when the Richmonds would join them for the first supper uniting the two families.

Four hours later . . .
The Dining Room, Hamilton House

Dinner that evening took place under the glow of dozens of candles, with the warm light reflecting off the crystals and glass of the chandeliers. It illuminated the murals on the walls depicting epic battles in English history, the elaborate place settings comprised of all the very best silver, delicately etched glasses, precious china, fine linen and lace tablecloths, bouquets of pink and white tea roses, two attending servants per guest, and the clock.

Brandon had checked the hour four times before the first course had even been served. One hour and twenty-three minutes later, he was still in agonies.

At the far end of the table, the Duke of Richmond had engaged Amelia's husband, John, Lord Brentford, in a discussion upon his preferred subject.

Above the murmurs of the ladies' chatter, Brandon could just discern their conversation. Among Brentford's many fine traits was that he was a good listener. That he was also genuinely interested in the subject, having land and horses of his own, meant that, for once, the duke had a suitable companion.

John asked questions. The duke answered at length.

"A stallion has two duties," the duke lectured loudly. "Protection of the herd and mating, of course. Occasionally, however, he must be kept from the first in order to ensure the second. It can be lonely being a stallion at times, I should think." Here he paused thoughtfully, and took a sip of wine while John nodded with interest.

Brandon thought the role of a man was much the same. It did not escape Brandon's notice that the introduction of the Richmonds had greatly and obviously diminished the liveliness of his herd. He suspected that Sophie might integrate with much more success. It was something to consider.

If only . . .

Did he dare . . . ?

Brandon wondered where Sophie was at this very moment. Was she upset? Was she, heaven forbid, sobbing alone in her room? Or was she at the theater with Alistair, or waltzing with some other man? Merely considering any of those options pained him

If she were here, they would certainly share sly smiles and winks and bite back laughter at the conversations and dynamics around them. Then again, if she were here, as his fiancée, the Richmonds would not be. There would be no talk of horses, no mention of prestigious friends—and there would be much more laughter.

If only . . .

Could he do it . . . ?

Brandon drummed his fingers on the table. She ought to be here, sitting next to him. He glanced at Clarissa, seated at his right-hand side. Her back was rigid, her hands were folded in her lap, and she was twisting the betrothal ring around and around. While she had responded politely to his attempts at conversation, she would not meet his eye. Even in the glow of candlelight, she seemed pale.

Sophie would be chattering away with him and everyone, and secretly holding his hand under the table. She was not terrified of him, as Clarissa seemed to be.

If only . . .

Did he dare . . . ?

Lady Richmond glowered at her husband's conversation—when she wasn't presenting faux smiles to his mother and sisters, who were nodding politely and murmuring "hmm" when Lady Richmond paused to breathe between mentioning her deep friendships with Lady Endicott and Lady Chesterfield. They nicely asked "Is that so?" when Lady Richmond mentioned the sweet gift that Lady Carrington gave to her. And they said "How wonderful for you" when Lady Richmond declared how blessed she was in her friendships. And then she proceeded to list them. Name after name . . .

Occasionally, Brandon received curious glances from his two oldest sisters. His mother was, by now, desensitized to Lady Richmond and her more grating qualities. Charlotte, however . . .

Charlotte was fiendishly amusing. She made him resent that he had to maintain an appearance of patriarchal foreboding for, dear God, how he wanted to laugh at her latest mischief:

"Are you perchance acquainted with Walter Smythson?" she asked innocently. He was the blacksmith in the village near Thornbridge Manor.

"Of course, dear. Everyone knows him," Lady Richmond responded patronizingly. Amelia looked up and blinked rapidly a few times, trying to make sense of it, because there was absolutely no way Lady Richmond would know him, or admit to it if she did.

"Ah, how silly of me," Charlotte continued. "So then you must know Lady Millicent Strange. She moves in the most select circles, as it seems that you do. You must be familiar with her."

Miss Millicent Strange had been Charlotte's imaginary childhood friend who was the regular instigator of all sorts of trouble. *"Miss Millicent Strange did it,"* Charlotte would say, *"and she's so very, very sorry."*

"Lady Strange and I correspond regularly," Lady

Richmond declared, taking another sip of her wine and then dabbing at the corners of her mouth with her napkin.

Lady Hamilton pursed her lips.

"You must be a favorite, then, given that it is so difficult for her to write after the accident," Charlotte said. Brandon raised his brow, but his sister ignored him.

"Oh, a dreadful occurrence. We were all devastated when it happened," Lady Richmond responded, affecting a sorrowful expression.

"And shocking. To lose a hand to the jaws of a wild boar!" Charlotte exclaimed. "One never expects that."

Indeed, one did not.

Brandon took note of his family's expressions: Amelia was holding her napkin over her mouth, and Penelope had her lips pressed firmly together. Their husbands, Brentford and Lord Addison, were similarly occupied with restraining their laughter. His mother was smiling as she smoothed out invisible creases in the tablecloth.

The Duke of Richmond lavished his attentions upon dessert. His daughter was not paying the slightest bit of attention. Round and around that emerald ring went on her finger.

"Her handwriting has never been the same, and it makes her letters a trifle difficult to read," Lady Richmond carried on.

"Charlotte, I'm curious as to how you are familiar with this Miss Millicent Strange," Brandon interrupted.

"She's a *lady*," Charlotte gasped. "I attend school with her daughter, Miss Araminta Strange," Charlotte answered breezily. "We call her Minty. Miss Minty Strange."

Amelia began to choke and her husband handed her a glass of water.

"One of your school friend's mum has had her hand bitten off by a wild boar," Brandon reiterated. Brentford excused himself and left the table.

"Yes. Tragic, is it not?" Charlotte remarked, first dabbing a tear that was presumably as fake as Lady Millicent Strange and her daughter, Araminta.

No, the real tragedy would be a lifetime of dinners like this one.

Brandon felt his heart begin to beat harder, faster. He looked at the clock. Again. It was nearly eleven. Footmen stepped forward to clear the dessert plates. This dinner was almost over, thank God.

But there would be more. He could look forward to a lifetime of dinner-table conversation consisting of minutia about the breeding of horses, lists of every ton member that had even the most fleeting acquaintance with Lady Richmond, and a bride who could not conceal her wish to be somewhere else.

Such a demeanor was uncomfortable at the dinner table. He imagined it would be as unbearable, uncomfortable, and painful on their wedding night. Brandon did not imagine it would improve significantly with practice.

With Sophie, though . . . By God, how he wanted her in such a primal, earthly way. The way a man ought to desire a woman. Brandon wanted to claim her mouth, grasp her breasts, hold her hips, and completely possess her. He wanted to make her gasp, moan, and cry with pleasure. He knew their lovemaking would be just that—lovemaking, and it would be earth-shatteringly exquisite.

He reminded himself that gentlemen did not think about lovemaking at the dinner table.

Perhaps he wasn't as much of a gentleman as he thought he was. Perhaps there was a little more rogue in him than he knew. Perhaps it was time to simply be a man, call upon logic and reason, and consider the facts:

His fiancée was in love with someone else.

He, and his notion of honor, stood in the way of her happiness. Would it not be more noble to release her from her obligation to him?

His future in-laws were terrible bores.

And most importantly, there was the simple, undeniable fact that he was in love with Miss Sophie Harlow.

He was also an outrageously wealthy and powerful double duke, which meant that he could marry whomever he wished and could afford the expense of a dozen breech-of-contract suits and still shower his rightful bride with jewels.

He was also a gentleman, which meant he knew exactly when to stop being one. Right now, for example.

Brandon stood and excused himself. There was an urgent matter he needed to attend to. He walked briskly away from the table. His pace increased when he reached the hall, and quickened further when he reached the foyer. When his boots hit the cobblestones outside, he broke into a run.

Chapter 43

The night before the wedding . . .

Brandon heard only the pounding of his boots on the road and of his heart in his chest. He raced down the street, paused for a carriage to pass at an intersection. He sprinted past a brawl outside of the Queen's Head pub. He ran past numerous illicit activities occurring in darkened corners and back alleys. His lungs burned. His muscles screamed for him to stop.

Brandon ran faster.

Finally, he arrived at Sophie's door. He was covered in a slick sheen of sweat, and his shirt clung to him in a very common way. Somewhere along the way, his cravat had loosened and gotten lost. He was breathing hard. He pounded on the door with his fists.

Bessy opened the door.

"Bessy. Hello. I need to see Sophie please."

"Did you run here, Your Grace?" she asked.

"I did," he panted. "Because I need to speak to your mistress urgently."

"I'll see if she's at home to callers," Bessy told him. He gave her the ducal stare.

"Bessy, who is it?" It was Sophie.

"It's yer double duke," her impertinent servant said.

"Let him in."

He stepped inside and wasted not a second.

"I love you," he said. He was out of breath, his heart was pounding, and not entirely from his recent exertions.

"I love you, too," she said plainly as if it were a perfectly natural way to greet each other. *Good evening, I love you.*

"Come away with me, Sophie," Brandon said breathlessly, but firmly. "Tonight."

"But tomorrow . . ."

"You. Me. Gretna Green. Tonight. I want to be with you, Sophie, as man and wife."

Brandon was absolutely certain. Sophie hesitated.

He could not understand why and he could not accept it.

"Sophie, I love you." He said it again, because it couldn't be said enough. "I want to be with you, as husband and wife. I want a family with you, and a life with you."

"I love you, too. I want all those things, too," she answered, and then she added, "but I need you to be at the church tomorrow."

That was not a rational wish. It was not logical. It was such a struggle for his brain to comprehend it, that he stopped thinking entirely and acted strictly upon instinct.

He kissed her.

Their last kiss had been fierce and urgent, and this was one, too. With this kiss, he had to make her understand that he absolutely should not be at the church tomorrow and, instead, they should be kissing and making love in a carriage on its way to Gretna Green. After all, she hated weddings, so an elopement would be perfect.

But those thoughts could not compete with the sensations arising from Sophie's kiss. Her small hands clutched at his shirt, as if desperately holding on to him. He pulled her closer to him, and tightened his embrace. He would never let her go.

Vaguely, he was aware of the clattering of a carriage, followed by silence. Sophie must have heard it, too, and made sense of it. She broke off the kiss, took his hand, and led him up the stairs.

"It's Julianna arriving home from a ball," she whispered. And then she pulled him into her bedroom.

Sophie led Brandon up the stairs and into her darkened bedroom. She could not let him go just yet, and she could not bear to have a confrontation with Julianna at the moment.

Brandon seemed to understand because she shut the door.

She was alone with her true love. In the dark. In her bedroom. They could be interrupted at any second. She shivered in anticipation of pure, hot bliss because he was here, and because he loved her.

He loved her!

She loved him, too, with a fierce intensity she had never imagined possible. He was hers, he belonged to her, which is why his marriage to another was so wrong. That would all be sorted out in the morning, and, frankly, she was having a tremendously difficult time focusing upon anything other than the fact that he loved her, and they were alone, in the dark, in her bedroom.

She reached out for him, and after some sweet fumbling, she was captured in his embrace. His mouth crashed upon hers, and she parted her lips to let him in. She sucked on his bottom lip, and he nibbled at hers. His hands were splayed upon her lower back, and then lower, to her backside. Still kissing him, she sighed at the thought of all that had transpired from their first moment to this one.

She loved him, and he loved her, too!

Brandon moved his grasp from her bottom to her hips, and then he slowly but firmly brushed his hands up her sides, pausing at her breasts, and then he tugged her sleeves down. She trembled at the sensation of his open mouth upon her bare shoulders.

Kisses, one after another, were feathered upon her shoulders, to her neck, across the hollow at the bottom of her throat, and then on the other side because one must be thorough and there wasn't an inch of skin that was not deserving and achingly in need of his lavish attention.

Sophie sighed and swayed upon her feet.

Brandon laughed slightly, a low, knowing-man's laugh. She realized just then that he hadn't always been as good as he seemed. In fact, this man was capable of some very deliciously wicked things, indeed. Another shiver of anticipation . . .

He kissed her mouth again, and time passed, and it was lovely. Brandon mumbled something, and it was lost in the kiss.

"To the bed," he commanded. She happily obeyed.

It was impossible to see in this darkness, so she guided them to the mattress. They took hesitant steps, and paused to remove articles of clothing. She found it strange that she should be warmer with her dress and underthings off, but she attributed it to a blush that was surely stealing across her skin. It was too dark to tell.

Sophie reached out, and placed her palms upon his chest. She explored the contours and ridges of his muscles, and savored the sensation of his hot, smooth skin with a slight covering of hair under her touch.

She moved her hands lower. He sucked in his breath. She took the hot, thick length of his arousal in her hands. He moaned, and clasped her wrists.

"Bed," he said again, firmly, ducally.

She followed his order.

After some fumbling steps in the dark, they collapsed onto the mattress. She lay on her back, and he lay on his side, next to her, cradling her in his arms. He stroked her hair away from her face, and kissed her mouth with more hot, tender kisses. And then . . .

He traced his fingertips from her shoulders to the pink center of her breasts, and he circled there and she couldn't help but shiver and sigh, and arch her back. His fingertips continued their path lower, across the smooth plane of her belly with a delicate almost ticklish touch, and then slowly, tauntingly he found the magical place between her legs.

He stroked her lightly and she gasped.

He increased the pressure and her body was owned by feverish trembles. His mouth closed over her breast. She moaned.

Brandon continued to stroke and caress her in a steady rhythm. He flicked his tongue back and forth, over the peak of her breast slowly and then quickly. And then when she could barely stand the masses of exquisite sensation, he did it again on the other one. Vaguely, she was aware of not being able to get enough air, but really, who needed to breathe at a time like this?

The pressure within her was swelling and heating up, and something had to happen soon because she really couldn't stand much more of this. She rocked her hips, and she couldn't help but writhe because she felt his touch everywhere.

"Oh," she sighed, and then she moaned. And then

she murmured again because he did that sensational, outrageously magnificent, wicked thing with his mouth to her breasts. And his hands, oh god, he slid one finger inside of her and still stroked the magical place and . . . *oh* . . .

She moved with him. He took one pink peak into his mouth and sucked. She arched her back and opened her mouth to cry out. His own mouth came crashing down upon hers, capturing the sound of her climax as that intense pressure exploded all at once, and she felt the white-hot waves of pleasure course through her. She throbbed under his touch, and sighed into his kiss.

And still, there was more.

"Sophie . . ."

"I love you," she whispered.

"I love you," he whispered back, and he caressed the length of her, from the curve of her hips to the swell of her breasts. "Sophie . . ."

"Yes," she murmured. Anything he wanted . . . she would give to him.

Brandon eased himself above her. The real sensation of her naked body beneath him was a million times more potent, intoxicating, and arousing than his most vivid dreams.

Between the recollection of all those dreams and the reality, Brandon knew that complete abandon was only a breath or a heartbeat away. His cock was aching to be inside of her. She whispered yes again, and he couldn't imagine holding back much longer, especially when she tilted her hips up to his. Using the last delicate shreds of his infamous self-control, he entered her slowly.

She gasped, and his cock throbbed inside of her. And then he began to move, thrusting slowly at first so that he could experience every possible sensation and savor every possible second. She wrapped her legs around his lower back, and he groaned as he pushed deeper into her. Still, he needed more of her.

It was a daze, a blur after that, as his brain ceased to function and the instinctive urge to possess her took over. He was aware of frantic kisses as she moved with him, and of raking his hands along her because he desperately needed to touch as much of her as possible all at once.

Her soft sighs and moans only spurred him on to move faster, and harder. He clasped her cheek, kissed her feverishly, and then he buried his face into that place where her neck curved into her shoulder. She clasped him to her, and as she climaxed again, those pulses drove him over the edge, beyond the physical possibility of control, and then he groaned, and shuddered, and let go completely.

As he held her in his arms afterward, Brandon felt triumphant, and contentment. His heart, which had earlier ached at the expected loss of her, now beat lazily and happily in his chest.

She was completely mad to insist that he go to the church tomorrow. He would respect her wishes, though, because gentlemen respected the wishes of women.

Rogues, however, came up with plans of their own.

The Dryden Hotel
Approximately four in the morning

At first Brandon knocked. Then he pounded with his fist. And then, finally, von Vennigan answered the door.

The prince was attired in boots, breeches, and a shirt with the buttons undone and sleeves rolled up. His bare hands were ink stained; one held a pen, the other held a bottle. Von Vennigan's hair was disheveled, his eyes were dark, and his mouth was grim. He stank of cigar smoke. Brandon suspected that he had interrupted the composition of brandy-fueled tragic odes of star-crossed lovers and heartbreaking tales of woe.

It was his pleasure to do so.

"I need you to be my best man," Brandon said.

Von Vennigan slammed the door in his face.

Chapter 44

On the day of the wedding . . .

Richmond House

Clarissa took a deep breath. Her maid, Nancy, tugged the laces of her corset tight.

"Only ten more minutes . . ." her mother said, glancing at her pocket watch. She was overseeing the dressing of the bride with military precision.

The good thing about getting married, Clarissa thought, was that it would get her away from her mother. She meant well. But Clarissa had developed her wings and was ready to leave the nest.

"Let's put the dress on, dear."

"Yes, Mother," she said obediently, because old habits were hard to break and because it was part of the plan.

The dress—a frothy concoction of white satin, silver lace, and pink sapphires swished over her head. Nancy began to do up the buttons at the back.

"And the veil."

Her maid secured the veil, at Her Grace's command.

"You are such a beautiful bride, my lady," Nancy gushed.

"You are, Clarissa. I am very pleased with you," her mother said, and Clarissa tried not to think of the crushing disappointment she would experience later. "I must depart now, and you shall follow shortly."

Lady Richmond was going first to ensure everything was just so. Clarissa and the duke would arrive shortly after.

"I will see you at the church," Clarissa said, uttering the first lie of her life.

"That's my girl." And then she was gone in a flurry of violet satin, and Clarissa felt a lump in her throat as she realized that might be the last time they saw each other. She was a hard woman, but she only wanted what was best, and she only wanted to be a success at the one thing life had asked of her.

But she could not back out now. Too much depended on her today.

Clarissa moved quickly to her desk and, from a secret drawer, recovered the stash of writing things that had escaped confiscation. She and Sophie had agreed upon the two things that it must say: she was leaving him, and he was to stay and wait for Sophie. After the first line, the ink ran dry.

"Lady Clarissa, His Grace is ready for you now," a maid said, interrupting.

The hallway clock chimed loud and long. It was time to go.

And then her gaze fell upon a bottle of the Tonic for the Cure of Unsuitable Affections. Her mother had included it on her dinner tray from the other night. The tonic was a strange shade of blue—to cool the overheated blood, the label said. Clarissa thought it might also do as ink. She quickly scrawled the second line, and then she quickly descended the stairs and climbed into the carriage that had been provided by the Duke of Hamilton and Brandon, her soon-to-be former fiancé.

24 Bloomsbury Place

"Oh, blast," Sophie muttered to herself. This could not be happening. Of all the things to lose, and of all the times to lose it!

Her voucher was missing. Her ticket to the wedding was gone. The ceremony was due to start in thirty minutes. It took twenty-five minutes to travel from her home to St. George's. She would never be admitted to the church without it!

Was this a sign?

Since when had she become superstitious?

It wasn't on her desk. It wasn't in any of her desk drawers, either—but she found her silver bracelet that she had misplaced last month. The voucher was not on her bedside table, or inside the wardrobe. Nor was it on the bed, with its rumpled bedsheets and pillows bearing the imprint of two heads.

Brandon. Last night. Heat suffused her cheeks, her limbs, everywhere, as she indulged in a fleeting recollection of their lovemaking. To be so intimate with him was beyond anything she'd ever dreamed of. She was sorry to wake up alone, but it was for the best. Hopefully, he would be at the church, as she asked him to do, because she needed to ensure that the passionate lovemaking of last night happened again and again, and thus, she needed that damned voucher.

"Oh, blast" was not sufficient language for a moment like this. *"Oh, bloody hell and damnation!"* she cried.

The wedding was due to start in twenty-eight minutes. There was no way that she'd be admitted without that damned voucher. Which meant that Brandon would be left at the altar. She could not allow that to happen.

"Julianna!" she hollered.

"What is it?" her friend answered, coming into Sophie's room. "Oh, lovely dress! Where did you get it?"

"I can't find my voucher for the wedding," Sophie said, now utterly panicked.

"It looks very expensive," Julianna said, still marveling at the dress. It really was lovely and spectacular and flattered her perfectly. Presently, that was irrelevant.

"Voucher, Julianna," Sophie said. "Urgent. Problem."

"Have you looked for it? Oh, yes, I see that you have," Julianna murmured, surveying the damage. Drawers were upturned, and the wardrobe doors were flung open, and there was a pile of random things upon the carpet.

"What do I do?" Sophie cried.

"Where was the last place you saw it?" Julianna asked calmly. They'd gone through this routine together a thousand times before.

"I don't know! If I knew I'd look there, and it wouldn't be lost and—" Sophie couldn't breathe. Suddenly, she was overwhelmed with heat and thus, massively uncomfortable. And panicked. Had she mentioned panicked? Her future happiness was at stake!

"Calm down," Julianna said calmly. "A hysterical fit will not help."

"Can I have yours?" Sophie asked.

"You are desperate to go to this wedding," Julianna remarked.

"Yes. Please."

"You are desperate and pleading to attend the wedding of the man you love to another woman," her friend said slowly. It was not making sense to Julianna, and that was understandable. It wouldn't make sense to anyone, unless they knew the truth.

"It might be my wedding."

"The dress . . ."

"I have a plan."

"Does Brandon know about your plan?" Julianna asked.

"No. I didn't get a chance to explain it to him." She had been too busy kissing him, and loving him, and offering herself completely to him. Talking hadn't really happened.

"What about Clarissa? And what about Lord Brandon's wishes?" Julianna challenged.

It dawned on Sophie at this moment how far apart they'd grown. Because Clarissa was in on the plan, and Sophie was very sure of Brandon's wishes. She hadn't told her best friend any of it, really, because she had been met with such censure every time. And now, she needed a favor and there was no time to explain.

"Please, Julianna?"

St. George's, Hanover Square
At the Altar . . .

It was a queer feeling standing here, at the altar, looking out at all the guests. *His* wedding guests. Brandon hadn't given much thought to this moment. In fact, he had avoided thinking about it entirely. Now it was here, *he* was here, and . . .

His heart ached for Sophie.

She was his now, and he would not surrender her. Or himself. So it was strange that he was standing here, at the altar of St. George's at his wedding to another woman.

What he wouldn't give to see Sophie at the far end

of the aisle, walking toward him with a smile on her
face. It would be a nervous smile, he knew that. And he
would smile at her in encouragement, as if to tell her
that all was fine, everything would be well, that they
would live happily ever after.

But not today.

His stomach ached, too. Nerves. Regret. Very well—
he could admit it—terror. Sophie had asked him to be
here—by what madness he knew not. A gentleman
always obeys the wishes of a lady, even if it destroys
him to do so.

St. George's, Hanover Square
The Carriage, Just Outside

The carriage carrying Clarissa and Lord Richmond
pulled up in front of St. George's. Throngs of people
had gathered to see the arrival of the wedding party,
the guests, and most of all her, Clarissa, the bride.

This was the moment where Clarissa chose her fate.
This was her very last chance. Once she exited the carriage there would be no returning to it until after the
wedding . . . to Brandon.

Duty or true love? Respectability or scandal? The
duke or the prince?

"Father, before I come in, I need you to give this
note directly to Lord Brandon."

"Eh?"

"Oh, please, Father."

And then she feared that he would insist she come
in with him. But he merely looked at her oddly for
a moment and acquiesced. Maybe it was because he
had begged her to marry this man, and he thought
she would, and he felt indebted to her. Or maybe he

couldn't resist the pleas of a girl he believed to be his natural daughter, and his child.

He pocketed the note and exited the carriage.

And if only for him, she hoped that Frederick would marry her and provide for her parents. She hoped that no one ever discovered her secret.

Her father walked toward the church. And then the carriage of a most distinguished guest arrived, pulled by six gorgeous, gleaming, and matching carriage horses.

"Oh, no," Clarissa muttered.

Her father stopped to engage the driver in conversation about the blasted horses. Minutes passed. Her anxiety was approaching a fever pitch when she saw Nancy coming out, most likely to assist Clarissa out of the carriage.

And then her father concluded his conversation and disappeared into the church. Before the maid could get any closer, Clarissa banged on the roof of the carriage.

"To the docks!" she called out.

The driver, in the employ of the duchess of Hamilton and Brandon, followed Clarissa's directions as he had been instructed to do.

St. George's, Hanover Square
At the Altar . . .

There was a delay. Brandon hated delays. He especially hated delays when he was standing in front of two hundred people who were starting to wonder. And whisper.

Brandon held a particular loathing for this one. If he knew what he was waiting for, perhaps he'd be better able to endure it. But he did not, and people were staring, and there was nothing he could do but wait and have faith that all would go according to plan.

Exactly whose plan, he knew not. He certainly had one of his own, and had doubts as to its success.

"Where is she?" Brandon's best man muttered.

"I don't know," he replied to von Vennigan's question.

"She should be here by now," von Vennigan said quietly, through clenched teeth.

"She'll be here," Brandon said with a confidence that he feigned. Clarissa was the most dutiful creature in the world. Their plan—hatched late last night (or was it early this morning?)—absolutely depended upon Clarissa walking down the aisle.

At the very last possible moment, Brandon and von Vennigan would switch places. Clarissa would get her wedding to the man she loved.

And Brandon would find Sophie, and marry her.

He didn't see Sophie in the crowd, so he kept looking. She didn't know about this plan, and he did not even know if she would be in attendance this morning. All he knew is that the brides were not where he required them to be. He frowned, and set off a flurry of whispers.

St. George's, Hanover Square
Outside, in the Crush

Sophie arrived in a hired hack, alone. It was not how one traditionally planned to arrive at one's own wedding. In her gloved hands, she clutched the prized voucher that Julianna had relinquished to her.

She had taken the time to explain, and her heart had clenched at the sadness she saw in Julianna's eyes, because she had been the last to know about all of this and she should have been the first. Sophie, then, understood that her disapproval of the Brandon affair was not simply due to moral objections but because she was afraid of losing her friend.

Things would change; it was inevitable. They had survived so much together: Julianna's marriage and then widowhood; Sophie and Matthew and all of that; living together in London, taking the town and the newspaper world by storm; being christened the Writing Girls and, until Annabelle and Eliza joined, having only each other.

Sophie hoped that Brandon was waiting for her at the altar, but she also prayed that her friendship would survive with an equal fervency. And with that, she paid the hackney driver, quit the carriage, walked through the crowds, and stepped into the church.

She'd been here hundreds of times before, for hundreds of other weddings. Now, she was here for her own. It being a wedding of hers, it was not complete without some unexpected, unnecessary, and most unwelcome drama.

St. George's, Hanover Square
Interior

Lord Roxbury did not attend the wedding with either Lady Derby or Lady Belmont, thanks to an item in *The London Weekly*'s gossip column "Fashionable Intelligence." Its author, A Lady of Distinction, had betrayed his secret—that he was simultaneously carrying on affairs with both ladies. Neither of them was pleased.

As they were entering the church, coincidentally at the same time, Lady Derby took the opportunity to step upon the other lady's hem, resulting in a tear. Lady Belmont responded by stopping suddenly, and swiftly jabbing her elbow backward into the abdomen of Lady Derby, who had not foreseen this maneuver.

It descended into an incredibly rare occurrence: a female bout of fisticuffs.

These sworn enemies battled each other, until the man that divided them arrived, giving them cause to unite against a common foe.

They expressed their great displeasure upon his person as he stepped into the aisle of the church.

This petite brawl had some unintended and unsuspected consequences: it temporarily prevented His Grace, the Duke of Richmond, from walking down the aisle to hand a very important missive to the groom. And thus, it allowed Clarissa's carriage to unsuspectingly make great headway toward the docks.

St. George's, Hanover Square
At the Altar . . .

"What's the old man doing?" von Vennigan asked, after the two brawling ladies and unfortunate gentleman had been escorted out. Brandon had a sinking feeling he knew exactly who the actors were in that drama.

"It appears that he is walking up the aisle to us," Brandon replied, stating the obvious.

"Good morning, Lord Brandon. Your Highness," the Duke of Richmond said. "Lovely day for a wedding, eh?"

Brandon and von Vennigan muttered their agreement.

"Quite shocking to see those two lasses fighting as such. Jostling for the position of broodmare, it seems," the duke said with a knowing wink. It was doubtful that either lady wished to breed, but his point was taken. "Well, I have a little message for you from the bride.

She's just outside in the carriage," Richmond said, handing over a small, folded sheet of paper.

"Thank you." Brandon opened the paper. Behind him, he heard his best man exhale with relief.

He read it once. He read it twice. It couldn't possibly say what he thought it did.

"Scheisse!" von Vennigan swore under his breath, having rudely but understandably, read the note over Brandon's shoulder.

He read it again.

I'm sorry, Lord Brandon, but I cannot marry you when I love another.

Each word was lighter than the last, suggesting she had run out of ink. There was a second line, but it had faded so that it was illegible. He hoped it wasn't important.

But one thing was clear: He was a free man.

Brandon lifted his gaze from the paper to the crowds. Two hundred very curious expressions peered back at him.

"But where is she?" von Vennigan demanded.

Brandon shrugged and stepped away from the altar. Von Vennigan shoved him aside and sprinted down the aisle.

The sound of a woman wailing silenced the crowd and echoed throughout the church. It was a sound so gut-wrenching and ghastly that one had to stop and look.

It was Lady Richmond, staring him down murderously and stalking toward him. Her intentions were clear: she meant to stop him.

And then Charlotte, who had been standing next to Lady Richmond, began to sway. She wavered on her feet. A moan escaped her lips. Her eyelashes fluttered. Her hand went to her forehead. Brandon saw her lips move but could not hear what she said. He'd wager it was something along the lines of "I feel faint" because at the perfect moment, Charlotte fainted into the arms of Lady Richmond.

Catching her was instinct. Immediately, however, Lady Richmond tried to pass her off to someone else. Had the best of the *ton* not been present, she surely would have dropped her.

Penelope and Amelia were there and refused to take the unconscious body of their younger sister.

Brandon took this opportunity to flee, but unfortunately, was not able to travel far, for his path was blocked by a gaggle of females—four, he counted— that he could not recall becoming acquainted with. His heart sank as he realized that they were most likely dear, dear friends of Lady Richmond.

"Excuse me, ladies." He raised himself up to his full height and looked down upon them in all senses of the term. They were not impressed, though one of them did bat her eyelashes and fan herself with a little more speed. On the whole, they stood their ground and blocked his passage to Sophie, to true love, to happily-ever-after.

It seemed that Lady Richmond did, in fact, have some dear, *dear* friends in truth. He looked behind him, at her, and saw that she was smirking while still holding a faint, but similarly smirking, Charlotte.

Brandon sighed. He could push through, and knock over a peeress or two. He could bully his way through one of the pews, but would likely be severely slowed, if not stopped, by all the guests. Or he could take another path.

He grinned. And then, he turned and ran.

* * *

St. George's, Hanover Square
In the Vestibule

First, there had been the commotion with Lord Roxbury and his women. And then, Sophie had glanced into the church to see the duke giving the note to Brandon (he was here!) and von Vennigan (he was not supposed to be here!).

The plan had gone awry. *Curses!*

She heard that awful wail, and knew it was Lady Richmond. She saw von Vennigan racing toward her. He skidded on the stone floor, stopping inches from her person.

"Where is Clarissa" he panted.

"Off to meet you at the docks!" she exclaimed, and he dashed off.

"Sophie!" she turned at the sound of a familiar voice to see Julianna.

"I found your voucher," she explained. "It was under the . . . oh, never mind. Have I missed it?"

"No. It's a catastrophic commotion, again!" Sophie said, her voice wavering. Though she hadn't much time to imagine this, she certainly had not anticipated this devolving so quickly into chaos.

Julianna understood, and took Sophie's hand in hers. She'd stood by her during one disastrous wedding and would do so for another, and that meant the world to her.

"Why are you standing in the vestibule?" Julianna asked.

Because she was terrified to go in there alone. She couldn't even say it aloud.

Sophie peeked into the church again. She saw an uproar, and Brandon running away. He was supposed

to stay put—Clarissa was to include those instructions
in her note, which they had decided should say: *"I'm
sorry, Lord Brandon, but I cannot marry you when I
love another. Wait here for the woman you love."*

Perhaps it didn't. But there was also the chance that
he was running away from her. Was it so damned hard
for a man to stand at the altar and wait for her?

She turned to go.

At the Docks

Upon her arrival at the docks, Clarissa realized that
she hadn't completely thought this through. She was an
unchaperoned young woman in a spectacularly fancy
gown studded with pink sapphires, waiting in an obviously fine carriage at the docks. Alone.

Her heart thudded, and not purely with pleasurable
anticipation.

Frederick was supposed to be here. She did not see
him waiting with open arms, as expected. In fact, there
was no sign of him.

She did not know which ship was his. She was not
sure if she should get out and ask someone for directions to the ship owned by the Prince of Bavaria, or if
she should wait here and send the driver. *Oh, dear.*

Sophie and Brandon were likely married by now. If
this didn't work out, she was in Big Trouble.

Trouble so massive that she couldn't comprehend
it. Penniless trouble. Her mother's freezing, merciless
fury. Her father's disappointment and embarrassment.
Perhaps she should climb aboard the first ship she could
and hightail it out of London entirely.

Before she could, the carriage door was flung open.

Clarissa shrieked.

"Your prince has come, my darling." It was Frederick climbing in, thank the Lord, and not a marauding sailor with dubious intentions, as she had feared.

She launched herself into his arms and allowed herself to feel relief, having found him before he sailed away from her forever. She nestled into his embrace, feeling safe, and enjoying his scent and the way his long, soft hair brushed against her cheek.

Eventually, his mouth found hers for a kiss. It was sweet, tender, and passionate all at once. She knew that this kiss was the prelude to so many more and her heart swelled at the thought.

"I love you," he said. "I love you because you can't sing, and because you are even more beautiful on the inside, because you write such good letters, and because the mere sight of your handwriting makes me happy. To gaze upon you, to touch you, to love you . . . Oh, Clarissa," he said, and his voice tapered off. "I love everything about you."

From the way he held her gaze she wondered if he knew her secret. She could not be sure, but she knew that if he was aware, it did not matter to him. They would have time to know everything there was to know about each other.

"I love you," she told him. "Because of you, I have become the woman I always wanted to be, but never thought I could. I love you for helping me find myself. I love your long hair, and your dramatic scars, and your passion for everything. I love everything about you."

"Will you come away with me?" he asked.

"Yes. Anywhere," she answered.

"Then we will live in Bavaria, but we shall return to England to introduce your parents to their grandchildren."

"That is perfect," Clarissa said.

"We'll not leave just yet. We shall marry first. Right now, in fact."

"But Sophie and Brandon . . ."

St. George's, Hanover Square
Near the Altar . . .

Lady Hamilton ordered Charlotte to recover her senses, which the girl did promptly. Lady Richmond shook out her arms and glowered at the girl who had thwarted her, and then stepped into the way of Brandon, blocking the exit to the aisle.

He swore. This was getting ridiculous now. All he wanted to do was marry Sophie. She was here, as was he, they were in a church, with a clergyman standing by a special license around somewhere. *Why was this so damned hard?*

"They said you were a good man," she said coldly to him.

"I have taken steps to ensure your daughter's future happiness." He knew this to be true, just as he knew that he was a good man.

"What have you done with her?"

"She is with von Vennigan," Lady Hamilton said, taking her by the arm and guiding her out of the way. "She is with a prince. A very rich prince."

The path to the altar was clear now.

The path behind him, to the vestibule, was still clogged with dear, dear friends whom he was finding very, very annoying. Beyond them, he saw Sophie turning to leave.

He felt a wail, not unlike the one Lady Richmond emitted, building up inside him but he contained it.

He could run, out the back, around the building,

and push through the throngs in front and maybe, hopefully catch Sophie before she left forever. He knew her and thus knew that she was at her most vulnerable now, waiting for a groom to stand up and be there for her.

So Brandon adopted his Obey Me I Am a Duke posture, with long straight spine, broad shoulder thrown back, and head held high.

"Ladies and Gentlemen," he said loudly, though he didn't yell, for that was undignified. Enough people in the vicinity quieted, prompted the rest of the church to fall silent as well. "Ladies and Gentlemen. We are going to have a wedding today. If you'll all regain your composure and manners, my bride and I would appreciate it."

And then, to the dear, dear friends of Lady Richmond, he said, "Ladies, please do kindly remove yourselves from the path of true love and happily-ever-after." Members of the congregation who heard that, laughed, and someone hollered that he ought to "get the cows out of the way" and the ladies fluttered away, pink with embarrassment and fury, and the aisle was clear.

He saw Sophie's delicious backside, and she paused, as if gathering her courage to turn and brave the long walk down the aisle before two hundred strangers, then say her vows, and become his wife. Courage, too, to redefine herself once again from Miss Harlow, to Mrs. Fletcher, to a Writing Girl, to the next Duchess of Hamilton and Brandon.

Brandon waited patiently, in front of all those curious faces, all the more so because he stood in the middle of the aisle, halfway to the altar.

In the vestibule, Sophie had paused to catch her breath and gather her wits. In a moment of damp palms, frantic shallow breaths, and a stomach in a dozen different kinds of knots, she had turned to flee the church, leaving behind the man she loved and the future she longed for.

Madness!

Sophie recovered her senses, turned around and saw everyone in their seats, quiet and expectant. She saw the aisle was clear, save for Brandon.

He was waiting for her, still and steady and assured, in the place she feared most of all. It was the spot halfway down the aisle, where she'd been standing when Matthew jilted her, when the veil obscuring her vision had been ripped away and her life had forever altered.

And though she was afraid to go there again, and could barely fathom walking past it, all the way down the aisle, Sophie remembered that she was a brave woman and that she'd already trusted the man waiting for her with her heart. Now it was time to trust him with the rest of her life.

She took a deep breath. She placed one foot in front of the other. And then another. He waited.

As Sophie got closer to Brandon, the feelings of fear melted away. He waited. She smiled.

And when she stood before him, halfway down the aisle, Brandon lowered to one knee and clasped her hands in his. When he spoke his voice was firm and confident.

"I love you, Sophie Harlow. You are everything I never thought I wanted, but exactly what I need. I want you with me forever. I will never leave you, not because I am honorable, reliable, and about to make a sacred vow before God. I will never leave you because I love you, and will always love you. There is no greater reason, or greater bond than that."

"Oh, Brandon," she sighed. Honestly, it was all she could manage. It was the perfect thing for him to say.

A few hot, happy tears stung her eyes because this was, in a way, the same as shouting one's love from the rooftops.

He grinned and continued.

"I could list all the things I adore about you . . ."

"You and your lists," she said with a little laugh. She loved him *and* his lists.

"But I think we ought to get married first, because we've waited long enough."

"Yes," she said, even though he hadn't asked yet. And a few people in the crowd couldn't help themselves and yelled, *"YES."*

"Will you marry me, Miss Harlow?" Brandon asked.

"Yes," she said again. "Yes!"

He stood, and wrapped his arms around her, and lowered his mouth to hers. The kiss was sweet, and a promise of forever. And then she whispered, "I love you, too"—and then she whispered it again.

"What about the wedding?" someone shouted.

"We came for a wedding!" another called out.

"Shall we, then?" Brandon asked offering his arm. He would walk her down the aisle, because he knew she was terrified to do it alone.

Oh, her heart wanted to burst with happiness.

"No, we must do this properly," Julianna cut in, bustling down the aisle, issuing directions. "Lord Brandon, you go stand at the altar and do not leave it until you are married to our girl." She turned to Sophie and spoke softly, "Sophie, I shall give you away."

Sophie offered a wavering smile, because now she really feared that she might cry. Even though Julianna hadn't approved, and hadn't believed this moment would ever happen, now that it was here, she wasn't fighting her best friend but standing up for her. But then again, that's what best friends did. They both knew that things were going to change, but that their friendship wasn't going to fade.

Sophie threw her arms around her for an embrace.

And then someone forgot their manners and asked loudly if she was going to walk down the aisle or not.

And then she did, all the way.

Julianna escorted her, which might have been re-markable, except that it was the least scandalous thing that had happened all day.

And then the Duke of Hamilton and Brandon made Miss Sophie Harlow—formerly of Chesham, lately of London, and famously of *The London Weekly*—his wife and his duchess.

Chapter 45

Ten minutes after the first wedding . . .

Still at St. George's

Because Lady Hamilton and Sophie had thought of everything, there was a special license awaiting Clarissa and von Vennigan when they arrived at the church, to go with the one that Sophie and Brandon completed as soon as their ceremony was over.

Lord Richmond gave his consent upon learning of the prince's wealth, his intention to share it, and the pair of Holsteiner horses he planned to gift as well. Lady Richmond wept copiously through the ceremony. And Clarissa and Frederick said, "I do."

A few hours after the weddings . . .

The wedding breakfast hadn't begun until late in the afternoon, and it was late in the evening when the guests, very well entertained, wined and dined, stumbled to their carriages.

Brandon escorted his new bride up to the ducal bedchambers—she would have gotten horribly lost, otherwise.

When she saw the massive bed, she promptly collapsed upon it. Oh, how her feet ached from all that dancing! And her cheeks hurt a little, too, from so much smiling. Not that she was complaining. Those were very good problems to have.

Her husband—Oh, how it thrilled her to say that, and to think of him as such!—would solve another problem of hers: how to get out of this dress without a lady's maid assisting.

But first she admired her ring, the Hamilton and Brandon family heirloom, which Clarissa had given to her. The emerald reminded her of her husband's eyes.

He joined her on the bed, and they lay side by side, looking at the canopy.

"I had a plan," she informed him. "Because one must always have a plan."

"I know. I as well," he said.

"From now on, we shall have to plan together," she said.

"Yes. I have something in mind right now." He grinned wickedly at her.

"You're planning to ravish me, are you not?" she said, knowing him so well.

"Exactly. Shall I list all the things I will do as part of this ravishment?"

"Oh, yes," she said. Then he listed all the places he would kiss her—her mouth, of course, and then the curve where her neck met her shoulder. Then he would explore the hollow of her throat, and move lower to her breasts, which he would lavish attention upon with his mouth, and his hands. He told her how he would take the pink center in his mouth and, at that, she moaned because she could almost feel it, and she needed to feel it completely. He continued on with his list, detailing all the other places he would explore, like the curve of her hip, and shockingly, between her legs, and then the inside of her thighs, and then back up to her belly, and higher to her breasts.

"Enough with your lists!" she cried, aching to feel his touch for real. "Kiss me," she commanded. And he did, because a gentleman honors a woman's wishes, especially involving long, hot, loving kisses.

Epilogue

Six months after the wedding . . .

Fashionable Intelligence
By A Lady of Distinction

After a whirlwind, secret courtship and a surprise switch at the Wedding of the Year, the Duchess of Hamilton and Brandon, formerly *The Weekly*'s own Miss Harlow, is settling into her new home with the help of a map commissioned by her devoted and besotted husband. It is with the duchess's permission that I announce that Her Grace will soon need to find her way to the nursery.

The duke's former intended, Her Highness, the Princess of Bavaria, née Lady Clarissa Richmond, has recently arrived at the Bavarian Court after an extended honeymoon with her new husband, the Prince of Bavaria. An official state wedding is in the works.

Author's Note

In every age, there are women who buck conventions and defy expectations. Those are the women I've found most fascinating and inspiring, and those were the characters I wanted to write. And so, Sophie Harlow and the Writing Girls were born.

Nothing like them actually existed in the Regency Era. However, at that time and earlier women were active in publishing. Mary de la Riviere Manley was the editor and founder of *The Female Tatler* (1709), and later of *The Examiner* (1711). Eliza Haywood launched *The Female Spectator,* the first magazine created by women specifically for women, in 1744. Mrs. Elizabeth Johnson, a printer, published the first Sunday paper, *The British Gazette and Sunday Monitor,* in 1779. *La Belle Assemblee*, a Regency era women's fashion periodical, employed women.

Furthermore, virtually all articles in newspapers and periodicals were published anonymously, so who's to say there weren't women writing?

The London Weekly is based on papers like *John Bull* or *The Age*—very gossipy weekly papers—or, more contemporarily, the *New York Post.* Sophie's column is based on one called "Marriage In High Life," that appeared in *The Illustrated London News* in 1842. For more information about women writers, my books, and the Writing Girl world please visit www.mayarodale.com.

Next month, don't miss these exciting new love stories only from Avon Books

Seventh Heaven by Catherine Anderson
When Joe Lakota returns to his hometown and his first love, he wants nothing more than to rekindle the passion he shared with the beautiful Marilee Nelson. But Marilee is no longer the self-assured girl he once knew, and though she yearns for his tender touch, she is hiding a most horrible secret.

A Highland Duchess by Karen Ranney
The beautiful but haughty Duchess of Herridge is known to all as the "Ice Queen"—to all but the powerful Earl of Buchane, Ian McNair. Emma is nothing like the rumors. Sensual and passionate, she moves him like no woman has before. If only she were his wife and not his captive...

Swept Away by a Kiss by Katharine Ashe
A viscount with a taste for revenge, a lady shunned for her reckless past, and a villain who will stop at nothing to crush them both. *USA Today* bestselling author Lisa Kleypas calls Ashe's debut romance "breathtaking."

Green Eyes by Karen Robards
Anna Traverne will never forget the dark and daring jewel thief who crept into her chambers and inflamed her passions with a brazen caress. She thwarted the dashing rogue then, but now he's returned for what he believes is rightfully his... and to take tender revenge on the angel who stole his heart in a single, incomparable moment.

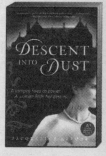

*Unforgettable, enthralling love stories,
sparkling with passion and adventure
from Romance's bestselling authors*

PASSION UNTAMED   *by Pamela Palmer*
978-0-06-166753-4

OUT OF THE DARKNESS   *by Jaime Rush*
978-0-06-169036-5

SILENT NIGHT, HAUNTED NIGHT   *by Terri Garey*
978-0-06-158204-2

SOLD TO A LAIRD   *by Karen Ranney*
978-0-06-177175-0

DARK OF THE MOON   *by Karen Robards*
978-0-380-75437-3

MY DARLING CAROLINE   *by Adele Ashworth*
978-0-06-190587-2

UPON A WICKED TIME   *by Karen Ranney*
978-0-380-79583-3

IN SCANDAL THEY WED   *by Sophie Jordan*
978-0-06-157921-9

IN PURSUIT OF A SCANDALOUS LADY   *by Gayle Callen*
978-0-06-178341-8

SEVEN SECRETS OF SEDUCTION   *by Anne Mallory*
978-0-06-157915-8